KU-199-171

LEIGH RIKER

A former contestant herself in the singles' Dating Challenge, Leigh Riker has lived in both New York City and Cincinnati – perhaps unconscious preparation for writing *Strapless*. An award-winning author of nine previous novels, she had 'the most fun of my life' with heroine Darcie Baxter's friends, foe and family.

When she's not tweaking or tormenting her own characters, Leigh teaches creative writing. She also enjoys travel – most recently with her husband to Australia – and in her 'spare time' at home indulges her cat Jasmine's many whims. Leigh is at work on a new novel.

Strapless

Leigh Riker

RED
DRESS
INK

Life's little curves.™

www.reddressink.com

DID YOU PURCHASE THIS BOOK WITHOUT A COVER?

If you did, you should be aware it is **stolen property** as it was reported *unsold and destroyed* by a retailer. Neither the author nor the publisher has received any payment for this book.

All the characters in this book have no existence outside the imagination of the author, and have no relation whatsoever to anyone bearing the same name or names. They are not even distantly inspired by any individual known or unknown to the author, and all the incidents are pure invention.

All Rights Reserved including the right of reproduction in whole or in part in any form. This edition is published by arrangement with Harlequin Enterprises II B.V. The text of this publication or any part thereof may not be reproduced or transmitted in any form or by any means, electronic or mechanical, including photocopying, recording, storage in an information retrieval system, or otherwise, without the written permission of the publisher.

This book is sold subject to the condition that it shall not, by way of trade or otherwise, be lent, resold, hired out or otherwise circulated without the prior consent of the publisher in any form of binding or cover other than that in which it is published and without a similar condition including this condition being imposed on the subsequent purchaser.

A Red Dress Ink™ novel
® and ™ are trademarks of the publisher

First published in Great Britain 2003
Red Dress Ink, Eton House, 18-24 Paradise Road,
Richmond, Surrey TW9 1SR

STRAPLESS © Leigh Riker 2002

ISBN 0 373 25018 5

140-0603

Printed and bound in Spain
by Litografia Rosés S.A., Barcelona

For Kristi Goldberg, who first urged me to tell this story
– and take a new direction. Your ongoing support and
encouragement mean so much.
Thanks, dear friend, and fellow writer.

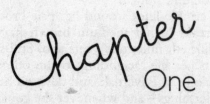

Chapter One

"I mean, it's just logical—stuff happens. Right?"

Like muttering to herself, Darcie Elizabeth Baxter thought, or trying to make sense of things, this was nothing new. Stuff happened, especially to a twenty-nine-year-old woman trying to figure out her life. Happiness. Men. Work. You name it.

So on a sleet-drizzled Monday morning in January, it didn't surprise Darcie to march into her cubicle at Wunderthings Lingerie International six floors above the Avenue of the Americas—and find Greta Hinckley rifling her desk. Again. Still, Darcie's heart stalled. Even her grandmother told her she could be too trustingly naive. Although Wunderthings was not a huge corporation on the order of Warner, Maidenform, or Victoria's Secret—the industry superstar—the smaller company had potential. Darcie wanted to be part of that, but she felt a sinking sensation. Had she left the draft of her proposal for this week's development meeting in plain view?

"Morning, Greta."

The other woman jumped—not high enough for Darcie's taste—then whirled around, a sickly smile pasted on her narrow mouth. It made Darcie feel lush, as if she'd sprung for those silicone lip injections like all the female news anchors on TV. Everything about Greta Hinckley seemed narrow. Her horsey face, her shoulders, her blade-slim body...her mind.

"Take anything that appeals to you." Darcie set down her foam container of coffee, determined not to let her incipient PMS this morning send her over the edge. "Don't let me stop you. *Mi casa es su casa.*" She didn't know the Spanish word for desk. House would have to do. Greta wouldn't notice.

From the crinkle lines around her pale brown eyes, the faint gray streaks in her medium brown hair, Greta had passed her thirtieth milestone years ago. Still single, without a man in her life, according to the office grapevine, Greta lived alone in Riverdale and devoted her entire being to Wunderthings—and whenever she could, to stealing Darcie's creative output.

Too bad Darcie was the only person who knew that.

It was enough to make her yearn for a full bag of red licorice whips for comfort. Darcie didn't like confrontation, especially with Greta, and usually Greta's "borrowing" concerned lesser issues. A suggested design to showcase next season's bras or bustiers. An Un-Valentine's Day Sale. New, high-traffic quarters for a not-quite-profitable-enough branch store. Not this time. A glance at the pile of papers on Darcie's desk confirmed that her proposal for Wednesday was missing. Her global plan.

She opened her coffee, took a sip, and burned her tongue. *"Damn."* She liked to think of herself as a controlled person, even today when she knew better. With difficulty she mellowed her tone. "If there's anything I can clarify, let me know."

"Clarify?"

Darcie perched on the edge of her desk, crowding Greta. She hated the dumb act. As if this wasn't enough of a disaster, Darcie's mother was in town—the worst week she could pick for one of her surprise visits to check on Darcie's "decadent" lifestyle in the big city. If only a fraction of *that* were true, Darcie thought, and struggled to remain calm. Maybe if she explained her position to Greta...

"We've done so well in the States, in Europe, blah, blah, as Walt Corwin said at last week's staff meeting, that the board has voted—as you know—to open up the Pacific Rim market. With the imminent recovery of the Japanese economy—let us pray—the decline of the Australian and New Zealand dollars, which gives us a growth opportunity at bargain prices, I'm suggesting..."

Greta straightened. "I have no idea what you're talking about."

Darcie arched a brow. "Then may the best woman win."

"Walter will decide—" Instantly, with their boss's name, Darcie noticed Greta's expression soften. "We'll know then, depending on the board's input, who will become his new Assistant to the Manager of Global Expansion. With my experience—"

"Your brilliance," Darcie supplied, her astonishment growing. Did she only imagine it, or did Greta's tone turn to maple syrup when she mentioned Walter? Interesting.

"Morning, ladies."

As if Darcie had cued her, Walt Corwin's administrative assistant swept along the aisle between cubicles, dispensing her usual brand of daily cheer and memos. Greta beamed. If nothing more, Greta was a political barracuda, but Darcie, shaking over this latest intrusion into her space, into her *mind,* could only smile weakly in response. And wonder if Greta really had a yen for their boss, the least of her problems.

This reminded Darcie of her own precarious hormonal state. Tonight, she would see the man in her life—a loose term to be sure—for their weekly "get together." With luck, those few hours between the sheets might help her forget Greta and her own mother.

As she passed by, Nancy Braddock brushed the edge of Greta's desk across the way. The in-basket wobbled and a sheaf of papers that had been sticking out slid onto the floor. In the midst of her morning parade, Nancy paused.

"Sorry, Greta."

Deliberately, she picked up the stack, tamped the pages into precise order—for Nancy, everything had to be in order, a habit Darcie admired—and started to set them back on the desk. Then she stopped again, glancing up with an intent frown in Greta's direction, the most expression the unflappable Nancy ever showed.

After a brief inspection, she handed the papers to Darcie then walked on.

Darcie stared down at them. *My proposal.* How long would it have taken Greta to scan the document, change the author's name, then print out a fresh copy for Walter Corwin—and even more important, for the Board of Directors?

Darcie nudged Greta away from her desk. "Excuse me. This has to be in Walt's office by ten today and I need to make a few additions. I can't imagine how it ended up on your desk, Hinckley."

The words didn't satisfy. She couldn't seem to blast Greta, except in her mind, and mentally Darcie stiffened her spine. She would let the proposal speak for itself. Damned if she would go under without a fight.

"If my hormones weren't on a total rampage, I'd just leave."

Ever since Greta that morning, Darcie's day had gone downhill. Muttering to herself that night, she stared into the mirror of the usual room at the Grand Hyatt Hotel and shuddered at the sight. She always cringed at this time of the month, so that was certainly nothing new. She had a dozen friends who felt the same way about their appearance—*miserable fat slut no one could love*—twelve times each year. Darcie was in her own puffer fish phase: four extra pounds, cheeks too full, breasts engorged and aching, belly out to here...

PMS Psycho.

Unfortunately, she also felt horny.

Darcie caught Merrick Lowell's reflection in the glass and frowned. Only moments ago he'd plied her with kisses, soft and hard, a caress or two of her tender nipples, before he abandoned foreplay, and her, for the telephone.

"I mean, go. As in, 'I'm outta here.' Let Mary Thumb and her four daughters 'handle' his problem."

The selfish thought couldn't be avoided. What about *her* problem? Why stand less than six feet away from a man who obviously wanted her only one night a week? Darcie considered moving straight toward the door, into the hall, down in the elevator and out onto Forty-Second Street. Since she'd begun to think of chain saw murder, tonight no longer held the promise of passion. She'd just grab the shuttle to the ferry, then cross the Hudson for home. Merrick seemed more interested in checking his voice mail— again—than in making love.

When Darcie turned away from the mirror into the room, he held up a finger. *Wait a minute. Then we'll screw.* And her resolve tightened.

Lovely. She *should* leave him.

Her friend Claire told her so, repeatedly.

Give up, Claire said. Darcie's relationship with Merrick—Darcie couldn't even call it that—wouldn't go anywhere. And when Darcie, who prided herself on logic, began to believe the same thing...

As if he knew what she was thinking, Merrick put down the phone with a smile that could melt granite.

"Sorry."

And that fast, her mood lifted. No more holdover from this morning with Greta Hinckley. No more chain saws. No more PMS. Again, she was a normal person, sort of, with regular moods instead of periodic plumpness, a human being with a job at risk, Darcie admitted, a woman who needed a man. *Now.*

"No problem," she murmured.

She reminded herself that Merrick liked schedules, which Darcie—since her migration from Cincinnati—was trying to despise, a minor glitch in their quasi-affair. So what? Marriage wasn't her top priority—even if Merrick would be her parents' Catch of the Day—and one reason Darcie had come to New York.

Darcie wouldn't want a big home in some fancy sub-urban development facing a golf course. She wasn't ready for Janet Baxter's statistical two point four children—how could you manage that?—and a new gas-guzzling SUV in the three-car garage. Or the adoring husband who would come home every night to do half the chores and parenting. Ha. Darcie's father never helped around the house, and Janet Baxter hadn't worked outside their home in thirty-four years.

Darcie didn't want a husband yet. Someday she might, assuming marriage improved her lot, but until then Merrick Lowell turned her on—every Monday night. Sex wasn't everything either, she admitted, but theirs was a pragmatic arrangement. At the moment, like an opportunity to climb the company ladder right over Greta Hinckley, it suited Darcie.

She even smiled. "Oh, suck it up."

Merrick was undoing his shirt, not looking at her. Instead, Darcie looked at him. Button by button, inch by inch of bared male skin, she felt her heart beat quicken. *Hurry*.

"What?" he finally said.

She cocked her head. "I'm admiring the view."

"Well, come over here. I like your admiration hands-on."

So he could be a little egocentric. Merrick had his faults, but he also looked gorgeous, which made up for a lot where her wayward hormones were concerned. Not that she wanted to seem shallow. Not that he was, really, her type.

His thick, honey-blond hair, in contrast to Darcie's fine, straight but often unruly dark bob, didn't bother her. Lighter hairs even sprinkled the backs of his hands, re-deeming him as a too-pretty boy in her mind, strong hands that could make Darcie moan. Soon, she hoped. Important point in his favor. He had deep-blue eyes to her own bland hazel gaze, a sexy mouth that made Darcie feel positively thin-lipped without those silicone shots. But of course he dressed like a GQ model—*Ick*—and had a too-cool name, when hers was just a name, and he came from old Connecticut money while she sprang from middle-class Ohio. He made Darcie, a product of public schools, feel she didn't have the inside track somehow. His education—Choate and Yale—reeked of class and privilege and had, naturally, led straight to his job on Wall Street where, without a Greta Hinckley in his path, he made tons of money…as he kept telling Darcie.

So he was a jerk.

Holding her smile, she started across the room. And felt a swift kick of anticipation when Merrick didn't smile back. He didn't seem distracted now. His eyes had taken on that darker, intent male look that meant business, and heat streaked along Darcie's spine. Sexual business.

He said, "You're sure taking your time."

"I'm meditating. On your sheer physical perfection."

"Jesus, Darce, will you just get over here before I lose my hard-on?"

Despite her own practical mood, a flutter of disappointment slowed her steps.

"That's romantic," she murmured.

He frowned. "I don't have time for romance. It's not like we only met, or something. I have to get up at 5:00 a.m."

Slightly peeved again, Darcie reached out to help him unfasten his French cuffs. Those gold-and-onyx links must have cost a fortune. Well, he had one to spare. Another thing they didn't have in common. Sex would have to do. She peeled off his shirt, dropped it to the carpet, then moved in close to run her fingers over his warm, naked chest, down to his belt buckle. She purred in his ear.

"I thought you were already up." *Big Boy.*

"Ha-ha. You know, comedy in the bedroom isn't the biggest turn-on."

Darcie made a pouty face. "Gee, now I'm losing my hard-on."

Merrick didn't respond. Apparently tired of talk, he

hauled her tight against his chest and kissed her. Darcie felt his teeth push hard at her lips, then his tongue entered her mouth and she went limp in his arms. She was such an easy mark tonight, it was pathetic.

Her knees weakened. Her thighs loosened. Desire oozed from every pore.

When Merrick started breathing fast, so did Darcie. His hands were all over her now, pulling up her sweater, then with one deft flick of a finger, opening her bra. Darcie's breasts spilled free. Or so she liked to think. They weren't really big enough to spill or jiggle with any degree of success.

With a growl he palmed her breasts, and another streak of fire flashed through Darcie so fast she thought she'd eaten too big a wad of the *wasabi*—Japanese horseradish—that Merrick always encouraged her to try. It sure opened the sinuses. His touch, his mouth on her, did the same now to every orifice of her frustrated body.

Darcie fumbled at his belt. If only she didn't have these reservations, and she didn't mean about the hotel room they were in. She pushed away her misgivings but couldn't manage to deal with Merrick's fly.

"Move a little. I can't unzip your pants."

He eased back. "Do it quick."

The zipper jammed. "Merrick…"

"*Quicker.*"

He pushed off her skirt, tossing it aside. Next her panties flew across the room, landing on a chair like one of her grandmother's tea cozies. Except that Gran was more the sort for peach schnapps or Jell-O shooters. Darcie slipped off her shoes, he did too, and then they were naked. Phew. The air-conditioned room felt suddenly too cool, and her nipples hardened into knots—not love knots exactly, but oh well.

Legs entangled, they stumbled toward the king-size bed. Darcie hit the pillow-top mattress and Merrick rolled beside her. He took her in his hard, health-club muscled arms and kissed her with a hint of tongue. Not bad. Maybe she'd overlook his earlier rejection.

"You hot yet, babe?"

Darcie gasped. "I'd say so. Yes."

"Then let's do it. That's why we're here."

His words lacked something, the stuff of her mother's dreams—Janet would agree if Darcie ever talked about her "love" life, which she didn't—but it was the twenty-first century and knights in armor on white horses were long gone. Men were...men. In the postsexual revolution, in the middle of a societal upheaval littered with women like Greta who had no partners, Darcie took her pleasure where she could find it.

"Ready?" he said.

"Move right in."

Merrick braced himself above her. Silently, she opened her legs, and without another word he slid inside her, deep and full.

"Man," he murmured in obvious appreciation.

"Woman," she managed because she wouldn't let him be a Neanderthal alone.

He started moving and she stopped caring about Janet's plans for her, her own dubious future at Wunderthings or some elusive happiness she couldn't quite grasp. Eagerly, she joined his rhythm. When orgasm caught them, it hit hard and fast—first Merrick, then Darcie. Nothing new there, either, in a whole day of nothing new. Merrick Lowell wasn't her dream, but even as an optimist she'd never had that kind of luck—or for that matter, a mutual climax. He would do. They would. For now.

Until the "right man" came along.

Like *that* would happen any time soon.

"He's lying, Darcie. Don't believe a word he tells you."

In Claire Spencer's opinion, for which she was highly paid in her job, Merrick Lowell was a bigger problem for Darcie than Greta Hinckley. Worried about her friend, on Tuesday night Claire watched Darcie pace the living room of her grandmother's apartment, which Darcie shared. Roommates? The odd couple, she thought. The duplex apartment, perched high on the Jersey Palisades in the same building where Claire lived with her husband two floors down, overlooked the Hudson River but, too tired to care about the view, she couldn't enjoy it. Even here, she imagined she could hear tiny Samantha's wail from her apartment's new nursery.

"Why would Merrick lie?" Darcie wondered, bringing Claire back to reality.

"You can't be that naive."

"Oh, yes I can. I'm from Ohio."

Her grandmother was watching television in another room, Claire knew, with her demonic cat, and Claire gave thanks for privacy. That, and Eden Baxter's famous macadamia chocolate chip cookies. Claire snatched another one from the Wedgwood plate on the coffee table. Maybe Darcie should eat more of them, add twenty pounds to her frame, turn her legs into protective pin cushions, and forget men, especially Merrick Lowell. How could she stand him?

"We don't do sophisticated in Cincinnati," Darcie pointed out. "It's a simpler place. People trust each other there. They leave their cars unlocked—at least in their driveways. They gesture to one another at Stop signs."

"With middle fingers?"

Darcie sighed. "No, with polite waves of the hand to go ahead."

"You can't be serious." Claire was a New Yorker. Middle fingers were like another borough dialect. Staten Island or the Bronx.

"They're so courteous, they stop in the merge lane on the interstates."

"I can see the pileups now."

While Claire fought against a yawn—lack of rest, not boredom—Darcie stalked to the windows and stared out at a balcony like Claire's own. Off to the left the majestic George Washington Bridge stretched across the river, but, used to the same view, Claire munched her cookie and studied Darcie's rich, dark hair. Straight and silky, it gleamed in the light, putting her own carefully frosted curls to shame. And what she wouldn't give for Darcie's slim figure just now, or her hazel eyes ringed with darker pigment, not the black circles from no sleep beneath Claire's generic blue eyes. She wondered if Darcie knew her own value.

"After yesterday with Greta and what you're saying about Merrick, maybe I *should* go home," Darcie said. "That would make Mom and Dad happy. If I lose this chance at Wunderthings, if Merrick *is* lying to me—"

"You're in love with that ass?"

Darcie backpedaled. "Well, no. But Merrick's pretty good in bed."

Claire wouldn't ask about last night. She'd only end up angry with Merrick, and sad for Darcie. Running on three hours' sleep herself, with her postnatal hormones all over the place, she'd just start crying. For a single instant she envied Darcie. Her figure. Her single life. Her chances.

"I wouldn't compromise. I'd look for damn good. Make that stupendous. Lights and laser shows. Fireworks. Excitement, Darcie," Claire insisted. "Thirty—the big 3-0— is staring us both in the face. You first." She couldn't help gloating. "Six months, sweetie. From then on, you don't settle for third-rate when you choose a man. Or a career, for Pete's sake—not to take my own husband's name in vain."

"Peter the Great. He's crazy about you."

Was he? Claire didn't feel certain these days. She thrust her shoulders back to emphasize her newly maternal shape. She needed to remember that she was still a *woman*. A bigger woman right now but… "Since the baby was born, I'm a goddess. At least after a night's sleep, which is rare, I am. Did I tell you? He loves my new chest."

Darcie turned and rolled her eyes. "He always did."

Not that Claire let him touch her yet. "Peter's a breast man, I admit."

"The man is completely obsessed."

"He loves all of me," Claire murmured to convince herself. She worried sometimes…most of the time…about going back to work soon, about marriage and being a good mother—what a change from her freewheeling, prebaby life with Peter—and about not being sexy to him now. Talk about obsessive. Silly, she supposed. Once they made love again…when she felt ready…

"Maybe you and Peter are a fluke." Darcie hesitated. "A hunky husband, a beautiful baby, that fancy job of yours. Vice President, Heritage Insurance, Inc.," she intoned, making Claire smile. "A new shape that stops traffic…."

The smile faded. "Except for my oh-so-generous and saggy-to-my-knees belly."

"You fit my mother's profile of Woman perfectly."

"Uh-oh." Claire knew Janet Baxter could be a handful, but she had Darcie's best interest at heart, too. They both wanted to see Darcie happy. Claire picked up another cookie, wondering why, if she was so happy, she cried all the time. "Your turn will come."

"To be pregnant, with morning sickness? I watched you, remember. I need that at the moment like a pink slip from Walter Corwin."

Claire frowned. The small but upscale women's lingerie company had seemed like a good opportunity for Darcie four years ago, but she'd gotten stuck behind Greta Hinckley—who wasn't naive at all—and Claire feared she would lose her creative momentum to Greta's continued sabotage. She pushed aside her own muddled emotions and the topic of Merrick Lowell.

"You're really worried about your job?"

With a groan Darcie strode away from the windows and Claire regrouped. She'd heard all about Greta.

"Listen. Hinckley's so caught up in her own underwire, gel-enhanced bra—top-of-the-line of course—she doesn't hear people whispering behind her T-strap back."

"Whispering what?" Darcie said. "About her stealing underwear, or getting the new assignment we're competing for in Expansion?"

"She won't get it, sweetie."

"She's a shark." Darcie told Claire more about the stolen proposal yesterday and Nancy Braddock's rescue, then forced a smile. "I'll know whether she mentioned that to anyone else by noon tomorrow. Either way I'm having lunch with Walt. If he chooses me, I won't have time for men," she added. When Claire snorted, Darcie said, "I may need sex but that's all. Until I get my life in order."

Claire bobbed her head. "I see. Then sex is why you stay with Merrick. What a deal. He gets laid with no strings. You get screwed with no consideration...."

"If so, that's my choice. Temporarily." She plucked a throw pillow from the sofa and threw it at Claire, who dropped the last of her cookie. "End of discussion."

Claire retrieved the chocolate macadamia nut crumbs from the carpet. "A new assignment is the least you deserve for all your hard work. For instance, rewriting Corwin's reports so they sound like a form of intelligent life wrote them in the first place. Working late three nights out of four on *his* projects—then coming in on weekends. If that slimeball Hinckley does get the spot, I swear—"

"I'll kill her myself. Walt, too."

"Give me a call. In this case I don't mind being an accessory to murder."

"We get along so well. We could share a cell."

Claire grinned. "Hang curtains, lay rugs...a few pictures, and it'll be home."

"Listen to us. Home for the Criminally Insane."

Claire joined her in a snicker then sobered. "But about Merrick..."

"He's okay. He takes me out, opens doors like a gentleman—"

"Once a month. The rest of the time he just pokes you."

Darcie couldn't argue except to add, "He's smart, makes good conversation—"

"When he's not on top of you."

"And he loves his nephew," Darcie finished.

Claire gaped at her, her own fatigue forgotten. "See?"

"What? Now you're saying his nephew doesn't exist? Merrick carries his picture in his wallet, and why would he lie? He's a sweet little boy with fair hair, the Lowell smile..." But she grabbed a cookie from the plate and so did Claire.

"I'm telling you, Darce. Wake up. The guy is married."

At noon the next day on the corner of Fifty-Fourth and Fifth, Merrick Lowell was the last thing on Darcie's mind. She stepped off the curb reciting her own vital statistics.

"Darcie Baxter. Twenty-nine years old and, possibly, about to be cast aside. I stand five feet four in my panty hose, which are soaked at the moment—no, not with lust but, like the rest of me, from this freaking rain." On the other side she marched along the sidewalk in the freezing January downpour. "I live with my grandmother, whose cat despises me. I'm sleeping with a man who likes his cell phone better than me, and obviously—" she drew a deep breath "—I talk to myself."

A yellow cab rushed past splattering slush over her down trench coat and nearly running Darcie over.

"I have a college degree, right? I'm not a total washout in the brains department, if some might disagree. I shower every day, use deodorant. I shave my legs before the hair even needs curlers. I don't lie—except for tiny fibs now and then, usually to protect someone's feelings. And only this morning I helped a little old lady cross the street." Or did Gran's daily trip to the convenience store next to her apartment building count? She'd been half a block ahead of Darcie the whole way. "I can't be that bad. Oh—and I do my job." In fact, she thought her presentation that morning to the board had gone well. She hadn't fainted or lost the power of speech. "So why give the goodies to someone else?"

She walked on, mumbling. No one noticed. On a dismal, gray day in Manhattan with a raw wind whipping off the East River and blowing through the canyons of skyscrapers, turning hats and people into sails, no one would. In New York, unlike Cincinnati, they scurried from meeting to deal, from glossy restaurant to trendy bar. They fought for cabs on the street. Except in times of crisis, they left others to their own devices.

Which proved to Darcie that she was in real trouble.

Maybe she should have stayed in Ohio. Bite your tongue, Gran would say.

In the middle of the block, she turned in at The Grand Vitesse. Its burgundy canopy looked to be the priciest thing about the place.

Inside, she spied Walt Corwin immediately. His thin hair lay plastered, as usual, against his scalp and he was— what else?—reading the *Wall Street Journal*.

Darcie waved off the waiter, who tried to take her damp coat. She plopped down across from Walt, propped her chin on her hands and beamed at him. Think positive. "Well?"

"Well what?" He continued to peruse the paper and her heart sank.

"Unless you're reading the fourth column—one of those cutesy feature stories—would you mind putting that down?" Another deep breath. Might as well get this over with. Then she could go home, peel off her sodden panty hose, pour a stiff belt of scotch—even though she hated liquor—and cry. "Did I lose out this morning?"

Walt's myopic blue eyes winked into some kind of watery focus.

"What makes you think that?"

She shook out her napkin. Real linen. Maybe the place wasn't that cheap, or Walt.

"I didn't lose?"

"Darcie, you need confidence. Why would you assume—"

"Desperation." Greta Hinckley, she thought.

"Take my advice. In the corporate jungle, never let 'em see you sweat."

"Walt, I need a raise in order to eat. I need this assignment to Global so my brain won't rot." She paused, not daring to hope. "You're my boss. Tell me. The board meeting…"

"Went to hell in less than five minutes." He glanced up again from the paper. "Four minutes after we dealt with your presentation. Order anything you like. I'm told the daily special—coq au vin—is pretty good. Chicken," he said when Darcie just blinked.

Blindly, she took the menu she was handed. She couldn't decipher a word, but not because it was in French. Even the translation didn't register. Her mind whirred in circles. Walt had warned her only yesterday that as a relatively junior employee it was unlikely the board would approve her appointment. And, Darcie knew, with Greta Hinckley in contention...

Hope skipped inside her. She scanned the entrees for the most expensive item, testing the waters. "How about lobster Newburg?"

"Go for it."

Her pulse sped. "You mean..."

He laid the newspaper beside his salad plate. His lips twitched. "Let's order wine. Or would you prefer champagne?"

Her mouth went dry.

"I...don't like champagne."

Could it happen? More money...a *future?* As if signaling the start of her imagined prosperity, Walt snapped his fingers. The waiter appeared with a bottle of chilled Chardonnay. Darcie watched him pour a pale-golden stream into her glass after Walt had tasted the wine. Her heart hammered harder than it did whenever Gran's pet Persian cat cornered Darcie in a surprise attack. When they were alone again, he lifted his stemmed goblet.

"Here's to my new Assistant to the Manager of Global Expansion for—"

"Walt! I love you!" She shouted it through the whole restaurant.

"—Wunderthings International."

"Oh. Oh Jesus. God. Oh—" She knocked over her wine. "I can't believe this."

She had talent, ability, good ideas. She wasn't (except with Greta) afraid to speak her mind. But fickle luck, actually coming her way? Darcie tried not to grin. *I'll never be hungry again, Scarlett.*

Walt sopped up the wine with his napkin. She knew he

hated messes. Hated the display of emotion for which Darcie had become justly famous in his department.

"Don't get your panties in another twist," he said, scowling at the wet tablecloth. "There won't be a lot more money."

Giddy, Darcie didn't care. She could manage. The opportunity, a title...

"A title, Walt." She grinned. "Can I have that on my office door?"

"What office?"

"I don't get an office?"

"Honey, I have an office. You're still on the cubicle farm...until next year when the board can see how you've done with this first assignment."

"I'll prove to them—" she waved an airy hand "—whatever they need me to prove." Had they actually accepted her plan? "I'll work twenty hours a day."

"You'll have to," he said.

"I can do that. Jeez, I can do anything." She drew herself up straighter. What was it Gran said? "'I am Woman, hear me roar.'" Her voice rose again over the room full of diners. Heads turned—well, whaddya know? Some New Yorkers weren't that jaded.

Walt laid a hand over her lips. "Christ, keep it down, will you? I went to bat for you over Hinckley, and I expect you to slave for me. I expect to be pleased."

Pleased? For a single instant Darcie thought she'd discovered the worm in the apple of paradise. Was he propositioning her? She fought back a mental image of herself on her knees in front of Walt at his desk. Her face on a level with his swollen lap. No, never. Despite Greta's possible fantasies about him, Darcie doubted that Walt, who was a widower, had a sex life at home or at work. If he did, she sure didn't want to be part of it.

"Your wish is my command."

Fighting a smile, he shook his head. "You're so full of shit." After the waiter took their orders, he poured more wine into her empty water glass. New York in the midst of a torrential winter downpour was also under a water rationing edict. Darcie couldn't imagine why—something about the reservoirs—but you had to beg for the stuff, even in five-star restaurants. As if she knew about those. Walt raised his glass. "Congratulations, Darce. Others may doubt but *I* have every confidence you'll do a fine job— make me proud. Make sure you do," he said, then, "I hope your passport's in order."

"Passport?"

He nodded toward the front windows where icy rain slid down the glass.

"I said, Global." He grinned. "Isn't that what you wanted? The Pacific Rim. It's like a reprieve from hell. Nancy told me what happened—and tipped the balance in your favor. Hinckley stays here. Good presentation, Baxter—for which you get your fondest wish—the opening of Wunderthings, Sydney. It's summer there."

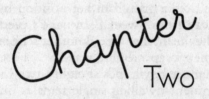

Chapter Two

"Balmy ocean breezes," Darcie told her grandmother. "Hot sun…"

"That's a shame." In the early evening after her trip home from Wunderthings, she watched Eden Baxter fluff another Oriental pillow on the oyster-white sofa. "I doubt you'll have time for the beach. Corwin will expect you to work."

True. She had her chance now to prove herself—much to Greta Hinckley's dismay—and didn't intend to blow it, but excitement still flowed through Darcie's veins.

"The guidebooks tell me I can spend nine to five in the city, then be lying on the sand at Manly after a thirty-minute ferry ride." Her specialty, Darcie supposed, owing to her daily commute across the Hudson. She might be new to this assignment, but she was a pro with ferries.

Eyeing Gran's huge gray Persian cat, which had just entered the room, Darcie felt her pulse hitch. She stepped back into the dining area. She never relaxed until she pinned down Sweet Baby Jane's location—and took up her own position as far away as possible.

"Maybe I'll reverse commute into the city. Then I could run in the mornings at the beach, grab a few rays—"

"Ah, to be young-er."

Eden flicked a feather duster over a spotless walnut end table. Another perk of living with Gran, Darcie acknowledged. She didn't have to clean. Neither did Gran but that didn't bear pointing out. Nor did the fact that in the glow of light from the end table lamp, her grandmother's carefully groomed, rich auburn hair had an apricot cast. And white showed at her roots. She needed a touch-up.

"You'll always be young, Gran."

She couldn't see a grin from her position by the dining table, well away from Sweet Baby Jane's predatory feline prowl, but she heard her grandmother's cheeky tone of voice. "My men keep me that way."

"You have more boyfriends at eighty-two than an entire block of apartment-dwelling single females on the Upper East Side."

"Isn't that *bad?*" Meaning good. Darcie eased away from the table. In the living room Eden rubbed a slender finger over a gold picture frame, checking for dust. The eagle in the expensive print seemed to glare back in disapproval, as Darcie's mother might.

"You're famed for your liaisons—in this building anyway."

Gran paused. "Has that naughty doorman been talking again?"

"Julio?" Darcie raised her eyebrows. "I hear he's the soul of discretion."

Eden snorted delicately. "As long as he gets his weekly tip for bringing up my groceries—gets that huge wad of bills I slip him every Christmas. I'm telling you, the list of maintenance people here who deserve 'appreciation' every holiday season is the nearest thing to extortion."

"Julio just likes the feel of your soft little hand in his pocket."

"Nothing soft about *him*." Eden turned. "Myra Goldstein says he has a shaft the size of Long Island. And she should know."

"Jealous, Gran?"

"Who, me? If I took half an interest in that man, he wouldn't be able to walk for a month. Make that a year. Myra is no competition."

Darcie grinned but let a few beats pass while her grandmother scooped up a stack of newspapers, some magazines. She was addicted to the *New York Times* crossword puzzle and at least twenty financial publications. Since being widowed fifteen years ago, Eden had become a success in the stock market. Her love life was equally legendary.

"If you don't behave, I'll have to tell Mom."

Eden made the sign of the cross. "Spare me, you thankless child. That son of mine could have married well. Instead, look at him. Henpecked by that virago of a wife in Via Spiga pumps and—have you seen it?—that faux fur jacket. It looks like road kill." She admired her own thinly strapped sandals with three-inch heels. Sweet Baby Jane wound around Eden's slim ankles before moving on. "Still, if it weren't for Janet Harrington Baxter, I wouldn't have you."

In spite of herself—Eden said such things a hundred times a day—Darcie felt her eyes mist. "I love you, too, Gran."

She waved away the sentiment. "You, and every man in this building."

"That's hardly the same thing."

"God be praised." Eden's blue-green eyes twinkled like peridots. "I'm going to miss you, you know. There'll be no one to keep those wolves from my door."

"With that sign dangling from the bell saying Abandon Trousers, All Ye Who Enter Here? I suppose not." As she spoke, she tracked the cat's slow saunter in her direction. Every time Sweet Baby Jane got near, she clawed the hell out of Darcie—on purpose, Darcie felt sure. She'd never known an animal so vicious at heart *(dogs usually like me)* but the small injuries seemed worth the free rent at Gran's. Never mind the traffic.

"Darcie Elizabeth Baxter, there is no such sign."

"There should be," she had just said when, without

warning, Sweet Baby Jane's sharp teeth suddenly clamped down on her calf. Darcie yelped, but Eden chose not to notice. Her beloved pet could do no wrong.

"I am far from being a promiscuous woman. At my age?" She covered her heart with scarlet-tipped fingernails. With the exception of her one mild heart attack years ago, Eden remained in excellent health, allowing for occasional bouts of angina during stress. "Don't be ridiculous. If you even think of spreading that vicious rumor, no one will believe you."

Darcie shook off the cat, trying not to draw Eden's attention, her leg stinging.

"They won't listen," she teased. "They know you."

"Well." Eden raised a perfectly penciled brow. "The last man who slept in my bed did leave with a big smile on his face."

"Norman?"

"No, not Norman. Jerome Langley."

Darcie rubbed her injured calf. "The little bald Jewish guy who never holds open the elevator door? He picks his nose, Gran. I'm disappointed in you. Again."

"The last man—it may have been Norman at that—was six months ago." Eden spun Darcie toward the stairs that led to the second level of the apartment. "How promiscuous is that?"

"Not very. But you're lying."

Her grandmother marched her across the pale-beige carpet, Sweet Baby Jane following Eden like a devoted dog. "You'll never know. And although I'll miss you, it's time to pack instead of snooping in my romantic business."

"You're right. But did I tell you? They sun topless over there."

Gran's steps faltered. "That southern hemisphere sun is strong, I'm told, and the new hole in the ozone doesn't help. Be careful then—but do show your wares, Darcie. You have nice breasts, which some Australian hunk is bound to appreciate. With a bit of 'exposure' there's no telling what you'll find."

"You want me to look for a man?" And bare herself so he'd even notice?

"You're not getting younger yourself, dear. It's time you considered a home of your own, several children…not right away…but still, a nice hard organ to bump up against you every night." She repeated, "Every night, Darcie."

She groaned. "I'll see Merrick twice this week."

Darcie had a sudden image of him on Monday, Palm Pilot in hand. *Thursday night's free, too. Same time, same place.*

"Then by all means," Eden murmured, "let's fling open the patio doors and shout. Loud enough that those idiots trying to kill each other in traffic on the bridge can hear—" she waved toward the George Washington "—that *man* has seen fit to bestow his presence *and* his sexual attributes—"

"Down, Gran." She was blushing. When Sweet Baby Jane smirked at her, Darcie sidestepped the cat. While Eden wasn't looking she booted SBJ gently in the rear. With a shriek of outrage, the animal streaked upstairs to lie in wait for her.

"Why, what happened, my little furball?" Eden called. As if she didn't know.

Darcie cleared her throat for attention. "It's not only Merrick's fault we don't see each other often. I have the trip across the river to consider."

"Horse pucky."

At the stairs to the upper floor Eden dumped her duster in a teak stand by the shorter flight of steps that led down to her small foyer. No cloud rose from the clump of feathers, which seemed to satisfy her.

"I know you don't welcome my meddling. But if I were you," she said, "I'd kick Merrick's highly toned ass right down an elevator shaft at the Grand Hyatt. You can do better. Remember your father's mistake."

Gran had a point. Her words about Merrick only echoed Claire's.

"Merrick does like Via Spigas, too," Darcie admitted.

Eden grinned. "I *am* going to miss you. You always make me laugh."

But before Darcie could put a foot on the first step to go upstairs, and shut her bedroom door before the cat could find her, Eden caught her arm. "Here's more advice—which I urge you to heed, dear. It's a very good sign for future happiness. Never—but *never*—marry a man who can't make you roar with laughter."

"Assuming I find this paragon of masculinity while I'm in Sydney *working,* would you like me to bring you one, too?"

"Don't stop there. A pair would be nice. In those sexy Akubra hats."

"Roll over, babe. You know you love it from behind."

Darcie couldn't imagine what she'd done to deserve such sweet nothings in her ear—just as she couldn't comprehend Merrick's indifference to her news last night that she was going to Australia. He'd barely said a word. In the dark hotel room on Friday near dawn she came awake to the murmured male voice beside her. A hard arm lightly covered with honeyed hair wrapped around her waist to drag her closer across the warm sheets, then turned her. A hard appendage jutted against her spine, insistently moving in a provocative rhythm Darcie recognized too well—but at the moment didn't welcome.

His delivery left something to be desired, too. His attitude.

"Would you stop? Merrick, quit." She shoved hair out of her eyes and struggled up in bed. She stared at him, bleary-eyed, then squinted at the clock on the night table. How had she slept so long? "It's almost 5:00 a.m. I need to get home to change for work. You know Gran worries when I don't come back all night."

"That's what you get for living with an eighty-two-year-old woman." His laugh turned into a groan when she jabbed his ribs. "Ouch. I bet she hasn't made love in four decades."

"You're wrong." So wrong he couldn't imagine. "And rude."

"Come on, I'm joking. I could tell, the one night we had dinner at her place, that she had eyes for me." He reached for Darcie again, his long-fingered hand grazing a breast before she scooted away. "You wouldn't run off and leave a man in need, would you?"

Darcie didn't plan them. The words popped out.

"Claire thinks you're married."

Merrick sat up. "Claire should mind her own business."

"Are you?" Darcie persisted.

"If I was, I wouldn't tell her."

"Or me?" she couldn't help saying.

His gaze flickered. "What is this, Darce? We went to dinner. Fell into bed. Had a good time. Just like usual. Didn't we?"

"Did we?" She wasn't sure at the moment.

"Christ's sake." He rolled out of bed, raising the scent of stale sheets. "If you're going to get funky on me with the relationship thing, I'm gone."

"The relationship thing?"

"You know. 'It's time for us to talk about commitment.' Wedding rings. Honeymoons on Maui or St. Kitt's." He grimaced. "Babies."

"What's wrong with children? You always tell me you love kids."

"Sure, somebody else's." He leaned over to plant a kiss on her mouth while an image of his sweet-faced nephew, then Claire's newborn daughter flashed through Darcie's mind. "Why would you want to get fat and gassy carrying some guy's brat?"

"I don't. Yet. But someday..." With someone, she thought.

He brushed another kiss along her collarbone. "You sure can't see me walking the floor with a squalling infant, can you?"

Hmm. With that image, another flash of memory caught her. Merrick in a dimly lit bar the night they met. Merrick, with his smooth blond hair, his dark-blue eyes, his upper-class smile, talking her into bed that first time. Then a newer fantasy came to mind: Merrick, pushing a baby carriage. Obviously, a far-off vision he didn't share.

"No, I suppose not." She didn't know why but disappointment surged inside her. "I suppose your nephew's birthday party is enough for a man of your stature...."

"What, are you being sarcastic?"

Darcie slid from bed to face him, toes digging in the carpet. "No. Are you?"

"What nephew?" he said.

She frowned. "The little boy you told me about. Remember? The one who learned to ride a tricycle before he was two. The favorite nephew who could throw a baseball at five and knew how to swim when he turned six. You bragged about him."

"Oh. That nephew."

Darcie blinked. "Merrick, how could you forget?"

"I didn't. Jesus, I'm only half-awake." He turned toward the bathroom. "Since we're both up—" he gestured at her wild hair, at his jutting boxer shorts "—and there's nothing happening here, between us that is, I guess I'll get moving. The earlier I get to work, the more money I'll make today—if the market's up, too."

Darcie stared after him. Claire's words, then Gran's, kept running through her brain. *You can do better. Never marry (or sleep with?) a man who can't make you roar with laughter.*

She *should* have stayed in Ohio. She should never have met Merrick.

No, it was only that she didn't expect things to work out with men just because they never had. But some day they would... Until then, logically it didn't make sense to give up regular sex with Merrick, even if he could be a pain otherwise.

Right now, she didn't like him, not in a dim bar, in a hotel bed, or anywhere else—especially a little kid's birthday party he claimed not to remember.

Australia looked better and better.

* * *

The next day Darcie popped an analgesic tablet in her mouth and washed it down, praying it would at least kill her cramps. Still in a mood after Merrick yesterday—not all owing to PMS—across the small table in a crowded coffee shop just off Broadway, she watched her mother ease a manicured finger around the inner lining of her black pump. Thank heaven Darcie had been busy packing until now. She sure wasn't in the mood for this.

"I must have stood in line at that ticket kiosk in Times Square for over an hour," Janet Baxter said, one reason they were meeting here. "This is still a filthy neighborhood. I hope I don't regret even the half price. Most of these shows have no substance."

"The audience, either. That's what you get on Wednesday and Saturday matinees."

Only tourists and suburbanites from Connecticut and New Jersey filled the seats then. In town from Cincinnati, Janet Baxter belonged to the former group, and had come with friends from Ohio, but of course she must have another purpose, too—something even beyond this visit with her older daughter, Darcie had decided. Her mother's clear brow furrowed before she seemed to remember that a frown could cause lines. Permanent ones at fifty-five. Her expression smoothed out like a banana peel.

"I'm deeply concerned about your grandmother," she said, apparently the real reason for their chat over tea (for Janet) and black coffee (for Darcie). Cheap tobacco, sweat and bad perfume roiled in the heavy air around them. So did conversation from the other tables, and Darcie had to raise her voice.

"About Gran? Why?"

Naturally, Darcie thought she knew. But in her current frame of mind she'd enjoy hearing her mother talk about a subject Janet found distasteful and uncomfortable.

"Your father and I sent you to live with Eden for two reasons."

"Cheap rent. Free utilities."

"And…" She obviously wanted Darcie to recite this part of the old litany, and one of Darcie's hot buttons. It was all about security, a safe place for their firstborn daughter to live. Darcie felt she could take care of herself.

"There's a third? You go ahead, Mom."

Janet squirmed in her chair. She pursed her lips, then just as quickly stretched her mouth to erase the tension. Toying with her cup of Darjeeling, she avoided Darcie's all-knowing gaze. Darcie let the moment—and her own chance to escape her bad mood—build. Until her mother surprised her.

"We wanted you—" Janet cleared her throat "—to keep an eye on her."

"There's a new slant. I'm supposed to baby-sit my eighty-two-year-old grandmother?" Darcie paused for effect. "Mom, she's had more dates in a month than you and I combined, in our entire lives. You should see the guys she comes up with."

Janet turned pale. "You're joking. Aren't you?"

Sure, but why let her off that easy? "I tell you, those men are already wearing a path in the brand-new carpet she had installed in December—a trail from her front door to her bedroom." *Let her tell you what's in Julio's pocket.*

Janet plucked lint from her navy Talbot's suit, straight from the Kenwood Mall store in Cincinnati. "You're trying to upset me."

"Go see for yourself."

Janet looked around the narrow shop, at the various array of Saturday-in-Times Square characters, as if only just aware of them, and wrinkled her nose. "I wouldn't cross the river to stay with her. I'm not welcome. Eden has always hated me."

"*Hate*'s a strong word." Darcie couldn't even use it on Merrick yesterday.

"I'm sorry we ever suggested you share her apartment for a few months."

With the seemingly casual statement, Darcie's instincts went on full alert. Uh-oh. Checking up on her wasn't the issue, but neither was Eden's sex life. Darcie had lived in Fort Lee for her four years in the East. Both she and Gran liked the arrangement. Although Darcie planned to get an apartment of her own, in the meantime, except for Sweet Baby Jane, they didn't get in each other's way and Gran was as tolerant of Darcie's lifestyle as Darcie had become of hers. She liked to think Eden's social life was mainly invention (good grief, she's my *grandmother*) even when she knew better. But obviously, she'd missed something. Janet had still other ideas.

"Perhaps we should find you a place now. With your pay increase—"

"It's not that much."

Which seemed to play right into her mother's hands. "You could get a roommate to share the rent. A real roommate."

"Mmm." Darcie remembered her college days sleeping with the lights in her face because her art student roomie needed to finish a project. All night. Tripping over someone else's clothes, someone else's boyfriend. Finding used tampons on the dresser and spent condoms on the rug. "I'll pass. At Gran's I have my own room and no one bothers me."

Janet was undaunted. "When you get back from Australia, we'll see."

"See what?" Darcie shook her head. "Mom, I don't need help." Not from her Midwestern parents anyway. "What's this really about?"

"Your sister," her mother finally murmured, sending Darcie's sharpened senses into another spin. Janet studied her lap. "She graduated from Smith last June. Seven months ago."

"Now there's a tragedy." UC—the local university— for Darcie, the Ivy League for her kid sister. "I was *at* the ceremony. What's she done?" Darcie smiled to soften the words. So Annie was the bottom line here. Annie, who didn't give a damn what other people thought. Darcie wouldn't mind if she had gotten herself into some sort of trouble for the first time in her life. Not serious trouble, of course. "Speeding ticket?" she said. "Didn't register to vote Republican?"

Janet waved a hand. "She's headstrong, you know how

she is. She wants to come to New York." Her mother said this as if Annie's career goal was to become a prostitute—though Janet would likely say "lady of the night." She pushed her cup aside, a drift of pungent Darjeeling rising into the stuffy air. "I honestly can't imagine her living with your grandmother."

"Corruption, Incorporated."

"Yes. Well. You may smirk but it's true. Eden is a bad influence." She dragged the cup back for another swallow, and another little frisson of discomfort trickled down Darcie's spine. "Your father and I are adamantly opposed to Annie's wishes—unless, as her big sister, you could look out for her. If you shared an apartment—"

"Mom, Annie's a slob."

Clearly defeated for the moment, Janet surged to her feet, then ruined her exit by stumbling in her Via Spigas. "I'll be late for the theater. Please think about what I've said." Recovering her balance, she gave Darcie a tight smile. "It was good to see you. I'll phone tomorrow. Perhaps we can do something together before you leave."

"I leave tomorrow night."

"Sunday brunch, then. We'll talk more about Annie."

Darcie rose, too, determined not to make any logical decision until after her trip to Sydney. But the devil rode her heels. "And I can tell you all about Julio."

Darcie was still smiling to herself when she whipped through the revolving doors at FAO Schwarz into the Saturday afternoon chaos that always reigned there. She didn't often venture into such stores—after all, she didn't have kids, as Janet might point out—but before she left the States she wanted to buy a gift for Claire's new baby. Her goddaughter.

A little thrill went through her. She'd only seen the baby once, but already she loved the tiny girl. And the promise she represented. Maybe this one fragrant little human being would get everything right. No errors, no strikeouts. Just a solid crack of the bat, and a home run down the center line of life into the bleachers.

Darcie wasn't a sporting person. "I'm the last one chosen for the softball team," she murmured and swept past a display of basketballs and soccer pads. "You should have seen me when I took horseback riding lessons. Ever watched someone end up backward in a saddle? And don't forget swim camp. I sank like a rock."

"May I help you, miss?"

A clerk stepped into the aisle, his gaze curious.

"No, thank you." She gave him a bland, unfocused smile.

"I heard you talking...."

"Was I? Oh, I must have forgotten to take one of my medications." She zipped onto the escalator to the second floor, and waved at a mountain of Bob the Builder toys on display. "Gotta watch it, Darce. Even in New York." She grinned. "But gee, he noticed."

She wandered through the video games department, then stopped to watch two boys tap out a tune on the giant keyboard that had become famous years ago when Tom Hanks played it in *Big,* still one of Gran's favorite movies. Eden espoused its same whimsical, youthful view of life. By the time Darcie located the baby area, she had nearly forgotten tea with Janet. *An apartment with Annie?* The possibility raised the hairs on her neck.

Darcie lingered over a table full of stuffed animals. She tried to envision herself holding an infant like Claire's daughter, standing at an altar for the christening beside her own husband—handsome, well-dressed, with a look of absolute devotion on his face as he gazed at his new family. The image was her mother's, not Darcie's right now...but was she seeing Merrick?

The fantasy ended when she remembered Merrick's vagueness about his nephew. And her need to figure out her own life first. Darcie surveyed the pile of animals, discarding the usual bears and bunnies. She had just paid for a cross-eyed zebra sporting a huge red bow when, across the aisle in the doll department, she spied a familiar form.

What would he be doing here? In a toy store?

It didn't fit his image, but Darcie sidestepped a woman

pushing a stroller so she could get a better look. Dark-blond hair, not a strand out of place, that recognizable GQ look even on Saturday in khakis and an Irish fisherman's sweater. Her heartbeat tripled in alarm. Since leaving Janet, she hadn't combed her hair, couldn't have any lipstick left. And her dark-green eyeliner, which tended to run when she got warm, probably streaked her face. It was too hot in the store. She must look a mess.

What difference does it make? You're you, *with or without makeup.*

He moved and so did she. Darcie saw a flash of profile— straight nose, not a bump or deviation—that tilt of his head, a little imperious, a lot commanding, even arrogant. The set of his shoulders. And wouldn't she recognize those hands anywhere? Especially on her bare body. It must be...

"Merrick," she called softly just as he lifted a hand to someone—not Darcie. Mad at her? He'd left in a mood yesterday morning. So did she. Once he saw her, and they talked... She didn't want to leave for Australia in a snit. Claire was wrong about him, she tried to tell herself. So was Gran.

When a little blond girl rushed toward him, Darcie didn't react. Someone's child had run headlong into a stranger—not unusual here, except that he seemed to know her. Merrick caught her slight shoulders with a laugh, said something, then watched her skip away. An odd look on his face...like adoration.

Her pulse thudding (the zebra's head sticking out of its bag with apparent suspicion, too) Darcie crossed the aisle into the doll department. It was pink. Hundreds— thousands—of Barbie dolls dominated the display space. Dentist Barbie. Wedding Barbie. Olympic Barbie. A host of international Barbies, the Dolls of the World collection. A little too crowded for Darcie's taste. She wouldn't make that mistake in Sydney. "Her" store would be clean, un-cluttered, sophisticated.

"Merrick." He stood in front of a rack of miniature clothing, his back to her, and Darcie saw him stiffen. When he turned, his smile looked wooden.

"I thought I heard your voice."

She shrugged. "Just talking to myself again. Or Buster." She held up the zebra bag then closed the distance between them, wondering why she didn't feel better about this chance meeting in a city they both shared. "Shopping for your nephew?"

Again, he looked blank. Carefully blank this time.

"Guess not," she said, gazing at the pink all around them. Like onlookers at a circus, scores of Barbies smiled at her, at Merrick from their plastic-windowed boxes. "I mean, what would an eight-year-old boy want in this department?"

"What are you doing here, Darcie?" His voice sharp, his eyes harder.

"Talking to you. Now." She brightened her tone. "I wondered...before I leave town...if we might..." *Fall into bed again in apology?*

"Daddy!" The same little girl pelted full-tilt into his knees.

Merrick set her away, smoothing her dress—Saks Fifth Avenue, Laura Ashley...?—running a hand down the length of her sleek blond hair. Hair almost like his. She wore a blue plaid ribbon to hold it back, and had Merrick's eyes, too.

Darcie's unwanted coffee sloshed in her stomach. No, this wasn't a circus for the Barbies to watch. It was the Roman Colosseum. Lions, gladiators, victims...

Daddy. Darcie bent down until she reached eye level with the child.

"Hi."

Merrick stepped between them. "Uh, why don't you run over there, kiddo." He pointed at a pyramid of dolls on a nearby table "Pick out one you like."

Assuming he was talking to the child, not to her, Darcie straightened and the little girl said, "Can I? *Can I?*"

"Yes," he said. "You may."

Her mission approved, she scampered off. A heavy silence hung in the air.

Claire had been right. *He's lying, Darcie.*

She squished her package in rigid fingers, choking the zebra. Buster goggled at Merrick and so did Darcie—without her eyes crossed. Shoppers pushed by. A baby, like Claire's, fussed. Over the PA system a male voice announced a sale in Electronic Games.

She felt sick.

"Well. Now I know."

"Darcie, don't make a big deal of this."

She reeled back at his weary tone.

"No big deal? Just call me naive…" To her horror, she choked up. She hadn't thought this would really matter, if it proved true.

"It isn't what you think."

"Oh, that's too tacky. What a classic line." She swallowed hard. She could smell his aftershave, expensive, woodsy. Smell popcorn on the air. Smell the more acrid scent of…betrayal. "Are you saying you're *not* married?"

He turned away. Darcie snagged his arm.

"Merrick, you owe me an explanation." When he remained silent, she said, "No wonder you didn't remember your 'nephew.' Or are you more used to calling him your *son?*" She flicked a glance toward the table nearby. "Your daughter looks like you. So does he. How old is she?"

"Six. Yes," he said. "I'm married." The words came out loud, and he deliberately lowered his voice, color slashing across his cheeks as if Darcie had slapped him. Not a bad idea. "I've been married for ten years. Is that what you want to hear?"

"No, I want to hear why you're screwing me instead of your wife!"

His tight schedule. His one-night-a-week free. Two this week, lucky her. *You wouldn't leave a man in need, would you?*

"It doesn't work between us," he said.

"What doesn't work? Sex? You and me? *What?*" She'd never felt so mortified, so hurt, in her life. Which was saying a lot.

He tried to lead her to a quieter corner but Darcie dug

in her heels. She thrust the zebra bag between them like a shield.

"Just say it here." And if there was anyplace more absurd, more public, than the doll department of FAO Schwarz, she couldn't think where. That didn't matter now. Then he shocked her again.

"I love you, Darcie."

"Oh. You bastard." A first, she thought. It was a wonder he didn't strangle.

"No, I mean it. It's over between Jacqueline and me. She won't even care."

"Her name's Jacqueline?" He nodded, looking at the floor, and Darcie's mouth tightened like a prune. His wife had probably gone to Smith, like Annie.

He glanced up through a screen of thick lashes. "Do you hate me?"

"Right now, I'd say that's a definite yes."

For several moments neither of them spoke. Darcie clutched the zebra and listened to her own breathing. It seemed capable of overriding the noise around them. Roared like an oncoming subway train. She might drop dead right here on the floor. *Attention, please. Emergency. Would Medic Barbie go to Aisle Four...*

"When do you leave?" he said.

"I told you, tomorrow."

"I can't see you before then?"

"I don't want to see you."

He looked miserable. "How long will you be gone?"

"I don't know. Days, weeks." She'd already told him that, too. Didn't he *listen?* "Whatever it takes to negotiate the space we want for the new store." Whatever it took, not just in Sydney, to heal her broken heart. *Forever.*

Darcie tried not to focus on Merrick. When his beautiful child bolted from the nearby table straight into his arms, Darcie flinched at her sweet voice.

"Would you buy me this one, Daddy?"

She thrust a pink, plastic-windowed package in his face. International Barbie. Dolls of the World. It seemed just right to Darcie.

Holding Darcie's gaze, Merrick grasped the box hard. "Sure, kiddo."

The little girl gave him a coy smile. "Do you want one, too?"

Merrick managed a small laugh. "Nice try. We'll just buy this today."

Darcie stared over his daughter's head into Merrick's dark-blue eyes. Then she tightened her grip on Buster the zebra—and marched toward the escalator.

"Darcie. Wait!"

She kept going. She didn't look back. It was the upside escalator, of course, but Darcie only needed to escape. Suddenly the setting, the noise, the displays seemed absolutely fitting. For once, she had the last word.

"Daddy already bought himself a doll—or so he thought."

Merrick didn't know it, but he needed the Returns Department. As for herself...

Australian Barbie.

Merrick Lowell would never see her—a.k.a. Darcie Elizabeth Baxter—again.

Chapter Three

"'**W**altzing Matilda,'" Darcie sang to herself. "'Once a jolly swagman...'" Losing the lyrics again, she hummed a few bars. "'Dum-de-dum...his billabong...'" For some reason her eyes filled.

Jet lag, she thought, and tipped her head back. She hadn't thought it would be this bad. The new Westin Sydney, with its open expanse of chrome, glass and satiny wood led her gaze upward to a vast skylight showing a night-black canopy full of twinkling, but unidentifiable, stars. New to the southern hemisphere, Darcie sat in the hotel bar digesting the beef tenderloin *en croute* she'd eaten earlier in one of the trendy lower level restaurants with Walt, and nursing a glass of local Chardonnay to settle things.

Wearing her pinstripe suit, even alone she shouldn't feel this out of place. In New York—ten thousand miles to the east, as her long, sleepless night on a Boeing 747 from San Francisco could attest—women wore black, too, particularly after five. With a good strand of pearls, her mother would advise. In most big cities of the world, you couldn't go wrong in dark colors, but Darcie frowned into her glass. She wasn't wearing pearls, and opals seemed the gem of choice in Australia, if she believed the many shop displays she'd passed on her way to the hotel tonight. And according to the group of what appeared to be thirtyish executives at the next table, beer had it over wine.

Idly, Darcie studied them.

She couldn't concentrate. A continued low-down cramping had made her order the glass of wine she didn't really want, or need.

"Thank God he didn't get me pregnant," she said of Merrick.

Bastard.

His being married wasn't the issue. She might be naive at times but she was no brainless ingenue. As a woman of the new millennium, sexually free and unencumbered, she could handle his being married—even if that little fact rankled some deep down remnant of tradition in her own character. *Thanks, Mom and Dad.* But Merrick's failure to reveal the truth? That still hurt.

Darcie hated lying. Liars, most of all.

Blinking, she straightened in her roomy club chair. Her glass clicked onto the marble tabletop. What if he carried some STD? That's all she needed to remember Merrick Lowell—genital herpes or warts. As if she didn't feel enough of a sexual outcast.

She pressed a hand to her suddenly thumping heart. But they had used protection. Every time. Remember, Merrick didn't relish having kids. Darcie grimaced. Then why did he seem to have two of them? Maybe it was only *her* imagined children he didn't want. Her middle-class genes.

With a sigh, she fell back into the deep chair again.

Twirling the stem of her glass, she gazed around the dimly lit room—and oh, as if a band had struck up the national anthem, "Advance Australia Fair," would you look at that. Yummy. A lone man stood talking to the bartender, another Aussie male Darcie had noticed earlier. Now, she barely saw him. Eclipsing every other man in the room, this one had dark hair, unlike Merrick's (a point in his favor) thicker, longer. Hair a woman could twine her fingers through, letting its sinuous silk send a message of desire straight to her achy loins.

His broad shoulders blocked out the bartender to his left, behind the bar. He lounged in three-quarter profile to her, an amazing profile if she bothered to linger on it. Better than Merrick's. Busily, Darcie's gaze swept like a huntress down his long frame, from those incredible shoulders and well-developed deltoids—bunched, and nicely rounded, under his chambray shirt—to his washboard belly, then his muscled, jeans-clad legs and, finally, his feet. Boots, she saw. Good ones, if she could judge from this distance. His fingers looked lean and graceful wrapped around the beer bottle in his hand, and when he lifted it for a long swallow, Darcie watched his Adam's apple work in his strong, beautiful throat. It was true. Australian men were not to be believed.

Could he be any more perfect? Like a fantasy come true, even the Akubra hat from Gran's wish list lay next to him on the bar. Darcie decided it was on her agenda, too.

"You jolly swagman," she murmured, sending him a flirty smile.

Heck, why not? She was on her own, for tonight at least, in an exotic foreign environment—for once in her life. No one watched her, certainly not all the executives at the next table who were telling loud jokes and laughing among themselves. Their cigarette smoke created a cloud of anonymity, like the famed Blue Mountains with their eucalyptus haze. Janet Baxter—or Darcie's father—were nowhere to be seen. And Cincinnati, though not quite as far away as New York, could be ignored for one night. Not that she needed to care. For good measure, feeling defiant after Merrick, she tipped her glass in salute.

She detected no response to the smile or the toast, but his steady gaze did even crazier things to her equilibrium, to her lower abdomen, and Darcie swallowed hard. With her nod in his direction—*three strikes, you're out*—the beer bottle stopped halfway down and he stared at her. Then he glanced over his shoulder as if to see whether she'd been signaling the bartender for a refill, not coming on to

him. He picked up his hat. What else could she do? Darcie
looked down into her half-full glass, and waited. Pulse
pounding. Stomach clenched.

Would he come over?

When a tall shadow fell across the table a moment later,
she realized she'd been holding her breath. Raising her
eyes, Darcie exhaled. Seeing him up close, she struggled
not to slip out of her chair onto the floor in a puddle of
need.

"If you were a mate—" he pronounced it "might"
"—which you're clearly not, I'd say G'day, but we Aussies
don't use the expression between the sexes." The word
hung between them. "You're a blow-in, eh? Welcome to
Sydney."

"Blow-in?"

"That's Ozspeak—for newcomer. Or you could say
Strine."

Ozspeak? "A stranger is a Strine?"

"No." He smiled. "That's how we say Aus-tra-lian."
He tangled the syllables.

Darcie smiled, too. "And I thought you spoke English
here."

His wasn't the smoothest line she'd ever heard, and he'd
guessed she was a tourist, but that voice could warm the
polar ice cap—which wasn't all *that* far away. Darcie
gripped both arms of her seat. His gray-green hat, plopped
at a jaunty angle on his head, the lightweight sport coat
that dangled from one finger over his shoulder, shouted
Take me. I'm yours.

She couldn't help herself. Darcie hummed the first few
bars again of "Waltzing Matilda," for his benefit this time,
and he laughed.

"Mind if I sit down?"

She gestured at the opposite club chair. "Park your
'tucker' right there."

He grinned—a gorgeous grin. "Already had my tucker,
thanks."

Darcie had no idea what *tucker* meant either. All she

knew was, it was in the song and that her abdomen, even her thighs, had begun to ache in a different way.

His grin widening, he leaned back in his chair. "Puffaloons, yabbies, Vegemite, a nice bit of Pavlova... What're you drinking?"

What was he talking about?

"Uh, Chardonnay. Anything...Strine."

"It's really *Or-strall-yan.* Since you're trying so hard to fit in here, I thought I'd point that out." Charmingly, in addition to his mangled vowels, his deep voice lifted at the end of each sentence, as if asking her approval of the thought. He raised a finger—which Darcie didn't resent as she had with Merrick at the Hyatt—to a passing waiter who'd delivered another tray of beer to the next table. A shout rose up at someone's latest joke. "Tucker means food," he explained.

"That was food you mentioned?'

"Puffaloons are fried-dough scones, yabbies are little freshwater crayfish, Vegemite's a national treasure—yeast extract. Pavlova's dessert. Meringue, whipped cream, fruit..."

"You were teasing me."

He nodded. "Besides, the tucker you meant is from the bush, often carried in a backpack."

Darcie smiled. "By a swagman like yourself?"

He glanced at his blue shirt. "Do I look that bad?" Then down at his jeans. "Sorry. A swagman's a bum. A hobo." Darcie flushed at her error and he said, "I came in from the station this afternoon. Didn't take time to change." He looked at the executives' table. They all appeared as well-dressed as Merrick. "Left my good bag of fruit upstairs."

Station? "I didn't see any trains."

He grinned again. "There are some. But that's not what I'm talking about."

Blinded by his smile, Darcie ran a finger around the rim of her glass, his gaze instantly homing in on the motion. "You're a cowboy?"

His eyes had darkened. So did her blood.

"Yes, ma'am. I raise sheep. On what you'd call a ranch."

Surprised, she took a breath. The air felt thick with smoke and...lust.

"Bag of fruit?" she repeated, recalling what else he'd said.

"Aussie rhyming slang. For suit."

"Oh. I didn't mean to insult you. You look nice." *Understatement of the entire timeline of mankind, Darcie.* She could put him in a display window—oh God, yes—and with his body draped like a coat hanger with filmy lingerie, wouldn't that sell undies? Or she could send him down a fashion-show runway with a skimpily dressed model on each arm. "And that hat..."

He removed it, as if suddenly remembering his manners, then playfully plunked it on Darcie's hair. When his hand brushed her cheek, she felt a flash of frenzied desire.

"There you go," he said, and her ache grew more insistent, her blood thicker. She couldn't stop staring. He wore a gold signet ring on his right little finger and even that melted her. His touch lingered, his tone softened. "Now you look just like an Aussie." He gave her a long once-over she couldn't read. "Guess I need to teach you a few things."

Darcie's libido puckered. "We can trade."

He held her gaze. "All right, I'll help you learn Ozspeak. My language—the language of a convict subculture full of rebellion. For what? Your...straight-laced English grammar?" He laughed, then offered his hand, his dark eyes warm and too direct. Could they see right into her more than friendly fantasies? She couldn't tell. Until he said, "Or maybe we'll work out a different bargain. Something more interesting." He paused when she took his hand. "Good to meet you. I'm—"

Before he could say his name, Darcie reared back. His firm grasp, the feel of his fingers around hers, the whisper-light brush of his thumb over her palm threatened to turn her to pudding. Butterscotch. Her whole body tightened. Too perfect.

"Let's not," she said.

"Not what?"

"Exchange names." She fiddled with the hat, tilting it rakishly over one eye. She'd had enough of Merrick Lowell and his lies. If she ended up with this Aussie hunk—oh, Gran, you should see him—she wouldn't regret it in the morning. "Let's keep things...mysterious."

He went still in his chair. He waited until the bartender set their fresh drinks on the table and left. The growing heat in his eyes had cooled. Considerably.

"You're not working here, are you?"

Working? "Not at the moment." Why did he ask?

He gazed at Darcie with suspicion.

"I finished at five today," she continued, "your time, whatever it's called."

"Eastern Standard Time in New South Wales. Greenwich mean time plus ten."

In New York that would be...yesterday sometime. Darcie felt too jet-lagged, too enthralled by him, too unsettled by his look to do the math. She waved a hand. Why did he seem...disappointed?

She hurried on. "The man I work for told me to go home. I can't seem to get my clock turned around, though. I don't know whether to yawn or do my morning bends and stretches." Then she knew. Shocked, Darcie swallowed. *A working girl.*

"You think I'm—" *A lady of the night?*

"Darling, I think you're the cutest thing I've seen. But I don't do hookers."

"I'm glad to hear that."

Hoping she'd convinced him of her relative innocence, Darcie leaned against the up button at the bank of elevators opposite the Westin gift shop. It was closed now. In the past hour the executives in the bar next door had raised their level of laughter and camaraderie another few decibels, and several women in trendy power suits had joined them. She and the cowboy had also taken their new "relationship" onto a different plane. Talk about verbal foreplay—once she made him understand that Walt Corwin

wasn't her pimp. The elevator doors glided open. Darcie
and the sheep farmer entered the car.

He punched his floor, she punched her button...so to
speak...then with his hand catching hers, he nailed her up
against the rail along the wall. His gold signet ring clinked
against the wood. Darcie still wore his Akubra hat when
his mouth lowered to her throat. His warm breath sent a
thrill of lust from the roots of her hair to her too-high
shoes, toes cramped like her uterus into a suddenly too-
tight space.

Murmuring, he kissed her neck, her earlobe, then drew
it between his teeth. Beautiful teeth, she remembered. His
hands began to roam. "So, you're in retail."

She'd had to tell him something about herself. That
wary look on his face had threatened to spoil their evening.
Darcie kept things general, though, except now he knew
she was staying here. Well, of course he did. Her head
swam a little from the wine but she could still think. More
or less. They were in the elevator, rising quickly to the
upper floors, not out on the street saying goodbye. Darcie
had a sinking feeling of déjà vu. Monday nights with Merrick at the Grand Hyatt...

"It's a new job," she said. "I'm not sure I'll be able to
do it."

His low tone sent flame along her already singed nerve
ends.

"I imagine you can do anything you set your mind to."

She paused, remembering Walt. "My boss is sleeping,"
she informed him.

"With you?"

"Next door. In his own room."

He drew back to smile at her. "You're *drongo*. Funny,
that is."

Or did the slang mean *idiot?* Her stomach sank another
notch. Men and hotel rooms were becoming a habit. And
who wanted a comedienne—as Merrick said? Now, the
Aussie would laugh at her, pat her on the head—smashing
his own Akubra hat with the motion—then send her to
her room. Darcie's Big Night in Sydney Goes Belly Up.

"Funny in a good way," he added.

"Let's see." She watched him move in again, felt his lips trail along the column of her neck to the first button on her white silk blouse. "I'm cute. I'm a laugh riot. I'm—"

"You're—" A big, pathetic joke with jet lag, PMS and no chance now of getting "close" tonight. "Sexy as hell," he finished. With his low words of reprieve, Darcie's legs went weak. She leaned her head back farther to give him access to her throat. His tongue swept across the hollow there, down to her breasts, into the slight cleft that passed for cleavage—when she wore the right bra. She wasn't.

And for a moment Darcie's sensible side prevailed. Walt was upstairs. They were here to work. In any case she shouldn't take a stranger to her room. Was she nuts? Forget Merrick Lowell. Not only were hotels becoming her second home, a bad habit, but this seemed risky. Possibly dangerous, Darcie cautioned herself. Certainly the rash notion showed a lack of common sense on her part. She couldn't help asking.

"You're not a serial killer, are you?"

His tongue whisked along the valley of her breasts.

"Like I'd tell you." At the droll statement she could feel him smile against her skin. He lifted his head, his dark eyes meeting hers. "Which floor are you on?"

"Uh, thirty-three."

He took her mouth, sent the words inside. His tongue, too. His husky tone.

"I'm on thirty-one. Let's go there. It's closer."

Her pulse soared like the rising elevator and Darcie stopped finding reasons to resist. Hell, take a chance—like Annie. By the time the doors opened onto the quiet hall, his hat had flopped over her left eye. By then, Darcie supposed the hotel security staff had had their fill of elevator foreplay, verbal and physical, on the video monitors. He took her hand, led her to the corner room on the corridor, and, while kissing her again, slipped his key card into the chrome slot beside the door that flashed red when no visitors were wanted. The light turned green—*go, Darcie*—and they tumbled inside.

Darcie had a quick impression of light wood, butter-cream walls, the frosted celadon-green glass door of the bathroom—like her own room. Before she breathed again, he had her up against the mirrored closet doors in the entryway. Still kissing, he caught her hips in his hands and bumped up against her, better than Gran had said.

Darcie wound her arms around his sturdy neck. With her head tipped back, the Akubra smashed against the glass, she hung on tight. Oh, God, he could kiss. God, he could...

In about five seconds, with his hand flicking open buttons like this down the front of her blouse, then his chambray shirt (he obviously didn't need practice) Darcie wouldn't even be breathing.

His hand dropped to his buckle. The belt snapped from the loops. It clanked onto the marble floor. Outside, through the plate glass window wall on the opposite side of the room, the stars—those unidentified constellations—sparkled in the black nighttime sky. Blocks away, down the long slope of King Street, which Darcie couldn't see from here, at Darling Harbour people danced and drank. It didn't matter. With his shirt open, her blouse undone, he pressed his chest to her breasts and Darcie whimpered at the low-down ache in her abdomen. They'd never reach the bed.

"Feel good?" He dragged down his zipper. She heard a foil packet tear before he sheathed himself. "I'll make it better. I promise."

"Don't let me down."

With her request, he whisked her panties off so fast Darcie never felt them fall. He cupped her bottom in both hands. That aching spot down low needed his attention so badly she couldn't speak—comedy was the last thing on her mind now—and his hardness pushed at the ready opening of her body. He raised his head.

"You're clean, right?"

She gasped. "I'm clean."

"Me, too. So let me...show you...my *billabong*," he whispered hotly.

Then he slid inside. Deep. Hard. Full. Heaven. Her breath rushed out.

"Ohhh."

"Unhhh."

The stars twinkled. The moon shone. The cold beige marble floor made her toes curl—or was that him? His arousal felt velvety hot. The mirror felt slick and cool against her bare bottom. If he opened his eyes, would he see her big behind squashed flatter than his hat to the glass? When his heat engulfed her, Darcie no longer cared about her exposed rear end, about hotel rooms with men who didn't love her.

His tempo increased. He stroked her, in, out, in, out until they both seemed to lose their minds from the very motion, like the lilting strains of the song she only half remembered.

"You little *swag…woman…*" he gasped.

"You…big *tucker…man…*"

She didn't know how long they lasted. Seconds. Minutes. Hours. Not long enough. At some point while the moon still gleamed and the stars still shone and Darcie still wore the Akubra, the climax caught her, swift and shattering.

With one last hard thrust, on a groan he came, too.

When he stopped shuddering and she finally stopped shaking, her head fell back against the mirrored closet. She didn't mind if he saw her rear now, plastered to the glass, reflected in all its formless, naked glory. When his head dropped to the juncture of her neck, his mouth hot and open on her damp skin, Darcie peeled herself away from the mirror. And the Akubra hat thumped onto the marble floor. She couldn't tell which of them was breathing in the most ragged rhythm. Or a complete lack of one.

Her heart beat like fury. His thicker, stronger pulse thudded against her breast.

He whispered a low, erotic word, and Darcie cried out, ready to begin all over again what they had just finished…but, like him, not quite finished. When he kissed her, long and sweet and silky, she hoped this one night would never end.

"'Waltzing Matilda,'" Darcie breathed into his mouth like a prayer.

"Want another beer?" Like a pagan god, hours later he stood naked at the minibar, a perfect sight in the open fridge door that shafted light over his loins, upward along his taut belly to his muscled chest and shoulders, to the renewed glitter in his dark eyes. Darcie wanted him, again, too.

Swathed in the white cotton duvet, she lay on the king-size bed amid big goose down pillows and grinned at him. Even though she didn't like beer, she said yes.

"And after that…?" she added, hoping for more.

"We'll rehydrate, then negotiate."

Like Scarlett O'Hara the morning after Rhett, she couldn't seem to stop smiling.

I'll make it better. "I won't give you a fight."

"I hoped you wouldn't."

"I have to say, I like a man who keeps his promise."

With a wolfish smile of his own, he slammed the fridge door and walked—strolled in all his male splendor, which Darcie suspected he did on purpose—across the room to her. Darcie lifted the duvet to invite him in. Now the city lights coming through the wide windows illuminated him, too. Gilded his sunbrowned skin. Deepened the interesting creases in his cheeks, the smile lines around his mouth.

"How old are you?" she asked idly, reaching for the beer he held out.

"Thirty-four." He didn't ask her the same question. "Why?"

"You're well preserved." She trailed a hand over his shoulder. "I'm twenty-nine."

"Thanks. We're both old enough." For what, he didn't say. He rubbed his bare chest. "Most women don't like telling, though."

"Are you always this polite?"

"My mum hopes so." Oh Lord, a chink in the walls of

pleasure. His mother. He had one, maybe just like Janet. He fell onto the bed, held his beer can to one side, and lowered his head to kiss her open mouth. "But no, ma'am. I'm not *that* polite. Now."

"I'm glad to hear that." She repeated her earlier words.

He frowned. "Hey. I didn't really think you were a working girl."

"Yes, you did."

He seemed to take most things literally, which Darcie tried not to mind, either. After all, she'd taken Merrick at face value. There was a lesson there but right now she wouldn't give it any credence.

"Well, I didn't want to think so," he said.

"Why not? Other than the fact you don't pay for sex?"

"I'd *never* pay for it. Even if I was ugly as a fence post."

Her gaze wandered over him. "Believe me. You have nothing to worry about."

"No worries, darling," he corrected her. "We're behind on our lessons here."

"No worries." Repeating the mantra, Darcie folded him close. *Darling*. "But on second thought, isn't this subject too personal for our first date?"

"What, sex? Have another beer," he said. "Then you won't care." He paused. "Is that what this is?" He glanced at the duvet, the pillows, Darcie. "A *date?*"

"Well. I guess not." She murmured, "No strings."

Warm and scented with sex, with each other, they lay close under the covers, drinking tall cans of Foster's lager. Another, then another. Ugh. Still, beer didn't taste so bad by the third bottle. Or was it fourth? At some point he'd called room service after they finished the minibar supply to have it restocked.

"For a woman who hates beer," he finally said, "you're holding your own here."

The room spun a little. "It's cheaper than the hard stuff."

He kissed her again, tasting of beer and man. "You live where?"

She hadn't told him. "New York."

"*City?*"

He sounded horrified. She took another swallow. "Uh-huh. Right outside of Manhattan. You know, the island the Native Americans sold to the Dutch."

"By yourself?"

No, with my grandmother. She couldn't say that, either. Didn't want him to know too much about her. Darcie pushed away the memory of home, even of Gran, who would appreciate more than anyone else this little tryst, and of course banished any thought of her mother. Tonight was tonight. Her one-time, one-night stand. Tomorrow was...

"No way. I have a roommate."

"Male or female?"

"Uh...female." Two actually. Eden Baxter and Sweet Baby Jane, the devil's spawn. Nearly a week later Darcie's punctured calf still hurt. She tried to recall her last tetanus shot but couldn't.

He frowned again. It made him look totally endearing, even if he did show signs—serious ones—of being too much like her family. "If I was your father," he said, proving the point, "I wouldn't let you live in such a big city. Too dangerous."

"Let me? You're not my father." Darcie ran one finger down his belly, then lower. "*This* is too dangerous."

That distracted him. All over again. Just as she hoped, he reached for another packet on the night table. "What happens when I run out of condoms?"

"We'll...renegotiate." She took him in her hand to help. Silk and velvet, strength and vulnerability. "We'll improvise."

"Sounds like a plan."

He made it sound like a question, but Darcie agreed. All she would let herself think about was this: lovemaking, long and lazy, to be relished, the likes of which she'd never known before—take that, Merrick—or perhaps ever would again. They shared the last of the beer...five, or was it six? And over and over Darcie indulged herself, her fantasies, the tug of need low inside, for the rest of the night.

In his arms, she dreaded the dawn—and ignored the first flutters of nausea.

Until a few faint fingers of light finally penetrated the wall of windows in room 3101 of the upscale Westin Sydney. Then Darcie Elizabeth Baxter startled awake, hot bile in her throat—and bolted for the bathroom.

Darcie gave one last gasp, swallowed twice, and straightened. Resting back on her heels on the marble floor, in the doorway of the toilet stall, she swiped the moistened washcloth over her face again, her parched lips, then drew long, deep breaths to steady her stomach.

There. She would live now. Worse luck.

Then she realized she was no longer alone.

Without looking up, Darcie knew he was there, leaning a strong, broad shoulder against the green frosted glass of the bathroom door—and shirtless of course. A quick glance in the vanity mirror confirmed his naked chest. Darcie shuddered while her heart did a little tap dance of appreciation. All that expanse of sunbrowned skin over sleek muscle, warm and smooth under her fingers during the only half-remembered night of casual sex and talk...the feel of the silky dark hair that swept across his breastbone...the lure of tight, dark twin male nipples...

"Hi. How's it going?" he said.

Deep, throaty morning voice. Hint of amusement.

"It's not. I hope."

He laughed, low and intimate, reminding Darcie not only of her illness—wretched, so wretched to be sick away from home, sick in a strange man's company—well, not exactly a stranger now, she had to admit—reminding her of the intimacies they'd shared. Now this...she heard the familiar chink of a can against the gold signet ring on his little finger. Darcie's nose wrinkled at the smell of hops, malt and yeast.

Oh God, he was drinking a beer.

"What time is it?" she said, aghast.

"Almost six."

"Six *a.m.?*"

"Down Under. I can't tell you what time it is in the States. You drank too much."

"I screwed too much," she muttered.

"The beer, the time difference, jet lag. I couldn't help but hear the chunder here."

Her stomach rolled again. "Chunder?"

"A local term for kissing the porcelain god. Aussie-style." He took another swig. "Chunder on the Paramatta," he mused. "Now there's a name for a movie."

"Paramatta?"

"It's the river that flows into Sydney Harbour. I know, that doesn't make any sense, but you have to admit it's got title appeal. Still, there can't be a worse sound for another human being to listen to," he said.

Which didn't seem to bother him. If he could drink beer at this time of day he had a stomach like steel. The six-pack abs, she could certainly vouch for. That is, until she'd suddenly jolted from bed.

"Believe me. I'd gladly trade places."

"I wouldn't." She heard the smile in his voice, the concern, too, but couldn't face him. "I've done my time. Thought I'd let you have your privacy here. You sure you're all right now?"

She cleared her throat, her voice shaky. "I'm fine."

"You look kind of gray—like a battleship."

"How flattering."

But then, forget the closet mirror last night. Probably her wide behind spread over half the floor in this position. Tightening her muscles, she shot a glance in his direction. A better view, for sure. Bare chest, flat belly, jeans zipped but not snapped. And, oh dear lord, there was that heavy bulge again behind his fly. What kind of man got an erection looking at a sick woman? But Darcie's face flushed with heat, and memory. Her own fingers twitched. She couldn't keep her hands off...*it*...all night. Was half a memory better than none? She couldn't recall much else.

Maybe she didn't need to, and eight—possibly nine—fully packed inches was sufficient. *Or what's a heaven for?*

Darcie groaned inwardly. Her thighs tingled. The depths of depravity to which she'd sunk since crossing the Pacific a day ago—or was it three?—continued to amaze her. Thirteen-plus hours on a jet from San Francisco with a good tail wind and she'd turned into a slut. A drunken…what was the Aussie term he'd taught her sometime during the night?…*bit of a brothel*. A mess, all right.

After this interlude on her knees, how could she feel aroused by even a sunbrowned, muscled god of an Outback male? A cowboy, no less. The sudden image of his slate-green Akubra hat—*what the hell had they done with that in the throes of their one-night stand passion?*—flashed through the remnant of her mind. And she hadn't even passed the city limits of Sydney to fall under his spell.

As if he could have any interest left in her now. She'd picked him up in the Westin bar…practically dragged him to his own room. She could feel him watching her, most likely wondering whether to call the local version of those little men in the white coats. Or the vice squad. A doctor…but he had his own diagnosis.

"It must have been the beer. You're not pregnant. Are you?"

"Pregnant? *Me?*"

Her gaze shot to him again. His dark eyes clear and direct—no hangover for him, no matter how much he drank—he shifted his weight against the door frame. Early sun shafted through the bedroom window that overlooked Darling Harbour blocks away, penetrated the clear glass wall into the bathroom like a lover, and gilded him in soft rose-gold light.

"I don't mean from last night, darling—" in the mirror his eyebrows, darker than his hair, lifted "—but what about before?"

"Not a problem, I haven't had sex since 1985."

When she finally turned, he was scowling, perplexed. Darcie figured the teasing lie was payback for his comments about tucker.

"How is that possible? You said you were a virgin till you were twenty-three. Six years, that would be—"

"A joke."

"Which thing?"

"Both."

He didn't look like he believed her. Not the brightest bulb in the pack, she'd decided, but that body of his simply wouldn't give up. Maybe, after Merrick, it was enough. She stared at him, her bout of nausea forgotten, then stared some more.

To her utter disgust, fresh, fierce desire snaked through her. He followed her inspection with his eyes.

"See something you like? Again?"

Darcie gave in. What the hell. An ounce of Scope and she'd be good as new.

Almost.

Rising, she swished out her mouth then crossed the room to him on shaky limbs. *You're history, Merrick Lowell.* If she didn't make love again until the next half of the twenty-first century, she would darn well make some memories with this Australian sheep rancher to tide her over. She looped her arms around his neck to whisper in his ear.

"Hi. I'm Darcie Baxter. And you are...?"

Chapter Four

"Dylan Rafferty."

With a heavy sigh, Darcie came clean about her last-night lover. She sank gratefully onto a bench in Hyde Park that afternoon then stared down the allée of eucalyptus trees opposite the center fountain in front of her, not really seeing their silvery trunks or feathery branches. Not smelling their heady scent every time those limbs moved in the light breeze. Not hearing the splash of water, the twitter of birds. Not even responding to the name she'd finally uttered to Walt Corwin.

"He farms sheep?"

He'd been pressuring her all day. Hank Baxter in disguise.

She said, "Like a million other Aussies with millions of sheep, yes."

Walt scowled harder. "And you just had to go to bed with him our first night in Sydney?"

"Gee, I didn't know you missed me."

"Very funny."

"I was off duty. You were brain dead from the trip,

already asleep. WLI—Wunderthings—had no claim on me from 5:00 p.m. yesterday to nine this morning."

At which point she and Walt had met for a quick breakfast in the Westin club lounge before their morning meeting with a group of Aussie businessmen and representatives from city government, all of whom seemed concerned with a U.S. lingerie firm encroaching on New South Wales territory.

"We're trying to develop *Australian* business," they said.

"Yes. Australia is poised to become a world power, financially speaking," Walt had agreed. "We can help. It's time to bring one of America's best-known and well-regarded corporations for women's wear to this continent."

The word *knickers* kept coming up. And *underpinnings*.

Odd. For most of the day, Darcie had wished for Dylan Rafferty's presence—and not, this time, in bed. Maybe she could hire him as a translator.

"We're concerned, Mr. Corwin," said the crisply dressed executive who seemed to head the group, "with preserving and creating *Australian* jobs."

"Wunderthings will bring more jobs." Walt fumbled in his briefcase.

Darcie came to his rescue. Swiftly, she handed out papers around the table. "I think you'll find these projections mean serious revenue for Sydney."

Walt flashed her a look of naked gratitude. "And once we prove ourselves here, the rest of the country will benefit. Canberra, Adelaide, Melbourne…"

Well, that didn't prove the right thing to say. Apparently, a great rivalry existed between the cities of Melbourne and Sydney. To the old-guard social set from Melbourne, Sydneysiders were merely a bunch of ex-convicts, as Dylan had implied. Upstarts, someone said.

It had been a grueling meeting and Darcie hadn't recovered yet.

Worse, her feet hurt.

At four o'clock she wanted nothing more than to slip off her shoes and rub her toes until they stopped cramping.

Please. If it wasn't one cramp for a woman, it was another. And just like a man, Walt had dragged her up and downhill the rest of the day, heedless of the fact that she was wearing heels. Chunky ones, yes. But Darcie could scream from the pressure on her insteps now. The canted incline of the streets had turned her mood from morning-after tingles, courtesy of Dylan Rafferty, to late-afternoon agony. At least she was wearing a cotton dress. Summer in January? She couldn't hate that.

"How many storefronts do you think we looked at to-day?" she asked.

"Not enough."

"Walt, I think you're taking the wrong approach." When he glared at her, Darcie hastily added, "*We* are, I mean." It wouldn't do to offend him. Team Player Darcie at your service, Mr. Corwin. Sir. She reminded herself that she was a long way from home, and at least Walt spoke normal English. He didn't murder his vowels and he didn't lift his voice at the end of every sentence.

Not that it wasn't a charming effect coming from Dylan Rafferty. His "language lessons," too.

Was Walt really angry with her for staying out all night? *Gee*, she thought. *I was only two floors down, practically underneath you.* She shuddered at that image of Walt. Dylan Rafferty in bed was one thing...

Too bad she'd never see him again.

"Go on," Walt said.

"What?"

"Say what's on your mind."

I'd like to spend the night, for the next two weeks, with a sheep farmer.

Yet it was Darcie who'd set their boundaries. No names. Then names but no plans for the future...even for tonight. "Let's play it by ear," whatever that meant. She was too tired to figure it out. Like the rest of her life.

"You don't think we should look at that place on Gloucester Walk?" Walt said.

"Well, it's trendy—"

"The Rocks is one of the best neighborhoods in the

city these days. Maybe it used to be a slum but no longer.
We're talking upscale with a vengeance. I don't see how
we could lose, Darce. It's high traffic—"

"Not on weekdays, and after five the restaurants get all
the business."

"Your suggestion would be…?" His voice held an edge.
Walt gazed down the eucalyptus allée, across Park Street,
toward the Anzac Memorial. A flock of ibis strutted past
to peck at a bed of marigolds.

Careful, Darcie. Walk soft but carry a big stick.

She shuddered when another spasm of pain shot through
her instep.

"Damn. I give up." She yanked off her shoe, massaged,
and groaned. "God, that's better than sex." Oops.

"Must have been a great night with the sheep farmer."

"It was. But right now I need this even more."

Impatient, Walt got to his feet. *He* wasn't limping and
he didn't have a run in his panty hose. Darcie straightened
on the park bench then let him off the hook. Walt was a
fine boss, a good mentor, and he'd been with Wunderthings from the start. But five years didn't turn him into a
woman—a woman on limited time these days with too
many obligations to juggle.

"From my research, I learned that Australian women are
just now joining the rest of the world. It's become an
economic necessity. They used to be stay-at-home moms,
but two wage earners are needed to pay the bills, just as
in America, and no one has time to hike around looking
for underwear, even in The Rocks."

"So?"

"Our best stores in the U.S.—the majority of our
branches—are where?"

She knew she'd be wise to let him take the credit.

"Malls," Walt said, but as if he'd never heard the word
before.

"Right. Like the Barrack Street Mall, the Pitt Street
Mall." Darcie paused. "Any of them here are in the center
of the action. They'd make shopping convenient, quick,
accessible. Let's look there."

He groaned. "My back's killing me. Come on," he said, "we have one more today. Then you can buy me dinner. Tomorrow we'll try your idea."

"You have an expense account."

"So do you right now. It's your turn."

Darcie hesitated. "You just want to keep an eye on me tonight, make sure I don't have any fun." No, that wasn't wise, either. "I mean, get myself in trouble."

Walt shook his head. "With Dylan Rafferty."

"He must be Irish. You know what they say about those Irish men."

He gave her a look. "Don't believe everything you read. He's an Aussie, too."

"And the combination is *magnifique*." Was, she added silently.

She'd been out of her mind to go to his room. She'd been even crazier to let him out of her sight after their one-night stand.

Story of my life, Darcie thought. Ships passing in the morning…and all that. She remembered the sight of him then, not in jeans but in his well-tailored suit. Her mouth watered. That white shirt against his tanned skin, and overlaying his muscles…

Walt's scowl returned. "You gonna see him again?"

"I doubt it."

"Just as well," he told her. "We have a lot to accomplish in two weeks."

He led her back through the park to Elizabeth Street.

"I'm telling you," Darcie said. "We're wasting our time with this location."

"Knowledge is power."

"Walt—do you have a *life?*" Did she?

Greta liked getting to work early. She loved dawn in Manhattan and French crullers on her way to the office, carrying hot black coffee in a cardboard cup. She enjoyed being alone when no one else was around, and the elevator, the aisles on her floor, the cubicles everywhere, stood empty. She adored the chance each morning to go through someone else's desk.

Slinking past the big copy machines at the end of the row, toting her coffee and pastry, Greta wandered into Nancy Braddock's space. Just outside Walter Corwin's office, the anteroom wasn't quite its own room—but close. Certainly closer than Greta's cubicle, and far more private.

Breathing a sigh of relief, she cast off her heavy black winter coat, flinging it across Nancy's desk chair, then pushed up her sweater sleeves. An acrylic sweater, of course. Greta couldn't afford cashmere. She couldn't even afford Darcie's silk-wool blends. Greta knew because she sneaked looks at Baxter's labels whenever the opportunity arose. Setting her coffee and cruller bag on the desk, she went to work. Nancy deserved this round of snooping. So did Walter.

Even the thought of his name made Greta's heart bump.

As for Darcie... With a brisk sense of purpose, she set about her task.

At Wunderthings, no one locked drawers. Greta had worked in offices where privacy, and security, were matters for paranoia. Not so here. Thank goodness. It amazed her, but in her five years with the company—she and Walter had started on the same day—she had learned a lot in these early morning sessions.

If only Nancy hadn't caught her with Darcie's proposal.

The office felt more empty than usual this morning—and the solitude fairly shrieked of her own defeat.

Thanks to Nancy, Darcie Baxter was now in Sydney. With Walter.

The double insult was not to be borne.

After a brief foray through the desk drawers, Greta pulled Nancy's in-basket toward her. She plowed through monthly reports, expense account renderings, phone messages...finding nothing of interest. Still, you never knew.

Darcie's naiveté would be her downfall—if Greta had anything to say about it. She just needed to wait for her next opportunity, and keep searching. No way would that dark-haired, hazel-eyed, trim little witch from Ohio trump her ace again. With Nancy's help, of course.

She ruffled through a stack of invoices, including Walter's AmEx bill for his tickets to Australia, and felt a heavy rush of desire that pooled down low in her stomach. *Walter...*

He never noticed her. Not really. But that, too, would change.

When the elevator doors whooshed open at the end of the hall, Greta crouched low behind Nancy's desk. What eager beaver had shown up early this morning? Not Nancy, she hoped. Not Walter. Certainly not Darcie, who was probably at this very moment wrapped around him in some Sydney hotel room. Why couldn't Baxter be satisfied with her new job assignment? Wasn't that enough? Did she need Walter Corwin, too?

Anger boiled in her veins.

Greta cocked her head to listen for a moment, but the person who exited the elevator—whoever it might be— walked down an adjacent corridor, and his footsteps faded. Probably one of the big brass...none of whom had ever acknowledged her contributions to Wunderthings International.

She would outlast them all.

One of these days Walter would recognize her value. He would overlook the rumblings from the office malcontents who tried to blame her for their own creative shortcomings. Darcie Baxter among them.

Greta's hand stilled on the next to last paper in the pile.

Aha. So Nancy was no brighter than Darcie. No more resourceful.

It took Greta Hinckley to pull things off. Someday Walter would reward her.

The medium-size yellow note had nearly escaped her notice.

Just as Walter, and the board, and everyone at Wunderthings failed to realize her talents. Oh, Nancy, she thought. You shouldn't have done this.

Walt, the message read, using the familiar form of his

name. *I've just seen Darcie's proposal—attached—in Greta Hinckley's in-basket. This idea is Darcie Baxter's. Maybe you should reconsider Greta's "suggestions" for global expansion.*

How dare she?

Furious, Greta tore the note into pieces, then into smaller scraps until not a single word remained intact. Darcie Baxter had already been on her list. Now, Nancy Braddock joined her.

Greta shoved the paper pieces into her gray slacks pocket. She grabbed her coat from the chair, draped it over her arm, aand marched down the hall to her own cubicle. In her other hand she carried her cardboard container of coffee, the greasy bag with the cruller swinging with it. No one would mistake her space for an anteroom, surely not for an actual office.

But someday...

She would triumph.

Darcie had no idea who she was dealing with. None at all. Nancy, either.

Bitches.

She would plow them both under. Laughing all the way.

In the night-dark acrylic tunnel of the Sydney Aquarium, Darcie gazed up in wonder. Above and to either side along the curving route past one tank after another, manta rays, sharks and eels dipped and glided and flowed around her. Their graceful motions tightened her throat in awe. The variety of the coral reef that decorated the display made her mouth water. So did her companion.

She couldn't believe she had linked up again...and again...with Dylan Rafferty. He seemed too good to be true—most of the time. Like this splendid place.

"What I wouldn't give to capture these colors," she told Dylan. Meaning, *Take you home in my luggage and keep you for myself.*

His hand squeezed hers in the darkness, his gold signet ring imprinting her skin. She doubted he knew what she meant about color, but his broad-shouldered presence be-

side her enhanced the Saturday sight-seeing experience. It
had been a wonderful few days.

"I'd use them at the new store. I'd reproduce them in
scarves, in lingerie. Wunderthings would churn—like these
magnificent animals—with spectacular hues and shades, all
light and shadow...."

Dylan slipped his arm around her.

"Don't tell me I'm *drongo*," she murmured. "It's my
job."

Instead, he said, "Walt Corwin doesn't like me."

Surprised, she said, "Walt doesn't like anyone."

That wasn't quite true, but she didn't want to hurt Dylan's feelings. He'd been quiet during their tour of the
aquarium—her choice of activity—and at first she'd
thought he was simply, like Darcie, taking in the beauty
of their surroundings. Apparently, he'd been brooding.

"He took one look at me and nearly hauled you off to
your room. Alone."

"Dylan, we had a one-minute chance meeting with him
in the hotel lobby. No big deal." Or was it? She sounded
just like Merrick Lowell about his marriage. "Walt's not
my father, either." She didn't know which would be
worse, him or Hank Baxter. "You're not upset, are you?"

"Nope." His mouth tightened.

"You sound upset."

The crowd funneled around them, and Dylan drew her
off to the side, midway down a straight stretch of tunnel.
He pointed out a yellow-and-black striped tiger fish.
"Nice pair of briefs," he suggested, then, "I'm not upset."

"Just because that wouldn't be macho, or because you're
really not?"

"Really not."

He leaned to kiss the nape of her neck and a thrill shot
along her nerves.

"Oh. Look." She didn't want their outing spoiled. Darcie dragged him by the hand to another section of the tank
where a brilliant clump of fuschia waved in the water.
"What is that?"

"Anemone. See?" He pointed again. "The purple one? The blue?"

"It's teal."

"Looks plain blue to me." With a laugh, Dylan stood beside her at the glass while Darcie counted colors and sighed in appreciation.

"They're gorgeous."

He bent to nuzzle her throat. "So are you."

She spun to face him, feeling hot color in her own cheeks, and nearly clipped his chin with the top of her head. Was he serious? *Her,* gorgeous? Dylan liked to speak his mind, and he didn't bother to hide his impressions— of her or anything else. She liked that about him—loved it, really—at the same time he took her by surprise. Darcie was accustomed to men like Merrick who either didn't share emotion or didn't feel it in the first place. She never knew which. Her father, too.

Darcie blinked.

"My eyes are too far apart," she said. "My fingers are stumpy and I—"

Dylan looked around, saw that they were relatively alone in the dark tunnel, and drew her close. "Last night, all night, you seemed exactly right to me."

At the heated memory she could barely speak.

"You're a charmer, Dylan Rafferty."

How did I get this lucky, for once?

So why not overlook the little differences she'd discovered during the past few days? Dylan's outspoken opinion of men and women and the roles they should play was…antiquated, courtly. Likewise, his attitude that children should be uppermost in a couple's relationship, and quickly. And his continuing praise of his mum. Darcie agreed with him about a love of children, but she'd soon realized he was thirty years behind the times. And stubborn. As for his views on women with careers, like Darcie…

"Not by half as charmed as I am. By you," he said, linking his strong hand with her fingers. He led Darcie around a bend to the next aquarium where a school of reef fish in even more vibrant colors swam and turned and glided through the water. Sparkling and bright, it appeared sunlit from above. "You want to leave soon? Go back to the hotel?"

His suggestive tone dissolved Darcie to mush.

"Pretty soon. Let's see the rest first."

If he wasn't upset, was he bored? She hoped not. But maybe his interest in her was in bed, nowhere else. Darcie wouldn't let it matter. Three nights ago she had come home after "house hunting" with Walt at The Rocks to find Dylan in the hotel bar. Not that she'd looked in hoping to spot him…or run back downstairs the instant Walt dropped onto his bed for a quick nap before dinner. She almost didn't need the elevator.

Walt hadn't been happy with Darcie, who didn't show up again until morning. She supposed she couldn't blame him, in the days since, for his continued sourness or his cool greeting when he finally met Dylan. Her fault. But to be honest, spending her nights with Dylan in his room was like getting a big bag of her favorite red licorice whips as an unexpected present. She'd make herself wait for tonight, anticipate.

She walked through the darkened tunnels holding his hand, feeling the beat of her own pulse against his skin. Or was that Dylan's heart? Given a second chance, after her original "mystery" and "play it by ear" remarks, she wouldn't make that mistake again. As long as she was here, she would see Dylan.

At the aquarium. And later, in his bed.

The tunnel bent again, soft classical music piped into the atmosphere as if keeping time with the bubbling water around them. Darcie's eyes filled with tears. When the magical tunnel ended near an enormous tank filled with coral, anemones, and fish of every description, she spied a set of carpeted steps. She drew Dylan down to sit beside her. For a few moments she listened and felt an inexplicable urge to cry at the beauty of the darkened tunnels, the spectacular life contained within the tanks…or because she'd found this beautiful man all for herself?

For now.

Dylan slipped her into the crook of his arm and she leaned her head against his shoulder. Darcie's hair slid over his other hand at the nape of her neck. Dylan shuddered a little then pulled her closer. A teenage couple nearby on the steps was making out in the dark. A pair of rowdy toddlers raced up and down the stairs. Their frazzled parents scrambled after them. Darcie sat very still, absorbing the heat and power of Dylan's embrace. When he lowered his head to kiss her, she felt every cell of her body ignite.

Darcie touched his face. "This is the nicest date I've ever had."

"Ah. So it's a date now, is it?"

"Definitely."

Dylan lifted his head. "What if it was more than a date?"

"You mean after this, in the room?" She whispered the words.

"No, in my life," he said. "Your life."

Darcie pulled back a little. "My, you're a fast one." Her tone sounded flippant, but she was suddenly trembling.

"I like you, Darcie." *I love you,* Merrick had said. "We're...compatible, for sure." He grinned. That gorgeous grin. Then he bent his head again to take her mouth, and for an instant Darcie forgot what he was saying. "I've known you just less than four days and I feel like it's...forever."

"That would be a trick."

"What would?" he asked.

"If you and I tried to..."

"Have a serious relationship?"

"You said it, not me." She didn't have relationships. Like Merrick, they never lasted. She had Wunderthings to consider—Walt was right—New York, Gran and even Sweet Baby Jane. That was her life.

Dylan took her hand between his. Strong, lean, callused from his work.

"What are you scared of?"

"I'm not scared. I barely know you."

He gave her a slow smile. "Pretty well, wouldn't you say?"

Darcie swallowed. "Three nights in bed, here at the aquarium—" she gestured at a school of zebra fish in the tank "—breakfast this morning in the lounge..." She shook her head.

"Don't forget dinner last night."

"That was in bed, too. We didn't even finish."

"Doesn't count, then?" He frowned. "Or doesn't this mean to you what it means to me?"

"Great sex?" Darcie tried. "Ozspeak lessons? Strine?"

His gaze lowered. "You want to make fun, I can't stop you."

"Dylan." She eased her hand from his. "I'm not trying to hurt you, but after my boss and I find the space we want here, I'll be leaving for New York. Do you know how far away that is?"

"It's a big ocean."

"Yes, and what would be the point of our even keeping in touch?"

"You'll be back. Won't you?"

"Maybe, but..." She had no idea when. Or if Walt would suddenly decide—after her wayward nights on this trip—to bring Greta in her place. Then what did she want of Dylan? "I know it seems shallow, enjoying each other for a time..."

He drew back against the next step to rest on his elbows. His face went taut.

"I'm not using you."

"I'm not using you either. But where...where could this go?"

"Anywhere we want."

Oh, God, he would turn her into a permanent mess of Silly Putty. That voice, those eyes, his hands, even this new edge to him...

"Besides," she said, "you seem to want things that I don't. Not yet anyway." She waved a hand again. "I don't want to become my mother."

"What's wrong with her?"

"Nothing, except she lives a very different lifestyle from the one I've chosen."

He cocked his head. "Don't tell me you pick up strangers in bars everywhere?"

She flushed. "No, of course not. You were the first." *And last.* She tried to explain. "Look. My mother named me Darcie. Darcie Elizabeth Baxter. Do you know what my initials make together?"

He looked perplexed. Which only melted her heart.

"D.E.B.," she told him. "DEB. In the U.S. that's a girl raised to be socially proper, to "come out" at eighteen at a dance where she wears a white dress and gloves, to meet the exactly right man who will elevate her position—" No, that didn't sound right, it sounded kinky. "I mean, raise her standard of living to new heights, beyond even her parents' and—"

Dylan guessed right. "You didn't want to be a deb."

"No! That's such an old-fashioned system. I wanted to be my own person—not that we were rich enough for me to be presented to society. I want to choose the man I'll marry someday, after my own career is in motion. I need to be able to take care of myself first. I *want* to be independent."

"Is this some of that women's lib stuff?"

She didn't want to blow this. "It was. Years ago some women—not my mother—took a stand, and because of those women opportunities opened up for the next generation. Now, in my generation I can be anyone I want to be, do anything I wish. This trip to Sydney is my first chance to prove myself."

"And I'm part of that. Temporarily." He paused. "Was that what picking me up in the bar was about? Is that why you went over the top that first night? Made yourself sick? Were you trying to prove how *independent* you are, as free with sex as any man? That's not even possible, Darcie. Women get pregnant, men don't. Were you showing your mother you aren't like her at all?"

This wasn't going well. She didn't know what else to say.

"You know," Dylan went on, "my mum's probably like yours. Only she grew up on a farm, not in Cincinnati. She married my dad, had three kids—I have two sisters—stayed home to raise them." He frowned harder. "She nurtured us, and him. He took care of her. I don't see what's wrong with that."

"It's not wrong. But isn't this more than premature?"

"We're having an intellectual discussion." He gazed at her in the dark. The noisy toddlers had scampered off back down the tunnel. Their tired-looking parents trailed after them. The two teenagers were still necking in the corner. "But you think the opportunity will last forever?"

She didn't see why not, except for that biological clock Claire had mentioned. Darcie wasn't ready to face that yet, either, much less a "relationship" with Dylan that had little chance of working out. On either side.

"Do we have to have this conversation? I thought we were having fun."

She tried to rise but Dylan tugged her back down onto the step.

He drew her into his arms and she didn't—couldn't—resist. Her heart pounded furiously, in excitement or alarm, she couldn't distinguish. He moved closer, gathered her in, covered her half-open mouth with his.

"Dylan." She would dissolve if he didn't stop.

But what about Dylan's view that a woman's place was still in the home? The last thing she wanted was a Cincinnati clone—a man from the Outback instead of suburban Ohio, but with the same notions. The last thing Dylan wanted was a city girl with a mind of her own. Or did he?

"This is us," he said, "not your mother or mine. Not just some date, not a few nights in the rack..." His next kiss rocked her. His tongue twined with hers and Darcie lost her senses. She clung to him, the poignant classical music swirling around them, through them, like a school of graceful fish. "Don't you see?"

Before Darcie could object, Dylan's hand slipped inside her blazer to capture a breast. Still kissing her, he kneaded it softly, tweaked the nipple into a hard, tight peak of need. Darcie couldn't help that, either. She moaned. In the corner, the teenagers jerked apart.

And Dylan smiled into the seductive dark, his features lit by the glow of artificial sunlight from the tank. After that, she was gone—no matter how different his outlook might be. Darcie would define her own life—and happiness—later.

"Your room?" he said into her mouth. "Or mine?"

Chapter Five

Claire Spencer walked the nursery floor with her four-week-old daughter. At this rate she would soon be in the best aerobic shape of her life. How many miles tonight? Four, six? Right now, at midnight, the room stayed quiet, peaceful. The very silence—the first since 5:00 p.m.—sounded like a shout. Samantha's small dark head lay nestled on Claire's breast, and at the faint pressure Claire felt a slight leak of milk. Too soon to nurse, she thought with an inner groan. *Please don't wake up again.*

Peter had given out an hour ago. Tossing her a bleary scowl, he'd disappeared into their adjoining bedroom and she could hear him now, snoring through the open door.

Men. There at the instant of conception, there at the moment of birth.

Claire arched an eyebrow. After that, Peter—like most of her friends' husbands or significant others—seemed to feel their duties had been discharged. Oh, he loved Samantha. Worshipped her, really. Daddy's Girl. But forget the sexual revolution, the equality of roles. His love didn't include more than one diaper change per day, no BMs thank you very much, one support bottle of formula on the rare occasions when Claire managed to escape. She hadn't been out of their apartment for more than two hours at a stretch since giving birth.

Motherhood was a bond. Like cement. No, more like Krazy Glue, and she'd stuck all her fingers together.

Immediately, Claire scolded herself. How could she think this way? She didn't just love Samantha, she would give her life for her child—and in those horrid moments during transition labor, before she felt the insane urge to push her entire insides out into the world along with her about-to-be-born infant, Claire had feared she just might end up dying for the cause.

Middle-of-the-night madness.

Samantha stirred and Claire's smile softened.

"We won't tell anyone, will we, sweetie?"

Hell, she was alive. Healthy, in fact. Her bottom had finally stopped burning. She would be able to bear the thought of sex again—in a year or two. And wasn't some of her flab starting to jell?

When Claire slipped a hand to her waist, checking its firmness, Samantha snuffled at her chest. Then she whimpered. A second later she was working herself into another first-rate howl and Claire felt tempted to join her.

"Listen, baby love. It's time to sleep. Get it?"

As if to say *I had my rest,* Samantha squirmed in her embrace and Claire's grip spasmed, making the baby scream. My God, had she nearly dropped her own child? It amazed Claire how strong an eight-pound infant could be.

"Peter," she called in panic.

No answer. Except for his continued rumblings. It amazed Claire how much noise, in infinite varieties, a man could make in his sleep.

"Did I really want this?" she muttered to herself, about her marriage or her baby, Claire wasn't sure.

Samantha cried harder.

Where is my mother when I need her? But Claire was a nearly thirty-year-old woman with a home, a husband, a career and a baby—and her own mother's postcard from

Fiji had come in the morning mail. Claire knew her parents hadn't even heard yet about Samantha's birth. Hopping from island paradise to exotic resort for the past six weeks, they hadn't called in more than a month. In her current state of total disorganization, Claire had misplaced their itinerary.

"What is wrong with me?" she asked Samantha, tears in her eyes.

No matter how hard she cried, Samantha would shed no tears, the doctor said, for another few weeks. Claire shed them for her. In copious amounts.

Jiggling the baby, shushing her softly so Peter wouldn't wake, she headed for the changing table. Of course. Why didn't she think before? An infant had basic needs. Last diaper change…she calculated madly…was an hour before, just after Peter went to bed. He smelled "poo," he said, and that was all it took to send him padding into the other room.

Claire didn't even glance at his bare feet when he scooted across the carpet. She loved his long, elegant feet. His soft brown eyes, his sandy-gold hair. Loved everything about him, really. Except that his image as a newborn father wasn't holding up well. This wasn't how they'd planned things. Blinking, Claire laid Samantha on the cushioned table and fumbled with the snaps of her yellow sleeper.

Samantha screamed.

"I always thought of myself as a fairly dexterous person," Claire mumbled. "Good thing I'm not a rabid conservationist—into cloth diapers with sharp pins."

She'd probably skewer Samantha.

Oh damn, now she was picking up Darcie's habit. Well, why not? Like an unmarried woman living alone, Claire had no one else to talk to. For a single second she disliked Darcie. Off in Australia, drinking good wine and eating great beef—with no fear of Mad Cow disease—meeting scads of Aussie men who seemed to have cornered the good genes market in looks, except for Peter of course. Visions of *Breaker Morant* and *Gallipoli,* of Bryan Brown at his peak and Mel Gibson any time raced through her weary mind. More tears. Even the thought of Russell Crowe didn't stop them.

"I am a disaster. Me, Claire Kimberly Spencer, VP."

Sniffling, crooning to herself as much as to Samantha, hands shaking, she managed to wrestle off the wet diaper printed with smiling nursery characters, then unfolded the paper glob. Ugh. Not again, she thought, glad her nose had stuffed up from crying so she couldn't smell. "More poo, sweetie?"

Swallowing, holding her breath, she cleaned, then swabbed Samantha's bottom with baby oil, but the lighter fragrance didn't permeate Claire's nostrils.

Samantha wouldn't stop crying. How could she wail that loud at the same time she wriggled like a crazed Slinky? At this rate, she'd be turning over before four months. She'd crawl at six and stand at seven and be walking by eight. Then watch out, folks. In no time she'd be ripping around the apartment, falling down the steps, pulling things off shelves, gashing her cheek on the coffee table...

"Oh, hell."

It certainly was, at least at midnight without any sleep for the past four weeks. She envied Darcie her freedom, and she loathed men. Especially, at the moment, her own. The instigator of all her inadequacies.

"What's going on in here?" As if she had conjured him up, he appeared in the nursery doorway in pajama bottoms, raking his fingers through his chest hair.

Claire glared at him. Samantha's decibel level shrieked higher.

"Was this your idea?"

"What?"

"Having a..." She caught herself. "B-a-b-y. Because I have to tell you—"

"Hey, there, Samson." Peter strolled across the room. In seconds he'd come wide-awake, like a fireman on call, and his soft brown eyes filled with such obvious love for their child that Claire had to turn away. It embarrassed her to see Peter look like that—and not for her. *Now I'm a jealous witch,* Claire thought. He bent over the changing table to plant a wet kiss on Samantha's bare belly. "You're going for the record, kid. Keepin' your mom up every night of your life so far."

"Hear me laughing." Claire's throat tightened again.

When it suddenly turned quiet in the room, her ears rang. She risked a glance at the baby. Samantha lay staring up at Peter with the same adoring look in her blue eyes. Straightening, he grinned. "She's crazy about me. What can I say?"

"She's the first baby ever born that doesn't love her mother." Her voice quavered. "I thought they didn't smile until at least six weeks."

Nudging her aside, he picked up the baby, cradling her like an old pro. Claire tried not to remember that she'd nearly dropped Samantha moments ago. Apparently, Peter had paid closer attention to their preparenting classes. Claire was still all thumbs. She couldn't hold back her frustration.

"How do you do that?"

Like an inept acolyte she followed him across the room to the walnut rocker they'd bought. Peter settled into it with the baby. Claire stood watching with her hands on her hips. Pure cellulite. They felt like unset gelatin.

"How?" Peter said, gazing into Samantha's eyes. She gazed back. "Practice."

"*Practice?* You're at work all day. You come home, pick her up, play cootchy coo, then watch Fox News. While I've been cooped up here all day, changing yucky diapers every five minutes—how can one small bundle her size pee that much?—and nursing every second between changes."

Peter's gaze shifted to her breasts. His eyes darkened.

"I love it when you talk dirty."

She turned on her heel. "I'll leave you two alone."

"Claire," he said, sounding genuinely puzzled.

"I was wondering how I could go back to work on half an hour's sleep—that is, if you stay in here rocking for thirty minutes every night."

"My pleasure."

"I wondered how I'll pump enough milk for Samantha every morning before I leave here." She marched toward the bedroom. "Now I wonder how I'll ever drag myself home." In the doorway she turned, blinking. "Peter, I'm not cut out to be a mother."

"You're just tired, babe." He yawned. "More tired than I am."

Claire went into the other room before her fresh tears spilled over. Samantha was the most perfect, most adorable baby in the world. She was part of Peter, part of Claire. But Claire had never imagined this job would be so hard.

"Maybe it's time to hire a nanny."

Leasing suitable space for Wunderthings' first Australian store had proved to be as frustrating for Darcie as finding the right man. Not one to give up in either case, the next Thursday she stalked ahead of Walt up the steep slant of King Street to the corner of George and the entrance to the Queen Victoria Building.

"This is a long shot," Walt complained, huffing mildly at the climb from Darling Harbour. "The real estate agent must be out of her mind."

"No, she's perfectly sane. Otherwise she'd be walking with us, not sitting back at her office at the bottom of this hill answering her voice mail."

"You have a point. She won't even show up here." Scowling, he reached out to open the heavy door into the first-floor level of the mall. "She knows better than I do that this is a wild-goose chase."

"Reserve judgment."

Walt had been grumbling all day and Darcie wanted to snap back at him, but *she* knew better. By their second week in Sydney, she'd convinced him that her evenings with Dylan were harmless recreation after the long days of hunting for retail space. Dinner, a few drinks—Darcie omitted the rest of Dylan's "entertainment"—kept her sharp for work the next day, she argued. She didn't want to destroy all her progress now.

On the main floor they picked their way through the throng of shoppers. Smartly dressed women, men in suits and ties. Darcie made a mental note then voiced it. She needed points with Walt. She suspected he would be difficult about spending this much money on rent.

"See? Busy executives, career women, uppercrust young moms with fancy strollers." She blocked out an image of herself at FAO Schwarz, with Merrick. "We'd need to stock mostly the top of our line here. These people aren't shopping for bargains. They want quality and style."

"Hmm," Walt murmured, turning his shoulder to avoid a man on the run. He eyed the guy's charcoal-gray suit, his paisley tie. "You could be right."

Darcie didn't give him time to doubt. "None of your sale bras in this store. These guys will buy lace-trimmed bustiers for that Valentine's Day gift. Thong panties in silk."

Walt shushed her. "No need to announce it over your personal PA system." He glanced around, as if embarrassed.

"Sometimes I wonder why you took a job with an underwear company."

Walt was a prude.

He merely glared. "Where did you say the empty shop is?"

"Second level. Right in the middle. Perfect."

"For Victoria's Secret, maybe. We have a long way to go."

"We're young, we're enthusiastic, we're energetic—" she flung out both arms "—we're *Wunderthings!*"

"Jesus."

Smiling, Darcie led him past the other shops—evening gowns, swimwear, trendy casual clothes, jewelry galore, opals everywhere—to the escalator. On the way they passed stained-glass windows, lots of gleaming dark wood, floors inlaid with intricate tiles. Innovative storefront displays.

"This is a beautiful building. I like what it says to me for our products."

"I knew I should have brought Greta Hinckley instead."

Darcie grinned over her shoulder. "Greta would have talked you into some tiny storefront in The Rocks, The Strand, the Pitt Street Mall—remember that last place with all the jeans and T-shirt stores?—and you'd curse the day for the next three years until the lease expired."

Darcie crossed her fingers in front of her so Walt wouldn't see and said, "I think you'll be impressed with what the QVB offers."

"The Accounting Department won't. And Legal—"

"We'll take care of them."

At the top of the escalator, she stood and gasped. Right in front of them, across the aisles running along either side of the central railing that wound around the long oval and showcased the other levels—a popular "people watching" attraction, she realized—sat the empty shop. Sparkling clean display windows, an inviting entrance…

She grabbed Walt's hand. In her other she clutched the door key.

"Let's take a look." Darcie didn't have to. She was already convinced.

In another five minutes, so was Walt.

"We can try to argue them down on the monthly rent," she told him. "Oh, Walt." Darcie spun around in the center of the empty room. When she walked toward the rear and the tiny adjoining office, the storage area, her heels tapped on the wooden floor. "This needs refinishing, but they should throw in a bit of sanding and polyurethane for the price, don't you think?"

"Not unless they want our business here. The city fathers didn't."

"There's not another lingerie shop like ours. They'll snap up Wunderthings. They'd be crazy not to." She gazed from the rear of the store to the front windows. People walking past glanced in, a woman with a kindergartner gazed inside, looking curious. Darcie dug in her bag for a business card, held it up so the woman would wait, then strode to the open door and handed it out. "Please, take this. And do stop by again when we've opened."

"I will, thanks."

Walt followed her. "We haven't even seen a lease, Darcie."

"Details, details." She peeked outside at their nearest neighbors. "We're between an opal shop and a store that sells power suits. We can't lose. From the skin out, it's three-stop shopping, right on this level. How much better can it get?"

In her bones, Darcie knew this was perfect.

"And downstairs, on the lower level, there are food stores galore. What could be more convenient?"

"A few hundred thousand in the account," Walt muttered.

"You're so cheap."

The real estate agent stepped in from the hall, a smile on her face. She'd known how Darcie would react to this site. She'd given them time to fall in love with the place.

"Marvelous, isn't it?"

"We'll take it," Darcie said.

"Now wait a minute—" Walt protested.

"You know I'm right."

Or so she needed him to think.

He sidled close to her. "What's that Aussie doing to you every night? I'm supposed to be the boss here."

"You are the boss." She batted her eyelashes demurely. And gestured at the real estate agent waiting in the doorway. "Now, please, deal with the nice lady."

"What's it like, buying—I mean, dealing for—a sheep?"

On the following Monday Darcie asked Dylan the question, her hand in his while they strolled along at Circular Quay. He gave her a lazy smile that nearly lightened her growing sense of impending loss. With hot dark eyes.

"Not like buying a pair of bikini pants."

"No, I wouldn't think so." She flushed faintly but plowed on. In an abstract fashion Dylan's sheep station fascinated her. She couldn't imagine living in the middle of nowhere, as he did, but the business itself impressed her. So did his continued presence right here. Buying sheep was Dylan's official reason for lingering in Sydney, for which she was grateful, but Darcie was another. His time, he'd assured her, was flexible. "You need a new ram for your herd, right? Breeding stock."

"Flock, not herd. A herd is cattle."

"Do you have the cow-sheep thing going on here? War between the ranchers like in the Old West?"

He smiled. "Where do you get your information?"

Darcie tapped her forehead with her free hand. "Right here."

Dylan tucked a strand of her hair behind one ear, sending a shivery sensation through Darcie's whole body. "Your mind is a scary place, darling."

"It's an active place. Creative. My mother always said so—not in a complimentary way."

"I'm surprised you didn't conform then just to prove her wrong."

Uh-oh. Dangerous territory. Darcie wasn't going there. Not now, not again.

"Let's just celebrate Australia Day, and leave our mothers at home."

As if he remembered their conversation at the aquarium, Dylan didn't disagree. Swinging hands between them, he walked her to the catamaran that had started its tour at Darling Harbour, then stopped to pick up passengers here. The sun shone, the breeze stayed light, the day seemed perfect, really, like the QVB. Darcie meant to enjoy it. And Dylan. It was her last day in Australia, a fact she wouldn't dwell on. Yesterday he'd taken her to a shop on Crown Street filled with stunning Aboriginal art, as if they had all the time in the world. But Darcie suspected, despite his reassurances, that he should get home. Tomorrow, she and Walt would be on their United flight to Los Angeles and Dylan Rafferty would become part of her past. There seemed no way to avoid it.

"What'd I say?" he asked. "You're frowning."

"Nothing. I was just...pondering sheep."

"Counting," he said. "You tired? We can go back if you want."

To Dylan's room? He always seemed eager to end their

sight-seeing. Part of her didn't want to spend this precious day anywhere but in his bed. But the rest—because she might never come here again, no matter how sweetly he asked, allowed Dylan to help her on board the boat. It was named *Aussie One*. Oh, he certainly was.

Within minutes the catamaran was underway again, and Darcie tried to forget her misgivings, her mixed feelings, about going home. At the exit of the Quay, the boat glided into the harbor past the Sydney Opera House but Darcie scarcely noticed. What if she *could* stay here for a while? Oversee the needed renovations to Wunderthings' new space in the QVB, assuming the contract was approved? Become Walt's point man—woman—for the store? Put her own stamp on its display windows, its interior design?

Recalling her fantasy of Dylan as a model in the window, Darcie felt the breeze blow through her hair. She watched it lift Dylan's darker silk strands, inhaled the ocean scents and watched the smile play on his lips and in his dark eyes. She couldn't get close enough to him today, and crowded nearer. He slipped one arm around her shoulders, the other around her waist and held her tight at the rail.

"Watch."

With his chin, he gestured at the opera house, the boat sliding past it, and Darcie's breath caught at the up-close view.

One of the most readily recognized buildings in the world had disappointed her at first sight. From the distance the Sydney Opera House appeared smaller than expected, not as impressive, and instead of the sparkling white she'd anticipated, it had looked dull, almost muddy. But here, looking up at its famous roofline of "sails," she could see the individual tiles that comprised it and the awesome view brought tears to her eyes.

"It's immense, really."

"Tons and tons of concrete, ceramic..." Dylan turned her face-on toward it. "Keep looking."

Darcie did, then couldn't believe her eyes. In the shifting play of light and shadow across the water, the roof

changed color—from that flat brown to beige and then to
cream, and finally, to a sheer, dazzling white. In the space
of seconds it changed completely, magnificent and startling
and graceful. She blinked harder.

Hormones, she might tell herself. But on her second day
in Sydney they'd kicked in (thank goodness that hadn't
bothered Dylan) and her period had been over for a week.
Then why so blue?

All around her boat horns blared, people called greetings
from the decks, the water churned with celebration. Aussies certainly knew how to handle their national holiday.
As joyously, she thought, as Dylan handled her.

"Beautiful," she whispered around the lump in her
throat.

Dylan tipped up her face to kiss her and the word went
through her again.

Darcie gazed back at the receding view of the opera
house, glistening in the full sunlight now. She wished for
a camera. But the postcards she'd bought would have to
do. So would her memories of these two weeks, with Dylan Rafferty.

"What do you want to do next?"

"Eat lunch."

"And then?"

"I'm waiting for the fireworks." Darcie meant that
night, with Dylan in his room, their last night, but she
would indulge him. He was crazy about the actual star-
bursts that would illuminate the harbor, he'd told her. All
Aussies were.

"Any excuse will do," he said, and kissed her again.

On the beach at Manly, their next stop that afternoon,
Darcie's senses heated another ten degrees. The sun blazed
hotter in the blue Australian sky. In her new bikini she
basked in its warmth, and the ever growing heat in Dylan's
eyes.

But if Darcie had felt naked before, she felt positively
exposed now. The crescent of beach, half an hour's ferry
ride north from Sydney, was jammed with sun worship-

pers, half of whom seemed to be cavorting on the sand or taking in the rays without most of their clothes. The women did sun topless here, she could report to Gran, and Darcie wanted to crawl inside her own skin to hide. *You have nice breasts,* Eden had said. But *yowsah.* Look at that. And that. And those.

By comparison with other women here, she felt her breasts looked skimpy, malnourished. Famine Barbie At the Beach.

Fanned out around her on every square inch of golden sand from the water that lapped against the shore in the sheltered cove to the row of towering Norfolk pines by the nearby street lay dozens—hundreds?—of sleek Aussie females, darkly tanned, scantily dressed. Bikinis, like opals, seemed to be the choice for most.

"Good grief," she murmured, though Dylan seemed unimpressed.

His mouth touched her ear, making her shudder in reaction.

"Take off your bra." Darcie started to protest and he said, "Shy, darling?"

"No. I just...we don't do that in America."

And in Cincinnati? Ha. Her mother, her father, if not Annie would die if they knew Darcie had even considered baring herself to the sun, the crowd and Dylan. Not that *he* hadn't seen her "wares" before.

He propped himself on an elbow and studied her.

"Chicken."

"Sheep," she said, tracing a line with her index finger across his smile. "You think I should follow the flock? When I see the men around us taking off their skinny little Speedos, and you join them, I'll reconsider."

"I think you're chicken." He smiled behind his sunglasses then trailed a finger down her side. Her mostly nude side. "I also think you want to...almost as much as I want you to. Truth or dare."

"I'm not playing."

Dylan sighed in obvious disappointment. "See that girl over there?" He craned his neck to look back over his shoulder at a nearby blanket. A woman was lying on her back, alone. "She's about your size, but hers are tilted. And her nip—"

Darcie slapped his hand. "Pervert. Voyeur."

"I'd rather watch you. I'd rather..." He trailed off, frowning. Dylan flopped back onto one of the beach towels they'd bought several blocks away in one of the souvenir shops. "Hell," he nearly whispered, "I can't bear the thought of you leaving tomorrow."

Alarmed, Darcie gently put her hand over his mouth to silence him.

"Don't. Let's not talk about that today." She couldn't bear it.

He turned his head away from her touch.

"I wish we didn't live so far apart."

"Me, too." She couldn't deny that. But Darcie had almost conquered her earlier sorrow about her flight tomorrow over thousands of miles of open ocean—not something she cared to dwell on in any circumstance. Now that she was leaving Dylan...

As if he sensed her renewed unhappiness, he rolled onto his elbow again and smiled at her, a sexy glint in his eyes, she supposed, though she couldn't see them behind his shades, a definitely intent slant to his lips.

"I know how you can make me forget."

He moved closer until his hip nudged hers. His hard, warm thigh touched Darcie's and she tingled. She could feel herself loosen, tighten in different places, right here on the beach. Across the street, where traffic moved up and down in front of the hotels, where horns tooted and boom boxes vibrated on the warm summer air, people walked and bicyclists rode and skate boarders glided. Hardly private.

"Take off the top, Matilda. Please."

"You're a very bad man."

As if to prove the point, he tugged at the string around Darcie's neck. Before she could move to stop him, Dylan had drawn her bikini top down. He reached behind her to pull the tie at her back and she felt a sensuous slither along her skin.

Darcie tried to turn over onto her stomach but he splayed a hand across her abdomen. "Oh. God," she managed.

And then she was naked to the hot sun, and Dylan's eyes. And those of anyone else who walked by or glanced over.

"Spread your fingers on your chest."

She gazed up at him blankly. The sun felt good, actually. *Look at me, Ma.* The closest thing to skinny-dipping. Janet would turn ten shades of red, not from sunburn. But all at once, with the warmth upon her skin, everywhere, Darcie liked it. When she still didn't move, Dylan lifted her hands, placing them over her breasts, covering her. Except that her nipples poked between her fingers. Hard. Like diamonds, not opals.

Dylan's gaze narrowed, heated.

He scooted down the beach towel, along Darcie's side, until his mouth reached the level of her breasts. He used one hand to turn her, slightly, so he could...

Dear God. He had drawn her erect nipple into his mouth. His tongue flicked against Darcie's fingers and she moaned aloud.

"You want to get a room here?" he whispered.

"No." No, she didn't. She doubted they could rent a room today, despite the many hotels at hand. All would be booked by now. And she wanted him to go on kissing her like this forever, right here, out in the open on the beach at Manly where the whole world could see them— or at least all the Sydneysiders here to celebrate Australia Day. "No," Darcie repeated as he gently sucked and sensation pooled low inside her and Dylan's arousal jutted against her thigh. "I'm...still waiting for the fireworks."

"How's it coming?" Dylan asked late that night.

"Just...fine." Darcie groaned into his mouth. Back from Manly, they were lying on Dylan's bed, in Dylan's room at the Westin, and if Sydney had created the most awesome spectacle of fireworks ever seen over Darling Harbour a few hours ago, that was nothing. In Dylan's inspired hands she was turning into an incendiary device. "I'd say another minute, two at the most and I'll—"

He moved against her, inside her. Silk and velvet. Heat and oiled friction.

"Let me join you."

You don't settle for third-rate, Darcie. You deserve lights and laser shows, Claire had said. *Fireworks.*

Darcie didn't know whether she could ever convey the barest outline of these past two weeks to Claire, Gran, anyone she knew.

Thank the stars—and a few pinwheels, some rockets— for Walter Corwin. He'd barely blinked when Darcie asked to spend the day, the whole day, with Dylan. Walt had an appointment, he said. He and the real estate agent would have brunch, then nail down the last details of the rental contract for the QVB. After that, he'd "keep busy" with a stroll near the harbor, a bite of dinner somewhere, an early night—if he could sleep with the pyrotechnics going off all over the city.

Dylan's hands caught her hips to hold Darcie still.

"Don't move," he murmured. "I'll go off too soon."

How could he, again? Darcie wondered. Didn't men need recovery time? After watching the light show from The Rocks, they'd wandered back to their hotel, stopping here and there along the way to kiss or touch or both, pausing now and then to have another drink somewhere. Then, in Dylan's room for this last night together, they'd fallen into bed. Made love. Once, three times...now four?

"I'm glad you have such staying power."

"Just for you." Even if he didn't mean them, the words sent another wave of desire through her body. Taking a deep breath, Dylan framed her face between his hands. Leaning on his elbows over her, he looked into her eyes. "I want you so much. I keep wanting you. I keep thinking..."

Bending his head, he kissed her mouth.

"Thinking what?" Darcie whispered against his lips.

"How you'd look—" he pressed one hand to her belly "—swollen here, ripe with a baby growing inside you, moving—" his hand slid upward over her rib cage "—your skin flushed, radiant—" then up again to her breasts "—your nipples larger, darker—" he kissed one then the other "—beginning to leak with first milk..."

"Dylan," she said on a moan. Talk about old-fashioned. Primal.

"You'd taste so sweet...."

The notion shocked her. His words shot through her from breast to thighs, and deep between. "Don't—"

He sipped at her. "It's how you should be. Sometime," he said.

It was only a fantasy. Harmless, sexy. She let him have it, let the forbidden thrill roll through her body too because it was just that—like these two weeks. Pretend.

He licked and nibbled, then kissed her some more. Her breasts, her collarbone, her jawline, her earlobe, her cheeks, her eyes, her mouth again until Darcie was gasping with need. And all the while he moved inside her, slow and deep, light and shallow, then hard and fast again. Darcie held on, her arms around his neck, her legs around his waist, her heart around his soul.

Until a fresh spurt of alarm hit her squarely in the solar plexus. Maybe, for him, this was more than a fantasy.

"You are wearing a condom?"

Dylan grunted. "Want me to double-bag it?"

She had no answer for that. No heart. When the climax came, it came at once—for both of them again.

"I could get addicted to this," Darcie whispered in the darkness when she caught her breath. "I never had a mutual orgasm until you."

"It doesn't have to stop."

His voice suddenly edgy, Dylan rolled away from her. She heard him deal with the latest condom before he lay back on the bed and pulled the white duvet over them. Darcie felt chilled anyway.

"We're not going to fight about this. Are we?"

"You could stay."

"No, Dylan. I can't." She stroked her fingers down his
cheek. Five-o'clock shadow…no, 3:00 a.m. shadow now.
"I have a job, you have a farm."

"Station," he said, his jaw set.

"You live in the Outback, I live in New York."

He had left his widowed mother with the sheep. But
she had called more frequently this second week and Darcie knew that Dylan was stalling not to go home. Yesterday, finally, he'd found a ram to be shipped from England
if the deal was right. He had duties, obligations, responsibilities. So did she. Then there were his attitudes about
a woman's place in a man's life…the kitchen, the bedroom, the nursery. Oh, Lord, the nursery. That erotic
playacting of his rolled through her mind again. If she
stayed any longer, she would start to feel tempted by the
very values she was trying to escape.

A hundred times, she thought. With Dylan. Over the
past two weeks.

"Call me," he said. "Here, when you get back. Or I'll
call you."

Darcie couldn't answer. All she could do was cling to
him for the rest of this last night, then go home—and keep
trying to fit her life pieces together in their balky puzzle.

She turned her face into his neck and breathed deeply
of his scent. Soap, beer, man.

She'd stayed away from the beer tonight herself. She
wasn't getting sick this last time.

Darcie had no time for sleep, either.

Long after Dylan fell into a restless doze, she lay awake
watching him. Touching him. Why? she asked herself.
Why do the good ones always turn out to be impossible?
In some way or other, they were always Mr. Wrong for
Darcie Elizabeth Baxter.

Fireworks.

She felt as if she'd set off a flotilla of barges loaded,
programmed, with every conceivable mortar and starburst.

It would be hard to say goodbye.

So she wouldn't.

When light filtered through the windows that overlooked Darling Harbour, she didn't bolt from the bed this time to humiliate herself in Dylan's bathroom. No. When dawn came in the morning, she slipped out from under the hand he'd rested on her hip all night, pressed a feathery kiss on his forehead—and, cold sober, left the room. Left Dylan.

Chapter Six

Darcie had just drifted off to sleep—blessed relief—when a small body thumped onto her stomach. Sharp claws kneaded her tender skin through Darcie's soft-knit Wunderthings pajamas, last season's biggest seller in the clothing line, and she startled awake. Cursing.

Sweet Baby Jane blinked at her in the dark, fierce cat eyes glowing.

"Don't even think about it."

If those stiletto nails sank into her any deeper, Darcie would abandon all pretense of politically correct treatment of animals. Knowing better than to spring up in bed, she moved slowly, cautiously. Intent upon removing the beastly animal from her abdomen, from her room, from her life if possible, she sat up. Shifting her weight, she hoped to dislodge SBJ without actually touching her. No such luck.

"All right. War."

She plucked Jane away from her stomach—a stomach Dylan Rafferty had kissed only nights before—and dumped her on the floor. Sweet Baby Jane hissed.

"Back off," Darcie warned her.

It was no use.

If she went back to bed now, Jane would only take advantage. As soon as Darcie fell into a restless slumber again, she would jump on her. Wide-awake in the middle of the night, Darcie padded across the hall. Avoiding Sweet Baby Jane's stalking, she hop-scotched into the bathroom. When she came out, the cat instantly pounced.

Darcie shrieked. Jumping from one foot to the other, she inadvertently stomped on the cat's tail. SBJ yowled. A second later, her grandmother opened her own bedroom door to peer out into the hall.

"Jane, my sweet?"

"It's her. And me."

"Darcie. Why aren't you asleep?"

"Other than a virulent case of jet lag? It's worse flying east than west." She sidestepped Sweet Baby Jane. Eden scooped her up, crooning, but Darcie said, "That's why."

"Did the bad girl hurt you, Janie? Ah, poor lamb."

Lambs, *sheep,* were not Darcie's favorite topic this week, either.

"I didn't touch her...but, Gran, this cat is vicious."

"Nonsense. Julio said only last night—no, night before last, just before you came home—that he's never met a cat like Jane."

The doorman? "I'm sure."

"He meant that in a good way, Darcie." Eden turned back into her room. "I'm delighted to have you home, dear, but I do hope your mood improves. Soon."

"My mood is fine," Darcie snapped. "But this...this *feline* needs a muzzle."

"Don't be silly. She loves everyone."

Darcie followed Eden into her room, safe now that the cat was in her grandmother's arms. Purring, of course, loud enough to wake Claire, Peter, and the baby two floors down. Sweet Baby Jane looked angelic.

"That animal should get a prime role in the next sequel to *The Exorcist.* I swear, she must be a familiar."

"My Jane a witch's companion? I should say not."

"You would if you'd ever turned your back on her."

"She wouldn't hurt a soul. Julio says…"

At the second mention of his name, Darcie let her gaze whip to the bedside telephone. Then the book lying open on Eden's bed.

"*How To Make Love to a Man?*" Darcie read the cover. "Honestly, Gran. Are you sleeping with *him* now?"

Eden blushed.

"We haven't gotten that far. He's Spanish, you know. Hot-blooded but a gentleman. A charming combination."

Like Dylan's mellow, laid-back style, his attitude.

"You're dating him?"

"Well, now and then. His night shift interferes with our social life."

"You could always go down to the lobby and help him open doors."

"What does that mean, Darcie?" Her grandmother eyed her with obvious disapproval. "That comment is so unlike you that I can only assume its source is your own lack of…satisfaction these days."

"No, I like Julio. He's cool. He seems very nice." *Very…young.*

"Go on," Eden murmured.

"That's all I know about him."

"Then please don't pass judgment on our alliance." She carried Sweet Baby Jane—who gave Darcie a triumphant look—to bed with her. Nestled in the covers again, Eden fluffed her filmy peignoir. Where had she gotten such a garment? Bergdorf Goodman, Darcie guessed. Circa 1954. Gran followed Darcie's gaze to the silent telephone.

"He still hasn't called?"

She played innocent. "Who?"

"Dylan Rafferty. I do love that name. Strong, masculine. Very inspiring," Eden decided aloud. "Tell me again. What was it like in the Land of Oz?"

"Busy."

"More," her grandmother urged.

"Hot."

"Ummm. That's better. What else?"

"All right. Sexy." She couldn't help the smile. Darcie

plunked herself down on the end of the bed, far enough away from SBJ that she couldn't get scratched. As if waiting, too, for this latest retelling of her skin adventures with Dylan Rafferty, the cat sent her a Cheshire grin. Maybe they could find common ground after all.

"You can't imagine, Gran. I've never felt the way he made me feel. He was like a drug...or so I suppose." She couldn't vouch for her sister Annie, but Darcie wasn't into substance experimentation. "He has these dark eyes, that melting smile, a blowtorch mouth—"

"He's a good kisser."

"Among other things, yes."

"You lucky girl."

Darcie suppressed the strong wave of need, then of anguish, that rolled through her. She shouldn't have started, even to entertain Eden or to fill her own sleepless hours. In the few days she'd been back in New York, the telephone had remained stubbornly silent. Her nights—so recently Darcie's days in Sydney—stayed perversely mixed up. Sleep deprived, upside down in time and emotions, she was turning into a "virago" like her mother. For very different reasons. Her grandmother was right. A horny virago. She didn't regret walking out on Dylan that last morning. It seemed better than a long goodbye she'd only have trouble forgetting. Like Dylan himself. But...

"Tell me again about the Akubra."

"In the elevator, or in his room?"

"Both."

By the time she finished, they were laughing. Even Sweet Baby Jane looked pleased with the stories that had lightened Darcie's jet-lagged heart at the same time they plunged her back into despair.

"I think you should call him," Eden said, riffling through the book in her lap. The cat lay on her pillow, vibrating, blinking, on the verge of sleep. "He must have been hurt...even angry when he woke up to find you gone. Without a word, I might add. How could you, Darcie?"

"It's better this way."

Or so she tried to tell herself.

"Distance, occupation, I should think those could be overcome. Any relationship requires compromise. Just look at Julio and me. The beautiful little man has me thoroughly on the other side of the clock—just like you with Dylan—because I can't bear the thought of falling off to sleep in a warm bed alone while he stands in that cold lobby, the wind blowing through his jacket every time the door opens and some rude tenant stalks in. What's the harm in calling Dylan to discuss your situation?"

"He won't compromise." *We'll rehydrate then negotiate.* Ha. Sexually, perhaps, but otherwise... "It didn't take me long to realize how stubborn he can be."

"So was your grandfather, but we lived together for forty-five years. Well, forty-six if you count the love nest we shared in the Village before our wedding."

"You and Gramps lived together?"

"And why not? We couldn't keep our hands off each other." She paused. "It sounds as if you and your Aussie feel the same."

"Felt," Darcie corrected her. "I'm not spending my life with a man who still thinks a woman should be barefoot and pregnant."

"He didn't say that. I won't believe it."

"Not in those words, but that's what he means." *Your nipples larger, darker, first milk...*

"I can think of worse scenarios."

Darcie brushed nonexistent lint from the comforter.

Brushed Dylan Rafferty from her life. Her dreams.

"He hasn't called you. You won't call him." Eden ticked off those points on her well-manicured fingers. "That's that, then. Too bad."

"It's for the best, Gran," Darcie repeated. "It is," she said when Eden arched a perfect eyebrow as only she could do so well.

"Two stubborn people. Sleeping apart."

"That's life in the new millennium. Haven't you heard?"

Then why did the thought sadden her? Like the too-silent telephone.

Darcie hopped off the bed. She had other considerations—the ones that paid her bills. She would focus on her job, the new store. "I have work tomorrow. Walt's presenting the contract for the Sydney store to the board. I need to get in early." Then there was Greta Hinckley, who in Darcie's absence had vowed revenge.

"If I were you," Eden said, "I'd convince Walter Corwin that Darcie Elizabeth Baxter is the only person to handle the entire process for Wunderthings' opening in Australia. Where Dylan Rafferty just happens to live. If you get my drift…"

The old saying made Darcie smile a little.

"He lives in the Outback." Before she left the bedroom, she cast one last look at the quiet telephone in resignation. Then another at Sweet Baby Jane, before she reminded herself, "I live right here. In full view of the New York skyline."

The next evening Darcie still sat at her desk on the sixth floor at Wunderthings and tried not to gloat. Hallelujah.

"Why didn't you tell me this afternoon?" she asked Walt.

"The board met at four o'clock."

"It's seven-thirty now." And her telephone hadn't rung in the past hour. Strange, since all day she'd gotten mysterious calls; hang-ups every time. Darcie tried not to stare at it, willing it to ring again. Convinced the caller could have been Dylan Rafferty, she kept trying to suppress her growing anticipation. "You mean the board meeting just ended?"

Walt Corwin perched on the corner of her desk. "Board meeting was over at five-fifteen."

"I thought I saw a bunch of suits drifting out to the elevators." She gave him a look. "So it's a done deal?" Wunderthings Sydney was a Go. Now, it had funding. Darcie's heartbeat sped. "What does that mean for me?"

She remembered Eden's advice to make herself

indispensable—to return to Australia, and Dylan Rafferty. With whom Darcie didn't want a relationship.

She did, however, want her job. Darcie never came to work in the morning without expecting a pink slip in her in-basket. *You're history, Ms. Baxter. You've outlived your usefulness. Do not pass Go. Do not collect $200. Head straight for the unemployment office.* One reason she was working late tonight.

She'd gotten behind in other projects during the trip. She needed to catch up. She wasn't really waiting for a phone call, she told herself.

"We can handle the Sydney project from here," Walt informed her, and Darcie's spirits sank. Not that she intended to heed Gran's advice and look up Dylan the minute she arrived on Aussie soil. "We're a little shallow in the pockets—budget isn't that great. I told the board we could fax, phone, whatever, on this, let the agent over there supervise the contractors we retained before we left."

Darcie swallowed. "Walt, we can't set up a new store secondhand. Someone should oversee things. You know the stuff that happens. Just when you think everything's going smoothly, some wrench gets thrown in the gears. This shop will set the whole tone for the Pacific Rim."

"I never thought of that," he said in a dry tone.

Chastened, Darcie slumped back in her chair. "I didn't mean you weren't aware of the problems that can crop up...."

"No, you meant 'send me on the first flight to Sydney, Walter.'" He paused to meet her gaze. "You think I haven't noticed you slumping around this office since we got back? Dragging into work late every morning?"

"I'm jet-lagged."

"Me, too. But I'm still at my desk on time."

She stiffened. "Has Greta been sending memos again?"

He waved a hand.

"Let's just say she's noticed the same things I have. Who could help it? She's heard the rumors going around the cafeteria, in the washrooms, too. Your little 'adventure' at the Westin has reached legendary status. So Darcie, for the time being we'll phone and fax. If anyone goes to Sydney, it'll be me."

Walt slid off the edge of her desk. He walked to the entry of her cubicle but didn't leave. With his back turned, he said, "Be careful. Greta's on a rampage. Nancy's so upset, I had to send her home early. In tears."

"Greta needs to get laid." Darcie murmured. "Maybe that would sweeten her disposition. At least then she'd be occupied with her own life, not everyone else's," she finished. Too tired to temper her tongue, Darcie smiled. "Maybe you should ask her to dinner, Walt. Or have *you* missed the office gossip? She has a definite yen for you."

Walt spun around. His face had turned pale in obvious shock.

"Greta Hinckley?" he said. "Me?"

"Greta Hinckley. And you."

Walt shook his head. "Boy, I must be slipping. She's a real coyote."

"Congratulations." Darcie grinned. "On the Sydney project."

"It was your idea."

"Congratulations to me, then." Walt hadn't said so, and that bothered her. Had she blown her integrity in Australia? With Dylan Rafferty? At least she had her memories— and that string of anonymous phone calls today.

She was still pondering the situation when Walt sent her a backward wave, then disappeared into the darkened aisle between the cubicles. "Give me more good stuff on Monday," he said.

Darcie didn't realize why he'd avoided her with news of the board meeting—and the funding for the Sydney store—until his footsteps faded into silence.

Who else but Walter Corwin knew about Dylan Rafferty?

"Can you believe it?"

Still seething over his indiscretion regarding her indiscretion, Darcie banged into the closed elevator doors the instant the car settled onto the ground floor of Wunderthings' building. She couldn't get out fast enough. She couldn't trust anyone—especially Walt Corwin. More paranoia. As for Greta... Taking a step back, she waited for the doors to glide open, then marched out into the foyer.

Her heels echoed on the terrazzo floor.

At 8:00 p.m. no one was around. Even the security guard had left his post, probably for his scheduled walk of the main level perimeter.

But then she did see the man waiting by the bank of elevators, leaning one shoulder against the marble wall.

For a single instant she hoped it was Dylan Rafferty of today's phone calls.

Darcie's pulse skipped. Was it possible he'd followed her to New York? So enraptured by their two weeks together that he couldn't stay away? She envisioned the abandoned lambs in his fields, the new ram without any ewes, his mother tearfully bidding him goodbye. *I hope she's worth it, Dylan.*

Of course I am.

Wasn't she? Her spirits soared.

Dylan might be wrong for her over the long-term, but she'd be ecstatic to see him again tonight. She couldn't sleep anyway. Might as well spend the nighttime hours between the sheets with her Aussie hunk. Darcie took two more steps, then realized the man waiting didn't wear an Akubra hat.

Bare-headed, he ran a hand through his blond—not dark—hair.

And Darcie froze like the Statue of Liberty.

Merrick Lowell tried a wry smile that once, before he'd betrayed her like the rotten weasel he was, would have made Darcie's blood flow faster through her veins. On Monday nights. She stopped and stared at him until his smile died.

"What are you doing here?"

"I've been calling all day. I couldn't bring myself to speak when you answered. Welcome home, Darce."

Disappointment swamped her again. The caller hadn't been Dylan.

"Go to hell," she said weakly.

He made a sound. "Now, now. I'd hoped you would feel better about us after your trip to Australia. Bet you're still jet-lagged, huh?"

Finding the will to move again, she walked past him without a word. Before she reached the revolving doors, Merrick stepped in front of her.

"Come on, Darce."

"What? Be a good sport? Forget about Jacqueline and the two kids? Pretend that my total humiliation in the doll department at FAO Schwarz never happened?"

"Forget Jacqueline," he murmured.

"I'm sure she'd be as thrilled to hear you say that as I am."

"We're separated."

Well, knock me over with Barbie's feather boa.

Darcie stared at him, one hand poised to push the revolving door into motion. "Separated." She pressed her lips together in thought. "I imagine that means for the evening. Does Jacqueline have a Girl Scout meeting with your daughter tonight? Is she picking up your son at hockey practice, so you're free?"

"She went home to her parents in Greenwich."

"Ah."

"Not for dinner," he said before Darcie could voice the same words. "Permanently. Right now I get the kids on weekends. We haven't negotiated a custody agreement yet or the kids' support..."

We'll negotiate, Dylan had said. It had become a schtick for them, a sexy gimmick. She felt a wave of sadness. She almost hated Merrick all over again for stealing Dylan's memory. For not being him.

"Don't let me keep you," Darcie murmured. She pushed the door. "You must need to sell quite a few chunks of stock to cover those new expenses. Keep that in mind next time you get a girlfriend. I hope your clients cooperate. The market's not in very good shape right now, Eden tells me...."

With a sigh—difficult women, it said—Merrick followed her out of the building to Sixth Avenue.

Cabs flashed by, horns blew, neon signs blinked. Darcie inhaled the familiar aromas of car exhaust, subway gas, and the river. She loved those smells. But they didn't comfort her now.

Shivering at a sudden gust of wind, she drew her coat closer to her throat.

"Darcie." Merrick caught her arm. "Have a drink with me."

"I need to eat."

"Dinner then. We'll talk."

"I couldn't swallow."

"Please," he murmured. "I know I was a jerk. A real prick. But that's behind me now. I've missed you. Give me another chance?"

Remembering his look of utter misery at the toy store, Darcie realized that a few weeks ago she might have felt tempted. On one level she missed their Monday nights at the Hyatt. She even missed Merrick's smile, his deep-blue eyes, his silky blond hair. But she could do without his GQ style, his Yale accent, his...*family*.

Then there was Dylan. With him in her past...

"I met someone in Australia. He'd be a hard act to follow."

"You're here now." Merrick walked with her to the corner, his hands shoved in the pockets of his camel hair coat, his head down against the wind—or Darcie's rejection? "So am I," he said. "Let me try."

Chapter Seven

"Amazing. Merrick Lowell, begging me to come back."

On the ferry across the Hudson, Darcie scrunched low in her seat, closed her eyes and imagined the dark water spraying out to either side of the bow as the boat cut cleanly through the current. It didn't calm her. She envisioned the high rock cliffs of the Jersey Palisades—like the climb she faced at work over Greta Hinckley. They didn't help, either. She daydreamed about Australia Day with Dylan, overriding tonight's encounter with Merrick.

The thought of Dylan—who hadn't called after all—only made her sit up straight in her seat to stare out at the lights on the other side of the river. Beckoning? Or reminding her that she was Darcie Elizabeth Baxter, Girl Wunder, single female living with her grandmother.

By the time she reached home, Dylan seemed more a part of her past than could be possible in just four days and four lonely nights.

"Wasn't that what you wanted, Baxter?"

News flash: After Dylan—after Merrick—she didn't know what she wanted.

When she opened the duplex door with her key to find

Gran cozied up on her oyster-white sofa with Julio Perez, Darcie ground her teeth. They had their arms hooked, like newlyweds, each holding the other's glass for a taste. Their eyes sparkled, Gran's peridot blue-green, Julio's dark-brown and glazed with obvious lust. Startled, they moved apart.

"Dinner, Darcie?" Eden bounded off the sofa. "You must be starving."

With her usual radar, she had sensed immediately that a) she and Julio were no longer alone and b) something was wrong. Eden put Darcie's coat and attaché case in the closet.

"I'm not hungry, Gran."

"I made pot roast." Eden's tone tempted her, as it was meant to. "Dark, sweet carrots. Crusted golden potatoes. Onions cooked just the way you like them."

"You never make pot roast for me." She waved toward the sofa. "Evening, Julio. Your night off?"

"Sí."

"Gran's a good cook. Isn't she?"

"*Muy bueno,* Señorita Darcie." The petite doorman wore skinny jeans and a green polo shirt that screamed Latin Lover. His black hair lay sleeked against his skull like an otter's pelt. "You are well, yes?"

"No."

"What's the matter, dear?" Gran rushed to feel her forehead.

"I don't have a fever." Darcie ducked away but made her habitual quick check of the room. Sweet Baby Jane was nowhere in sight. Thank God for small favors.

Julio sipped his drink, which appeared to be a gin and tonic from its clear liquid and the slice of lime hanging over the edge of the glass. He angled his head around the fruit to drink. Darcie thought she might like one herself.

"I ran into Merrick tonight."

Gran's face registered quick alarm. "That man had better not be in my building," she said, shooting a look at Julio. "I'll have him thrown into the street. With luck, a cab will run over him."

"He is a bad man?" Julio inquired.

"Yes." Gran smiled at him. "Not at all a gentleman like you, *mi corazón*." She patted her hair, which still looked apricot to Darcie. Hmm. Maybe Julio kept her too busy these days to take time for the hairdresser. "Merrick Lowell broke my poor Darcie's heart," Eden explained. "And now he has the nerve to show his face again? And he wanted…what?"

Darcie sighed. "Reconciliation."

"That's why you were late. I was beginning to worry." But not too much, Darcie thought, to prevent her tryst with Julio and the wedding glasses. Eden frowned. "I hope you didn't—"

"No, I came home. He wanted to take me to dinner, have a drink."

"He wanted to lure you into his bed again. I have half a mind to call his wife."

Darcie smiled a little. "He tells me they're separated. I'm not sure whether to believe him."

"He's a liar and a cheat. In my day your grandfather Harold would have taken a shotgun to him. Or at the very least, manipulated his clients' stock and run him right out of Wall Street. Come to think, some buckshot in his ass would be a nice finishing touch."

She couldn't help laughing. "Gran, thanks. I appreciate your support."

"Now that Harold's not around, I can offer you Julio."

"I will do whatever you wish," he said.

Gran gave him a grateful—or was that lascivious?—smile.

"And later, we'll see about *that*," she murmured. "In the meantime help me twist Darcie's arm to eat some of this pot roast. What will I do with the leftovers?"

"Serve them again, like you always do," Darcie said with a smile.

"I'd prefer you finish them tonight. You look thin. All that jet lag, no sleep—and now, Merrick Lowell. Not to mention Dylan Rafferty."

Ouch. "No woman is ever too thin."

"Nonsense. I won't have eating disorders in my house."
She gestured at the dining room table. "Sit. I'll get you a
plate."

"Gran…"

"I didn't hear you." Eden bustled into the kitchen, letting her hips sway, probably for Julio's benefit, beneath
her tight stretch pants. She still had a good butt, Darcie
admitted. But she and Perez certainly made another Odd
Couple. No, the Odder Couple. "Do you want gin and
tonic or wine?"

"Both. Just mix 'em."

She didn't mean it, but the combination sounded almost
appealing.

Darcie kept seeing the obvious pain in Merrick's deep-
blue eyes. That boyish lock of silky blond hair that always
fell over his forehead when he looked down—as he always
had in bed, lying over her. Until his betrayal.

"Take my advice, Darcie," Eden called from the kitchen
where Darcie heard cabinet doors slamming, dishes bang-
ing onto the counter, silverware rattling in the drawer.
"The next time you see that poor little rich boy, kick him
where it counts."

Instead, Darcie kept remembering Dylan and the silent
telephone in her room.

And her grandmother who, as soon as Darcie vanished
into that too-quiet bed to try to sleep, would undoubtedly
crawl over Julio's fragile frame like a marine hitting the
beach at Iwo Jima.

Latin lover?

The world wasn't perfect.

Maybe Merrick wasn't that big a bastard.

"Maybe I should give him another chance."

"Give her another chance? Even Eden's vicious cat has
only nine lives."

Claire Spencer strode from the nursery into the bedroom, keeping her voice low not to wake the baby. Samantha had slept through the night last night, and Claire

had high hopes for a repeat. Claire might survive after all. She had less confidence in Tildy Lewis, the new nanny.

"She's just getting the feel of the job," Peter argued, lying in their bed with his hands stacked behind his head. He looked thoroughly relaxed. "She's young."

"So is Samantha. We need quality care for her, Peter." It infuriated her how relaxed he could be with their daughter's welfare at stake. "The first day Tildy was here, she let Samantha sit in a poopy diaper for hours."

"Yeah. I know. The next day she boiled the supplemental formula—but she didn't hurt Sam, sweetheart. She had the sense to let the milk cool first."

"It probably had no nutritional value left."

Today Claire had come home early to find the girl watching "Oprah," sobbing over Oprah's latest fiction pick for her book club. Another depressing, sordid account of someone's dysfunctional behavior, she supposed. Claire didn't need that in her own home.

"I'm tempted to call the agency."

"And go through all that interviewing again? Samantha is too young herself to be seriously traumatized by her baby-sitter's tears over a maudlin piece of fiction. Give Tildy a break, Claire."

Suspicion reared its ugly head.

"Why do you like her so much?"

"Samantha?"

"No. Tildy." Claire had to admit, she was attractive in her own way. A few pounds heavier than she might be—with terrible taste in clothes—but Tildy had thick reddish hair and gorgeous green eyes and Claire wasn't sure she wanted her around. "Don't tell me you haven't noticed."

"Noticed what?"

Claire waggled a hand. "Her...looks."

"She's cute enough, I guess. In a kind of Disneyland way."

Wishing for Mary Poppins or Mrs. Doubtfire—did such paragons of child care really exist?—Claire tried to relax. The apartment was quiet. She and Peter had managed a civilized dinner for the first time in weeks. Samantha lay tucked into her crib in the dream nursery Claire had designed, surrounded by stuffed animals, her dolphin mobile chiming softly in the distance.

"Is that what this is all about?"

Claire gave him a baffled look.

"My presumed attraction to Tildy," he said. "What's the matter, Claire? Too much work at the office, too soon after maternity leave?"

She could have groaned. Not even a week, and Claire had a pile of folders on her desk, a screen full of e-mail, a full tape of voice messages that she might never wade through. Every night she came home to another of Tildy Lewis's disasters.

Claire bit her lip.

"I worry," she confessed. "I worry about everything these days."

"Tell me. You're a professional brooder." Peter motioned her over to the bed. "Come here, sweetheart. Let me refresh your memory about our marriage...."

"What part?"

He grinned. "The sex part."

Mild panic skittered through her. "Peter, tonight's not a good time."

His mouth tightened. "What now? You don't have your period, do you? I thought as long as you nurse—"

"That's not always the case, but no. No period." Her milk wasn't that plentiful either. Her body remained all messed up. So did her life. And Claire didn't know how to make it the way she wanted it to be. What had happened to her careful schedule, her neat apartment, her sex drive? "I'm just tired."

"Headache?"

"I never get headaches."

He kept his tone casual. "I just wondered because women who don't want to have sex with their husbands usually claim a headache. When you get one, then I'll know that you've really moved into some new phase of existence—in which I am no longer required."

"That's silly."

"So is this obsession about Tildy and leaving Samantha all day with someone else and how the hell to get your work done." He didn't look relaxed now. Peter had taken his hands down and folded them over his bare chest. His mouth turned grim. "I've tried to help, Claire. But we're coming apart here and I don't know what to do about it."

Pulse thumping, she eased into bed beside him. Claire tried to clear her mind, her guilt. It was her turn now to reassure Peter. It wasn't as easy as she'd hoped, adding another little human being to their household. Not as easy as she'd expected to return to work. Not as easy to...make love again when she felt like a sow. "We'll be fine, Peter."

If a woman had ever needed a mantra, Claire decided, this was it.

She also needed to talk to Darcie. She hadn't seen her since Australia.

"Twist my arm," Darcie murmured, "and I'll tell you more," enjoying herself that Saturday for the first time since she'd come back to New York.

"You can be so cruel."

Claire gazed at her across the table at Phantasmagoria, their favorite luncheon spot. In the mid-sixties off Lexington not far from Bloomingdale's, the basement-level restaurant served crunchy salads drizzled with balsamic vinaigrette, and the trendy *panini*s Darcie adored. She tried not to grin around her ham-and-cheese-stuffed, grilled sandwich.

What could be better than a chat over lunch with a friend who understood you?

"There's really nothing more to tell," she said.

"I take one look at that sparkle in your eye—you hussy—and I know better. He sounds yummy. So he has dark hair, dark eyes...and looks like a cowboy?"

"Australian-style. Sheepboy."

Claire laughed.

"Tall, broad-shouldered."

"Umm." Claire took a bite of her BLT. "And you spent

most of your time in Sydney in bed with him at the Westin?"

"My free time." The distinction seemed important to Darcie. She didn't want Claire to think she was a slut. "Just good old, healthy recreational sex."

"You make me pine for the 'good old' days before Peter and I were married. Before the baby came."

Darcie's *panini* stopped halfway to her mouth.

"Are you trying to tell me something?"

Claire studied a piece of bacon hanging from her sandwich. "You don't want to know. Motherhood is a far more complex event than I anticipated."

Darcie thoughtfully stirred her coffee. "I read once—in *Glamour,* or was it *Cosmo?*—that sex after childbirth can be a traumatic notion for a new mother. Do you find that to be the case?"

"We don't have sex."

Darcie's mouth dropped. "You and Peter the Great? Give me a break. That man—like Dylan—has double his share of testosterone. You told me he loves your new figure, your breasts...."

Claire shushed her, although she knew there was usually a younger crowd here, too intent like Claire and Darcie upon their personal problems, including men, to eavesdrop.

"He's not obsessed?"

Claire admitted, "He wanted to make love the other night, but Darcie, I just can't. It doesn't seem sexy. It would be clinical." She set her sandwich aside. "My God, six weeks ago I was in the delivery room—all that mess, all the blood—and now I'm supposed to think Peter sticking his cock in me is the best idea since Adam and Eve?" She shuddered.

"You should talk to your doctor about this, Claire."

Her gaze snapped up. "You think I'm neurotic?"

"No, I think you're having a few 'conflicted' feelings."

"Maybe, but I don't know *why.* I'm healed, I'm healthy. Samantha's even sleeping through the night—now and then."

"Is she?" Darcie perked up at the mention of her god-daughter. "I need to see her again. I brought her a present from Australia."

"Another gift? She loves the cross-eyed zebra."

Buster. Memories of FAO Schwarz danced in Darcie's brain and she frowned.

"I'm glad. I should have taken it back, though. After Merrick—"

"The son of a bitch."

"So true," Darcie said. "Did I tell you I saw him?"

"You *didn't.*"

Remembering Gran's similar reaction, Darcie took a breath then related their impromptu meeting in the Wunderthings lobby, plus Merrick's new single state, assuming he told the truth.

"And he had the nerve to ask you out? I hope you said no. I hope you screamed loud enough for the security guard to hear—and pitch him out the door at gunpoint."

"Gran's suggestion." Darcie swirled her spoon through her cooling coffee. "He looked so forlorn, Claire. I think he's really sorry about what happened."

"I'll bet his wife is, too." Claire eyed her. "He could be lying. He's good at it."

"And I'm so naive I'd probably fall for him all over again?" Taking a sip of coffee, Darcie made a face. "What if Merrick *is* telling the truth?"

"I'm not happy that I was right about him before. But what are you saying?" Claire leaned closer to look into her eyes.

"That Australia's a long way off. There's no sense thinking about Dylan."

"How could you help it?" Claire raised an eyebrow. "You weren't just making up all that stuff about the Akubra hat, the man's endurance, were you?" She shook her head. "No, you couldn't have invented making out among the reef fish and manta rays."

"I'm a very creative person," Darcie said with a smile. "But not that creative. Claire—" she sighed "—I'll never see him again. I didn't leave my business card, didn't give him my home number. And he hasn't tried to call me at Wunderthings, which would be easy enough to find."

"You must have really ticked him off."

"Gran thinks so, too." She paused again. "Besides, he's a dweeb about women."

"Maybe he was teasing. Maybe that's his way of avoiding commitment."

Darcie didn't think so. "It works then," she said. "Really well."

"Most men are at least halfway into the cave." Claire grimaced. "Even Peter. His pressure to have sex...his refusal to change Sam's dirty diapers. He picks and chooses how to help, you know. I don't have the same choices."

"The nanny's not working out?"

Claire shivered. "Don't get me started. Yesterday Tildy wheeled Samantha to the grocery store—and left her in the carriage outside 'for just a minute.'"

Darcie frowned. "That's dangerous. Anyone could snatch the baby."

"My point exactly. Why Peter can't see that is beyond me."

"I must admit, I'm disappointed in Peter the Great," Darcie murmured, patting Claire's hand.

"I'm disappointed in me." Claire waved a hand, her eyes too bright. "I mean, I should be able to handle the baby, my job, the apartment, my marriage. Tildy." She shuddered again. "I think I'm losing my mind. I know for sure I've lost my libido. I may as well give up—apply for Social Security. I'm no good at my career or raising a child."

"Claire, Claire."

She blinked. "Excuse me. I am such a...*mess*. At first I worried that Peter wouldn't find me attractive anymore. Now that I know he does, I worry I won't want to do the deed. Ever."

"Your hormones are probably out of whack. It happens."

"What are you, the voice of experience?" Claire rolled her eyes. "I am a raving lunatic. With leaky breasts. I smell like an old baby bottle all the time. It takes half a dram of Passion every morning to make me presentable for work. Ha," she said. "Passion. That's a laugh."

Darcie gave her a moment to collect herself. Their conversations tended to circle around, as female conversations do, covering a lot of territory. Now they were back to Peter and Claire and motherhood. Darcie didn't know what to tell her; she had no experience in such matters. And with men in general…well, Claire already knew her track record there.

"So." Claire straightened in her wicker chair. She traced a finger over the paisley tablecloth. She moved the salt and pepper shakers around. "What are you going to do about Dylan Rafferty?"

"Nothing."

"Merrick Lowell?"

"I'm thinking that over."

"I'm warning you, girlfriend. He's still a snake."

"The one-eyed trouser snake." They both snickered, then Darcie added, "I heard that with Gran in a Monty Python movie."

"It's a good one," Claire agreed.

True to form, the snake himself was waiting for Darcie again on Monday when she left her office. This time she didn't feel quite surprised to find him leaning against the wall by the elevators. But this time he gave her that rueful smile from the sixth-floor lobby, not on the main level. Interception with no chance of escape. Darcie saw this as an escalation of intent. He didn't want her slipping past in the five o'clock rush.

"Did we make an appointment?" she asked him.

Merrick straightened from the marble wall. His smile faded.

"I'm taking you to dinner."

People brushed by them. A secretary from Marketing gave Merrick a quick once-over, then winked at Darcie in approval. If she only knew.

"A woman likes to be asked, not shanghaied."

He leaned close, lowering his voice. "Don't tell me to take a hike."

She smiled, too sweetly.

"Bad day, Darce?"

"Please don't ask." In the past few days Greta Hinckley had changed tactics. She had attached herself to Darcie like a malevolent shadow.

"Come on, you know you're hungry."

Merrick took her elbow, guiding her onto the elevator when the car doors opened. It was empty and they stepped inside, and Darcie remembered the elevator in the Westin, with Dylan Rafferty. His Akubra. His hands, and his kisses. When Merrick tried the same tactic, without the hat, she pushed him away.

With a hurt look, he propped his shoulder against the chrome-faced wall.

"So. How long is this going to last?"

"Merrick, you can't possibly think that we'll just pick up where we left off. You lied to me. How am I supposed to overlook that?"

"You're a kind woman."

Darcie stared at him. "You really think I'm easy, don't you?"

He smiled, winningly. "I think you're hot. I'd say that's reason enough to share a few drinks. Zoe's has sea bass on the menu this week...." He lifted his eyebrows.

"All the way down in SoHo?"

"Your favorite recipe."

"Evil." Her stomach growled. Her tongue tingled at the thought of succulent tomatoes, basil, garlic and sour cream with just a hint of lemon. He sweetened the pot.

"We'll catch a cab."

"All right. Feed me. Then I'll decide whether to put a curse on your head."

With a broadened smile, he must think he had her. Darcie could feel confidence fairly oozing from Merrick's pores. Nothing unusual about that, but the last time she'd seen him—and in FAO Schwarz—he'd looked chastened. An appealing quality he might consider permanently incorporating into his character, because it softened Darcie toward him in spite of her resolve to hate his guts forever.

Be careful, she silently ordered herself.

Change was not Merrick Lowell's middle name. Any man's, perhaps.

She kept quiet until her second glass of Chardonnay at their corner table in Zoe's. Merrick's favorite restaurant, of course, not hers. Darcie liked the food, loved the pleasant service, but tonight its trendy, open kitchen and tin ceilings created too much din for her shattered nerves. The day with Greta had been too much for any sane person. Worried, too, about Claire, Darcie toyed with the stem of her glass. But she had enough of a buzz now to at least make conversation with Merrick.

"Tell me about your separation."

He winced. A good touch, Darcie thought.

"I went home the Saturday I saw you at FAO. Sara— my daughter—piped up to Jacqueline that she'd met this nice lady in the store. I would have told her myself, Darce—" he shrugged "—but Jackie picked up on it first. It was time. I'd told you that. We've had problems for a while now."

"Because of me?"

"I never mentioned you."

"Gee, I don't know whether to feel flattered by your discretion…or cheap because I was a hole-in-the-corner affair."

"Is that what you think we are?"

"Were."

He sighed. "I'll try to explain. Jackie and I were a bad match. Our families are friends and our mothers…well, our wedding was your classic social event of the season. Did you ever see *A Wedding?*"

"I've seen dozens of them." Darcie had a closet full of ugly bridesmaid dresses. Her cousins, if not her friends, kept getting married with depressing regularity.

"No, I meant the movie. Robert Altman. An all-star cast, and everything goes screwy at this big society bash."

"Oh, yeah. The grandmother—I think—dies in bed.

No one wants to admit it and spoil the party." Gran had made her watch that, too.

Darcie liked *Four Weddings and a Funeral* better, but Merrick had never opened up to her like this before. She couldn't help but be impressed by this new forthright side of him, assuming it could be trusted.

"It was a classic," he went on. "Could have been Fellini, really. Jackie's gown cost ten thousand dollars. People all over Greenwich were stabbing each other in the back to get invited. I realized by the time we fed each other wedding cake and ran for the limousine to catch our plane for Aruba—"

"Poor babies," Darcie murmured.

"—that we didn't love each other. Hell, we never liked each other that much. In bed it was okay at first—"

"With the lights out."

"Jackie's a beautiful woman. A nice woman. She's just not for me."

"You want something different." Like Darcie Baxter. "Something Midwestern and gullible." She gazed at him. "Some naive working girl—" she remembered Dylan in the Westin bar "—I mean that in the best sense—who will stare adoringly into your gorgeous blue eyes, tell you how wonderful you are in the sack—and never once question your commitment, or lack thereof."

"You're determined to stay angry. Aren't you?"

"I'm determined not to get hurt again."

Merrick sighed. "Darce, we never promised each other anything."

"That is another problem."

"What do you want from me?" He squirmed in his chair. He rolled his scotch glass between his palms. He stared at the white tablecloth. *"Marriage?"*

"Not unless you're into bigamy."

"We're getting a divorce. Jackie filed on Monday." It was Monday now. Maybe Merrick had come from the courthouse, or a lawyer's office, to Darcie. "Last week," he added when he glanced up and saw her suspicious look.

"I feel bad for your children, Merrick. But this has nothing to do with me."

He took a swig of scotch. "You claim you're not ready for commitment, either."

"But I like the possibility. Someday." She pushed her wineglass away. "I think I should go. When you get your life straightened out, don't give me a call."

He reached out to snatch her wrist. "Sit down. Please," he said when she tugged at his hold. "Don't make a scene, Darcie. Have a heart, will you?"

"I had a heart. You smashed it."

"All right," he said. "All *right*. We won't talk about Jackie. But you started it."

Darcie slid back into her chair. The waiter hustled over to the table, and plunked down two platters of sea bass, steaming and redolent of spices. Her stomach growled again. She was still easy.

"First, Greta Hinckley," she murmured.

"She giving you trouble again?"

Ah, now he would become her father confessor. And reel Darcie back in like the fish on her plate. She stared down at it. Eat, or run?

She picked up her fork. "She's hounding me. I don't trust her."

"A wise reaction."

Merrick had heard—had he actually *heard?*—all about Greta during their time together of nonconnubial bliss. She could trust him at least not to repeat what she said. "I found Greta fleshing out a design, so to speak, just before five o'clock. That's why I left early."

"I'm glad you did. I didn't relish waiting for you until seven."

Darcie shrugged. "She's working on this…weird plan. Hose for thin legs."

Merrick threw back his head and laughed aloud.

This seemed to set off a round of laughter in the restaurant, and guffaws could be heard from other tables. The sounds rose into the air, bounced off the tin ceiling, ricocheted into Darcie's ears. She had to smile.

"Ridiculous, isn't it?"

"Totally absurd. Will Walt go for it?"

"I doubt it, but I've been wrong before. As long as she doesn't stick my name on it, I guess I don't care."

"Unless she has something else—her real plan—under wraps."

She hadn't thought of that. "You're right. She could." Darcie dug into her sea bass. She was starving. It felt good to laugh, good to share with Merrick the details of her life. Her work life, at least.

"Darcie, come back to me. I need you."

Her fork clattered to the floor. It rang like a dinner bell. Or an alarm? *He's still a snake,* Claire had said. Stuck in the elevator, Darcie thought, without Dylan. *Merrick needed her?* Now, *that* was new, and Darcie needed to believe she had a life after Sydney. She'd think about forgiveness. Later.

Merrick leaned near and caught her hand.

When he drew her closer and his mouth moved the last inch toward hers, Darcie didn't resist.

He might be lying again. She might be naive. But she needed to be held.

Suddenly, Australia seemed even farther away than it really was.

"Okay," she murmured when his lips touched hers. "A friendly kiss. But no sex."

"We'll see."

Chapter Eight

"Hey, Matilda."

At the deep, mellow voice the next day, Darcie froze, her hand on the telephone. She cast a startled glance over her desk at Wunderthings then swallowed hard.

"Dylan?"

"Who else calls you Matilda?"

She took a scattered breath. Oh, God. Oh, God.

She'd given up on him, let Merrick kiss her again—just once—only last night. Now...she'd gone from zero men in her life to two at once.

"I didn't think you'd call."

"Kinda hard to put in a call, darling, to someone who fails to leave her phone number behind." Uh-oh. He sounded edgy. Her listing was in Gran's name. Guilt swamped her and Darcie swallowed before he spoke again. "Good thing I knew where you worked. The Internet's a great research tool, don't you think?"

"You found this number on the Web?"

"One of those programs that has every telephone directory in the world. I use it for business with my stud."

The last word went through her like a streak. She knew he meant *farm,* not *sex,* but still...

"That must have taken you a full minute to track me down."

Silence. So he hadn't tried to find her. Until now.

"What changed your mind after all this time?" Darcie asked.

Dylan's voice dropped lower. "You remember that thing we did...middle of the night...my room, my bed...you climbed on top...did that reverse and—"

"Dylan. I'm at work. I can't talk like this."

"I'll talk. You listen."

Darcie fidgeted in her desk chair. Across the aisle Greta turned to look at her, eyes sharp as an eagle about to consume its prey. Darcie shifted again, putting a shoulder to the cubicle entry. Damn. She'd said Dylan's name, more than once, and Greta likely hadn't missed it. The office rumors—Walt's rumor—were true, she'd realize. And resent Darcie even more.

"I'm not on a speaker phone, am I?" Dylan wanted to know.

"No. But if you're going to talk dirty..."

That wasn't what Dylan had in mind after all. His tone hardened.

"Actually, no. I've been pretty pissed."

"I thought maybe you were." So Claire and Gran had suggested, but Darcie felt her spirits rise. He hadn't called *not* because he didn't like her. He was just mad.

"Why'd you run out on me?" he said.

"We had fun, Dylan. Two weeks' worth. But I told you—"

"Let the other shoe drop. Dump me. I dare you."

"How could I—" She'd said too much. She didn't want to repeat the word *dump* with Greta's ears flapping just across the way "—when I'm in New York and you're—"

"—in the barn."

"You are so literal, Dylan." Every time she said his name, she lowered her voice another notch. She almost whispered now. "You know what I mean."

And then, as only Dylan could, he nailed her.

"It's past midnight here. I just doctored a sick lamb. I named her Darcie."

Surprised, touched, she felt her eyes fill. "That's…thank you."

"Welcome. I thought you'd like to know. So I picked up the dog and bone."

"Is that Aussie rhyming slang again?"

"For telephone."

"What does she look like? Darcie II."

He laughed a little. "She looks like a sheep. Merino. Top-quality, of course."

"You could send me a picture. On the Web."

"Yeah, I could. Maybe I will."

He was warming up again now. The anger, the obvious hurt she'd caused, was fading. So did her guilt. Darcie spun in her chair, and smiled.

"She has your eyes, your…determination," he continued. "She willed herself to pull through."

"Oh, Dylan…"

"I really like your eyes. And your hair. Your mouth, your br—"

She cleared her throat. Walt Corwin had appeared at her cubicle doorway. Greta leaped from her seat to stand beside him, and Darcie put a finger to the disconnect button. "My, uh, boss is here. I have to go."

She heard a panicked grunt. "Darcie, quick. Give me your home number."

She rattled it off, not even stopping to think this wasn't wise—any more than in Sydney the morning she walked out on him. Leaving Dylan in bed, bare all over.

Her heart beat triple time, her palms had left moist prints on the phone. Dylan Rafferty had called. He'd named a feisty sheep after her. No one…but no one…had ever done *that* before.

"I knew you were a hard act to follow," she murmured.

"Believe it, darling." He paused for a long moment. "Ever had phone sex?"

She blushed. "Um…"

"Tonight," he said, and she could hear his smile. "Unless I have trouble with your lamb again. If I do, then tomorrow."

"I'll...look forward to it."

Strange, that she might prefer telephone seduction to the real thing, not that she was ready—if she ever would be—to encourage Merrick, but there it was. She'd think about that later.

"Fair dinkum," Dylan murmured. Good enough.

She covered her grin with a hand. "Fair dinkum."

"Darcie." Walt wanted her *now.*

"I really have to go," she said into the phone.

"Don't bust a gut."

"What?" He'd lost her again. She was far behind in her Ozspeak lessons.

Dylan laughed. "Don't work too hard, Matilda."

He hung up, humming the tune that had become their song.

"You're blushing," Walt informed her.

She didn't meet his gaze. Or Greta's. They were both still standing in the entry to her cubicle, and Darcie had been avoiding Walt since Friday. She always avoided Greta when possible. Darcie grabbed a red licorice whip, a comfort treat, from her desk drawer.

"So it's true," Greta said. "You did meet an Aussie."

"You tell her, Walt," Darcie murmured, still irritated that he'd started the rumor.

"Big guy, shoulders, wearing a—what do you call it—an Outback hat?"

"An Akubra?" Greta said, making the word sound like a smutty joke. Her eyes narrowed another inch into venomous slits.

Darcie couldn't resist. "You can imagine what we found to do with that."

Greta folded her arms over her scrawny chest. Then she glanced at Walt, and her gaze warmed. "I am a woman of more than average imagination...."

She implied the opposite of Darcie and obviously remembering Greta's yen for him, Walt shot Darcie a frightened look.

"Can we talk in my office? I need your update on the Sydney project." He was gone before she answered.

Oh, Lord. Caught up in jet lag, Merrick's reappearance, and her nightly dreams of Dylan, she hadn't prepared a thing.

"Should I come, too, Walter?" Greta's voice followed him like a hound on the scent. "I wanted to discuss my idea...."

"Save it," Darcie murmured. Competition she didn't need just now.

"If Wunderthings puts my hose design into production right away, and starts the marketing campaign, Walter can launch it in Sydney."

"Look into the demographics," Darcie suggested. "With the growing weight problem in this country, I'd rethink your notion about hose for thin thighs."

Greta's face fell. "There are plenty of skinny women. Look at Hollywood."

"That's anorexia, bulimia..." Darcie whizzed from her cubicle into the hall. "We'll talk later, if you want. Walt's waiting."

With Dylan's phone call still buzzing through her mind, her senses, she whipped down the long aisle to the anteroom where Nancy Braddock sat nursing a cup of coffee.

"Greta barking at your heels again?" she said, and Darcie rolled her eyes then marched into Walt's office chewing on her licorice stick.

She could use the distraction of the Sydney opening to quell her own desire for Dylan, her confusion about Merrick, even her vision of Greta's beady eyes boring into her back. Too bad she didn't have any new ideas for Walt Corwin.

In his office she closed the door and leaned against it.

"That woman wants my blood."

"You and Nancy may have to form a vigilante group."

He was joking. Darcie wasn't.

"Couldn't they find something for Greta to do in Marketing?"

The department's offices were located two floors below, and Darcie hardly ever saw anyone who worked there. Mainly because she despised Marketing. It would be a good place for Greta.

"I wish." Walter obviously hadn't missed the yearning look on Greta's face. At least Darcie had warned him. He groaned. "She left some harebrained design on my desk before I got in this morning—"

"Probably when she read all your files. And plowed through your drawers looking for embarrassing personal items with which to blackmail you."

"She doesn't really do that."

"Get real, Walt. That, and more. Hide your condoms."

He frowned. "I thought Nancy was pulling my leg."

"Greta would like to pull something a bit higher up. See paragraph above."

He flushed. "Where did you get that mind of yours?"

"In a Happy Meal, where else?"

Filled with dread, Darcie plopped onto the chair in front of his desk. An actual office, she thought, gazing around with admiration. Pictures on the walls—bad water colors, but still, pictures in frames. Wood, or plastic? She couldn't tell. His walnut desk looked like an ocean compared to hers, and, as with any good executive, its top was mostly bare. As if he didn't have any work to do while peons like Darcie took care of the grunt jobs. True, she had to admit. Claire had been right about that, too. Walt dragged open a drawer, drew out a half-finished cigar, and clamped it between his teeth.

Darcie wished for more red licorice, like a security blanket.

"I've heard from the agent in Sydney. The contractor will rip out the old Sheetrock this week, then the electricians are scheduled to come in. We need to figure out where we'll want more outlets, that kind of thing."

Darcie rose to the challenge. And fibbed. "I've been working on that."

"You have?"

She needed to reassure him of her competence. Somehow. "I'm a self-starter, Walt. It was obvious when we got approval of the contract for the space in the QVB that things would start to move. Quickly, I hoped. Time is money."

He smiled in approval. "What have you got?"

She could see Walt was relieved. Nothing new. In the four years she'd worked for him—as Claire also pointed out—Darcie had anticipated his needs more often than not. More often than her own, just as she had with Merrick. She'd worked extra hours. Rewritten Walt's reports. Made him look good. He owed her, she figured.

Darcie hoped to collect—and secure her position in Wunderthings-Sydney. If she played her cards right, she might see Dylan again, which had become an especially appealing notion in the past hour.

Darcie suppressed an image of him...she could still hear his voice, yes, but those broad shoulders, too, that great smile. And those kisses...

"Greta threw me off a bit. I left my notes in my desk. I'll get them."

"Later. Just fill me in now."

"Well." She cleared her throat, mind whirring. Darcie plucked a brass paperweight off Walt's desk. "We're in a very upscale neighborhood there."

"That's news? Tell me something I don't know."

"Good hotels all around, Darling Harbour a stone's throw away—if you're walking downhill, that is, not up—other malls and restaurants."

"Get to the point, Darcie."

"Yes." Quick, get one. She hefted the paperweight. Not as good as red licorice, but it would do for comfort. "Uh—in the QVB we have a prime location. We need to showcase that, make the rest of the stores around us dim bulbs by comparison. We want the shopper's eye to home straight in on Wunderthings the instant that person gets to the second level."

"Right," he agreed, nodding, looking interested in her hasty concept.

"Man or woman," Darcie rushed on, improvising as she went. "Young mothers, lovers, newlyweds, hard-assed professional types..."

"Darcie. *What?*"

Her brain slipped into higher gear. Necessity being the mother of invention. "So besides the interior of the shop— which I believe should be highly sophisticated in appearance—we need a dramatic front window display."

"Define sophisticated."

Um... "Cream walls, maybe silk paper, gleaming wood floors, I think, yes, with scattered Oriental rugs...real ones. Dark, rich mahogany display cases, matching rods for the hanging displays, everything coordinated. Lush. Sensual." She took a breath, on a roll now. "A visual, auditory, tactile feast for the senses. We'll scent the air with expensive perfume. I think we should develop one of our own."

"Where have you been? We launched FloralMist last spring."

Momentarily derailed, Darcie wrinkled her nose.

"Too sweet. Too young. Too un-sexy."

"Customers love it."

She dropped the brass paperweight on her toe but didn't dare cringe. Pain throbbed through her. "They'll love the new one more. We'll call it...Australove. No, Sin-dney." She couldn't even say that and Darcie waved a hand in temporary dismissal of a bad idea. "I'll come up with something. Or Marketing can. But do you see the concept?" She didn't dare call it hers, take credit for the notion and further irritate Walt.

"It's different from any of our other stores."

"Exactly. So is the Pacific Rim market. Think Orient, Walt. We're talking a blend of cultures, lifestyles... diversity. We may want a few Japanese or Chinese models for the opening. No, a Eurasian girl. That's it. Exquisite, stylish, sensual herself."

"We can't afford a live model."

"Mannequin, then." She paused for another breath. "Or

would we be better going with a multiethnic look? Lots of mannequins. You know. Irish, English, Scots, Italian, German…along with the Asian angle. Kind of highlight Australia's melting pot quality."

Walt studied his empty desktop. He flicked a glance around the office, his gaze landing on a hazy water color of New York harbor, then glancing off a desk picture of his wife before her last illness. Something he never talked about. Darcie sometimes forgot he was a widower. He settled a look on her.

"What else?"

She didn't know. Suicide?

"Uh, um…"

"You don't have a plan written down. Do you?"

"No, but I think well on my feet." She stood up.

"Get me something by five o'clock. Something great."

"You don't like what I just told you?"

"I love it," he said.

Darcie drifted from his office, Greta Hinckley forgotten. Merrick Lowell temporarily eclipsed. Dylan Rafferty… she'd talk with him tonight.

Phone sex. You had to love that, too.

Giving herself a mental high-five, she floated back to her cubicle.

"Damn, but I'm good!"

Darcie worked late. She took the ten-fifteen ferry home, then couldn't find a cab. By the time she arrived at Eden's apartment building on the Palisades, it was almost midnight. Exhausted, Darcie barely noticed that Julio wasn't on duty in the lobby when she passed.

Scarcely remembering what night of the week it was, she punched the elevator button and rode upstairs, yawning. Tuesday, that was it. A week after Sydney. Would Walt like her concrete ideas? It had taken Darcie the rest of the afternoon to get them down on paper. Then, after his initial comments, she'd slaved through dinner—wonton soup and a bag of fried noodles delivered from the

Chinese deli on the corner—to revise her proposal, the only person on the sixth floor until nearly ten o'clock.

If she'd seen Merrick tonight, she might have been forced to make some decision about their new "relationship." But since she hadn't seen him, especially after Dylan's call, she wouldn't hate herself in the morning.

Oh, God. Dylan.

Jamming her key in the lock with sudden haste, Darcie let herself into the duplex. Intent on getting to the answering machine, the first thing she saw was Sweet Baby Jane blinking sleep from her eyes at the top of the foyer steps.

"Evening, SBJ."

The cat showed her teeth in a snarl.

"Well. If that's how you want to play..."

She'd been trying to treat the cat with kid gloves for days. Patting her on the head. Chucking her under the chin. But nothing helped Darcie where the evil feline was concerned. Not even last night's full can of turkey and giblets dinner before bed. Jane had vomited the rich food all over the carpet, and Darcie wasn't certain she had fully removed the stain from her grandmother's precious new possession.

Face it, she thought. "You hate me. Don't you?"

Shuffling sounds from the upper level caught SBJ's attention—and Darcie's. Her grandmother appeared on the landing, then smiled. Guiltily. Why did she look guilty?

"There you are, dear. I thought I heard you come in."

Eden's cheeks turned pink. She was wearing a silk wrapper—circa 1972, Bonwit Teller, Darcie guessed—a filmy nightie underneath, and scarlet nail polish on her toes. They were usually bare. And so was Eden, who preferred to sleep nude.

"Company?" Darcie murmured.

"You wicked girl."

"Me?"

"You would call attention to my visitor. We won't disturb you." Eden swirled around to head back along the upstairs hall. "Have some coconut cream pie. It's in the fridge." She stopped. "Oh, your man in the Akubra called."

"Dylan?" Who else.

Darn. Lost in her work, she'd forgotten for a time—how could she?—and now she'd missed him. He would think she was avoiding him.

"What did he say?"

Her tone softened. "His little lamb is doing fine."

"Me?" Darcie asked again.

"No, that's not right. He said *your* little lamb. I think he meant a sheep."

"Oh. Darcie II."

Eden pattered down the hall. "He has a marvelous voice, dear."

Darcie agreed. He had marvelous everything. Maybe she'd judged their lack of suitability too quickly. "I may be going back to Australia, Gran."

"I thought you should."

With no further explanation, Eden disappeared into her bedroom—from which Darcie heard, when she tried to avoid Sweet Baby Jane's flying claws and danced by in the hall, the unmistakable sounds of…definitely…lovemaking.

"Julio?" Darcie called, unable to resist.

"Sí…" he gasped. *"Señorita."*

"Welcome to the club."

Eden sang out, "You *wicked* girl."

"Me?" Darcie said, giggling. And went on into her room.

She slammed the door shut on Sweet Baby Jane—nearly catching her tail in it. My grandmother, she thought. Eighty-two years old. Hot as a silicone-enhanced Las Vegas showgirl. It was enough to make Darcie—alone in her bed without Dylan's voice to warm her after all—feel an emotion as strong as Greta Hinckley's threat of revenge.

"I do not believe in envy," Darcie muttered to herself.

She didn't believe in envy, but she did need to sleep. It wasn't Gran keeping her awake nights, she told herself. In the past three nights Darcie hadn't slept, and she could no longer blame jet lag for her bleary mornings.

By Friday Dylan still hadn't called.

Caught up in work at Wunderthings for Walt, she'd missed Dylan's phone sex date on Tuesday night. Wednesday and Thursday she'd spent lying on her bed, listening to Eden and Julio in the other room again. Earplugs were becoming a distinct possibility. For the fourth night in a row, she sprawled across the wide mattress and wished the telephone could let her off the hook.

Maybe he was giving her the business. After all, she'd stood him up the other night after his first call to the office. After "dumping" him in Sydney.

Her track record with men wasn't getting any better after all.

Merrick Lowell, either. Since his separation from Jacqueline, they no longer needed to rendezvous only on Mondays, but neither would Darcie meet him at the Grand Hyatt. They met in public now.

Why make it into anything more?

She didn't know what to do with the new Merrick, the wounded Merrick. Still, they were talking now, a little, and that was different.

As for Dylan…she blotted out an image of him.

Mr. Right hadn't materialized.

Darcie blanked out another vision, of Eden with Julio.

She even managed not to think about Claire, with Peter the Great. Or not.

No more waiting for the phone like a weepy teenage girl, she thought. No more envy of her own grandmother. She was back where she belonged. For now. For now, at least…

"You're seeing him again?" her sister Annie asked by phone the next night.

"Don't tell Mom."

"You know what she thinks about New York. And unless Merrick puts a ring on your finger, she'll think the same of him."

Darcie pleaded into the phone, "Annie, don't say a word. Promise."

"Is he good?"

She didn't answer. *Who knows?* She couldn't remember. A recent downturn in the stock market—it went up, it went down, Darcie thought, why get excited?—had Merrick stressed out, and his divorce made things worse. Or was she imagining the change in him?

Why didn't she feel any better today?

Annie wasn't helping, even when she changed the subject.

"You need to tell Mom that you're willing to room with me."

But I'm not. "She'll never allow it. Not with Gran."

Annie laughed. "No, an apartment of our own."

"Look, Annie. I'm busy at work—frantic now that Walt has me refining the Sydney project design, which he changes every day. I don't have time to look for an apartment and I'm happy enough where I am." Wasn't she?

"Listening to her with Julio every night?"

"Not every night. He works."

"What kind of life is that, big sister? Schloffing back and forth to Manhattan on the ferry—"

"Schlepping."

"—living with your *grandmother?* We'd have such fun fixing up a place. I'd get a job—something—and we could party every night."

"I don't want to live in a sorority house, Annie."

Her sister had been party girl of the year at Smith four years running, but she could almost hear Annie shaking her head now.

"You've been with Gran too long."

Darcie smiled. "She swings better than I ever could, believe me."

"And it's depressing you. I can tell. You need to be around younger people—like me—you need to be free and wild in New York."

"You talk like that and Mom will never let you leave Cincinnati."

"Oh, yes, she will. I'm wearing her down. Dad, too. All I need now is for you to—"

"Contribute to the delinquency of my baby sister? I'd never live down the shame. Mom and Dad—"

"Will relax if I'm with you. I won't be any trouble."

"Like a rogue elephant on a rampage?" Darcie sighed. "I can't talk about this now, Annie. I have to go."

"Are you meeting Merrick at the Hyatt?"

"Not tonight."

"Is your Aussie calling?"

Thanks for that reminder. "I doubt it."

"Phone sex," Annie said with a wistful sigh, then disconnected the call.

Wistful herself, Darcie lay back on her bed, and when she'd promised she wouldn't, waited for the telephone to ring.

As if she were Greta Hinckley. Without any life at all.

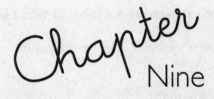
Chapter Nine

"Another night with Merrick, dear?" Gran's dry tone followed Darcie along the upstairs hall to the steps.

"It'll leave you and Julio the apartment to yourselves."

"I'd rather have you home."

Uh-oh, Darcie thought. Here we go again. Like another cue that this Wednesday evening wouldn't turn out well, Sweet Baby Jane wound around Eden's slim ankles, twined between Darcie's feet like a bobbin weaving cloth, and all but tripped her down the stairs—not an accident, Darcie felt sure.

Avoiding Jane's claws, she skimmed down the steps in front of Gran.

"Merrick's taking you to dinner?"

"And a movie," Darcie murmured. "Last week we went to a play."

"His son's third grade pageant? That's hardly Broadway, Darcie."

"No, an off-off-Broadway thing. But I've seen his son's picture from the pageant. He looked really cute dressed like a turnip."

In the center of the room, Eden whirled. "How could

one possibly dress like a turnip? Much less look appealing."
Clearly, she wanted a fight.

"Julio dresses like a doorman...and you seem to find
him fetching. That dark-brown uniform, those fake gold
epaulets, braid hanging everywhere."

"That isn't the part of Julio I like to see hanging."

Darcie arched a brow.

"Well, not hanging exactly," Gran said. Was that a faint
blush in her down-dusted cheeks? She patted her newly
tinted hair. No apricot tonight. She looked more like a
russet apple.

Darcie didn't respond about Julio. "I won't be late," she
told Eden.

"So it's just a quickie? He's a premature ejaculator. I
knew it."

"Gran!"

"Do I shock you?"

"Only every time you open your mouth. What would
Mom say?"

Gran bristled. "If she knows what's good for her, she
won't say squat until next Christmas. Do you know how
many telephone calls I've had from that woman this
week?"

Darcie silently groaned. Annie.

"Four," Darcie guessed.

"Ten. Three of them last night. She interrupted Julio
and me right in the middle of the most *delightful*—"

"I get the picture, Gran." Darcie tried not to shudder.
Like Merrick, Julio was far from her idea of a dream man.
"What did Mom say?"

"She threatened me. If I didn't know better, I'd tell you
that woman can see through fiber optics. Straight along
the telephone wires from Cincinnati to Fort Lee. She told
me if I didn't mend my ways, she'd have your father come
see me. I always knew she was nosy, but it was as if she
sat down right on my bed while Julio and I—"

"Please don't tell me she's putting Annie on a plane."

"Judging from the loud wails in the background, no.

Your sister may be fighting the good fight, but she hasn't won yet."

"You wouldn't want two of us in the apartment. Would you, Gran?"

"It won't come to that."

Darcie didn't quite know what that meant. Nothing new for her these days—at home or at work. She gathered her coat, her gloves, her tote bag and started for the entryway, Jane hissing at her heels. If she hurried, she could catch the next ferry to Manhattan.

"When is Merrick's divorce final?" Eden's question stopped her cold. Darcie wouldn't escape this evening, like most others lately, without the rest of her grandmother's lecture.

"We don't discuss it."

"You should, Darcie. Make the most of your life, not the least."

"Merrick Lowell is not the man I'm going to marry."

"And how well he knows that."

What do you want from me? At first, she'd assumed he was single but afraid of commitment; then she'd learned he was already married. Now, separated, he seemed too depressed to talk about another potential walk down the aisle. Or was that more naiveté on her part? "I probably couldn't live with him anyway," she added.

"I should say not. You're wasting your time."

"You met him once." Wishing Eden would drop the subject, Darcie danced away from Sweet Baby Jane's flashing teeth. "He thinks you had the hots for him."

"Darcie Elizabeth Baxter, that's absurd. I'm twice his age."

"And then some," she murmured. "What about Julio?"

Eden smoothed her candy-apple hair. "He's not that much older than Merrick."

"How old?"

"Forty-one, two." She was lying. He must be younger.

"Gran, you're twice *his* age."

"Ah, but love conquers all."

"You're in *love* with Julio?" Eden didn't answer. "I

thought he was just another of your boyfriends. Wait until Mom hears this."

"My relationship with Julio Perez is my…affair, so to speak." But Eden didn't smile, either. "He and I get on beautifully—in bed and out. Which is our business. Ours alone."

"I couldn't agree more. So is mine, with Merrick."

Gran's mouth thinned into a disapproving line.

"I'm well past childbearing, Darcie. It hardly matters whether Julio and I marry or spend the rest of our lives sleeping together. You, on the other hand…"

"I'm not ready to get married. To anyone."

She sighed. "If you hadn't turned off that Aussie hunk—"

Gran scored a point. Bull's-eye.

Darcie stiffened. She felt terrible quarreling with her grandmother, but, "I did nothing to 'turn off' Dylan Rafferty. He said he'd call, but he never did. His choice. I fail to understand how I could possibly ruin a relationship that a) never existed, b) isn't right for me and c) is probably the worst mistake of two weeks I ever made in my life." No matter how good they felt.

"You're pining for him."

"I am not 'pining'!"

"Then call him. Or would you blithely sacrifice a chance for a reasonable romance? Merrick Lowell's only relationship, I might add, has been with himself. Since birth. He's a narcissist. I won't tell you again, Darcie, that man is simply using you."

"You just told me."

"He'll hurt you again in the end." Eden looked exasperated. She reached out a hand to tuck a strand of Darcie's hair behind her ear, a placating gesture. "You're wearing that mutinous look. You inherited it from your mother. But I'm quite serious, dear. If both Claire and I have told you that you deserve better than Merrick Lowell, why won't you at least listen?"

"Because he—he—" She couldn't find the words to defend him, or herself.

Eden turned thoughtful, another bad sign. "Julio has an adorable nephew. I think you should meet him. His name is Juan—Juanito, to the family—and he—"

Just her luck. Before Darcie could shut the front door behind her on a dramatic statement, Sweet Baby Jane took a chunk out of her ankle. She hoped she didn't regret the yelped words, or the decision.

"I think I should look for my own apartment!"

"Jane, after all, is a big drawback to our living arrangement."

And Annie had a point, Darcie told herself, also for the hundredth time. So did Merrick. A few days later she flipped through the Sunday paper to the real estate section. "What sense does it make to live with your eighty-two-year-old grandmother?"

"There's a whole world waiting," Annie said through the receiver that Darcie cradled between her neck and shoulder. "Full of men. You know the saying, 'Girls just want to have fun.'"

Darcie sighed. Her last evening with Merrick hadn't improved once she left Fort Lee.

Forgetting all about Annie, Darcie rattled the open newspaper, folded it into a quarter width as if she were on the crowded ferry or a commuter train with other paper-readers jammed close. Occupy as little space as possible, urbanites. Dylan could probably spread a newspaper over hundreds of acres if he wanted. But lately in Gran's apartment, Darcie felt like an interloper prying into Eden's "affair" with Julio, listening—though she never meant to—through the bedroom walls at night.

Ugh.

Taking up too much room.

It didn't help that Gran's sex life seemed far superior to Darcie's, which had become nonexistent.

But did they have to fight about it?

In the past twenty-four hours neither of them had spoken to the other. Her fault? Poor Julio had become their go-between, their interpreter—and his English wasn't that great. If Eden was waiting for Darcie to apologize, to take back her threat to move from the duplex, she would wait until she turned 164.

Had Darcie outstayed her own welcome?

Running a finger down the column—Furnished Apts./ East Side—she gave a sigh. Either the rent seemed too high (all rents in New York were too high) or the advertised space sounded dreary. Sometimes both.

"Darcie," Annie whined in her ear.

"I'm reading."

"Anything good?"

"No. And Mom hasn't said you can come to New York."

"I think she's weakening. Look for some place big enough for both of us. Oh, and no tenements. No dangerous neighborhoods."

Hmm. That seemed almost worth the sacrifice to keep Annie in Cincinnati.

"A quote from Mom?"

Her gaze went blank on the real estate pages. Was she nuts to even consider this? Annie was a slob, while Gran was one of the neatest, hippest people she knew. Darcie regretted her angry outburst, yes, even her threat. But to stop hearing Julio and Eden in the throes of passion? To quit waltzing around Sweet Baby Jane? To decorate her own place…have parties…walk to work? She wouldn't have to ride the ferry again, unless she decided to visit Eden.

Once they weren't angry with each other anymore, that is.

A flash of sadness arced through her.

Maybe it was time to strike out on her own. More than time. She imagined Eden Baxter would be happy to get her duplex—and her privacy—back. Surely there was some logical order to be found in her own life.

And who knew? In the city Darcie might meet someone totally unlike Merrick—or Dylan Rafferty.

Hey, Matilda…

* * *

In her own apartment the next Thursday, Claire Spencer held on to the last of her temper.

"I'm sorry, Tildy. I can't continue this charade."

From beneath her fluffy red bangs, Tildy gazed at her blankly. "Charade?"

Claire reached into the bassinet where Samantha was squalling at a decibel level in the upper reaches of human hearing. Frantic, her heart pounding, Claire lifted the baby into her arms and gently rocked her until Sam's limbs stopped flailing and her rigid spine relaxed. "Shh, Mommy's here. You're fine."

"I only put her down for a minute, Mrs. Spencer."

Claire frowned. "I walked into this apartment more than *five* minutes ago. No one heard me—of course you didn't. Sam was crying too loud. I changed my shoes, put on a pair of jeans...and she's still crying."

"It's good for her lungs," Tildy said lamely, brushing hair from her eyes.

"Well, it's not good for mine." Claire's heart felt squeezed in her chest. "I'll write you a check for the whole week. But I want you to leave. Now."

"My references..."

"Tildy, if I were you, I'd go to computer school. Or take bartending lessons. Anything but child care, especially with a newborn."

Tildy's thin mouth set. "Babies can be difficult."

"Yes. I know. So can parents," Claire muttered, then jerked Tildy's coat from the nursery's buttery-yellow giraffe rack trimmed in coral-pink.

"I need the pay, Mrs. Spencer."

Tildy's whine set her teeth on edge. Her now hard green eyes frightened Claire but she wouldn't let it show.

"You are a lucky young woman. If I followed my worst instincts, I'd be on the phone to the agency. I thought I was hiring a competent, caring stand-in so I could return to my career. Instead, I've spent every moment at my office biting my nails, twining my hair until it snaps off in my fingers...*worrying* that some terrible mishap has befallen my only child!" Claire finished in a loud, spiraling tone that made Samantha's face squinch tight again. Her tiny body quivered. Claire was a breath away from screaming when she marched from the cheerful room. If she didn't leave, she would not only communicate her tension further to her nine-week-old daughter; she might strangle Tildy Lewis.

Claire strode into the living room, jiggling Sam in one arm and crooning to her while she searched with her other hand through Peter's desk for the checkbook. Her heart still thumping, she bent to scrawl her signature on the form. Tearing off the check, she shoved it at Tildy.

"I've added a small bonus to tide you over until you get another job. I pray it won't be as a nanny."

Claire had no sooner shut the door behind Tildy—with a shaky sigh of relief—when the bell rang. Thank goodness Peter hadn't been home yet to talk her out of firing the girl. Swearing under her breath, not with her usual creativity because of Samantha's presence, she yanked open the door again.

Darcie stood there, gaping. "Who was the red-faced girl I just saw stalking down the hall?"

"My ex-nanny."

"She looked barely out of diapers."

"Umm. That's where it starts." Claire held the door wide. Then took another look at Darcie's face. "What's wrong?"

"Nothing," Darcie tried but when she leaned to greet Samantha, Claire saw tears in Darcie's eyes. Samantha chortled.

"My daughter may not know a female disaster when she sees one, but I do. In fact, I am one. Now that I've ditched her nanny, before guilt overwhelms me for ruining someone's life, let me hear about your day."

"Oh, Claire."

She carried the baby back to her bassinet, turned on the dolphin mobile that hung above it, and listened for a moment to the chime of its nursery tune. "'The Itsy Bitsy Spider.'" Then Claire went to the kitchen, retrieved a half bottle of merlot from the refrigerator and poured it equally into two balloon glasses.

"Here." She handed one to Darcie. "Talk."

Darcie's sigh told her half the story. It was a man, of course. Claire wondered when it wasn't a man—and thanked the institution of marriage. It had its downside, but for the first time since Samantha's birth, Claire could appreciate being well out of the singles scene.

Only she was wrong. It wasn't Merrick, or the Australian.

"Come here, sweetie." When Darcie had related her quarrel with Eden, Claire tightened her arms around her friend on the living room sofa.

Darcie sniffed. "Maybe I should reconsider—before I make another mistake. I mean, I could apologize to Gran, stay with her, keep the status quo. Why not?"

Claire disagreed. Darcie's tone sounded brave, the emotion Claire had felt when she fired Tildy at last, but her own problems weren't resolved with that one action, and neither were Darcie's. She couldn't take a step forward, then three steps back.

"No. You can't. On second thought, you need to move into the city. Get closer to other people like yourself—men, that is—single, certifiably *unattached,* looking for Ms. Right. No kooks. There must be some."

Claire wanted her to find someone other than Merrick Lowell and his self-centered approach to their "relationship." It was taking its toll on Darcie's self-image. Which wasn't that solid to begin with.

"I'm conflicted," Darcie said, reaching for the merlot again. She took a healthy swig, holding the glass with both hands.

"Conflict?" Claire thought of Tildy, her own job, Peter, the baby... "I could write a book."

Darcie brightened. "Hey. Why don't we?" She forced a grin, obviously glad to change the subject no matter how silly it proved. "You know that new self-help book that just came out? *The Give-In Wife* or *Woman,* something like that? I wonder if she heard of that geek years ago—Gran told me—who thought women should meet their husbands at the door wrapped in see-through plastic every night." Darcie paused. "Barbie dolls," she added. "Real ones."

"*The Stepford Wives II*," Claire said with a laugh.

"We could do the realistic take—not the fantasy—on women's lives today. The turmoil, the demands...the whole dating scene. I mean, who *dates?* I am a perfect example, even with Merrick." She sat straighter, clearly in control again. "And what about marriage? The ticking clock. Kids. Add a career—could we focus this?"

"We'll deal with it."

"How?"

Darcie's eyes looked less shadowed. *But deal indeed, and how?* Claire wondered. They spoke at the same time and Claire's smile grew.

"I don't have a clue."

Darcie threw up her hands. "I don't have a freaking clue."

Chapter Ten

On a bright Saturday afternoon Darcie marched along East Seventy-Third Street, a newspaper clipping clutched in one tight fist. Behind her, Claire pushed Samantha in her fancy stroller—which must have cost as much as a low-end Jaguar—and every third step advised Darcie to relax.

"Don't get discouraged. We've been through this before." Claire leaned down to slip Sam's pacifier back into her mouth. "In SoHo, NoHo, Chelsea, Gramercy Park, Central Park West and South, Yorkville..."

Apartment after apartment over the past two weeks had disappointed them, but in those same weeks Claire hadn't let Darcie out of her sight. If she wanted to see a possible rental, Claire went with her, and more often than not Samantha rode shotgun.

"No, I have a good feeling today."

Darcie glanced left, then right. How could she not feel good on this quiet, tree-lined street on the Upper East side, flanked by rows of exquisite town houses. Some had been gutted, then renovated, and looked ultracontemporary with huge windows and chrome doors, but still, they blended with their older, brick-faced neighbors. Fingers crossed behind her back, Darcie hoped the address she was looking for would turn out to be perfect.

Her spirits instantly sank. In front of the brownstone—yes, a classic original—stood a small crowd of what appeared to be other house hunters. Well, what did she expect? Real estate was at a premium.

"You have as good a chance as anyone else," Claire whispered in her ear.

They hung off to one side, near the curb, and Claire rolled Samantha's carriage back and forth to keep her happy.

When she fussed, Darcie handed the baby a bright rattle from the small collection of toys tucked in around her. Sam's fingers tightened then fell open. She didn't get the concept of holding on yet. Distracted, Darcie held out the blue lion face again. She adored Samantha, but the milling group of would-be renters all looked more financially stable than Darcie.

Claire squeezed her shoulder.

"You're becoming a mother hen," Darcie said. "If you get any closer to being like Janet, I won't be responsible for my actions." She grinned but Claire's encouragement had made her eyes mist. "And I love Samantha, but don't you think she's getting a little bored? We've dragged her to every rental in Manhattan."

"Maybe she'll become a real estate agent when she grows up."

"If you're set on being part of this miserable process, you could leave her with Peter on Saturdays."

"Peter had to work. I should, too," Claire added, then hastily, "I don't mean I'm making some great sacrifice here."

"But you're behind in your job."

"Who isn't?"

"True," Darcie murmured, still feeling guilty that she'd kept Claire from her own duties, responsibilities, obligations. Hadn't they talked about the pressures on women recently? Neither of them had time to write the book. "What about a new nanny?"

Claire hesitated. "I've been thinking...my job's high enough on the food chain that I could take Samantha to work with me...oh, hell, like that would allow me to catch up. I'd just stay up all night at home—when Sam's finally sleeping through—and piss off Peter."

"Walt's a little impatient with my apartment search," Darcie put in.

"Men," Claire muttered. "They just don't get it."

"To be honest, he's a lot impatient. I scrambled to meet my deadline on the Sydney store design yesterday."

"Which must have thrilled Greta."

Darcie winced. "She offered to do it for me."

"Big of her."

"Walt nearly agreed." Darcie mused for a moment. "I've been wondering if I shouldn't try a different approach with her."

"A snake in her desk? Or no, why not rifle her belongings the way she sifts through yours? No telling what you might learn."

Darcie's frown quickly smoothed when Samantha peered up at her and started to pucker. "Don't cry. I'm fine, cupcake," she said, offering the baby a soft-stuffed alphabet block to gnaw on. *I keep thinking how you'd look, swollen, ripe...*

Claire grinned. "Sam's heard all about Greta Hinckley."

"She sits right across the aisle from me. If only I could stop feeling like the KGB is watching."

"The KGB *is* watching."

Darcie's next comment got swallowed. A woman wearing a tweed suit pushed through the knot of waiting apartment-hunters, and took her position on the stone steps leading to the front door.

"Sorry, people. Apartment's taken."

Disgruntled comments rose into the afternoon air.

"But I've been waiting...."

"I called...."

A man in a Burberry trench coat swore under his breath. A blond princess type in designer jeans and a leather jacket, wearing high-heeled skintight boots, stalked off looking furious.

A young couple, disappointed like Darcie, shuffled off down the street.

When the crowd dispersed, the agent disappeared, and Claire looked at Darcie who said, "This calls for a late lunch at Phantasmagoria. My treat."

"I can't, Darce. Peter wants to have dinner out tonight...."

"Then I'm your baby-sitter."

She and Samantha could read the want ads together. Like there was a reasonable apartment in New York with her name on it.

"Thanks," Clare said, "but we already have a sitter."

They were halfway to their favorite restaurant when Darcie pulled up short. Claire ran into her heels with the Perego stroller but Darcie didn't even yelp. She was used to Sweet Baby Jane.

"Claire," she said, pointing at a sign in a window.

The brownstone, two blocks farther east, didn't look as upscale as the false lead they'd just followed closer to Fifth Avenue, but Darcie stopped to stare. The building seemed decent. No garbage littered the scrap of iron-fenced concrete "yard" where a small wrought-iron table and two chairs held a flourishing green pothos plant. The windows on the basement and upper levels sparkled in the sunlight.

For Rent, the sign proclaimed.

Claire touched her arm. "Let's take a look."

An elderly woman answered the doorbell. So promptly, Darcie thought, that she might have been looking out the front window.

She led Darcie, Claire and Samantha—in Darcie's arms—into a first-floor apartment. Darcie lifted her eyebrows at the cleanliness of the living room, the light that flooded every corner.

"I'm giving up the apartment," the woman explained. "It's too much for me here in the city now. The noise, the traffic...my daughter convinced me to take a room in her house—and I admit, giving up this responsibility is welcome."

"You have a lovely place here."

"Yes, until my husband died. Now it's not quite home." Mrs. Lang studied Darcie who was carrying Samantha. "Are you married?"

"No."

Pity, the woman's expression said. "Let me show you the rest."

By the time they came full circle from the cute kitchen—it even had a small window—and the *two* bedrooms, the one bath, Darcie was in love. Forget men. She'd just stay here, figuring out her life, getting her work done at Wunderthings, climbing the ladder, enjoying her own space until she too needed to move in with...well, she wouldn't have a daughter, but one day Annie might. Or Darcie would be like Gran, who just kept going, even have boyfriends in her eighties...

That was, assuming a Mr. Near-Right even existed.

"If you don't have offers already, I'll take the apartment."

She liked its location, its layout, its space and light and ten-foot ceilings. Of course she'd repaint, but she spoke too soon.

Mrs. Lang named her price. And Darcie felt her spirits tumble down a hole.

When she and Claire stepped out again, in shared misery, onto the street, Claire's pricey stroller was missing.

Perfect.

Darcie couldn't afford this apartment. And now she owed Claire a carriage.

"Claire wouldn't hear of it," Darcie told her mother on the phone that night. "Peter says their homeowners' insurance should cover the theft. But I still feel bad."

"The city is no place for a young family. No place for *you,*" Janet Baxter insisted, making Darcie fervently wish she hadn't mentioned the subject. "Your father and I are willing to fly you home."

"I'd rather discuss a loan."

This being Darcie's original reason for calling, she held her breath. She liked to believe she was an independent woman. She had left a deposit on the brownstone apartment and she hated asking her parents for money, but this was an emergency.

Janet didn't seem as enthralled by Darcie's "find."

"Two bedrooms—miniscule, I'm sure, compared to what we have here—one bath. *One* bath, Darcie?"

"There's only one of me."

Her mother hesitated. "There can't be an adequate kitchen."

"The Langs lived there for forty years. They had plenty of time to furnish the place. In fact, Mrs. L wants to sell me the living room set, some end tables, outdoor furniture…"

"Is there a refrigerator?"

"Yes, Mom. A stove, a dishwasher, too—it's one of those narrow ones, but just right for the space beneath the counter."

Janet sighed into the receiver at the Cincinnati end of the call.

"Here in Symmes township you could rent a lovely place with three bedrooms, a dining area, even a garage. Or in Montgomery. Landen, too. What is the rent there again?"

She named Mrs. L's price—well into four figures—and Janet gasped.

"It's New York City, Mom. The cost of living isn't cheap. But it's exactly where I want to be."

"And your father and I are supposed to fund this madcap adventure?"

"I have a job. I have friends here. Now I'm a small loan away—a few months' rent, Mom, that's all I need—from having a place of my own." She paused for effect. With a partial rent subsidy, she could concentrate on Wunderthings, dazzle Walt with her creative input on the Sydney project and perhaps get a bigger raise.

"You want me to get away from Gran's influence, don't you?"

"Yes." Janet paused. "Very well."

Darcie's pulse stopped. "You'll send the money?" This seemed way too easy. "It doesn't have to be all at once. A monthly stipend would be great. Tell Daddy to add interest to the loan."

"No loan, Darcie."

"But you said..."

"Your father and I—" one of her favorite phrases "—are willing to spring for part of the rent, provided..."

Uh-oh. When Janet paused again, Darcie realized her comments had been leading to some condition she wouldn't want to consider. Lost in euphoria, she'd forgotten one thing. Filled with sudden dread, Darcie held her breath.

"...that you take Annie as a roommate."

Darcie groaned. "Oh, Mom. No. Please."

"We talked about this when I was in New York. Only last night your father concurred. Annie's job here is a dead-end. That boy she's been dating—Cliff—has nothing to offer her. He's still in grad school. Perhaps this change of scene is what she needs after all." Janet lowered her voice. "Frankly, your sister has been driving me mad since I first spoke to you. She is absolutely the most persistent twenty-three-year old girl I know. She's obsessed with the notion of moving to that city."

Darcie felt an unusual surge of empathy for her sister.

"Woman."

"I beg your pardon?"

"Annie's a woman, not a girl, Mom. So am I."

Even when she needed a loan to float her boat. Her mother made a sound that could mean agreement, or disagreement.

"Annie has improved. She's really not as messy as you remember."

This did not reassure Darcie. She had no doubt in her mind that Annie had been playing their parents like a

Stradivarius to get her way. Cleaning up her room once or twice wouldn't seem that much of a stretch.

Darcie's new apartment, or Annie, certainly didn't thrill Eden.

But Julio wasn't around—he was on duty in the lobby—and she had to do her own talking without an interpreter. Back stiff, hands laced together, she eyed Darcie with disfavor.

"You have a nice big room here. A small rent. No utilities. You don't need a loan from Hank and Janet. I can't understand why you need to move."

It was the first time Gran had spoken to her in more than monosyllables since their quarrel (or through Julio) and Darcie hated to upset her again. But she'd called Mrs. L the instant her mother hung up and would sign the lease tomorrow. Her stomach fluttered. There was no going back.

"It's not a loan."

"No, it's a pound of flesh. Janet does nothing without a motive—as you've discovered. Do you _want_ Annie living with you?"

"Not really." Still, flush with joy at her own first apartment, Darcie refused to face that yet. She flashed a look at Sweet Baby Jane, napping on the sofa. "But then, maybe it isn't such a bad idea." Safety in numbers, Darcie thought. "We'll keep each other company."

The cat would never again—except when Darcie visited—take swipes at her tender skin. Eden wouldn't want to hear that reason for her move, either. She pursed her lips then pressed a hand to her heart.

"I need my digitalis. Don't say I didn't warn you. I love Annie dearly but she'll drive you insane. I give it a month, tops."

"If that happens, you can say 'I told you so.'"

Eden only smiled, but with a sad edge.

"If you needed a loan, dear, why didn't you ask me?"

"That's what Claire said, too."

"And you told her 'no' because…?"

"Same reason I didn't ask you." Darcie couldn't. She and Gran weren't on the best terms, even now, but at eighty-two Eden needed her nest egg. More than she needed a too-young boyfriend. "Keep your money," she said gently. "I'll be fine."

Eden started to smile again, then her lips went straight as a walking stick.

"This moving. It's not because of Julio, is it?"

"Moving Day," Darcie muttered.

She sure couldn't call it a party, wild or otherwise. Yet this was her day and she made the most of it.

Struggling up the stone steps with yet another carton of junk, she ran smack into Claire's behind. "Ouch," they both said at once, then laughed.

"Look at yourself," Darcie said. Claire's sloppy sweatshirt, her torn jeans, her raggedy sneakers didn't suit her VP image, or that of Peter's wife or Samantha's mom. "This is so not you." She gestured at herself with one hand, then grabbed for the corner of the box again. "Or me," she added. "Too bad the weather didn't cooperate."

"I'm glad it's cloudy today."

"I won't ask why."

"Because it's a good omen. It always rains on moving day."

"It's not raining yet."

"It will. Ask Peter."

"Ask me what?" He appeared in the open front door, and propped one hand on the frame. Holding a beer, he grinned at Claire, looking boyish and sexy. "If I have time for a quick tumble on that big new bed Darcie bought?" He waggled his eyebrows at Claire. "With you, my love, of course."

"It hasn't been delivered yet. Don't be crude."

Peter gave Claire a look Darcie couldn't interpret, just as she couldn't keep juggling the heavy carton.

"Could you two settle your problems without me? If I don't put this stuff down in the next two seconds, my arms will fall off."

"Then you'd be no good to us at all," Peter agreed and stepped back. "I'd help you with that box, but I'm replenishing my precious bodily fluids." Another pointed look at Claire.

First through the doorway, she jabbed him lightly in the ribs.

Right behind Claire, Darcie found Merrick in the kitchen unloading a batch of housewares Gran had insisted on sending with her. Dumping the last box beside his feet, Darcie straightened with a hand at the small of her back to massage away the kinks.

She looked around.

"Not bad."

"Me?" Merrick said with a smile for his favorite subject.

Darcie rolled her eyes. "No, this apartment." She was beginning to wonder just how many beers the two men had consumed while they "helped" her move. But then, that comment could come from Merrick any time. "It's looking good."

Courtesy of Mrs. L, she had living room furniture, her kitchen would soon be equipped enough to cook the simple meals that were all Darcie knew how to prepare, and with luck, her bed would arrive by 5:00 p.m.

"Who's going for pizza?" she asked. "I'm hungry."

"Lift a few more cartons," Merrick suggested, "while I run to the corner. Pepperoni? Mushrooms?"

"Everything."

"Double cheese," Claire ordered. "No anchovies."

"More beer," Peter said. "I'll go with you."

Claire stepped in his path. "No you won't. You can drag the rest of those boxes off the truck. Darcie and I will unpack."

He looked at Merrick. "Worth a try."

"Give me your wallet," Claire said.

"Robbery. What's next? I'm now a pauper, at the mercy of two women."

Merrick said, "I promise not to open the beer before I get back."

"Good man."

Darcie grinned at her friends, so happy she could hardly speak. Within the week she'd be organized, well before Annie arrived. Annie had stayed in Cincinnati even after their parents' check winged its way to New York. She had to give notice at her job—not much, but some, she said—and handle Cliff, her disgruntled boyfriend. Oh, then pack her belongings. Darcie mentally groaned. She could imagine the boxes yet to come.

By the time Claire and Peter took the sleeping Samantha home hours later, Darcie felt exhausted but still content. Elated, in fact.

In the living room, after waving goodbye to the Spencers, Darcie crawled onto Merrick's lap in the big armchair she'd inherited from Mrs. L.

Merrick gently pushed her away.

"Do I smell bad?" Darcie frowned at him, but Merrick had his eyes closed and couldn't see her. "I must smell bad. Thank goodness it wasn't ninety-five degrees today with humidity to match. I mean, it's bad enough to lift all those cartons, and moving my desk from Gran's apartment was no easy feat—"

"Are you talking to yourself again?"

"No."

"Because I'm not listening. I'm asleep."

Trying not to feel hurt, Darcie slid off his lap. "If I get you another beer, will you wake up?"

Shaking his head, Merrick laughed. "Darce, relax, will you?"

"This is my first night in my first home. *My* home. I want it to be special."

"Then throw on a dress. Something racy. We'll go out to eat, have a few drinks—I'll buy you champagne—" He groaned softly. "Except I can't move."

Did she smell bad?

Darcie sniffed under both arms. Not too shabby, omitting her torn T-shirt, her ripped jeans. But she was *moving,* the world's messiest chore. So what was his problem? She couldn't quite figure it out.

"Tell me. Do you miss Jacqueline?" she asked.

"After what she did?" He snorted in apparent surprise, as if he were totally blameless. "I've learned my lesson. If I ever get married again, we'll sign a pre-nup."

"You and me?" Darcie said. "That won't happen."

He half smiled. "That's one thing I like about you. You're honest."

"What's another thing?"

"Excuse me?"

Suddenly this seemed important. "Tell me something else you like about me."

His hesitation told her more than she wanted to know. Still, she'd asked. "Don't be a witch tonight," he said. Merrick went into the kitchen, flicking off the living room light switch on his way. In the darkness, Darcie seethed.

Then she strode after him.

"Why do you do that?"

"What?" he said, his gaze blank when he turned from the refrigerator. He'd been perusing its contents.

"Every time you leave a room, you shut off the lights. On me."

He sighed. "The rich don't get wealthy from squandering every dollar. We turn off lights, we drive used cars..."

"I bet you never drove a used car in your life."

Merrick owned a Lexus. No, two of them. One was an SUV model, for weekends. The other had every gimmick and accessory known to materialistic man. But Darcie had to take his word. She'd never seen either of them. Just like his apartment—the one his wife had left along, Darcie supposed, with all her reminders of Merrick.

"What concern is it of yours if I make enough money— which I damn well do even in this market freefall—to buy myself a few trinkets?"

"I've never had a trinket," Darcie murmured. "Maybe a diamond and ruby bracelet...matching earrings for my birthday? When is my birthday, Merrick Lowell?" She singsonged the "tick-tock" of a game-show clock. "Beep. Time's up."

"Christ. Are you punishing me again for some reason?"

"Sorry. Only one of us is playing now."

He plunged back into the fridge and came out with a beer for himself. "What the hell do you think it felt like, Jackie taking the kids and running off like that?"

So it did matter to him. "Even if you weren't perfect for each other."

Darcie thought of Claire, of how difficult she found being a new mother. But for Merrick to lose his kids, even part-time...

"This isn't easy for you, I know."

Tonight, Darcie refused to feel irritated. Argument exhausted her, and it was getting late. In more ways than one. Was she going to spend the rest of her life having phone sex with Dylan instead of the real thing? Or was it time to really mend her fences with Merrick? Overlook his shortcomings? Soothe both their egos, at least for a while?

"You want a slice of this leftover pizza?" he said, apparently unconcerned.

"I thought we were having dinner at Luccio's."

"Pizza, Luccio's. It's all Italian."

"Let's order in, then. They'll deliver."

"See? I'm the big spender you always dreamed of."

"I was actually more interested in Pierce Brosnan tonight. Brad Pitt. Ben Affleck...definitely Ben."

"Ha-ha." But Merrick looked hurt. *No sex.* Had she injured his male ego that badly?

Taking pity on him, she ambled toward him. For old times' sake. Just as she got there, he tipped his beer to his mouth, but Darcie took it away. She trapped him against the counter, and twined her arms around his neck.

"Forget food. If this kitchen was a bit larger, this counter a foot longer, you'd be begging for mercy, Mr. Lowell."

For a brief spell, it seemed like a good idea. Then a collage of images from Australia flashed across her mind-screen, of Dylan, and Merrick stiffened, too.

He pried her fingers from his neck.

"I can't. Not now."

Deflated, Darcie stepped back.

"Maybe I should take a shower," she offered.

He yawned. "I should get going. It's been a long day."

Disappointed because tonight was important to her, she formed a pout. This never worked for anyone she knew except Annie, but Darcie tried.

"I thought you might stay." She added hastily, "We could just sleep."

"Sleep where?"

Oh. That *was* a problem. Eight o'clock and her bed hadn't been delivered.

"Some other time." He eased past her and headed for the front door. It would be nice if he opened his arms, inviting an embrace at least. "Darce, it's not you."

Watch out. She'd heard that phrase before. "Then what?"

He disappeared into the hall. A moment later he was gone.

Well. No answer, but no reason to get clingy, Darcie told herself.

No reason to fly into a snit.

So she had a decent job—most of the time it seemed decent—good friends, if she overlooked her recent set-to with Gran, and a family back in Cincinnati. Unless she murdered Annie the day she arrived in New York.

And above all, tonight, she had this.

"Happy New Apartment, Darcie Elizabeth Baxter," she said aloud, raising Merrick's beer bottle.

Because it seemed no one else was going to say it and Darcie needed to hear those very words. Even from herself.

At midnight the telephone startled Darcie from a restless sleep on the living room sofa, huddled under a comforter, and set her pulse racing. She bolted upright. For an instant she wondered who had her new number—or who had died in the middle of the night.

"Hey. Matilda."

Dylan's deep voice kicked her heart rate into highest gear. And just after she'd given up on him. For good. The men in her life were, if nothing else, consistent. They always surprised her.

"Hi," was all she could manage. Then, "How did you find me?"

"I just talked to your grandmother."

Oops. Darcie had never mentioned living with Eden.

"That is," he went on, "after someone named Julio answered. I didn't know your family was part Hispanic."

"I'm not. He's Gran's...friend."

"He sounded sleepy. Of course I didn't understand him very well. Between his broken English and my Aussie accent—"

"Believe me, you were better off. My grandmother's relationships get rather complicated."

"Is she sleeping with that guy?" Dylan sounded amused.

"Oh, yes." No sense denying it. "Julio is the flavor of the month."

Dylan laughed. "At eighty-two my granny was rocking in a chair, staring into space, talking to herself. That was all she could manage."

"Gran's different." Like me, Darcie thought. Except for the part about talking to herself. In that, she resembled Dylan's grandmother. "So she gave you my new number?"

"Gladly. Her word, not mine."

"I just moved," Darcie explained unnecessarily.

"Let me get this straight." She could almost hear him frowning. "You were living in New Jersey, relatively safe. Now you're in the big city by yourself."

Darcie half smiled. He was always so literal.

"Yes, tonight. But my sister's coming to live with me."

"Two women," he muttered, "with a flimsy door between them and some *drongo*—nutcase, loser, take your pick—with a knife."

Glancing around the dimly lit apartment, then at the blackness outside her windows (she didn't have draperies yet) Darcie shivered.

"Dylan, don't exaggerate." Scare me, she meant.

"I'm not. I think you should have stayed where you were."

Darcie hauled the comforter around her suddenly cold body. He was a gorgeous man, but Dylan's views remained very much at odds with hers. Alone in the apartment for the first time, she didn't need any reminders of her vulnerability.

"Could we change the subject, please?"

"Okay. How's this? I'm still half mad at you—one reason I haven't called."

"Is that your apology? Because it doesn't quite work."

"No, it's not an apology. I *wanted* to call, then things got whacko here and I realized in the middle of the whole mess that I was still angry enough to keep putting off another call. So I didn't. Call," he said.

"What mess?"

"Remember that ram I wanted to buy when you were in Sydney?"

"Yes." She remembered the lamb named Darcie, too.

"He was out of the U.K. where they've been having this hoof-and-mouth problem. So the deal fell through. I had to start looking all over again. Finally found another ram I want in New Zealand the other day. Bought him from the flamin' Kiwis last night. He gets shipped tomorrow." He sounded weary, but still on edge.

"How many sheep do you have?"

"A few."

More than that, she was sure. "How big is your... station?"

"Pretty big."

Huge, Darcie interpreted, like the rest of him. She suppressed a thrill of lust. Unlike Merrick, Dylan wasn't inclined to boast. "Why so modest?" she asked him.

"We Aussies don't care for tall poppies."

"Tall poppies? You mean, flowers?"

"No." He yawned. "It's somebody who stands out from the crowd, tries to show he's better than everyone else. Not a popular concept here."

But it was endearing in Dylan, even sweet. And he was obviously much brighter than she'd given him credit for at first. Successful. All that testosterone, too, she thought, under such tight control. Exciting.

"You've been busy," she murmured.

His voice dropped lower. "Not too busy to keep from thinking about you, Matilda." He didn't sound happy. "My last call held me for a week or two—"

"It's been six weeks," she acknowledged.

His tone warmed. "You been thinking about me, too?"

"Now and then." She half smiled into the receiver.

"Thinking about me how?"

"Naked." No point lying about it.

"Me, too, darling. You, that is."

Darcie stretched out on the sofa, wrapped herself tighter in the comforter, and grinned. "Any details you could share?"

"Oh, yeah. Gladly," he repeated Gran's word, then launched into a half-whispered but torrid description of what he would like to do to Darcie, his bed or hers, it didn't matter.

"Yours," she murmured. "I don't have a bed tonight."

By the time they hung up, she was tingling. All over. For Dylan Rafferty.

He might be half the world away. But tonight, she'd been totally alone except for his voice. With this move, of which Dylan disapproved, she had cut most of her ties. Gran was no longer her roommate. Claire didn't live two floors down. *Had* she made a mistake after all? Darcie wasn't sure.

With Dylan's murmured good-night still in her ear, she snuggled in her covers. "You know, I think this just might work out."

Darcie didn't ask herself whether that meant her new apartment, or Dylan.

Chapter Eleven

With a grin Annie Baxter surveyed the clutter in her new bedroom. Because of her position in the family as the younger of two daughters, she had never bothered about neatness—that was Darcie's responsibility—or, in fact, what other people thought of her.

Darcie, on the other hand, cared too much.

"I'm getting settled," Annie informed her, wanting to pinch herself. She wasn't dreaming. Was she? Her room in Cincy was nowhere by comparison, and Annie had plans for this place. She might even paint the walls black.

Darcie stood in the doorway with a frown. "You've been settling for the past week. I don't see any progress."

Annie dragged open a few drawers in her new pine chest with its fake rusted hardware. Very trendy. She flung the closet door wide, then flipped open an empty suitcase on the floor. "See?"

"Two pairs of jeans on hangers. Three shirts." Darcie ambled into the room to peer into the dresser drawers. "Your underwear thrown in a clump. Where's the rest of your stuff?"

"I'll get to it."

Darcie planted both hands on her hips (always a bad sign for Annie) and blew a stray strand of hair off her face.

"We need a few rules here."

"Yours, I suppose." Sometimes she felt tempted to hate her big sister, but Annie hated even more to waste energy. Most of the time she admired everything about Darcie, which had always been a problem for her. "I don't like rules."

"Tough. Number one," Darcie muttered, holding up a finger. "Your junk stays in this room—neat or not, I guess I won't worry about that. But the living room, the bathroom, my room especially, I do. Two, you wash your dishes and clean the pots you use. Every time. I do care about the kitchen, and last night you left burned spaghetti sauce in the pan." Another finger flew up to join the first two. "Number three, you try to be careful about meeting people. Honestly, Annie. This isn't Cincinnati. You can't just walk up to someone in a store and strike up a conversation."

"I worry about *you,* Darcie." Annie hesitated, something she normally didn't bother to do. Life had always been her play yard, from the day as a three-year-old when she'd charged out of the neighborhood park, found the larger world across a busy street, and become family legend. "You go to work—leave the house at precisely eight-oh-five every morning—you come home by six, fix dinner, watch one hour of television—a news show, what fun is that?—then go to bed."

"Unless I'm seeing Merrick."

When Darcie's eyes fell, Annie's gaze sharpened. "If you're not happy with him, get another guy." She grinned again. "Come to think, I heard you on the phone the other night. Is the Australian stud still calling?"

Darcie actually flushed. "Now and then."

"You're having phone sex, right?"

"Annie, that's none of your business."

"You *are.* That's great, Darce. What's he like?"

"Inventive," Darcie answered. "Number four...you need to get a job."

She should have known. Darcie wouldn't forget the last—Annie hoped it was the last—of her points. Annie had no intention of following them. She did as she pleased. Even her mother didn't step in her way anymore, not much at least.

"I need to find the right job," she said, fingering one of the four silver earrings in her right ear. "Not just any old thing."

"Have you called the agency I told you about?"

"The one you used to land that high-power position at Wunderthings?" Annie couldn't help it. She snickered.

"I'm earning a paycheck, Annie. That's more than I can say for you."

"Big whoop."

With an obviously disgusted sigh, Darcie turned her back. She started for the hall and her own room. Time for bed. Maybe she was expecting her Aussie to call. Annie hoped so. Maybe she'd listen in tonight.

"Gran warned me," Darcie murmured.

"Ask yourself this—would you rather share this fabulous place in the middle of all the action with me? Or commute to Jersey every night to watch Julio romance our grandmother?"

"I haven't decided."

Darcie's response came too quickly and Annie's spirits sank but only for a moment. She was used to disapproval. She considered herself to be a free spirit, and didn't have any inclination to change her outlook on life.

"I want a full report tomorrow night," Darcie told her. Annie could almost see their mother's finger poised in midair, another reminder to turn herself into a responsible human being. "I expect at least one job interview, preferably more."

"What are you? The career police?" Flinging her hair back over her shoulder, Annie dug into another of her mother's carefully packed cartons. She tossed a shimmery blue dress in the general direction of the open closet. Then picked it up again. Holding it in front of her Smith

T-shirt, she studied herself in the dresser mirror. Hmmm. She no longer liked the color with her new shade of hair.

What is that? Darcie had asked. *You had such pretty chestnut hair. Henna Sunrise,* Annie had told her, not as certain as she'd first been about the brighter color. Maybe she needed a quick trip to Saks in the morning. The party she was planning to launch her new life in New York—the life Annie was meant to have—required something really outrageous. In the meantime, "Relax," she advised Darcie. "Mom and Dad are paying half this rent."

Greta Hinckley had too many bills to pay. She needed money, she told herself on Monday morning. She needed Darcie Baxter's job. But she wasn't headed there anytime soon. Walter Corwin hadn't taken to Greta's hose-for-thin-thighs design. In fact, he'd told her she was nuts.

Greta was still smarting over his words, and she despised Darcie even more for being right. If she'd listened to Darcie's attempt to dissuade her from approaching Walter with the idea...

Her stomach turned at his rejection. If she didn't want to stay near him, she would look for a new job. As if she'd find one with all those leggy, young just-out-of-college types buzzing around the city, taking up all the really interesting positions. Like Darcie.

Greta stashed her uninspired, brown bag lunch in the side drawer of her desk.

She hadn't missed seeing the take-out meal Darcie had eaten yesterday. White albacore tuna. Fresh tomato. Whole-grain bread. A perfect red delicious apple.

Greta had wished for poison, like the fruit in Snow White.

And that new apartment Darcie kept talking about...

No long subway ride for her to Riverdale each night. Darcie wasn't living with her grandmother any longer—the only redeeming thing about her until now—but with that daffy-sounding sister of hers. Greta would gladly trade places. She felt her resentment growing, yellow-leafed, like one of the sulky houseplants in her apartment.

When she heard Darcie's heels click along the tile floor, she turned her back on the aisle. The job, the apartment, even her lunch only served as reminders for Greta that her own life sucked. And that didn't take into account Darcie's beau, Merrick Lowell, or the Aussie cowboy Greta had overheard Darcie telling Nancy about only yesterday.

Greta couldn't overlook Darcie's trip to Australia, either, particularly her hotel stay with Walter. *Never rains but it pours.*

"Morning, Greta." Darcie breezed past into her cubicle. "No desk-drawer adventures today?" She turned in the entryway. "Did you finish the memo Walt wanted on the Rochester mall?"

"He'll have it on time." She hadn't started it yet. Head down, she plunged into her middle drawer, looking for gum to ease her mood. "He's forgotten all about me—about it—by now."

"Don't count on that. Walt may look disengaged, but he has a mind like a trap."

Greta glanced up. Darcie was still standing there, arms crossed as if she were waiting. Or trying to decide how to broach another topic. "Did you need something?"

Darcie blindsided her. "No, actually, I've been thinking. We got off on the wrong foot here long ago. But we're neighbors, aren't we? In a manner of speaking. I—" she paused as if the next words might choke her. "I'd really like your input on the Sydney store, maybe some help with its opening."

"You what?"

"You have good ideas, Greta. Not the hose thing, but at times..." She trailed off. "I mean, there's no reason for us to work at cross purposes here. So feel free to give me any suggestions. I'll tell Walt we're going to work together."

Greta struggled not to let her mouth fall open. What did Baxter really want?

"And that's not all," she went on, proving Greta right. "I—I've decided to make a suggestion of my own that might help."

That'll be the day. "Help what?"

Darcie crossed the aisle to perch on Greta's desk without invitation. "Help you in return." Then she seemed to lose momentum. Leaning over the desk, she picked up a silver letter opener that Greta cherished. "This is beautiful. Where did you buy it?"

Buy it. No way. Greta flushed, then delved back into her drawer not to make eye contact with Baxter. She didn't care to explain where the gleaming piece had really come from, or how it happened to be on her desk. *None of your business.* "It belonged to...my mother. You were saying?"

"Oh." She put down the opener, and Greta heard her take a breath as if to brace herself. "Well, I mean, maybe it's time to...for lack of a better word, upgrade."

Greta's head shot up again. She emerged from her drawer without the gum. She shoved the silver opener back into her pen cup.

"Upgrade? What?"

Her job? She couldn't agree more.

"Yourself," Darcie said softly.

"If this is some kind of setup, Baxter..."

Sure it was. Ask for her assistance with the Sydney opening, snoop through her stuff, then spring the real trap. But Darcie looked serious, even thoughtful, if somewhat embarrassed by this subject. Greta had never given her credit for having a brain before, but she did make sense. Although Greta wanted to feel insulted, she knew as well as anyone else at Wunderthings that a girl could survive— thrive here—on a pair of willowy legs and a good chest. The sexual revolution hadn't changed that. Unlike Baxter, Greta possessed neither one. Did Darcie mean she needed a beauty makeover?

"I'm, uh, having a little party soon to celebrate my new apartment, and you're invited. I mean, this would be the perfect time. There's nothing like a new look to lift a woman's spirits. Different clothes, a good haircut..."

"What's wrong with my hair?" *Baxter wants me at her party?*

Darcie looked uncomfortable but didn't answer directly. "Let's have lunch, today. My treat. We can talk about this, then. Maybe I can give you a few tips—not that I'm an expert—"

"What's the punch line?"

Darcie took a deep breath as if to brace herself. "Greta, you need a better self-image. It takes one to know one."

Greta started to smile. This could be interesting. Lunch might give her some ideas, even show her Darcie's weak spots. If she wanted more money, a better position at Wunderthings, maybe a little shopping trip wouldn't hurt. And if she wanted Walter...certainly he'd be at the party, too?

"Are you paying?" she asked.

"Sure," Darcie said.

By Saturday afternoon Darcie wondered whether she had lost her mind.

"Why does my life never seem to fully resolve itself?"

Following Greta through the women's department at Macy's on Thirty-Fourth Street, Darcie gnashed her teeth. By nightfall she would have a mouthful of stumps.

How attractive would that be to all those single guys Annie insisted would flock to their planned housewarming party?

Yes, in a moment of total madness, Darcie had invited Greta, too.

"What about this?" Greta stopped at a rack of black jersey dresses.

"Definitely not you."

"You said that about the brown knit two-piece."

"Greta, think *color*."

In her determination to change their relationship, Darcie had treated her to lunch earlier in the week, then suggested shopping today. Darcie's reasoning had made sense to her at the time. Greta needed a real life. Asking for her ideas on the Sydney opening might keep her from stealing Darcie's. And given new responsibility, Greta would be happier in her job. There were all sorts of possibilities.

With Darcie's help and this "upgrade," Greta might also attract a man. Not Walt, of course. *She's a real coyote,* he had said. But with luck, Greta would meet someone— maybe at the party. Darcie let the fantasy build. Greta might fall in love, decide to follow her new man somewhere and leave Wunderthings—even leave the state.

That notion had begun to appeal to Darcie.

She wasn't sure this shopping spree was going to work. "You can attract more flies with honey than vinegar," according to Gran. But then, Greta wasn't a fly. She didn't seem to welcome Darcie's "help." Certainly she didn't seem inclined to take her advice.

"Red makes me look...pink. Like a serious drinker."

Darcie edged her away from the black jersey toward a rack of yellow-sprigged blouses with coordinating skirts.

"Here's something new. Try it. This is very springy looking."

"Sallow," Greta said. "My skin's too olive-toned to wear yellow." She turned, her gaze sharp. "What's this really about? You pay for lunch, invite me to your party when we've never even shared a coffee break before—"

"All right." Darcie admitted defeat. "I thought if maybe I helped you dress more up-to-the-minute, your life would become happier. You'd stop plotting revenge against me for the Sydney job."

"I deserve revenge for the Sydney project."

"In your mind, I suppose so. In mine, *not*." They glared at each other, lost for a moment in their everyday animosity.

"There's no reason we can't work together." Darcie stalked away before she gave in to the urge to smack Greta.

"But you need to do your own job!"

She'd never spoken so harshly before, but Darcie didn't get out the next words, whatever they might have been. Her gaze fell upon a center display of silky lounge pants with sleeveless tops and totally smashing jackets trimmed in brilliant colors.

"Greta, look. This is it. This is *you*." She ran the soft fabric through her fingers. "The black will make you feel...comfortable, and the sparkle will knock out every male eye at the party."

"I wouldn't go that far."

But Greta reluctantly joined her, and the two of them accidentally brushed hands on a beaded jacket. Green, silver, crystal. Darcie jerked it from the hanger and held it up to Greta's sturdy frame. The design looked slimming, too. Perfect.

Darcie loved perfection.

"It's...nice." Greta's pale eyes lit with what could only be female lust for the ideal outfit.

"Nice? Green's a good color. Brings out your eyes, complements your hair. It's sophisticated yet casual. You won't spend the whole night yanking at a too-tight skirt band or hitching up your panty hose."

Greta's mouth twitched. "That's hell, isn't it?"

"So true."

For a long moment they stood, joined by a feminine hunt now successfully completed. Darcie stared at the vibrancy she saw in Greta's eyes against that very becoming green. Really, it looked outstanding.

"Try it on. Go ahead." She pushed Greta toward the nearest dressing room.

When she came out, resplendent in the three pieces, Greta actually giggled.

Taking a step back, Darcie surveyed her masterpiece again.

Of course she didn't consider herself to be a fool.

She wouldn't trust Greta farther than she could drag her. Still...

"I'm sending you to my hairdresser. A few gold highlights, a brighter shade of brown...marvelous. Come on." She pushed Greta to the dressing room, then pulled her to the checkout counter. Back in her usual brown clothes, there was absolutely no doubt about it. The evening outfit had transformed Greta. "We're going downstairs next," Darcie informed her. "Some new makeup, and your phone will be ringing off the hook."

Hope sprang into Greta's eyes, despite her next words.

"My last date was ten years ago, with a janitor from my building. He didn't kiss me good-night. He never called again. He's dead now."

Dylan Rafferty phoned again that night.

Which would be his next midday.

Darcie couldn't figure out how he managed to sound so sexy during his lunch break—or was it afternoon tea in Australia? Lying across her bed, she smiled into the receiver, and continued to recount her day with Greta.

"By the time we left the makeup counter—" with three hundred dollars' worth of cosmetics in a small but gorgeous bag "—Greta was glowing. I mean, *radiant*, Dylan."

"Be careful. From what you tell me, she's a sticky beak."

"A what?"

"Nosy. She pokes it where it doesn't belong... Were *you* glowing?"

Uh-oh. His voice had dropped lower, as it had the other night, and Darcie figured his patience with her stories about shopping with Greta Hinckley had just fizzled.

"I'm always glowing."

"That's been my experience."

"Flatterer." Darcie felt a lowdown tug of answering interest, and her nipples tightened. She stared at her T-shirt. Two marbles under the worn cotton. Big marbles when Dylan continued in an even throatier voice.

"Remember the night we walked back to the Westin...and kept stopping along the way? Remember the kisses we shared right under the Coathanger—" the Sydney Harbour bridge "—and on every street corner, darling, in The Rocks?"

"I remember the bars we stopped in."

He laughed a little. "I was pretty ruined when we reached the hotel." His tone plunged another ten feet, like someone taking a high dive off the bridge. "You got friendly then and we..."

Darcie cleared her throat before she got carried away again.

"Dylan, I remember."

"How it felt when we stripped each other naked, then dropped into bed..."

She started breathing fast. "Perfect recall. Abso—yes—lutely." Her nipples strained against the cloth and Darcie rolled onto her stomach.

"I remember just how you tasted. The softness of your lips, our mouths together, slick and..."

Phone sex.

She couldn't help but play along. "Where are you now?"

"In my living room."

"With your *mother?*" Shocked, Darcie looked around to make sure Annie wasn't hovering in her bedroom doorway.

"She drove into Coowalla. I'm alone, darling."

Hmm. Maybe he wasn't quite as traditional as she'd thought.

"You don't have any lambs to doctor? What about that ram you ordered?"

"He's here, having the time of his life." His voice sounded husky. Even his sheep fostered their telephone foreplay. "We bred him this morning. Where are you? In bed, I hope."

"On top."

"I love it when you get on top." At his playful innuendo Darcie felt her cheeks heat, her breasts tingle, her inner thighs liquefy. She squirmed against the comforter. "What are you wearing?" he asked.

"A T-shirt. Old jeans. Nothing exciting, believe me."

"You excite me in anything...or nothing." She heard him swallow. "I go to bed at night and lie there in the dark, remembering the things we did, the things you wore or didn't wear. Guess what happens?"

"I, uh...you must get—" She broke off, hearing a sound across the hall. If Annie was listening in on their call, she'd kill her.

"Hard. I get hard. I'm hard right now. Darcie—"

"Ohhh." Her moan joined his at the erotic admission.

"Take off your shirt. I'm taking off mine." *Macho man.*

"In the living room?"

"Do it."

Obediently, wearing a wicked smile, she sat up and peeled off the old yellow T-shirt. *Sin,* it said across the front. Then, below, *We don't do that in Cincinnati.*

"Tell me. Did you do it?"

"Yes. You?"

"Oh, yeah. Now get rid of the jeans," he urged. "I'm peeling off my pants."

Darcie lay down and wiggled her hips to strip off her worn denims.

"Your knickers, too." Underpants. "What color are they?"

"White. Cotton."

He groaned. "Next, the bra. Is that white, too?"

"I'm not...I wasn't wearing a bra."

"God help me." Now he was whispering. "Touch yourself."

Startled, Darcie halted. "Dylan, my nosy sister may be listening."

"If she is, I don't care." She could hear him breathing. Rough, and ragged. "I'm pretending you're here. I can see you, feel you...."

She moaned again. Then suddenly, tears blurred her vision. In the background, on the opposite side of the world, she could hear Dylan groan, too. So out of reach. Only his voice could hold her.

"Remember when I said I'd like to see you pregnant? Your belly swollen, taut..."

"Yes." She had to admit, it made an erotic fantasy, especially if she involved Dylan in the event from a safe distance.

She heard his shaken sigh. "I'd touch you all over...lay my cheek against you...feel the baby...."

She would come apart if he didn't— "Stop. Please. Don't."

He must have heard the frantic steel in her tone. The regret.

He *was* far away. And as the fantasy proved, he had such very different values.

Dylan didn't want to stop. "You'd be beautiful. Even more beautiful."

"I'm not ready for a baby. I'm not ready for that."

She knew he could be stubborn, and heard him take a breath. "Cold showers never work. I think you've found the effective solution, though. Watch me shrivel."

"Dylan, I'm sorry. I just can't..."

"I gotta go. Talk to you tomorrow."

Right or wrong, she didn't want to let him go now. She *didn't*.

"Did you forget something, sheepboy?"

His soft, irritated laugh went through her like another thrill of lust.

"'Night, Matilda. Don't sleep too well. I know I won't."

Chapter Twelve

Darcie lay in her darkened bedroom and stared at the ceiling to which she had affixed dozens of sparkling stars, her own constellations in her very own apartment. Like phone sex or picking up Dylan in a bar, this was something she'd never done before, and Annie claimed to be proud of her.

Annie herself was losing it. She had come home only the day before sporting a brand-new hole in her navel, and that red punch mark in her left nostril looked raw.

Ick.

Not to mention the small tattoo of an owl—for night owl/party animal, Annie had explained—that now graced her right flank.

"Wait until Janet and Hank see those," Darcie told herself. "If they ever do."

Her ceiling stars wouldn't compare, but darned if she would mutilate her own body to make a statement of independence. Darcie hated blood. She hated pain even more.

With a sigh she rolled over in bed—and stifled a scream. A shadow had crossed the window that opened onto the fire escape. A large shadow with a deep chest, wide shoulders, a shaggy-haired head. Darcie watched in horror, her pulse racing madly, her throat bone-dry. Terrified that she would cough and alert the male intruder to her presence—no, to her state of full consciousness—she breathed, sharp but shallow, through her open mouth. *Please God, make him go away.*

Dylan's warning about two women living alone filled her brain. Images of her own dead body skittered through her awareness. Could this man hear her heart beating?

It slammed against the wall of her chest and Darcie pushed a hand to her breast in the hope he wouldn't see its movement.

The figure bent down. He still looked tall, solid, muscular. Dangerous to her health.

The window was forced open.

Darcie clamped a hand over her mouth not to scream after all.

If he didn't know Annie was in the apartment, too, they might have a chance. Annie could call 911. The police would arrive in the nick of time. Darcie could almost hear them on the stairs now...

"Goddammit." The dark shape of a man stepped inside, snagging his jacket on something sharp. Maybe a protruding nail or sliver of wood. "Make my day," he muttered.

Darcie didn't dare to breathe.

If she stayed silent—difficult for her even under normal circumstances—he might just steal her blind then leave without noticing her in the bed.

Tonight she couldn't be that lucky.

First Dylan Rafferty had sent her off to fantasyland with his sexy voice and that hint of irritated amusement after their aborted phone sex. Now a total stranger stood in the center of her bedroom surveying his new surroundings with an apparently practiced eye.

His gaze landed on the lump of covers that was Darcie.

When he took one step toward her bed, she did scream.

He lunged in her direction. His hand covered her mouth before Darcie's voice reached full power. *Help.* But there was a hole in her rescue fantasy. Annie Kathryn Baxter slept like a long-dead corpse herself. She wouldn't hear a sound.

"Mmmppfff." Darcie struggled against his restraining hand.

His hand smelled good. Like an expensive men's cologne.

"Take it easy." He eased back and Darcie froze. "Jesus. I won't hurt you."

Wait a minute. The enticing scent, the decent leather jacket, the smell of clean male skin. What kind of burglar-rapist climbed through a window in the middle of the night wearing good clothes? What burglar even owned good clothes? Besides, would he pick some singles apartment inhabited by two women with minimal assets?

They weren't worth robbing. She doubted that between them she and Annie had forty dollars in the apartment.

Not long ago Darcie hadn't even owned a bed.

"I'm going to take my hand off your mouth," he whispered, saying enough that she noticed a light drawl. "Don't yell again. Please."

A polite burglar, too?

As soon as he released her, Darcie shot upright in bed, no longer afraid.

"Who are you?"

He held a finger to his own lips this time. "Shh. It's okay."

"The hell it is." Her vocabulary seemed to be slipping. So did the shoulder of her oversize T-shirt, which Darcie had worn to bed. It slid down to her left bicep. His gaze homed in on the expanse of bare flesh—and stayed there.

"I never thought it actually happened," he said. "Skin. Gleaming in the moonlight." He shook his head. "Weird."

"Weird?" Darcie waved toward the open window. A soft but chill breeze blew through the sheer curtains, which had done nothing to guard her privacy or protect her safety. Tomorrow she would buy a metal grille to cover the glass. "In two seconds, if you don't go back through that window and close it behind you, I'll call the police."

"Oh, Christ. What a day."

She felt braver now. "This is *my* apartment. Unless you leave the premises—right now—you'll end up tonight with another blot on your record."

"My what?" He sank down on the end of her bed like an old chum. "I locked myself out of my apartment. Okay?" He glared at her in the dark. "It's not enough that I lost my keys down a subway grate on my way home from the crappiest date I've ever had? Then I tear the knee out of my best khakis, rip hell out of my new jacket on your windowsill…now I'm some kind of felon on my way to the slammer?" He ran a hand through thick, dark hair. "Just great."

"Your apartment?" Darcie seized upon his first statement because she didn't know how to deal with the rest.

"Hi, neighbor. I live upstairs."

"Two-A. Why didn't you climb in your own window?"

He assumed a too patient, lecturing tone. "Because a) there was a patrol car cruising this block when I got home, b) your apartment was conveniently located in the shadows on the lowest level of the fire escape and c) I get my kicks ruining the best clothes I own, clothes in which I planned to start my new job tomorrow—and frightening young women half to death in the middle of the night."

Darcie didn't know why she felt like apologizing. "I'm sorry."

"No, that's my line." He rose from the bed, weaving a little on his feet. "Hold the thought. I need to take a leak." Unerringly, he headed for her bathroom. His apartment obviously had the same layout as hers.

"So if you climb in my window, what good does that do you?"

He didn't answer. Darcie waited for him to come back into the room. Annie was still sleeping, oblivious to their late-night intruder.

"I figured if I could get inside the building, I could

jimmy my door lock. With luck, I might get a few hours' sleep before I blow the rest of my life—forget a career—tomorrow." He picked at a hangnail on his thumb.

Curious, Darcie asked, "What career?"

"I'm in advertising. Ha," he added. "Wouldn't you know? It's not bad enough the whole industry's in a slump. My date tonight left with another guy while I was in the men's room."

"You have a weak bladder?"

"Only when I drink six beers trying to anesthetize myself."

"Ah," Darcie said. She leaned over to switch on the bedside lamp—then almost shouted again. The man blinking against the sudden glare, like Darcie, just might be, after Dylan Rafferty and Merrick Lowell, one of the best-looking men she'd ever seen. New York, like Sydney, was full of them. How could you hate it?

Not perfect, she thought, taking a longer look. His otherwise straight nose had a slight hump in the middle. Broken once, probably. His left eye seemed ever so slightly larger than the right—not uncommon, either. Annie's right eye always looked just the least bit stunned, and Greta Hinckley always appeared to Darcie like someone whose genes had gotten jumbled at conception. On this guy, his little imperfections looked good. So did his scuffed leather jacket.

Much better than the Harley-and-black-leather type Annie had brought home earlier this week. Not trendy black leather in that case but hardcore.

Her visitor stared at her in return. Although light-haired, he wasn't *GQ* like Merrick, or *International Male* like Dylan. He fell somewhere in between. A glimmer of interest flickered in his gray eyes then was tamped down. Clearly, he was in no mood for sexual adventure. Her heart still thumping, neither was Darcie. "Would you like to sit down?"

He glanced around the room. "You have about as much furniture as I do. No, thanks. I'd better just—" he flipped a hand toward the outer room "—go."

Darcie had a better idea. She tiptoed across the hall in
her too-big T-shirt, feeling his gaze on her bare legs, and
filched Annie's hobo bag from her dresser. Annie snored
on, unaware of the excitement in Darcie's room. She returned to find their "neighbor" leaning against the wall by
the window. "Are you all right?"

"Yeah. Fine. You?" he said. "I didn't mean to scare
you."

"Nah. Strange men climb through my window almost
every night."

He grinned. "You wish."

Darcie handed him Annie's key ring. "My sister has
every key ever, you know, cut from a blank on one of
those funny machines at the hardware store. She collects
keys. When she was in college, she used them all the time
to get in the dorm after hours...check on her boyfriends..."

"Weird." He echoed her earlier statement.

"You should meet Greta."

"That's your sister's name?"

"No, someone else I work with. Never mind. Our relationship here hasn't progressed far enough for me to share
Greta just yet."

He took the keys. "Thanks. It should only take me the
rest of the night to figure out which one works. You been
in New York long? You're pretty trusting."

"A few years."

"Not long enough," he said.

"I'm from Ohio. It's a hard habit to break."

He held out his hand. A beautiful hand, long-fingered.
"I'm from Georgia. Cutter Longridge."

"That's your hometown?"

"No, my name." He grinned again. "All us Southern
boys have family names. What about you?"

She stood mesmerized by his soft drawl, by his soft gray
eyes. There was no way she'd wake up Annie now to share
the bounty. "Darcie Baxter. I'm in...underwear."

His glance dropped to the hem of her T-shirt. Her
panties.

"Wunderthings International," she added.

"No kidding." His grin widened. "Maybe we'll have a private fashion show one of these nights."

"In your dreams."

"They might be short tonight—if I ever get to bed— but I can guarantee you, they'll be excellent." He shut her window then walked to her bedroom door.

"Good night, Cutter."

"I'll drop your keys off in the morning." He gave a fingertip salute. "Nice to meet you, Darcie."

"See you."

Long after he left the apartment, Darcie lay in bed, alone again, smiling at the stars on her ceiling.

"Wow," she said aloud to the darkened room. "In New York you don't even have to leave your apartment to meet the most amazing men."

A week later Claire dashed from the bedroom into the kitchen. She wore her panty hose (black, of course, for tonight) her matching bra (Wunderthings Sexy'N Sleek, size 36B, $24.95, purchased from the store's online catalogue because she had no time to shop) and a slinky black skirt that hung, still unzipped, from her hips, which were still wide enough the skirt couldn't fall down. Claire checked the last round of potstickers on the stove, then dashed back into the nursery.

Samantha was howling.

"What's new, pussycat?" Claire hummed, worming a clumsy finger between Sam's round belly and her diaper. "Peter!" she said without turning.

"Right here." He peered into the crib. Sam had graduated from her bassinet, and she squirmed under Claire's restraining hand. "Wet again?" he echoed.

"Soaked. Fix her, will you? I'll never get dressed."

Peter raised his eyebrows. "Fine by me. We could stay home tonight—"

"Ruin Darcie's party?"

"—and see what kind of trouble we can get into on our own."

"With the baby-sitter in the next room?" Claire spun around, avoiding Peter's arms. "Is she here yet?"

"Any minute."

"I hope she doesn't bring her boyfriend this time. I don't trust him."

"With Danielle, or the silverware?"

"Both."

Claire charged back into their bedroom, leaving Peter with the wet diaper problem. He'd become a master at it, but still, only wet ones. No matter how she tried, Claire couldn't seem to develop the skill of changing, powdering, rediapering. She felt like a first-timer every time. This, from the VP of Heritage Insurance? A different set of skills, she told herself.

Peter called out from the nursery over Sam's squalling.

"Do you realize the last time we had sex was last year?"

"Don't exaggerate."

He strolled into the room, holding Sam. She looked dry and cozy and cute as a munchkin in her fresh sleeper with the lavender bunnies on it.

Claire looked about wildly for her top. "Could we discuss this some other time? In private?" She shot a glance at Sam, who grinned toothlessly at her and waved her arms. "Sweetie, I can't hold you right now. Daddy will play with you. Mommy's lost her clothes."

"I knew my wish would come true. Come here. Put me out of my misery."

Claire's pulse jumped.

He jostled the baby, making her giggle. "Sam wants Mom and Dad to...cuddle up together. Why, she asked me only yesterday about a baby brother or sister for Christmas."

"Won't happen. This is April."

"Might be early."

He sounded serious, and Claire felt her heart tighten. He'd also acted pushy the day they helped Darcie move.

"Peter, I can barely handle Samantha. It will take me years to feel comfortable with motherhood. I'm very disappointed in myself—"

"Claire Spencer, Overachiever."

"Well, I am. I can't help it. I'm usually good at what I do—anything I do."

"Sam adores you. So do I. What else do you need?"

"Competence."

He frowned. He looked so good dressed in dark pants and a collarless shirt, his sandy hair brushed and gleaming for Darcie's party, that Claire's breath caught. She almost felt tempted. Stay home, make love...she could scarcely remember what it felt like. Assuming her body still worked after Samantha had played Roto-Rooter through her vagina.

"You're totally competent, Claire. I can't believe you said that." Peter paused to stare down at his daughter. "You mean the three-days-a-week routine isn't working any better?"

"Think Tildy. Peter, I am the laughingstock of my office. On the phone with one hand, trying to nurse Sam who's propped up with my knee, signing letters with the other hand. At the end of the line some guy is saying, 'What? I can't hear you,' because she's crying, and I see my career flash in front of my eyes because I just realized I'm talking to the CEO of Heritage."

She dove into her dresser drawer, looking for her top. It wasn't in her closet. Half the time she couldn't remember what she was supposed to be doing—or had done in the past two minutes. Peter apparently agreed.

"Maybe you're right. We should go to the party. You need to get out more."

"Like I need a shrink?"

Peter strolled over to her, and something soft plopped onto the dresser top. "Your blouse. It was on the bed. In the *middle* of the bed. Funny, how red shows up against white."

Straightening, she made a futile gesture. And Claire's attempt at a party mood vanished with his next words.

"Good idea. See someone, Claire. You may not remember but I do. We had sex on December 24. Competence is not the issue."

* * *

"Where is Claire?" She'd promised to be on time.

When the doorbell rang, Darcie flew from her bedroom—the scene of more than one strange-middle-of-the-night meeting with Cutter Longridge—to answer it. But it wasn't Cutter or Claire who stood there.

"Merrick."

"Am I early?" Unsmiling, he peered around her into the empty living room. "You did say eight o'clock." He was a stickler for promptness.

"You're counterfashionable," Darcie assured him. "Did you bring the scotch?"

Wordlessly, he produced a bottle.

"Put it in the kitchen, will you? You'll see the bar we set up on the counter. Pour yourself a drink." He clearly needed one. "Oh, and take those pastry puffs from the oven, will you? It's Annie's job but she disappeared. They must be done."

A minute later, Merrick called out in a surly tone.

"They're burned."

Smoothing a hand across her hips in the slinky bronze dress she'd chosen for the party, Darcie muttered a cussword under her breath. He would continue to be difficult tonight—like all nights lately since her move. So much for her handsome date, her elegant soiree—if that was the word she wanted—and her apartment full of stylish guests. As if on cue, Annie appeared from her room with the Harley man in tow. Darcie groaned inwardly. He hadn't taken off his black leathers and a huge silver lightning bolt winked in one ear. His slicked-back dark hair made her shudder, so did his nearly black eyes, but Annie clung to him like a woman hanging on for dear life to the back of a motorcycle.

They both staggered a little, and their smiles looked silly. Alarm jolted Darcie. Had Annie been toking with him in the bedroom? Or were they playing slap and tickle?

"You burned the puffs," Darcie informed her. "Send Harley to the store for another batch. Hurry. Everyone will be here soon."

She hoped.

What if no one came?

Darcie wouldn't blame them. A cloud of smoke hung over the room, hazing her vision. The puffs were scorched, Claire hadn't shown up with the potstickers for which she'd once been famous among their friends, and for some reason Merrick looked like a thunderhead.

"His name's not Harley," Annie said, smoothing the skirt of her ultra mini-leather skirt. "It's Malcolm."

"Then send Malcolm to the store." When Annie started to go with him, Darcie said, "You stay here. Add a bit more garlic to the onion dip."

"Darcie, it's so strong now that unless everyone in the place takes a scoop, none of us will be able to stand each other."

"That could be true anyway."

Darcie rearranged a vase stuffed full of red licorice whips, her favorite, on the refreshments table. *Dammit, Claire.* And why was Merrick prowling the apartment like some lost animal from the zoo? She'd begun to pray for another of Cutter's forays through her bedroom window. Darcie had quickly decided against the metal grate for security.

And Gran should have been here by now.

"I need new friends," Darcie murmured.

By the time most of her invited guests did arrive, she felt certain of it.

"Mingle," she kept saying, but no one did.

Back from the store, Harley—Malcolm—fell bonelessly into the far corner of the living room with Annie on his lap. Most everyone else joined them, so to speak, by sitting down, and Darcie felt her heart sink. Long ago, Janet had tried to teach her how to entertain. A party on its feet was a successful one.

At least the food and drink were flowing. Merrick drank four scotches before Darcie stopped counting.

"Are you offended by Annie's date?" she asked him, following his gaze to the corner again.

"He makes me wonder about your upbringing in Ohio—but no. I could care less. She's an adolescent. Send her home." He glanced around, Britney Spears's voice spiraling through the room at the top of the stereo's volume. "Who are these people?"

"You know Eden. And that's Julio." She turned. Nothing surprised her tonight, but Gran and her latest man were quarreling in low voices.

"Excuse me," she told Merrick, and crossed the room to them.

"What's the problem?" she asked her grandmother.

"Julio took one look at your guests, then at me and decided he was too young."

Darcie stared at him. "Don't even think about hurting my grandmother."

"Oh, that helps," Eden said, blinking.

"It is not that I care less about you," Julio assured her. "It is that I do not wish to seem like a…" he searched for the phrase. "How do you say? 'Little toy.'"

"Boy toy?" Gran flushed. "Really, Julio. If I've ever treated you as if I thought—"

"No, *mi corazón*. But I am such a younger man…."

"One thing I adore about you."

"That's better," Darcie said, and with a kiss on Eden's cheek, she left them to work things out. Julio had a good point, though. She could see no future to their relationship. Sooner or later, Julio would leave Gran, even if he didn't intend to hurt her. They seemed as different from each other as she and Dylan. Troubled, Darcie slipped a hand through Merrick's arm.

"There's Claire with Peter—at last—no, wait," she added with a sinking feeling yet again, "they're not talking to each other. See how Claire is throttling her drink? And it's noncaffeinated soda because she's nursing. Peter has his shoulder turned to her, talking to Walt Corwin. You've met Walt…"

Merrick looked away. He seemed oddly disoriented.

"Come on," she said with a sigh of desperation. "I'll introduce you to Greta."

Greta's new sparkly outfit lit up the room. Leaving Merrick in Greta's clutches, talking about stocks, Darcie headed

across the room again. In her bedroom doorway Cutter
Longridge had just stepped in from the fire escape like an
answer to her prayers, and Darcie gave him a brilliant
smile.

"Cutter. I'm so glad you could come."

He sent her an amiable grin. "No sense ringing the bell
like everyone else."

She saw Merrick watching them. Or was he studying
Cutter in that assessing way? Across the living room laughter rose—Claire, sounding brittle? Annie, teasing Harley?—and another CD kicked in. Alicia Keys.

"You look amazing in that dress," Cutter said, his gaze
moving down then up to fix on her exposed throat. "That
coppery shade does wonderful things to your eyes."

"It does?" He'd never flirted with her, seriously, before.

"Better than black leather on Annie."

"That's Harley's jacket. She's in her biker phase. It'll
pass. I hope. She had a great dress for tonight. Wonder
where it went?"

When Cutter kissed her cheek then her mouth, Darcie's
pulse stalled. The night was looking up. Then he eased
back, and set her away from him almost before the kiss
could register, and Merrick frowned across the room, even
when Cutter left to find himself a drink. Merrick's gaze
tracked him. Over the blare of music and laughter, the
sound of a breaking glass, Alicia was singing, "How Come
U Don't Call Me?" Darcie heard the phone ring, and wel-
comed the intrusion.

Dylan raised his voice against the din at her end of the
line.

"Sounds like you're raging there. I mean, having a
party."

"I'm trying. It's supposed to be my housewarming."
Suddenly she wished he was here. Ready for a beer. Laid-
back, mellow, easy to talk to despite their differences.

"I'd be in for that," he said, "give it a go, but by the
time I got there, it'd be over. Wouldn't it? Even if, with
the time change, I'd arrive the same time I left."

After Dylan hung up, Darcie turned back into the room

and saw the front door close, softly, like one of her mother's rebukes. Cutter handed her a drink.

"Some guy in an Armani suit just left," he informed her.

Merrick. Guilt swept through Darcie. "Did he look angry?"

"No. He looked..." Cutter shrugged. "Puzzled."

"Why did Merrick leave?" Eden materialized beside them, a glass of wine in one hand, Julio held close with the other. "Did someone hurt *his* feelings, dear?"

"Me. I guess." But she didn't know why.

"Ah," her grandmother said, not in reproach. She turned toward Cutter, drawing Julio forward. "We haven't met. I'm Eden. This is my *inamorata*."

Apparently she and Julio had resolved their quarrel, at least for now.

"Cutter Longridge, ma'am. My pleasure."

"Oh, my. That southern drawl." Approval glittered in her eyes. "And closer at hand." She meant Dylan. "You must bring Mr. Longridge to dinner."

"Gran..."

"Never mind Merrick. Your taste is improving."

Then she disappeared with Julio, who ogled Eden with an adoring look.

At least Gran was speaking to her now.

That was a definite improvement. But at the moment, Darcie didn't care whether Merrick ever spoke to her again, whatever his problem might be.

To distract herself, she helped Cutter tease Walt Corwin into a smile. By the time they moved on, Darcie noticed with astonishment and some dismay that Greta and Walt were standing close together by the far wall, talking, gazing into each other's eyes. Then a game of craps in the middle of the living room carpet brought a round of shouts from the players, capturing her attention. Someone next door banged on the wall just as Claire twined an arm through Darcie's.

"I must say separation hasn't done a thing for Merrick's disposition. Too bad he left early. Not."

Darcie saw right through her. "You and Peter doing okay?"

"Peter who?"

"Claire," she said.

"Don't ask. Let's circulate."

They wandered through the crowded living room. Eden and Julio were dancing cheek to cheek now to a Ricky Martin samba. Someone had turned out the lights. In the corner, Annie lay plastered to Harley. No, Malcolm.

"Why is your sister taking her top off?" Claire asked.

"Oh, God. She isn't."

"Looks that way from here."

When Annie shook her chest for the whole room to see, Darcie felt the sense of doom that had filled her all night take form. Disappointment—in Merrick, in her sister, in their housewarming—rolled through her in waves.

It was only a moment later when the police arrived.

Chapter Thirteen

"Close call," Darcie muttered.

On Monday morning she slunk into the office, certain the grapevine had already circulated the story of her house-warming party and Annie's near-arrest. Whichever co-workers on the sixth floor hadn't been invited, or had chosen not to come, would be regaled with anecdotes about the squad of burly policemen—New York's finest in navy-blue with matching scowls—on Saturday night, responding to a complaint of noise.

Annie had covered her breasts just in time.

"Can't you just see it?" she murmured. "Janet and Hank blowing into town, packing up my belongings with Annie's, flying us both back to Cincinnati?"

A safer life, they'd claim. And add Darcie to their list of bad influences, topped only by Eden.

"Installment number 704 of Darcie Baxter in The Wicked City."

Then Darcie stopped. She almost didn't recognize the person sitting in her chair.

Pencil-slim black skirt. Red silky blouse. Like Claire the other night.

"I thought red made you look like a serious drinker."

Greta Hinckley glanced up from the paper on which she was writing.

"Walter said it's his favorite color." She paused. "You can get half a dozen wearings from a blouse if you let the wrinkles hang out each night and the perspiration dry." Greta's Fashion Tip of the Day.

"Hmm," Darcie murmured, trying to read upside down. "This may be a pointless question—but what are you doing in my cubicle?"

"Leaving you a note. I wanted to thank you."

"Unless you're also composing my note of resignation, I doubt that."

Greta looked hurt.

For a moment Darcie simply stood and stared, ashamed of herself. People change, she thought. They can.

"I'm sorry. You look smashing. I mean, you looked awesome at my party—but this morning..." Her gaze sharpened. "Great hair." The glossy rich brown shade Greta had picked out at Darcie's hair stylist's had been enhanced with strands of blond, gold, wheat and on Saturday night she had shimmered when she walked. "But it's not just the hair," she decided.

"I think Walter noticed."

Well, of course he had. Darcie hadn't seen that coming. Even Walt was a healthy man.

"I saw the looks he kept giving you."

Greta looked down at her scrawled signature. "He took me home."

"All the way to the Bronx?"

"In a cab."

"Not the subway?"

"No." Greta lowered her head, and her tone. "Then he asked me out."

"You're kidding." This wasn't at all what she'd hoped for.

"We had dinner last night." Greta waved the note she'd been writing.

Darcie snatched it from the air and read quickly, skimming over the words. *You have my undying gratitude. I couldn't have done this without you. Whatever you need me to do, I'll do. Thank you, Darcie. Thank you.*

Her eyes misted. "Greta," she said around the lump in her throat, "you're the one who 'did it.' New clothes, your hair, different makeup." *Let us pray.* "I think you've created a whole new Greta Hinckley."

Or so Darcie hoped until later that afternoon when she went into Walt Corwin's office, surprised the goofy male grin on his face—and saw that he, too, was reading some memo from Greta. Fresh suspicion jolted through her veins.

"What's that?"

"Hmm?" he said, not looking up. "Oh, just something for the Sydney store."

"From Hinckley?"

"It's brilliant." He glanced over the sheet again, a new pride in his tone. "She proposes an opening-day festival—snacks, soft drinks, prizes, a drawing for a romantic weekend at the Novotel or the Westin...."

Darcie lost her train of thought. After *Westin,* she heard nothing.

She held out a hand. "May I see?"

She had to admit, the proposed ideas weren't bad. Of course not.

A small frisson of betrayal raced down Darcie's spine and she felt her spirits sink. Greta had thrown her off balance with that thank-you note. Then—*bull's-eye*—she'd run straight to Walt with "her" ideas. Again, he was actually considering them. They were Darcie's, of course. She couldn't say that, though. She would look petty. She'd only mentioned the barest sketch of the notion to Greta during lunch last Saturday. Naive should be her middle name.

"So you guys had dinner last night, huh?"

"Greta told you?" He rubbed his neck. "I always thought Hinckley was...strange." His features softened. "But we have more in common than I thought—" He broke off, as if suddenly aware he might appear odd himself, or realizing he was letting Darcie in on his secret: *Walter Corwin has a personal life.* "Never mind. It was just dinner. Now about Sydney..."

Darcie sent him a wide-eyed look of innocence.

"Only the other day I told Greta we should work together on the Sydney opening. In fact, I asked for her input. I'm glad she's already given it to you."

The flies with honey approach clearly wasn't working as well as Darcie had prayed it would. But Gran wasn't entirely wrong. To be charitable, Greta's new clothes *had* given her a different image. Maybe they had given her the beginnings of a soul. Or could Darcie get that lucky?

"I thought I'd put Greta in charge of the festival," Walt was saying.

"Sure. Excellent."

He slanted her a wary look then ran a hand through his meager brown hair. Or did that too look better this morning? How long would it take the office rumor mill to forget Darcie's party and see the more interesting story here? "I'm surprised," he said. "Now what's your contribution?"

"I'm researching something."

"What?"

Darcie fought the urge to groan. With his every word she could feel herself losing control of the situation. Losing her mentor. "It's a secret. I'll let you know. Tomorrow."

"You'll let me know before you go home tonight. Did Gret—I mean, Hinckley tell you? The orders on the case pieces are behind schedule. The factory in Melbourne tells us the display furnishings won't be ready by opening."

"Yes, they will. I'll handle it. Personally." She didn't want him sending Greta into that breech.

Had she created a monster after all? Greta's revenge might well be Walter Corwin. But where Greta was concerned, Darcie had learned to think fast.

"A few details may be lacking but you'll have my ideas within the hour."

"See to it. Because if this is another of your half-baked—"

"You'll love it. I promise."

With panic gnawing in her stomach, Darcie scrabbled at her computer. First, she checked her e-mail—and discovered a download from Dylan. The color picture of a sheep scrolled down her screen. Darcie II. For a moment, his thoughtfulness and the opportunity to "meet" her namesake held her spellbound. Soft-looking, thick white coat, soulful brown eyes... Then as she blinked at the image, her thoughts regrouped.

"I can do this." Her sheep seemed like a sign, a good omen. Inspired all over again, she stared at the Internet's spinning globe for a few seconds then tapped in the key words she wanted.

Aboriginal Art.

A quick glance around told her Greta was nowhere to be seen. Darcie scanned through the merchant site that flowed onto her monitor.

The offered patterns that popped up looked wild, fanciful. Their rich, dark colors, their stark contrasts, their almost geometric images set her creativity whirling.

The notion had been in the back of her mind since Dylan had taken her into the same little store on Crown Street in Sydney.

His country had a strong, genuine tradition.

Darcie rolled through the listed products, but wasn't satisfied. She needed more than authenticity. She wanted... Original Designs. Hand-painted, one-of-a-kind patterns for Wunderthings alone. If she could find the right sources, if they would agree to license their art... If she found the right factory...

Darcie exited the site, checked her telephone index then tapped in to an outside line. She punched in Dylan's home number.

"Waltzing Matilda," she hummed softly to herself.

She could almost see her plane tickets in hand, the flight to Sydney, Dylan meeting her at the airport, taking her to view the best artists he could find...taking her to bed again. She'd have not only his voice in her ear then but his hands on her body, his mouth on hers, his...

"Hello, Dylan speaking. You've reached Rafferty Stud. Please leave your message at the sound of the beep...I'll get back to you."

"Darcie, I need that memo." Walt leaned against her cubicle doorway.

"Now?" She hung up without leaving a message. It hadn't been an hour.

"I'm talking to the VP in five minutes."

"You'll have it in four."

Her fingers were flying over the keys before he turned away.

By the time she finished the brief memo, and slashed her signature across the bottom of the printed page, Darcie was grinning.

Wild yet disciplined designs. Silky, sheer fabrics. Aboriginal-inspired lingerie. Australian made.

It was the best idea she'd had in four years. "And all mine."

Much later, Darcie let herself into her apartment. Relieved that all seemed dark and quiet, she tiptoed down the hall to her bedroom, dropping her tote bag onto the cushy tub chair she'd bought last weekend at a SoHo flea market. Of course getting it into a cab hadn't been fun, but Cutter Longridge's help (his lazy good looks, too) had gone a long way toward making the experience one Darcie would care to repeat. Next weekend they were renting a van to drive to Pennsylvania where Cutter thought he could find a Shaker armoire for his apartment.

He must earn a lot more money in advertising than Darcie did at Wunderthings, and she couldn't quite call it a date but...

With a heartfelt sigh, she sank onto the end of her bed to unlace her short boots. Then froze.

A sleepy drawl spoke from the corner, startling her. A voice she recognized.

"Take it easy, Sugar. I'm trying to sleep here."

She peered at the shadow propped up on her bed, of a large, obviously male form.

If a life has to be filled with "firsts," why are mine always weird?

"Cutter," she said. "Have you been drinking?"

He groaned. "My head's pounding, my gut's dizzy."

Darcie tossed a pillow at him, slouched in the dark corner, on top of her covers. "You throw up in this bed, and your stomach will be the least of your problems." She sniffed the stale air. "Do I smell beer?"

He shuddered. "Dark stout. This neat place in NoHo— it just opened—had two for one tonight."

"Wow. A beer sale. Wish I'd been there."

Tousle-haired, he managed a grin. Even bleary-eyed, he was a sight to behold. An always welcome sight. "No, you don't. You hate beer."

"And you had to share the experience?" For a moment she wondered whether she'd conjured him up simply because his presence cheered her. "Or is there some other reason for your visit this evening?"

He struggled to an upright position. "I'm locked out. Again."

"Cutter, you really should stop climbing in my window."

Because she couldn't summon any real anger over the situation, Darcie marched out of the bedroom, down the hall, into the living room. She flopped on the sofa. A minute later, Cutter appeared wearing a pair of black sweatpants, a ripped T-shirt and a very white-toothed smile that almost negated his obvious state of inebriation.

"I went running to sober up. No pockets. Forgot my key."

"Yeah, right."

His smile grew. "I knew you'd be home by now."

That statement stopped Darcie cold. "How did you know?"

"Your sister may be a flake who stays out all night. But

not you. Remember those white gloves girls used to wear for dancing class?"

"No." She wouldn't admit it.

"My mother made me go every week to learn my 'social graces.' That's real important—" he said *impahtant* "—down South."

"And your point would be?"

"I always imagine you with a drawer full of those gloves."

Darcie rolled her eyes. She wasn't carrying that much baggage from Cincinnati...was she? He hadn't been hoping to share her bed?

Long after Cutter slipped out her front door and padded upstairs, hours after she heard his apartment door close for the night, Darcie lay looking at the living room ceiling.

Frankly, she couldn't figure out their relationship. He flirted with her now, he'd kissed her the night of her party. But still...

She felt more like his Cousin Darciebelle from Atlanta than she did Cutter's potential girlfriend.

"Sigh," she murmured.

Reaching over, Darcie retrieved the cordless phone from the end table.

She hadn't connected with Dylan earlier about the Aboriginal designs she envisioned for Wunderthings. She needed to do so. Time being of the essence.

And in Australia right now it was...late afternoon, early evening? Tomorrow?

Or not.

"Oh, heck. He didn't return my call. If need be, I'll wake him up."

Darcie dialed then waited, anticipation racing through her veins.

Until—big surprise, her luck running below zero tonight—the rest of her day fizzled like an old balloon when a woman answered.

"Rafferty Stud," she purred.

Okay. Let's not panic. The woman could be his mother. If she was, why did she sound young? And sexy?

"Mrs. Rafferty?"

A small laugh. "Not yet. May I help you?"

"Just...I mean, tell Dylan that Darcie Baxter called."

With her tongue feeling twice its size, her heart, too, she hung up.

"So I can't figure out Merrick," she said aloud, "or Cutter."

Dylan Rafferty's problem, however, seemed plain enough.

Chapter Fourteen

"Another twisted first in my life," Darcie muttered to herself. Wouldn't you know, a woman would answer, a sultry-voiced woman with obvious plans for marriage to Dylan, reminding Darcie that she was the pot calling the kettle black.

One of Gran's old sayings, but it fit.

Why expect Dylan to be faithful? After all, Darcie was still seeing Merrick Lowell. Technically speaking. And, when he chose to climb through her window, Cutter Longridge.

Three days later, still waiting for some response from Australia, Darcie stared at her desktop. Two weeks in Sydney didn't make a relationship, which she hadn't wanted in the first place. Did she?

Maybe she should give up on men. Completely. They sure didn't make sense—and neither did her life.

Then, as if he were another omen, Walt Corwin appeared like a bad genie from a bottle. He was scowling. Darcie preferred his I've-just-been-infected-with-the-love-virus expression. Thank heaven Greta was away from her desk.

"What did you find out about that furniture holdup in Sydney?"

"You don't want to know."

"Yes, Darcie. I do." He came into her cubicle. His pale-blue eyes looked even more washed out than they'd been B.G. Before Greta. His mood seemed to match. "I don't want a memo from you tomorrow morning or by the time you leave here tonight. I need the update. Now."

"Is the board meeting again?"

"No, but I have a business to run. With your help, I hope. What's going on here? All week you've been sitting in this cubicle—which I happen to know you hate in the first place—moping around like some teenage girl whose boyfriend didn't call."

Because this happened to be very near the truth, Darcie said nothing. As if she could call Dylan Rafferty a boyfriend.

"You have troubles with Lowell? Come on, Baxter." He paused. "If there's a problem, I'm here to help."

At his urging tone, Darcie flicked a pencil across her desk. Walt wasn't known for his listening skills—or his compassion. "The problem is, Paramatta Design can't deliver those case pieces until two weeks after we open in Sydney."

"Why's that?"

"You really want to know? I warned you."

Walt wasn't the type to hope for the best.

"Spill your guts."

She had a quick flash of memory. Dylan's bathroom at the Westin Sydney. Chunder. Ugh.

"You won't like this."

"Trust me. I've heard worse."

Darcie took a breath. "No, you haven't. Greta changed the delivery date on the order."

Walt simply stared at her. *"Greta?"*

His gentle tone told Darcie more than *she* wanted to know. Obviously, Walt was still seeing Greta outside the office—and he wouldn't welcome learning that his new ladylove was a liar as well as a thief. After giving Greta unasked-for advice on clothes and makeup, trusting her a little, Darcie had no one to blame but herself.

Makeovers Deluxe had been too successful.

Now, as she'd suspected, she seemed to be losing her mentor. Would he believe Greta, not Darcie?

"You're trying to tell me Greta Hinckley despises you so much, she'd sabotage the Sydney opening?"

"You said it, not me."

"Why would she do that?"

"To get the revenge she threatened. Remember, Walt?"

"Since you brought her into the project? I don't think so."

Darcie sank lower in her chair. She felt like a slug. Despicable. Worse, she felt as if she were hanging herself with her own panty hose.

"Greta called Paramatta Design. You can check that yourself."

"She must have misread the date you gave her."

"It was Greta, I'm afraid, who picked the new date."

He dragged a hand through his thin hair. "And why would she choose a date—on her own—that leaves us with no shelving, no display cases, no goddamn *chairs* for the *fitting* rooms—" his voice kept rising "—for two weeks after we open for *business?*"

"I don't know."

His hand slammed down on her desk. "You and Greta have had this rivalry for four years. From the day you started. I'm beginning to wonder who the guilty party is— Greta, or you." He eyeballed her, obviously expecting a confession. "Whose memos are being 'stolen' and whose ideas are really getting 'borrowed.'"

Mine.

But she didn't say so. He wouldn't believe that either.

"I guess you'll have to figure it out for yourself, Walt." Darcie took a breath. "Of course there is my Aboriginal line of lingerie…"

Walt ran a hand over the back of his neck.

"Yeah, there's that."

"You liked my idea?" She put the slightest emphasis on *my*.

He grumbled to himself for a moment. "*If* we can get production on line in time for the opening," he said, looking unhappy. "What did you find out about licensing the prints we'll need?"

"I'm working on it."

He sighed. "Meaning you don't have a firm answer."

"I have several possibilities in mind. I'm waiting to hear from them. As soon as I do, with figures for your budget, I'll—"

"Write me a memo."

"Better than that, I'll hand deliver it." Darcie grinned, though she felt far from confident. The few Web sites she'd contacted had been slow to respond, and of course Dylan hadn't called back. Not that she wanted him to personally. Now. "I won't even stop by Nancy's desk. How's that? I'll barge into your office and slap it down in front of you."

"No surprise." He stood up.

"Walt—" she called him back, sounding panicked when she needed to appear strong and in command "—I can do this. I promise."

"I'll trust you not to run over Greta in the process."

Her heartbeat hitched. "Is that a warning?"

"No. That's a definite threat."

She couldn't keep quiet. "As in, my job depends on it?"

"You said it. Not me."

"Was he serious?" Cutter asked her that night.

They were lying companionably across Darcie's bed, and she had one ear cocked for Annie's return. Her sister hadn't come home for dinner—not that she always did—and in such silence, Cutter's visits, like Julio's interpretation for Gran, were becoming a necessity.

"Walt's always serious," she answered.

"He should lighten up."

Cutter pulled her close, nuzzling his cheek against her hair. A faint thrill spiraled down Darcie's back, but she tried to ignore it. Merrick hadn't called. Neither had Dylan, naturally. All that talk about some imaginary pregnancy, the sexy flirtations at midnight from Australia were over. How could even a long-distance *friendship*—if she would leave it at that—with a man like Dylan Rafferty survive?

Cutter drew back. "Did you know, when you're upset your eyes turn brown? When you're happy or interested they're really green." He studied her gaze. "You have all these shades and glints. Like your personality."

"Really." Intrigued, she tried to smile at him.

"See? Right now, you're forcing it. You're not happy tonight. Why? It's not only Corwin."

She gave him a look of exaggerated surprise. "I am amazed. What have I done to deserve you? A perceptive, sensitive male...under the age of forty...with a heart of gold, not to mention a very sexy body..."

"Stop changing the subject."

His soft drawl nearly undid her.

"Sometimes," Darcie murmured, "I wonder if you're real. I mean, this guy climbs through my bedroom window one night like part of a dream—and now he's one of my best buds. My confidant. My...cousin confessor."

"Cousin?"

"Kind, considerate, the best catch in four states..."

"Only four?" He grinned against her skin. "You should marry me."

Darcie's pulse lurched.

"Gee, a man who actually brings up marriage." Not pregnancy. "Now I know I'm a goner."

"And you're still avoiding the issue."

"Which is?" she stalled.

"Your eyes. Your gentle, well-brought-up, decent nature. Your tendency to not believe in yourself, despite all evidence to the contrary. Your—"

"Naiveté."

"Naive? You are, you know." He hugged her tight. "You can tell me, as long as I'm being cast in the role of cousin tonight. Which, I suppose, says more about me than

I'm willing to ponder." He paused. "What happened, Darcie? I get the feeling someone has broken your heart."

"My heart breaks all the time. It goes with being naive."

"Keep talking. I'll get it out of you sooner or later."

She sighed. "There's nothing to say." But then, Cutter Longridge brought out some chatterbox quality in her that she hadn't fully appreciated. Darcie rested her head on his shoulder, and told him all about Merrick and Jacqueline, about Walt Corwin and Greta Hinckley, about Dylan. By the time she finished, she was blinking.

Cutter thought a moment while his hand idly stroked her back. "I'd say your Aussie missed you so bad, he's taken up—temporarily—with another woman who can't hold a candle to you. He'll regret it."

"I didn't want him anyway."

"No?"

"He's too...traditional. Victorian, almost. He thinks women belong at home."

"Barefoot and pregnant. My daddy feels the same."

"But you don't."

"I believe women should be whatever, whoever, they please." He smiled. "That's my mama talkin'." Cutter thought some more. "I'd say Merrick Lowell has too much on his mind with the divorce. That must shake him up." He mulled over the next topic on which she had bared her soul. "I'd say Walt's thinking with his dick, not his brain."

Darcie laughed a little to release her tension.

Gently, having said his piece, Cutter kissed her. Like a friend. His mouth felt warm and soft, like his voice, like his southern drawl, and Darcie thought how easy it would be to love this man. To just give over and let him tell her who she was and what she really needed. For the rest of her life.

Forget Walt. Wunderthings. And Aboriginal panties. Consign Greta Hinckley to history.

"You're sighing again," he said. "Is there more?"

"No. You've seen my whole underbelly."

Cutter laughed. "I'd like very much to see your underbelly, Miss Darcie. We could play show-and-tell for the rest of the night...."

When he trailed off, Darcie moved back. Was he serious? She glanced up at him and noticed a perplexed look, like Merrick's, on his face. "What?" she said.

"I apologize. I never say things like that to women I respect." He frowned slightly. "What are we doin' here? I still haven't recovered from that kiss during your party...but I have to tell you something."

"What?"

"I'm not good at playing stand-in for other men. Rafferty, or Lowell. I get the feeling you think of me as a surrogate, not a true rival for your affections—or your bed." He gestured. "I mean, look at us. How many red-blooded Georgian rakes like me could spend a whole evening lyin' around with a gorgeous woman like yourself...and never try anything remotely scandalous?"

"You sound like Rhett Butler."

"I am Rhett Butler." He smiled halfheartedly, but Darcie could see he felt hurt. "My mama always says she raised her boys to be Southern gentlemen with a hint of the outrageous."

"The best kind. Except for climbing through my window."

"Harmless," he said.

Darcie smiled. "I wouldn't be too sure."

"Enjoy me while you can. I won't be around much for a while." His smile faded. "I have a deadline at work—a make-or-break project, if you know what I mean."

"Your job's at risk?"

"We might say that. My boss certainly does."

"Cutter, I'm sorry. But you'll do fine, I know you will. You'll probably even win a promotion." Darcie squeezed his arm. "I do love your visits—you know that, too, don't you—" She hesitated. "But, well, do you have a cell?"

"Phone? Just got one."

"Then next time you lock yourself out, call me. I'll let you in the front door."

He shook his head. "I dropped it," he said, "when I

hoisted myself onto the fire escape tonight. Guess I'm accident-prone." He didn't sound at all concerned. He was incorrigible. She felt almost flattered.

"I don't know how to say this…but some night there could be someone here."

"You mean another guy? All the more reason why you need me. To protect you."

"Well…it's possible. You never know."

Cutter settled back beside her, his arms loosely around her. She felt better now. She always did when Cutter "came to call."

"So." He lifted her hair, sifted it through his strong, lean fingers, kissed her throat, then—again—her mouth. He tasted like warm sun and safety. Definitely the kind of man she should home in on. "Are we goin' to develop this into something grand and passionate ourselves? Or should we just stay friends?"

Darcie drew his head down for another kiss. "I guess we'll see, Mr. Butler."

"I guess we will, Miss Scarlett."

Annie felt like Cinderella dumped at the ball without her prince—or a ride home. Her key scraped in the lock and she let herself into the darkened apartment she shared with Darcie, who was waiting up for her. Big shock. From her perch on the living room sofa, Darcie leaned over to snap on the lamp and Annie blinked against the sudden glare.

"What's the matter? Did Cutter Longridge drive you from your bed?"

Annie had spent her evening with Malcolm—Harley, Darcie called him—and a bunch of other friends at a series of downtown nightspots. Exhausted, still a little buzzed on beer, totally disillusioned by life, she squinted at the light.

Darcie ignored her question. But of course had one of her own.

"Why are you so late?"

"Curfew violation again? Write me a ticket. I left Cincy to avoid this nightly interrogation, but Mom and Dad are amateurs compared to you." Annie strolled across the room. "When I come home is my business."

"Not in a city the size of New York. Annie, your body could wash up in the East River some morning. Then what could I tell Mom and Dad?"

Annie grinned to disguise her real mood. "To stop sending half the rent every month." Who would miss her?

"That's a terrible thing to say."

"Hey, it's no secret. I'm not wanted here."

Darcie frowned. "You would be if you kept your room clean. Instead, you're way out of control. It's not fair, Annie, for Mom and Dad to pay your way. You're twenty-three years old. It's time you—"

"Oh, please. Listen to yourself. You sound just like them."

Annie's pulse thudded. She did not want to have this conversation again. Especially tonight. She didn't want to hear Darcie's disapproving tone or the blah, blah, blah of her words at least three times every week. "Give me a break. Haven't I tried? I went to the College Grads Employment Service. I did the stupid interviews to become a secretary or gofer. Is it my fault nobody will offer me a decent job?"

"You need to broaden your search," Darcie said, her voice firm. "Make applications elsewhere. Try a new placement service. You're bright, Annie. Use your brain to think of something other than new ways to open a beer bottle or wear your hair."

Was she that awful? She'd never cared what other people thought. But in Manhattan or Cincinnati, Darcie was the one who moved giant problems with a single shove.

She said more gently, "You just need to focus."

"I'm sowing my wild oats." But then, why did she keep thinking about Cliff lately, practically living next door in Cincinnati? Quiet, serious Cliff.

"That's for men, not women."

"Then I'm scattering my bright spirit to the four winds."

Darcie climbed off the sofa. She walked right up to Annie, who swayed on her feet, and planted both hands on Annie's shoulders. Darcie stared into her eyes.

"You are a good person. But—to coin an old phrase—'we can't go on like this.'"

"What does *that* mean?"

Darcie's stare intensified. "I don't like your friends. I don't want them in my home. I don't like all those new holes in your skin or the picture on your butt. Neither will the guy you marry someday. How will you explain this to him?"

Cliff's warm eyes, his soft smile, danced across her mind-screen. "I won't. I don't explain myself. To anyone. Even you," she said, trying not to flinch. "This isn't fun for me, either, Darcie. I thought it would be. I wanted so much to move here, spread my wings and fly. Just like you."

"Me?" Darcie managed a laugh. "The Sydney store's a mess of monumental proportions, I may not have a job myself by the time that's done... I have no idea what I want to be when I grow up...."

"You don't?"

"So whatever image you have in mind about me is just a crock." Darcie half smiled. "That doesn't change this. Read my lips, Annie. 'You have to get a job.'"

She pressed her mouth tight. Then she challenged, "Or what?"

Darcie's smile faded. "I send you home."

"You can't send me anywhere! I make my own decisions."

"Then decide to act like an adult."

"If you're not sure about your life, why do I need to be?"

"Because we're different people." She paused. "Because I count on you."

Annie was astonished. "Don't fold on me, Darce. You're my idol."

The room went absolutely still. So did her big sister. The truth was out—at last—and Annie minded, but only for an instant. Why not? Ever since she'd come to New York, she'd been hiding her secret, just as she had hidden it from the moment of her birth. *I'm a fraud. You're the real one.*

"I'm what?"

"I mean, how could I ever measure up?" Even the phrase *I mean* was Darcie's, not her own. *There's the original, and here's the photocopy.*

"Measure up to what, exactly?"

"This. *You*. You may have problems, Darce, but you also have real friends like Claire, a paycheck, men—even Merrick—who don't make you pay for everything and talk dirty and take your last dollar from your wallet—"

"Don't tell me. Harley?"

"Malcolm," she said. "I had to walk home. Stagger home, actually." Annie tried to swallow the big lump in her throat. It stuck there, as hard and prominent as all her unmet resolutions to be just like Darcie. "You're not as naive as people think. You pegged him right away. If only I had seen...but I never do."

"No? But you're tough, Annie. I admire that."

"If I'm so tough, why do I feel bad about some dork like him?"

Darcie slipped her arms around Annie again.

"He's a loser." She squeezed her hard, and Annie felt warmth flow through her veins, a better buzz than beer. "Oooh, I'm so mad I could spit like Sweet Baby Jane! How *could* he treat you like that? We should sic Jane on him with her sharp claws—"

Annie couldn't help it. She started laughing. All her life, Darcie had defended her, protected her, fought her battles for her. But that was just it. So now what?

Maybe Darcie was right. Maybe it was time to grow up.

The thought turned Annie's already sour stomach. But there it was.

Maybe she should even thank Harley for the wake-up call. She drew back to look at her big sister. Her champion.

"I love you, Darce."

"I love you, too."

Lay it all out now. "I've never wanted anything except to be like you. But I don't know how to be."

For a moment they hung there, in each other's arms, rocking. Secure.

Then Annie said, "You know what else? This move was supposed to be the biggest adventure of my life, a life filled with grand adventures. But then I met Malcolm...God, I don't even know his last name." She paused, trying hard to remember. *Did he ever tell me?* "I have this tattoo on my ass that isn't even cool..." Her eyes filled. "All these piercings."

Darcie wiped tears from her eyes. "Annie, stop."

"No, but this is the worst part." She was gasping now, not sure whether she was laughing at herself or crying because she'd really been a pathetic child after all. "I'm a welfare case to Mom and Dad...and I—I—"

"Say it."

Annie's voice dropped to a shamed whisper. *The truth— hidden even from myself—is out.* She couldn't believe it.

"I think I'm homesick, Darce."

Chapter Fifteen

The next night Darcie had barely reached home when the telephone rang. The well-remembered male voice sent a thrill of lust—and regret—trickling down her spine like warm syrup. Dylan Rafferty could get to her every time, the man if not his message.

"She reminded me of you."

"Oh, you...*jerk*."

Darcie's heart pounded at his transparent lie. Did he think she was still *that* naive?

"Hey," he said in the silence. "Are you mad at me?"

She huffed out a breath. Her finger poised over the disconnect button, but Dylan stopped her.

"Darcie, let me explain."

She tried a breezy tone—as if she didn't care. "No, we're both adults. Independent. You're free to see whoever you please." Significant pause. "We have no commitment to each other, Dylan. I'm just trying to make our positions clear."

"I can make them clear." His tone lowered. "What're you wearing?"

"Full body armor."

Dylan half laughed. "Seriously."

"Full body armor. High-gauge steel."

Her tone stayed flat, but Darcie knew she was rapidly getting into trouble. Dylan's seductive voice cut through her frozen emotions with the ease of that heavy syrup oozing into the nooks and crannies of a blueberry waffle. In another minute she'd forget all about the sultry-toned woman who had answered his phone. The one who obviously expected to become Mrs. Dylan of Rafferty Stud. The word zinged through her defenses. It was hard to hate a man whose very work reminded her of sex. Darcie realized the only way to keep herself safe would be to ask Dylan about Aboriginal art.

"The reason I called..."

But Dylan had that one-track male mind that refused to be derailed. "You don't need a reason to call, darling. That woman means nothing to me."

"How sad."

"She picked me up in a bar last time I was in Sydney." He'd sounded hesitant, as if a glimmer of unease had drifted through his oh-too-masculine brain, but Darcie had to bring this conversation back to business. Immediately.

"How familiar," she murmered.

She launched into a breathless explanation of her ideas for Wunderthings' newest line of lingerie, her need for authentic design. When she finished, he was silent for a long moment until Darcie cleared her throat.

"Yeah, I know a guy," he finally said. "Henry Goolong. He lives not far from me. He's full-blooded Aboriginal. He and his grandson work together. Mostly, they make didges—those musical instruments I showed you on Crown Street—but I expect he'd design some pretty wonderful stuff for your knickers...and for a reasonable fee."

Darcie's misplaced physical excitement for Dylan's beautiful body morphed into a more practical need. The job kind, which she hoped she could deal with better. "Our contract would provide him and his family with extra income—"

"—and you'd get what you need without bankrupting your company."

She took a breath. "Can you put me in touch with him?"

"Yes."

"Will you?"

"Sure," he said. "Got a pen?"

He rattled off the numbers as if he realized—at last—how important her career was to her, and Darcie dutifully took them down. A whole bunch of them for the cross-oceanic connection. She tried not to listen to the continued timber of Dylan's voice, its depth and richness, a voice that had always sent her senses into orbit. Never again, she promised herself.

She hadn't been surprised, really, to hear that female voice, or even to learn that Dylan had other interests concerning sex. Would an oh-so-virile man like him stay celibate waiting for Darcie who might never get back to Australia, never see him again?

When he finished, she said a polite, "Thank you."

"You're welcome." His tone sounded mocking, almost sarcastic.

"I'll give him a call. At a reasonable hour of the day—your time."

"Okay. Fine."

She held a finger over the button again to hang up.

"I appreciate your help," she said. Business only, then couldn't resist. "Thank you for the picture. Say hello to Darcie II for me."

"I will but..." He stopped her again. "Hey, Matilda."

"Goodbye, Dylan."

Darcie hung up, sorrow flowing through her veins not like rich, warm syrup now but like cold-thickened sludge.

It was over. The relationship that had never really begun.

Maybe she should remain single for the rest of her life and stop worrying about some Mr. Right—*not* Dylan—who probably didn't exist. So much for her elusive notions of happiness.

As if she'd read Darcie's mind, Claire was packing when Darcie walked into her office at Heritage Insurance on Monday wearing a soulful expression that could only mean a man problem. Knowing it would reveal itself soon enough, Claire turned back to a half-empty carton.

"What's this?" Darcie asked. "Management kick you up the corporate ladder again?" She waved at Samantha gurgling in her nearby playpen. "Not bad. Bet this time you'll get a corner office. Overlooking St. Patrick's Cathedral."

"I quit."

Darcie gave her a blank look.

"You're obviously caught up in some disaster of your own," Claire said, tossing a pair of bronze bookends into the box. "I'll make this simple. Man equals love equals marriage equals baby. That's where the buck stops." She glanced over her shoulder at Darcie. "I can't possibly spend half the night with a teething child then give my best to Heritage Insurance. I can't cook dinner, do the laundry and rush into work the next morning after another night of bad sleep…well, you get the picture."

"You're leaving your job?"

"Yep." Claire fought back a mild wave of regret.

"But Heritage Insurance is you—and vice versa."

"Not anymore." She smiled misty-eyed at Samantha, who wagged a rattle in her direction. "I'm trying my damnedest—darnedest—to be a halfway decent mother to this adorable daughter of mine. I just can't do anything else right now."

Darcie had apparently shelved whatever male trouble she had in her life in favor of curiosity. "Peter gave you an ultimatum, right?"

"No. I just couldn't take it any longer, Darcie. I need time with Samantha, time to get my energy back, time to…just *time.*"

"Hmm. I always thought they'd carry you out of here on a stretcher straight to the morgue, still tapping away on your Palm Pilot."

"Charming."

"No, I mean you'd just drop dead at your desk from

trying to be all things to everyone. Your career, Peter, Sam...even me."

"I've come to my senses."

Claire made a cooing noise toward Samantha, who flung the rattle. With a gleeful giggle, she watched it wing Claire right in the head.

"Ouch. Darn it, sweetie." She rubbed her temple. "No swearing in front of the baby, Peter's orders. Other than that, he is a self-contained support unit. In words, anyway."

"You sound resentful."

"Do I?" Claire added a stack of papers to the packing box, flipped the flaps shut, then carried the rattle back to Sam. Promptly, Samantha dumped it again. "I've made this decision on my own. Peter doesn't even know yet—though I'm sure he'll be glad to have a full-time mother for his child. Lord knows I interviewed most of the eligible nannies in all five boroughs, most of Jersey, too." She sighed. "I've certainly given the take-your-daughter-to-work program a run for its money, and I've ruined every Donna Karan suit I own. There isn't a Natori blouse without spitup all over it. I give up."

"Me, too." Darcie slumped onto a chair in front of Claire's desk.

"Okay. What is it?"

"First, Annie. She misses home. I think she even misses Mom and Dad, and this morning on my way out I saw her mooning over the picture of her old boyfriend. It appeared on her dresser—in the center of all her other junk—last week. I should have seen the signs then." Darcie sighed. "We had a big fight the other night. I don't think she's ever going to get a job—and you know what? I wonder if she wants one."

"If Annie found a job," Claire pointed out, "she'd be making a commitment to staying here."

"Exactly." Darcie forced a grin. "You and I make a team. Great minds."

"But if Annie left, you'd be stuck with the rent. All of it."

"You wouldn't want to board Samantha with me for the next eighteen years, would you? I'll cut you a deal." Darcie thought a moment. "I mean, then I wouldn't need to worry about getting married eventually...having kids of my own. I'd just raise Sam—of course, there is my job..."

"Don't tempt me." But Claire gazed fondly at her daughter. "Let's see. We have one dysfunctional sister who won't get a job, one dysfunctional friend who can't keep hers..."

"Gran, too," Darcie added. "She and Julio had another quarrel. She called me in tears at six this morning. I don't know what to do with her. We're not on the best terms still, and I can't run out to Jersey. I have a call in to Australia at the office." Claire's eyebrows lifted. "Not Dylan. Business. I need to get back soon, but I had to see you. The voice of reason."

"Ha." Claire plunged into another carton, blinking. Samantha must have picked up on her mood, and started to cry. Or was she just frustrated about the rattle, which lay on the office carpet again? Claire still couldn't decipher her various cries. "Women from infancy to eighty-two are falling apart," she said. "Isn't there anyone here who knows how to cope with life?"

"And men," Darcie murmured.

Claire emerged from the box. "I knew it. I knew that's why you're here."

"Actually, I did hear from Dylan."

"Ohmygod. He apologized, right? The woman on the phone was his mother, or no, she said not Mrs. Rafferty. She was his sister, his cousin..."

"None of the above. She was exactly what she seemed to be."

"He's got another girlfriend?"

"Claire, I was never his girlfriend. We had two lovely weeks in Sydney—"

"Darce, I've heard your song before. I hate to tell you, it's not headed for the top of the charts."

Samantha cried harder. Feeling guilty again, Claire

scooped her up, rocking the baby and staring at Darcie who, she could see, was a blink away from tears herself.

"He didn't apologize?"

"He tried. I couldn't see the point." She sighed again, her chin quivering. "It was sex, that's all."

"Works for me. Or would, if I had any libido." A big part of her problems.

"You're nursing. I read that nursing can suppress sex drive—kind of like a built-in birth control device."

"Would you come to the apartment and tell Peter that?"

"Sure, if you fix dinner. I love your chicken Florentine."

"It's yours. If you baby-sit while I take Peter out for drinks so I can tell him I quit my job. He's in San Francisco on business until Friday."

Darcie's face cleared. "Ah. I see. You self-destructed in the middle of last night with Sam shrieking in your ear because she's cutting teeth. You folded."

Claire hustled back to the carton, jiggling Sam on one arm.

"It was a weak moment, I admit, but overdue. I'll go back to work when Samantha enters first grade. I have plenty of time. In fact, I'm part of a growing professional women's revolution—a backlash movement."

"You might lose your job skills, Claire. Your edge."

"I lost my edge when my obstetrician said, 'the head is out.' But that's okay. I love Samantha, don't I, sweetie?" She nuzzled the baby's neck, and Sam's grumbling quieted into a gurgle. "Yes, Mama loves you. We'll be fine. Together."

Darcie snickered.

Claire mentally crossed her fingers. "I'm going to love wheeling Sam to the park, meeting other mothers, having picnic lunches, watching Sam play in the sandbox."

"You'll be chewing nails by the end of next week."

"Bite me, Darce."

"I won't have to. You're gnawing off your own leg."

"Well, what about you, Miss Independent Woman Who Doesn't Need a Man Right Now? Ms. Female Who

Can Figure Out Her Own Life?" Claire snorted, startling the baby. "For someone who's trying so hard to stay single, you look pretty miserable this morning." She paused. "I think you're still hot for Rafferty."

"Hot is one thing. Right is another. You're a fine one to talk. Look at this—" Darcie waved a hand at the office cluttered with boxes "—giving up the thing that's made you tick, quite happily I might add, since I've known you."

"Face it. We're all screwed up. You, me, Annie, even Eden, who knows more about life and men than all of us put together."

"That's what I tell Mom."

"Don't forget Greta." Claire kissed Sam's damp curls and put her back in the playpen. She was blinking again when she straightened. "What a mess. And I don't mean my office."

"I guess we're doing the best we can."

Claire couldn't let it go at that. This morning, charging into the president's office, even into Human Resources after that, she'd felt confident...free. And absolutely correct in her decision to give it all up.

Now, she wasn't that sure. And neither was her best friend.

"Darcie, you are such a Pollyanna."

By the end of the day, Darcie had to concede that Claire might be right. She'd no sooner reached the office at ten o'clock that morning—late by an hour—when Greta tried to sabotage her efforts to negotiate an agreement with Henry Goolong in Australia. Why did Darcie never learn? She couldn't trust the woman.

"You went over my head about this to Walt?"

"I thought we were a pair now, Baxter. And since you weren't here, I assumed you'd want me to handle it."

"When hell turns into a cherry Popsicle." So much for Greta's supporting role.

Thank goodness no real damage had been done. Henry finally agreed with Darcie by phone to send four Aboriginal designs suitable for Wunderthings lingerie patterns as soon as a contract was signed. She'd have to make sure Greta took no part in hammering out those details. And start making plans herself for production as quickly as possible, in time for the Sydney opening.

"What if he doesn't sign?" Greta asked as if she expected trouble, and probably she did. Trouble she would orchestrate herself. Wasn't it enough that she and Walt were thick as thieves these days? *I have created a monster.*

"Henry will sign. It's a simpler world down there." Darcie wished she could say the same.

Still furious with Greta, she left work. Merrick had phoned three times that afternoon but Darcie had been too busy to talk. His work number didn't answer now, his cell phone either, and his home phone was busy. Having finally weaseled his address from him not long ago, she decided to drop by. Maybe they would order in tonight, pizza or Chinese. Relax. Maybe they'd actually talk... about their "relationship," even about Greta. Darcie couldn't stop seething.

In the soft evening light, Darcie held up one hand to hail a passing cab. It flashed past without slowing, and she breathed out a sound of frustration and started talking to herself.

"I don't know whether I feel more angry with Greta Hinckley about Henry Goolong (why couldn't Walt see that?) or whether I'm mad at myself. If I hadn't stopped at Heritage to see Claire, who needed me, I would have been on time to work."

Or should she feel oddly relieved? Frankly, Darcie had been waiting for just such a power play from Greta since her trip to Australia.

Darcie leaned into the street again like one of those bronze figures that dotted the city's sidewalks and little parks. Whimsical, urban. Impervious to her growing fears, unlike the low clouds gathering overhead.

She should have taken the ferry to Gran's instead. Eden would comfort them both tonight, maybe with a bowl of homemade chicken soup laced with sherry. Her quarrel with Julio, Darcie's with Greta, would become minor blips on their personal radars, of no consequence.

Finally, a cab screeched to a halt just in front of Darcie's feet, and she climbed gratefully inside.

"Seventy-Eighth and Park, please."

No comment. Maybe her driver didn't speak English. Darcie yearned for the days she didn't actually remember when New York's cabbies had been articulate fountains of earthy wisdom they were only too willing to share with passengers. Eden claimed they had been a large part of her education.

Darcie gazed at the passing lights and store windows, trying not to clutch the sagging seat cushion with both hands while the taxi lurched through traffic.

At Merrick's apartment building, the doorman announced her on the intercom.

She heard a murmured drone of conversation then Merrick's voice.

"Send her up."

What if he had guests already? She hadn't thought of this. Maybe he and some friends were playing poker, having a few beers. Swearing and telling jokes. One of those male-bonding events. But that sounded more like Dylan.

What if Merrick had a date here—and Darcie was about to make another fool of herself, like that Saturday at FAO Schwarz?

Darcie preferred the former alternative. Wasn't one unpleasant surprise the limit in any relationship?

After her talk with Dylan, she had her doubts about men in general. She exited the elevator at the second floor. Merrick would invite her in, offer her a sandwich from a platter of pastrami on rye, hand her a beer. Maybe they'd play a few hands of poker. Not strip, of course, when they weren't alone but…

The door opened before she reached it. He must have been watching through the peephole. Darcie fixed a bright smile on her face. Expect the best.

"What are you doing here, Darcie?" Merrick stood in the doorway.

"You called. We didn't have a date tonight or anything. I just…" She peered around him. "Could I come in?" He obviously didn't intend to invite her. "I have something to tell you."

"Can't it wait? I'll see you tomorrow." He didn't step back. "What is this?"

"An invasion of your privacy, apparently." She rushed on. "I called, but I couldn't reach you. I left the office, pissed at Greta, and before I knew it…here I am."

He folded his arms over his chest.

And Darcie noticed he was wearing a skintight T-shirt that hugged every inch of his well-defined chest. She'd never seen him in casual mode. His arm muscles bulged. So did his jeans when she glanced down at his fly. Darcie remembered those qualities, which had attracted her to Merrick in the first place.

"Have you been working out?" No, that didn't sound right. He wouldn't have a semierection then. "I mean, at the gym tonight."

"No."

With a sigh of obvious defeat, Merrick moved back. He turned in the doorway and a second man stepped forward, smiling. He was tall, blond like Merrick. Wearing a form-fitting T-shirt and tight pants. He and Merrick might have been twins.

Number Two was also wearing an apron.

The Iron Chef, it read. Some TV show competition Darcie had watched once, with Gran. Because she rarely cooked, she hadn't liked all that high-speed slicing and dicing of exotic ingredients, none of which tempted her.

He held up a small platter. Curious, biding her time, Darcie went up on her tiptoes, and saw fresh sushi arrayed in a beautiful fan shape, neat as the plastic food in Japanese restaurant windows. She shuddered. Raw fish was not Darcie's favorite, either.

"No, thank you."

He kept holding the plate. "I'm Geoffrey."

"Hi." She stuck out a hand. "Darcie."

They shook.

Merrick made a strangled sound. "Look, this is ridiculous. We'll talk *tomorrow*," he told Darcie.

Her heart was suddenly pounding. She had a strange feeling.

No women's voices murmured from within. No pastrami on rye, or beer, could be glimpsed on the table. No deck of cards. All Darcie could see was a cozy scene—dinner about to be consumed like all those nights in Hank and Janet's dining room. Merrick cleared his throat.

"Geoffrey is my—"

"Partner." He lowered the platter of sushi and gave her another friendly grin. Then he slipped his hand into Merrick's.

Merrick's eyes begged her not to react. *No FAO Schwarz, please.*

Well. There was no answer Darcie could make to that. Plain enough.

Clear as glass. She imagined a shattering sound.

But what about me? She wouldn't yell or even cry. Never mind sex. What kind of *human being* was he to keep her in the dark?

Merrick said something to his "partner," then stepped out into the hall and closed the door behind him. He studied her as if he didn't quite know what to say. Neither did Darcie. She'd never been in this situation before.

"Geoff seems like a very nice man."

Merrick leaned against the door and scowled, his arms folded over his chest and the snug T-shirt. "I don't mean to hurt you. There's no reason why you and I can't keep seeing each other."

"Sure, why not?" Darcie's heart threatened to pound out of her chest. "You've 'entertained' me behind closed doors for years. I never knew where you lived, with whom you lived...even Jacqueline was a surprise...and I sure didn't realize you had two kids who could be desperately hurt by our 'arrangement.' Now, there's Geoffrey."

"You're getting melodramatic."

She adjusted her bag on her shoulder like a leather security blanket. "I've been your mistress, for God's sake. It wasn't humiliating enough to find out in the middle of FAO Schwarz that you had a wife and family—I had to stumble up your front steps tonight and find my replacement fixing dinner. I don't care about your sexual choices, Merrick—I hope you're happy—but dammit, why couldn't you just tell me? Instead, you lied to me. Again."

Merrick straightened. "Can we get past this? Please?"

"No. We can't. I've been deceived. Twice over. It won't happen again." Darcie started to leave but he caught her wrist and, with his eyes, soulfully asked her to stay. "What more is there to say?" she said, exasperated.

"I need your help."

Darcie gaped at him. "You what?"

"I like Geoff. A lot," he said, lowering his voice as if not to be heard inside the apartment. "But I'm not ready to...well, yes, commit. After all, Jackie and the kids are just gone—I'm not adjusted yet. I'm worried about my son and daughter's reaction to having a male live-in. It's a definite surprise for them. But I don't want to step on Geoff's feelings, either. What do you think I should do?"

Darcie's heart was beating like a small bird's in a panic. She couldn't believe this. Worse than Greta today. Worse than...all her nights with Merrick.

"Life is too strange. I come here thinking your calls today meant you wanted to see me. And all you're really after is some free help? Advice to the lovelorn?"

Her voice rose on each word.

"Darcie."

The truth dawned. His difficult mood, his puzzled expression. "Is that why you seemed so...confused at my party? Ah, I see. You weren't gauging my relationship with Cutter. You were sizing him up! No, I'm outta here. Someone is waiting for me at home," she lied. "Thank God."

Merrick's gaze narrowed. "I've heard that tone before. You mean the Australian guy?" His look turned mulish. "That's never going to work out."

"Oh, thank you. Then I'm batting a thousand tonight. What's new?"

"He's in New York?"

Darcie didn't answer. She hitched her bag higher on her shoulder—and strode to the elevator. Shocked, yes. But she didn't feel judgmental, or angry.

Anger was a wasted emotion on Merrick Lowell. Clueless.

"What about next Monday?" he called after her.

Chapter Sixteen

"A moment of truth," Darcie murmured when she reached home—by then the gray evening had turned to rain—and came to a dead halt on the sidewalk in front of her building. Gran had been right. Merrick Lowell was a complete, utter narcissist. He saw the world only through his own filter.

But no, even after the encounter with Merrick, she wasn't seeing things. He was no mirage. Smack in the middle of her steps, there sat Dylan in the drizzle. Wearing his gray-green Akubra hat, his chambray shirt and jeans, his jacket—and that mega-watt Aussie smile. Damn, she didn't want to feel this way, but her heartbeat sped.

Or, did Dylan's smile really seem that bright?

No, she decided. He looked...stunned by some life event, just as Darcie had felt meeting Merrick's boyfriend. She had to remind herself that, in her experience, Dylan deserved every nuance of the expression he wore. Darcie planted both hands on her hips.

"Are you lost? I mean, you're a little out of your way."

"I had to attend a livestock conference in Kansas City. While I was nearby, I decided to drop in and see you."

She wouldn't smile. She would *not*.

"Dylan, K.C. is fifteen hundred miles from here."

"Distances don't mean that much to us Aussies. It's a big country."

He hadn't moved, and Darcie wondered if he was afraid to get up, to face her, and risk a punch in the nose.

"You're getting wet," she pointed out.

Mustering her dignity with effort, she marched past him up the stone stairs and, taking care he didn't see her shaking hand, jammed her key in the front door lock. She needed to get inside, to be safe from further surprises, unpleasant or otherwise, tonight.

Talk about naive. "I should expect my engraved, gold-plated trophy in the mail any day now."

Dylan followed her. "Are you too mad to even say 'hello'?"

Darcie didn't turn around. "Hi."

He hesitated on the threshold behind her. "Does that mean I can come in?"

"Do whatever you like. I'm here by myself." No, that wasn't right. From the intense look in his dark eyes, he had things in mind that Darcie wouldn't even consider. "Stay out here in the rain if you want. Whatever you do, please don't touch me."

"You *are* still mad."

Maybe when she grew as old as Gran, she'd decide to forgive him. They could start over. Fall into bed again. Screw their brains out. Or was that screw out their brains?

Grammar didn't seem to be on Dylan's mind, either.

"Then there's hope," he decided aloud.

No sooner did Darcie close the door behind them than he threw his arms around her. She squirmed, trying to get out of her soaked trench coat so she could stop shivering, but despite her warning to keep his distance, Dylan held tight.

"I've missed you. God, you don't know how bad I missed you."

Darcie stopped struggling. She said nothing. The silent treatment was one of Janet's favorites, and Darcie had seen it work many times. Not that she admired herself for using it now. She made herself stand still until, finally, he lifted his head from the crook of her neck where possibly he'd been about to plant a moist kiss. She could feel the heat of his mouth almost touching her skin. His tone lowered.

"I lied."

"Well, that's a huge surprise. Is there some discount tonight? Or are all you guys taking a crash course in Ethics for extra credit at the New School?"

"All of us?" He released her and Darcie shrugged off her wet coat then strode by him toward her bedroom. *No, don't go there.* If he followed her, she might ignore the fact that she was royally pissed at Dylan Rafferty for reasons she couldn't justify, and jump his bones.

Instead, Darcie plunked down on the sofa and grabbed her afghan.

She wrapped herself in it but kept shaking. Merrick, Dylan... They were enough to make her overlook Greta Hinckley.

"You're cold," he said, rocking on his boot heels, hands shoved in the back pockets of his jeans. Wet jeans, she saw. How did he work his fingers inside that tight, dark denim? Wet boots. "Let me get you warm, darling."

He sat down beside her but Darcie scooted away like Little Miss Muffet.

All those nights of phone sex ran through her mind. Then that one call a woman had answered. Dylan had been just a pleasant diversion. Like Darcie for him.

Maybe if she told herself often enough, she'd believe it.

"What did you lie about?"

He said, "I'll dry you, then we'll talk."

"You can talk while we both get dry."

He gave her another look. "I can only do one thing at a time. Okay?"

"Okay." She held up her hands. "I meant separately."

He was here. She had to make allowances. He was a *man*...and she was still glad to see him.

So much for lies and the end of quasi-relationships.

As for her naiveté, if she wasn't careful, she'd fall for him all over again. And for how long this time?

Dylan rubbed the afghan over her arms, raising goose

bumps of cold and pleasure on her skin, then started on her body. Darcie stayed his hand, which had grazed her breast.

"I'll do this part."

"You can do all my parts, if you want."

She drew back. "Dylan, what are you doing here? Nobody, not even from Australia, flies halfway across another continent to see a woman he met in a bar."

"That's what I lied about—*her,* not you." Dylan settled them in the cushions, his arms around her, the slightly damp afghan warming their skin. She stopped shaking. "I didn't meet Deidre in a bar. She lives on the station closest to mine."

She was his *neighbor?* "Is she pretty?"

Darcie had no idea where the question had sprung from. It embarrassed her, but like any woman, she wanted to know the answer, no matter how painful.

"Yeah. She's real pretty. Long dark hair, big brown eyes. A figure that—"

"I don't need details."

She heard the frown in his voice. "She comes over sometimes. When we both get the urge to indulge our hormones."

"A practical arrangement on both sides."

"Yep."

Ouch. And where was his mother then?

"So then you two hop into bed. Is that supposed to make me feel better?"

"Does it?" he said.

Darcie sat up. She looked into his dark eyes, and tried not to see the confusion there. Her own confusion, too. "Why don't you just marry her?"

"I don't love her. She doesn't love me."

"Ha. You're kidding yourself. She has every intention of becoming Mrs. Dylan Rafferty. Someday."

Dylan looked startled by this news.

"Deidre? What makes you think that?"

"She told me. Not in those words, but I'd have to be deaf not to hear the message that was plainly coming through."

"Oh," he said. "Right. I get it now." Dylan grinned. "Deidre was just having her fun. She's a great joker. I told her about you and she prob'ly figured out who was calling that day."

"Now, there's a good story to tell my grandchildren."

"It's no story, Darcie. It's the truth."

"What a pal. The woman ruins your 'friendship' with me and you give her high marks for having a sense of humor."

He scowled again, clearly in over his head. "I don't think you understand the Aussie system."

"You're right. I don't." She didn't understand men. "Is this like the 'tall poppy'?"

Darcie bounded off the sofa and hurried to her room, heedless now of the fact that Dylan might pursue her. She needed dry clothes. She needed distance. She had just peeled off her blouse and unhooked her bra when he showed up in the doorway.

"Do you mind?" she said, stifling the urge to scream.

His eyes widened. "I don't mind at all." He tracked her body with his hot, dark gaze. "Keep going, darling. You're just getting to the most interesting parts."

Darcie turned her back.

Dylan took three strides and pressed himself against her spine. He slipped his arms around her waist, locked his strong hands in front of her. She glanced down at his gold signet ring. A patchwork of tiny cuts crisscrossed his wrists and he noticed her looking at them. "Barbed wire," he murmured. He ran his mouth along the nape of her neck, then her shoulder. "There's a Border collie's nip, too, on my calf, mean little devil." His lips brushed her bared skin and Darcie sucked in a breath. Desire shot straight from the base of her brain to her groin, darting through all the erogenous zones it could find en route. "Sheep kicked me the other day right where it hurts."

"You poor..." He nipped at her earlobe and she moaned, unable to continue.

"Injured man." His mouth roamed. "You ever think about becoming a nurse?"

"Not until this minute."

"Know who kicked me?" Shifting her, he trailed his lips across her collarbone and she smiled at the hard push of his arousal along her lower back. "Darcie II," he whispered. "Takes after her 'mother.'"

She wriggled against his hold. "I'm trying to be angry with you."

"Quit trying so hard. Why are you?" he said. "Because I showed up here in the rain? And didn't call first? Or are you going to keep Deidre between us until I have to leave New York? Waste all this precious time when we could be enjoying each other?"

Dylan swept a light touch over her breasts and Darcie's knees went weak. She nearly whimpered when his fingers tweaked her nipples. "Since you paid for an airline ticket, I guess that would be foolish."

"Definitely."

"I imagine we could…make better use of this opportunity."

"Oh, you bet."

He had her skirt off now. He stripped her panty hose, clammy and cold and clinging, from her legs, and flung them to the carpet. Her "knickers" followed, then she was naked. Darcie turned into his embrace, her hands homing in on his belt buckle like magnets. *Ka-chunk*. Dylan groaned.

"See? On the other hand, you know how to hurt a guy, too."

"Now, there's an idea. I could exact my revenge—" taking a page from Greta's book "—for a certain period of time. Like a jail sentence."

"I'm your willing prisoner."

"How long do you think? An hour?"

He pretended to consider that. "Hey, I've been a pretty bad boy."

"From my experience at the Westin, I'd say so." She smiled into his eyes, feeling warm all over now. "More than an hour, then." Tight in each other's arms, they side-stepped toward the bed. Thank heaven, she'd bought a queen-size mattress. Plenty of room for what Darcie had in mind.

It had been a rotten day, she told herself. She deserved to make him suffer.

Of course that meant "punishing" herself, too...

They landed on the bed, Dylan half covering her, Darcie's arms twined around his strong, suntanned neck. Dylan's signet ring clinked against the headboard.

"All night," she whispered. "Maybe that won't even be enough."

"No time off for good behavior."

She arched up against him. "No possibility of parole."

"Death row?" he asked, mock fear in his voice.

"I wouldn't go that far. But close."

She'd forgotten how beautiful he was, and Darcie felt tears spring to her eyes. He was funny but wise in his own, down-home way. He felt like heaven in her arms, and he certainly looked like a god with his sunbrowned skin and dark, mischievous eyes.

"You are a rascal, Dylan Rafferty."

"It got me in your bed again." His lips brushed hers, then her throat. He laughed a little, low and sexy and thoroughly male. "In like Flynn."

"Does that mean what I think it means?" Darcie tried to sound stern but his mouth was sending hot, erotic messages along her skin. "You're taking advantage—in this case, of a sexual situation."

"Seizing an opportunity," he corrected her. "So are you, Matilda."

True.

"All right. You're here." She drew his mouth down to hers. "Do your worst."

"Well. Since I'm clearly not capable of reform..."

He eased her legs wider with his knee. Then he raised onto his elbows and gazed down into Darcie's face. And smiled. Wicked sunshine. He was still wearing his hat, and the Akubra slid down over their faces as Dylan kissed her. When his body meshed with hers and he slid deep inside her, *in like Flynn,* Darcie moaned. She could feel his pectoral muscles against her breasts, his hips close to hers, his penis filling her, stretching her, loving her.

Dylan's tone sounded shaken, no longer glib.

"Say it, darling. You know you want to."

"It's...good to see you. I missed you, too."

"And you forgive me." He moved a little faster, harder.

"Yes. I...ohhh."

It was like the first time at the Westin, only better. Neither of them lasted long. In a few minutes, or was it seconds, Dylan's body withdrew from hers then held, suspended, before he entered her one last time—and Darcie lost it, went spinning over the edge.

So did he.

He was here, and she was thrilled to see him.

She was in even deeper trouble now, but she didn't care.

Darcie gasped into the hollow of his neck. "Moments of truth."

Back down to earth again, more or less, Darcie had just finished her overseas conference call a week later with Walt Corwin and Henry Goolong in Sydney, with Greta Hinckley listening from her cubicle, when Walt rang back again. Solo this time.

"It's not bad enough, I fly all the way to Australia." His voice sounded as if he were in the same room with Darcie, but he wasn't. She kicked back in her chair, putting her feet on the desk. "Then I find out the shipment of case pieces you ordered won't be late after all."

Great. Her whining had gotten results.

"Hello. That's a good thing, Walt."

"See if you think so when you hear the rest." Darcie straightened, dropping her feet to the floor. "Thanks to all the yelling you and I did, the order arrived yesterday. Or is it today? Damn, I can never get the time straight."

Neither could Darcie until now. All the more because Dylan Rafferty had taken up temporary residence in her apartment, in her bed. In fact, she was squirming right now to get home to him. Darcie glanced at her watch. Yesterday Dylan had bought it for her—a classy silver watch with two faces. For that reason, she would have thought it perfect for Greta Hinckley, except she wouldn't give Greta— ha-ha—the time of day. And Darcie wouldn't give it up.

She could now tell Walt exactly what time it was in both Sydney and New York, which didn't quite impress him.

"How did you get so smart?"

"I have friends in high places." For example, Dylan had hit her G-spot, dead-on, at least three times the night before. Darcie smirked at Greta, then into the phone. She tried to concentrate on what Walt was saying.

"Well, get this. We uncrated those case pieces last night. And—wait for it—they're all wrong. Pecan instead of walnut. Etched glass not frosted doors on the armoires."

Darcie's heart sank. "How do they look?"

"Like pecan armoires with etched glass doors."

"Well," she said, ever the optimist, "we can work with that. I mean, the etched glass will allow customers to see a product through the closed doors when the frosted model would mean leaving them open all the time. More flexibility. I hadn't thought of that."

"So you think we should keep the pecan?"

She wouldn't go that far. "It doesn't complement the rest of the décor. I'd rather have walnut."

"So would I. Let me see what I can do."

Darcie made a suggestion. "Maybe we could use the pecan for the store's opening, then switch to walnut as soon as it's available." She paused. "For a hefty discount, of course. Considering the inconvenience we've suffered."

"Baxter, sometimes you're a genius."

She grinned. "Remind yourself to give me a generous raise. A couple of vacation weeks, too." Right now, with Dylan in town, would be good.

"Let's not be premature." Walt sighed. "There's more."

"Don't tell me. Our mannequins showed up without any arms or legs."

Across the aisle Greta blinked and leaned closer into the space that separated their desks. Darcie turned a shoulder to her. She hadn't forgiven Greta for the Henry Goolong incident. Her mind scrambled. If there was a problem, they would use just torsos. With a bit of ingenuity, she'd come up with an innovative display that would make limbless models the newest trend in window design. Since Dylan's surprise appearance on her doorstep, she felt she could do anything. Multiple orgasms? Simultaneous climaxes? Her forte. His, too, it seemed.

"Wallpaper," Walt was saying.

"Excuse me?" He'd interrupted a quick, pleasant daydream of Dylan in the flesh, all of it, his impressive pecs beneath that crisp, sleek smattering of hair over his breastbone, the hard planes of his washboard belly...

"Are you listening? The *wallpaper*. It's on the walls. The wrong damn stuff."

Darcie froze. She could handle late orders. She could deal with the wrong display cases. With wallpaper, she hit overload.

"You mean they hung the wrong *pattern?*"

"You ordered Regency Stripe, right?"

"Yes, gold on a paler shade of gold. Very subtle. Classy."

"We got black stripes on white. Hell, the whole place looks like zebra hide."

Darcie groaned. "If we were in Africa..."

"We're not. And haven't you about exhausted your capacity for optimism here? Baxter, we're running out of time. Goolong's designs for the lingerie go into production next week, the soonest the factory can manage, which makes them only *possible* for the big day, not probable. What in hell do we do now?"

Miffed by his criticism of her personality, Darcie let the silence build. Finally, she said, "Henry's happy with his contract. We have the designs—and they're gorgeous, just what I hoped for. Even his faxes look wonderful. You take care of getting production flowing. I'll deal with the wallpaper."

"How?"

She threw up her hands. "I don't know, Walt. Maybe you should have sent me to Australia." Except then, she'd have missed Dylan. This time, here, might be all they'd have. "Okay. Rip off that paper with your own two hands if you have to. I'll call around to suppliers, see where I can get the Regency Stripe we need. By next week all of this will seem like a bad dream."

At her blithe tone, his voice twanged with suspicion. So

did Greta's gaze from across the aisle. "What's responsible for your Walt Disney mood today?"

"Who, not what," Darcie corrected. "I'll ring you back as soon as I can."

"You mean Rafferty?"

She hung up on his growled response. Nothing would spoil today, not even disaster at Wunderthings Sydney. She might be optimistic and naive, but she knew how to get things done.

Inspired by Dylan, who was waiting for her at home, Darcie had her calls made in half an hour. The Regency Stripe wallpaper was on its way from a Thirty-Fourth Street warehouse in Manhattan to the Queen Victoria Mall in Sydney. When Greta started across the aisle at last, as if no longer able to contain herself, Darcie grabbed her tote bag and stood up. She envisioned Dylan lying in her bed, bare-chested, those dark tufts of silky hair showing at his armpits...

"I'm leaving early." She blocked Greta's way, feeling strong and, for once with Greta, in command. "Stay, Hinckley. Don't take another step. And if you even think about sabotaging this project—again—I will personally cut out your heart."

Greta huffed out a breath. "Well. I only wanted to help."

"That's what Madame de Farge must have said while she watched all those heads roll into baskets at the guillotine in Paris. Keep knitting. I'll be home if anyone really needs me."

There was no telling how long Dylan could stay in New York. While he was here, Darcie meant to make the most of him. She promised herself she wouldn't expect more.

Girls just want to have fun. Annie's words.

Chapter Seventeen

Still shaking her head over Greta, Darcie walked into her apartment and heard conversation from the kitchen. Following the sound, she discovered Annie fixing dinner with Dylan.

Darcie's heart rolled over.

Her sister's hand was tucked beneath Dylan's on the handle of a big cooking pot. Darcie inhaled a mix of aromas she mostly didn't recognize. In the pan oil sizzled and spit. The oven light winked red, indicating that something was also baking.

"What's happening?"

They both looked up, guiltily, Darcie thought. Like Julio and Gran.

Then Annie giggled, looking back at Dylan, who, with a quick glance at Darcie, guided her other hand to stir whatever was in the pot. Annie wore a skintight spandex top that stopped above her navel and a pair of low-slung capri pants, also stretchy, that defined every inch of her long legs, and Darcie realized her sister had been giving Dylan too many approving glances since he'd come to stay with them. Annie grinned at her.

"Imagine me, learning to cook Australian."

"Meaning?" Despair joined Darcie's alarm. They were standing too close together and Dylan wore his Akubra, to Darcie always a sexy sign. She tried to distract herself. In Sydney, she had been subjected to both gourmet cuisine of various nationalities, with Walt, and—in Dylan's company—traditional Aussie fare. Her figure still hadn't recovered from the "meat pies," hefty portions of beef and gravy in a doughy pastry. And she'd never noticed before how tiny her kid sister's butt was.

A quick memory flashed through her mind: Annie, dressed for her prom in Cincinnati, getting help from her date who pinned on her corsage, his fingers brushing Annie's chest above her low-cut gown. He'd been Darcie's boyfriend, once, and too old for Annie, but "borrowing" him didn't bother him, or Annie, in the least.

Dylan sent Darcie a smile she couldn't interpret, then draped an arm over Annie's shoulder. In a dark shirt and worn jeans, he made Darcie's mouth water—and not from hunger. "We're making fish 'n chips tonight. You're late."

"I'll clean up the mess," Annie promised.

And steal Dylan in the process? The scene looked too cozy for Darcie's comfort. What had they been doing before she came in? She edged closer to the stove, then stepped back when the oil hissed at her. From a safer distance she craned her neck and saw clumps of battered fish floating, bubbling, in the grease. Potato slices bobbed among them. She could feel her mood going farther south.

"Please open a window. We'll all suffocate in here."

Releasing Annie, Dylan bent to examine the oven's contents, which Darcie couldn't see. His gold signet ring chinked against the side of the pan.

"Damper," he explained, straightening like Annie's prom date after he'd stuck the pin through her cleavage…no, corsage.

Darcie's stomach churned. "And that is…?"

"Unleavened wheat bread." Heavy, Darcie decided. "Usually, it's baked in the ashes of a campfire—but of course here in the big, dangerous city, you girls don't even have a barbie."

"You mean a grill?" Darcie frowned, not wanting to rise to his bait on this particular topic. "Our landlord won't allow it."

Annie jumped in. "This building is so old, one spark and everything we own would turn to ashes. After a really good blaze."

"See?" Dylan said. "This environment is lethal."

Darcie scowled. "I happen to love New York. If you're not happy here—"

He gave her a bland look of obvious reproach then continued, "The bushmen ate damper to kill their hunger."

"I'm sure it was effective."

She'd be digesting this meal for weeks.

"C'mon, Darce," Annie coaxed. "I think it's great Dylan's showing us how people eat in his country." She plucked the Akubra off his head and clamped it on her own red hair. "I may even visit someday myself."

"Make that September. I'll put you to work on the station. Shearing sheep."

Annie made a face. "Doesn't that hurt them?"

"Nope. Unless you're careless and give 'em a nick." He pulled Annie close again. "You come with her, Matilda. I'll let you shear Darcie II. You need practice."

"I've lost my appetite," she murmured, and left the room.

Her eyes stung—from the cooking oil, she assumed. Her vision blurred. She marched into her bedroom, slung her tote bag against the wall, and blinked. Idiot. She wasn't about to cry. Why should she?

So Dylan Rafferty obviously had the hots for her kid sister. Annie was a cute trick, she had to admit, and she didn't have Darcie's hangups, her confusion about life. Sure, Annie was homesick and she still hadn't gotten a job—probably never would, as long as Hank and Janet continued to pay her rent—but she had few inhibitions. Darcie could attest to her sexual freedom with Harley— and others.

But darned if she'd wind up like Greta Hinckley, hating other people for their good fortune.

"Hey, darling." Dylan's soft tone from the threshold made her eyes fill.

"Go away."

Behind her, he leaned one shoulder against the door frame. Darcie saw him in her peripheral vision but didn't turn around. "Annie's getting the fish 'n chips out of the pot. We even have newspaper to wrap them in—the *New York Times* ought to be right up your alley—and the damper's out of the oven." He spoke to her like her father. "Wash your hands and come sit down. We're ready."

"Bully," she muttered.

"Hey, you think I'm—"

"No, I meant 'goody' for you. And Annie. Enjoy your meal."

"You're acting like a little kid. What's wrong?"

"I have PMS. You've been warned."

Dylan stayed where he was but his tone softened.

"Your breasts ache tonight?"

She whirled around, her cheeks heating. *"What?"*

"Your belly feels swollen and tender?"

"You are playing with fire, Rafferty—and not from the barbie."

"Your temper's on the short fuse?" Dylan turned into the hall with a simple, "Okay, then," and went back to the kitchen. To Annie.

"Two for two," Darcie said, blinking again. "Perfect score."

Claire Spencer wondered whether she was, instead, self-destructive. Having quit her job, she sat at the dining room table in Fort Lee and picked at her dinner. At least she was losing weight. And Samantha was in bed at mealtime.

"You're not eating," Peter said, shoveling in more Caesar salad.

"I'm not hungry."

"After a day with Sam in the park?"

"She's not walking yet. Wait until she walks."

"So what do you do?" he asked. "Play in the sand..."

"Swing."

He half smiled. "I love a woman who swings. Both ways?"

She had to laugh. "No, I push Samantha—and talk with the other mothers."

"I'm glad you have company. I wondered when you left Heritage how long it would be until you realized that the companionship of your peers, the interaction all day, is important to you."

Claire recited her litany. "It's important. But Samantha's more important."

"Top priority, I agree."

But it wasn't Peter who shoved that swing at the park until Claire's arms ached. It wasn't Peter who took Saturdays off—just one day each week would help—to spell her. It wasn't Peter who felt utterly incompetent among all those earth mothers nursing their babies in public, quieting their cries with such skill that Claire wanted to dig a hole in the sandbox and hide her klutzy head.

"You didn't put your makeup on today," Peter pointed out.

"Samantha doesn't care if I wear Desert Mocha or Sunset Peach lip gloss. She told me only the other day that she hates mascara...and eyeliner? No way."

Peter ripped off another chunk of French bread.

"Samantha doesn't talk. I tell you, you're losing it, Claire."

"Five pounds so far," she said, deliberately misunderstanding. "By next summer I'll be a dead ringer for Naomi Campbell."

He grinned. "So," he said, leaning back in his chair, "you've almost lost your pregnancy weight. You're spending time with Samantha. You even talked with that therapist. How come you still look miserable?"

"I have no clue." Was it that obvious?

"The doctor gave you—us—the green light long ago. You're healed. We can do whatever we want. Resume sexual—"

"I know," she said. Heart suddenly pounding.

He rose from his chair. He picked up his plate, then gestured at hers, not meeting her eyes. "You done?"

"Yes. Thanks."

He disappeared into the kitchen, his sandy hair gleaming in the overhead light, his incredible tush looking just right in his tailored slacks. Claire's mouth went dry.

Drier still when he came back with a bottle of wine.

He didn't say a word.

Claire studied him again as he came toward her seat, then lost him behind her, while her pulse picked up more speed. Peter leaned over her at the table, brandishing the bottle.

"How much poetry would be required to get you to come with me? Right now," he said. "I remember 'The Charge of the Light Brigade' and a few stanzas from 'The Shooting of Dan McGrew.'"

She couldn't smile. "Samantha…"

"Is sleeping. All that fresh spring air makes her ready for bed at a decent hour these days. Nights," he corrected. "So how about it? Here, or the bedroom. Living room sofa if you'd rather. Your choice."

"Peter, what if I can't…?"

But in that moment, she knew. Her obsession over Samantha, about her job, were Claire's problems—concerns she hadn't shared with Peter. She saw the flash of irritation—and loss—move over his features, and realized she couldn't obsess forever. If she did, she would lose him. Above all, Claire loved Peter. And with her decision to open a dialogue between them, as if he also knew what she had risked, Peter helped.

He feathered kisses along the side of her throat, then nibbled her earlobe. Claire shivered and reached up behind her to slide her arms around his neck. Upside down, his face appeared as she tipped her head back, and they kissed. Gently at first, his lips barely touching hers, until Claire's mouth went slack and her breath shortened and she felt the old zing of sex zip through her postpregnant system.

She couldn't remember when they'd last felt this close. She opened her mouth to him. And they really kissed.

Peter groaned.

"I'm breaking your neck," she said.

"Feels good. Keep going." The bottle clunked down on the table and he wrapped his arms around her. After a long look into her eyes, Peter slid to his knees in front of her chair. He was breathing fast now, too, and he had that look on his face she loved. Hard, focused. Sex. "I want you, Claire. Don't say no this time."

It was a first step, she thought, back to where they belonged—with each other. He buried his cheek in her lap, nuzzled at the juncture of her thighs.

Through her jeans his touch burned. Inflamed.

Oh, God, she hadn't felt this good in such a long time. "Peter…"

He kissed her through the denim. "Please get these off."

"Do you think we should really…?"

"Yes. No question."

"But I'm afraid…"

"We'll be fine. We will, Claire."

Talking softly, he encouraged her with a few lines from "Dan McGrew," about Alaskan gold, but he didn't need poetry. Neither did she. With one hand on his silky hair, she watched him take off her running shoes, her socks. He unfastened her jeans, glided down the zipper, tugged at her pants. Lifting her hips, she helped him. First the Ralph Laurens, then her bikini briefs. Thank God, she'd dug them out of her drawer today—and they actually fit again. Then she was naked. And in less than a minute, so was he.

With his gaze fixed on hers, Peter held out a hand. He drew her off the chair, onto the carpeted floor.

"Here," he said. "Let's don't break the spell."

Claire agreed. She would talk to him later about her need to be by herself now and then. Her grief over leaving Heritage. Her inadequacies he already knew about.

But in Peter's arms, with his body poised above hers once more, Claire dismissed her shortcomings. Was this a big part of what she'd been lacking? Missing? Her husband. Her marriage. Her own sexuality, combined so meltingly with his.

"I'm not going to last long," he warned her. "My sex life has been a desert."

"Don't wait for me."

But then, he lowered his head to her breast and kissed her there, on her right nipple, the one that still felt sensitive to touch, and even when he sought her left one, the still-numbed one, Claire felt her whole body come to life again, too.

She could *feel*.

Slowly, he entered her, then halfway home, paused. Her body tightened. Her heart thumped. Peter smiled down at her.

"Okay? Or too much?"

"Lovely."

To her amazement, it was. Inch by inch, he filled her, stopping to make sure she was comfortable, and as it had been between them since the first time, Claire's body went liquid and soft and welcoming, and then—like a miracle she'd given up expecting—he was there. All the way. Moving easily at first, then as Claire moaned in his intimate embrace, faster and harder and deeper. Her body began to tighten, with his, in the good way. In the next instant, with a groan, Peter came—and with that, so did she. So did she.

During the quivering aftershocks, Claire clasped him tight, her head to his, their bodies pressed together, damp and hot. Home.

"I'm sorry," she whispered, tears in her eyes. "It's been too long."

"Don't be sorry. We're fine. I told you we would be." He drew her even closer. "I love you, Claire."

"Peter, I *love* you."

Darcie lay in the dark, alone, hating herself with the usual vehemence she reserved for the one week each month when she suffered PMS.

On her side, she burrowed deeper into her pillow but kept one ear cocked for sounds from the living room. She'd eaten dinner in sullen silence while Annie and Dylan kept each other company. Their laughter had gone through her like a corkscrew, making her even more unhappy with each delicious bite of Dylan's crispy fish 'n chips. The damper she left by her plate. What if they really hit it off—and Darcie was forced next spring to attend her sister's wedding to Dylan Rafferty?

Darcie had reached for another succulent hunk of the batter-laden seafood.

Ridiculous.

He couldn't make love to her the way (all the ways) he did then switch to Annie just because she liked his cooking.

Could he?

"I'll just close my eyes and try to sleep," she whispered.

Then Dylan's murmur from the other room changed her mind. Alert with her next heartbeat, Darcie raised up on an elbow in bed. She could hear her pulse rushing in her ears. Was Annie out there, too? Darcie listened but heard only Dylan's voice.

Still, what if he wasn't alone, like her? Worse, what if he was seducing Annie on the sofa? And Annie was too awed by his deep voice and clever hands and talented mouth to answer him?

Darcie bounced out of bed—and fell flat on the wooden floor in a tangle of covers. "Great, now I'm doing pratfalls."

Swearing, she struggled to her feet. Tearing the top sheet off the bed, she wrapped it around her and crept toward the living room.

If she found Dylan on top of Annie, she'd throw them both out in the street.

Where had this primitive urge come from to safeguard her territory?

Darcie didn't stop to ponder the question.

Creeping closer, she peered around the door frame into the living room.

Dylan was on the phone. To Darcie's relief Annie was nowhere to be seen.

Maybe she'd gone out.

"Charlie's doin' fine?" he said into the receiver. Darcie studied his long, lean form stretched out on the sofa and fought back a sigh of appreciation. Lord, he was good-looking. Too bad he'd grinned like that at Annie. "You're no match for that new ram," he said with a soft laugh. "No, I'm serious. Leave that to the men. That's why I pay them. They can handle Charlie—they understand his needs."

He listened for a moment and Darcie looked her fill. His shoulders were magnificent. Good trapezius develop-ment, too, she tried to think with objectivity. His biceps rounded out his T-shirt sleeves like ripe melons, and his flat belly, his slim hips, his long, well-muscled legs in those worn blue jeans made her pulse race faster. Too bad he could be such a Cro-Magnon man.

Despite her irritation, she was rapidly turning into a puddle of need.

Hormones? Or, something more?

"You're sure everything is all right?" Dylan said with a frown. "You're not just telling me it is and when I get home—even in the slow season—I'll find the whole place gone to hell?"

Even from across the room Darcie could hear feminine outrage at the other end of the line. It only made Dylan smile.

"Okay. All right. I understand. Yes, ma'am."

More higher-pitched protest sounded through the re-ceiver.

"I will remember my manners—from now on. Talk to you tomorrow. G'night, Mum. I love you."

She heard the sputtered sign-off clearly. Darcie leaned against the door frame, wrapped in her sheet. When he hung up, still smiling, and met her gaze, she arched an eyebrow.

"Your mother?"

"She's in charge of the station while I'm gone. It's not our busy time but if I *didn't* advise her—"

"She'd do just fine on her own."

"How do you know?" Dylan stretched out a hand to her, and Darcie peeled herself away from the door to join him on the sofa.

"I'm a woman, too."

He grinned. "No argument there."

She kept a small distance between them, still annoyed over the scene in the kitchen with Annie. "We're not just helpless females who can't make a decision without a man to guide us."

Dylan shrugged. "My dad died five years ago. Until then, Mum had raised us kids and kept the house. Oh, she nursed the sick lambs like Darcie II and the orphans—with a woman's touch—but my father made the decisions. Since he's been gone, those decisions have been mine. I make them. I pay the consequences."

"Then why leave her responsible now?"

Begrudgingly, he admitted, "Because gradually, over the last five years, she's involved herself more and more with the daily operations of the farm. Because there's no one else," he added.

"What about your hired help?"

His smile faded. "Sure, but if one of them makes the wrong choice, it's not his station that goes under. It's mine. And my mother's."

"Ah-ha," Darcie said, sitting closer beside him.

"What?"

"Then you agree, it's her station, too."

Dylan looked away. "Well, hers in the sense that she lives there. The Stud's been her home for the last forty years. I hope it will be her home until she dies. It's my job to preserve that. For my own wife and kids, too," he said. "Someday."

"And you call her every night to make sure she didn't mess up?"

"I have to."

She groaned. "I'm sure she appreciates that. Not."

"Meaning?"

"Your mother raised a wonderful son. I'm very partial to him sometimes. But how do you think she feels when you check up on her? And imply she's a breath away from bankrupting the place she obviously loves?"

Dylan remained silent for a long moment.

"You think that's why she was screaming at me?"

Darcie rolled her eyes. "It's a strong possibility."

He sighed, then draped an arm along the back of the sofa. His hand inched closer until he touched the nape of Darcie's neck and she shivered at the contact.

"Dylan, how can you be so dense about this? You and Deidre, for instance. She's obviously an intelligent person, independent and strong. She runs her own station right next to yours—"

He looked stubborn again. "It's her dad's station."

"You can't believe that. Red gingham curtains, and babies, as opposed to barns and sheep dip and tractors?" She snorted. "Guy stuff, women's business? Come on."

Dylan tried a smile but his eyes stayed serious. "Do we have to talk about this? Because I'd much rather take you to bed and make up for whatever was going on tonight at dinner."

She rubbed her cheek against his hand but wouldn't let the subject go. "I love a man who speaks his mind—even if it's to express his outdated attitudes. Is this the way you think about Deidre?"

"That's different."

"How, Dylan?"

He set his jaw. "Deidre's an only child. She'll inherit that station only because there's no one else."

Good grief, it's still the nineteenth century there. "So she runs it—successfully, I assume—by default."

."She and her father run it. For now."

"And he gets the deciding vote."

Dylan's fingers stopped moving on her skin.

"I wonder if it's a good idea for a woman to go to college."

"Oh!" Darcie leaped up from the sofa.

"Every guy I know thinks the same way."

"You see? This is why we should have ended whatever this…this is when I left Sydney. The sex was good, but—"

"The sex *is* great. In fact, we should do it again. Right now."

"Does that usually work for you? Manipulation?" She planted her hands on her hips and stared him down. "You're really cocky tonight."

He raised his eyebrows. "You better believe it."

His husky tone wouldn't sway her. Her own hormones, either, or—a quick glance at his jeans—Dylan's arousal.

"I am not crawling into bed with you after an argument."

"Why not?" His gaze darkening, Dylan caught her hand and drew it to the hard ridge of his fly. Darcie's fingers twitched on the denim. She felt her bones melt.

"I'm not in the mood," she lied.

"Yes you are. With me, you're always in the mood."

He was right. Darn him. The past days had been the best of her life.

But where could this lead? He was like some throwback to the 1950s. Still… "Things are changing, Dylan. Even in your country, they are. I saw that for myself in Sydney. Are you telling me your wife's income wouldn't help Rafferty Stud?"

"I don't want my wife to work. I earn my crust— enough for both of us."

"Oh, brother."

And she'd thought he understood about Henry Goolong, about her job. Darcie let out a breath of defeat. Like Dylan, her father pretended not to hear what he didn't want to deal with. No way could she get deeply involved—more deeply involved—with a man just like Hank Baxter. For a terrible moment, her mother's image flashed across the screen of her closed eyelids.

Then she opened them and Dylan was staring at her, serious and determined and very, very sexy. He drew her close.

"You're right. I'm a caveman." His eyes darkened another shade.

"I didn't say—"

"I'm also horny." His mouth covered hers before she
wiped away her grin. Their teeth clicked together, then
Dylan reangled his head and took her mouth again. And
this time he got it right. Oh, boy, was it right, even if he
wasn't right for her.

Before she realized his intention, Dylan had swung her
up into his arms.

"You'll break your back," she warned him, enjoying his
strength anyway.

"You're light as a Lamington."

"Is that good?"

"And just as sweet. Lamington is sponge cake," he told
her. "My favorite, squares with raspberry jam, chocolate
frosting, coconut…"

Her mouth watered again. For cake, for him. Dylan
carried her through the apartment, down the hall, into her
room. Laying Darcie on the tangled sheets, he followed
her down onto the bed and began to kiss her.

"Let's get basic here. Why do you think I tucked up
close to Annie in the kitchen? Teased her through dinner?
I wanted to prove to you—I guess just as my mother wants
to prove to me how capable she is—that it's fine to feel
jealous. About Annie. Or Deidre. Or any other woman."

"That's your point?" But of course she knew.

"And this." Dylan dipped down to her mouth for another soul-destroying kiss. His hands roamed over her
body, and her skin—that most sensitive of all organs—
leaped to instant life. "Matilda, you're as primitive as I
am." She tingled everywhere. Without planning to, she
raised her mouth to his again, seeking his tongue with hers.
And moaned.

"Point taken."

Dylan spooned them together in her warm, cozy bed,
and outside, a siren shrieked past. The garbage truck rolled
down the street, stopping every few feet to grind trash loud
enough to wake the dead. The smell of the river drifted

through the cracked-open window, and the complex scent
that was the subway's alone, an aroma that would always
remind Darcie of New York—and this night. Still, she
tried once more.

"Dylan, we're totally wrong for each other."

"You think so."

He half covered her with one strong leg, and that touch
of crisp hair and clean male skin reinvigorated her already
sensitized flesh. Dylan moved down her body, inch by area,
from shoulders, collarbone, breasts, to Darcie's never-small-
enough-to-suit-her waist, her bloated-at-the-moment belly,
her hips.

Dylan laid his cheek against her tender abdomen.
"When your stomach hurts and your breasts ache and your
temper's on the rise at every little thing, don't you know,
Matilda? I can help."

His hand played through the curls between her thighs
until he found her very center and Darcie gasped with
pleasure.

"Dylan!"

"See? We're absolutely…right."

In the next instant he shifted—and entered her on one
long, smooth, elegant stroke. And Darcie lost all thought
of wrong or right. Then or now. Man or woman. Time,
place—the rattle of the garbage truck fading into the distance around the corner onto Madison…even their differences ceased to exist.

Australia. New York.

City Girl. Country Boy.

Tradition. Feminism.

For now, Darcie pressed up into his embrace, into his
body, and let the joining take her. No points. Just being.
Together. Oh, so tightly together that they might have
been one.

He annoyed her, she irritated him, but until tomorrow
their differences could wait.

Perhaps, she thought, just maybe…

Dylan Rafferty might be trainable.

Chapter Eighteen

"If I were only fifty years younger..."

Her grandmother's first reaction to Dylan didn't surprise Darcie. She'd waited on purpose to introduce them until his last night in America. Having Eden put the moves on him was not Darcie's idea of fun, and after settling the matters of Deidre and Annie and her own unexpected jealousy, she still felt a bit raw about competition. Dylan had dazzled the entire office at Wunderthings the day before although she'd kept him away from Greta. Tonight Eden sported full warpaint and a diaphanous flow of sapphire hostess lounging pajamas.

"I wouldn't put it past you, Gran, to charm his pants off—literally."

When Dylan tipped his Akubra hat, "Pleased to meet you, ma'am," Eden pressed one hand to her chest. The other stayed clamped in Dylan's larger grasp. "Matilda—Darcie—has told me all about you."

Eden arched a penciled brow at her granddaughter. "I'll assume the news was good."

"Spectacular," he said, and winked.

With a flirtatious grin, Gran finally removed her hand

from his and stepped back out of the doorway to her duplex, motioning them inside.

The smells of pot roast and just right, oven-browned
potatoes greeted Darcie, who felt her toes curl. "Ahh. You
made my favorite dinner."

"Beef," Dylan said with an appreciative sniff. "Mine,
too."

"I thought it was lamb," Darcie said.

He winced. "I have a tough time with that. Makes me
glad I run a wool operation, not a meat business."

Glad to hear that—in all this time she hadn't wanted to
ask for fear her namesake was doomed to end up in a pot—
Darcie drew him into the living room with a quick glance
around for Sweet Baby Jane. She didn't want Dylan at-
tacked, especially when he was wearing his best dark pants
and a white shirt that wouldn't look good with gore on
it. The coast being clear, she led him to the sofa.

"Sit. Relax. What are you drinking?" Eden asked just
as the doorbell rang again. "Oh, this is fun. Here's Julio."

Dylan grinned at Darcie. He'd heard about Gran's boyfriend, too.

In no time the two men were fast friends, talking about
World Cup soccer as if they'd known each other for years.
Maybe their differing accents gave them a common bond
or something. In any case, Darcie was grateful. She'd envisioned a long evening of awkward conversation filled
only by her stiff attempts to draw everyone out. The
housewarming party was still too fresh in her mind.

No longer needed, she drifted into the kitchen.

"May I help you, Gran?"

Eden bear-hugged her, rooster-print potholders like
clumsy paws on both hands. She felt oddly fragile in Darcie's embrace and Darcie frowned despite Gran's chipper
tone. "It's good to have you home. And that young
man…" She lifted her eyebrows. "If you tire of him anytime soon, while I'm still 'available,' I can take him off
your hands."

"Don't you try. What do you mean 'available'?"

"You'll find out later. I told you, the hat's the key. But

what's under it—all the way down—is genuinely first-class, too. That man has *genes*...and I don't mean from Levi Strauss."

"He's not a side of beef like your pot roast."

"Don't be too sure. Even Janet couldn't disapprove."

"Mom won't get the chance." Darcie's smile faded. "He's leaving tomorrow."

She couldn't quite get used to the idea.

Eden pursed her lips, shiny mauve tonight. Still, Darcie thought her cheeks looked pale. Was Gran worried about her? "Please don't tell me you intend to let him go. You'd have beautiful children, dear. While I'm young enough to enjoy them, I hope."

"Let's not go there—or we'll end up fighting." Darcie took the potholders from her, then removed the roast from the oven. "You serve the drinks. I'll deal with this. Do you want gravy?"

"Would it be my pot roast without?"

"No, of course not. Silly me." She turned off the bubbling peas on the stove.

Eden bustled about, fixing Julio's Manhattan—giving him two plump maraschino cherries—then uncapping Dylan's beer. She pushed Darcie's white wine across the counter to her and set aside her own Merlot.

"I'll be right back. Then we'll talk."

"Gran."

But she was already gone. Darcie mixed water and flour for the gravy. She stirred it into the drippings to thicken, found Gran's best Limoges bowl and dumped the peas in, then looked for the electric knife to slice the meat.

She did anything to help—to keep herself from thinking about Dylan's departure. Would it be better to sleep apart tonight? Accustom herself to her solitary bed again? Or should she jump him as soon as they got home and make herself some memories to rival those of her trip to Sydney?

It didn't take long to make her decision.

"Here. Let me do that." Dylan appeared, took the knife from her and skillfully cut the pot roast. Between each slab, he leaned over to kiss her. The kisses got longer and hotter until Darcie heard herself gasping.

"Save yourself," she managed. "I have plans for you later."

"I hope they're the same plans I have for you."

She was about to agree when pain shot through her ankle. Darcie yelped—and glanced down to see Sweet Baby Jane, her sharp teeth piercing Darcie's skin. Bending, Dylan gently pried the cat away and scooped her up.

"Moving to my own apartment was the best decision. The word *kill* crosses my mind," Darcie murmured.

"This little sweetheart? She barely broke the skin." He held Jane up at face level, and Darcie waited for the beast to take out an eye, but Jane only purred, then settled against his chest. "See?" Dylan said. "She probably bit you because she was afraid you'd step on her. You have to know how to treat her."

Darcie remained skeptical. "Oh, sure. Was that the problem?"

Slipping Jane an end of pot roast, Dylan set her on the floor. With a devoted SBJ following, leaving Darcie speechless, he carried the platter into the dining room where Gran's table was set with her Haviland china and Waterford crystal and the heirloom Irish lace cloth she'd inherited from her own grandmother. *If I spill gravy on that,* Darcie told herself, *I'll die right here.*

Maybe that would save her another attack by Sweet Baby Jane—or dying tomorrow morning when Dylan left.

To keep from falling into a depression, she ate too much. Why not? She was hungry and after tonight, she wouldn't have a man to look good for. "As if I need to define myself through Dylan, or anyone else," Darcie reminded herself. Then another glass of Chardonnay seemed wise to wash everything down, and drown her growing misery. Thank heaven the conversation proved lively. By the time dessert rolled around, Darcie felt like a roly-poly clown from FAO Schwarz. A dizzy one.

How could she alternately enjoy an evening, and pray for it to end?

"I have the important news to announce," Julio said in his careful English before Darcie dug into her coconut cream pie. "Attention, all of us." He rapped his fork against his glass and the antique crystal chimed. Darcie's ears rang.

"Julio," Gran scolded gently but he didn't seem to hear.

He cleared his throat, the Waterford still ringing. "Señora Eden is to become—"

"His fiancée," Gran supplied, her pale cheeks suddenly flushed with color.

Dylan was the first to recover. "Beaut," he said.

"I—I—" Darcie tried twice but nothing else came out.

Eden's expression fell. "You're not pleased, dear?"

"Well, I—" Her eighty-two-year-old grandmother, a bride again? With a groom half her age? Not that it should matter...

Dylan's arm came around her shoulders. "Matilda's just surprised. It's good news. Isn't it, darling?" He squeezed her, prompting a response.

"It's—wonderful. Yes." Somehow, she found herself standing. On stiff legs, she moved to her grandmother's chair and leaned down to kiss her. When she clasped Eden's hands, they felt chilled. "Best wishes, Gran. I love you."

"You're not shocked?"

"Well. Only a little. I wasn't expecting this, that's all."

"Your mother and father will be mortified."

"That's their problem." Darcie turned to shake Julio's hand, then Dylan clapped him close in one of those male hugs that always looked embarrassing to both men, not to mention bone-breaking. Dylan's embrace all but smothered the smaller Julio.

"Good going, mate." He pronounced it *might*. "So you're set on a bit of Trouble and Strife," Dylan added with a smile. "That's Aussie slang for wife. Congratulations."

To Darcie the last sounded like a question. Many of his statements did, but to her the uncertainty fit the occasion.

"This calls for a celebration." Eden rose from the table.

Her cheeks had lost their brief high color, and Darcie again thought she looked ashen. Did she fear Darcie's opposition—like Janet's? It didn't seem like Eden. "Let me get the champagne."

"No, I will. You sit down, Gran."

Avoiding the snap of SBJ's teeth on her way past, back in the kitchen, buying herself time, Darcie hauled champagne flutes from the upper cabinet. Juggling four glasses and a cold bottle of Piper Heidsieck, she hurried to the dining room, her heart still pounding.

She and Eden had been buds—of very different ages, but still fast friends.

She would be the first of Darcie's friends to be married except for Claire. Darcie didn't count cousins. Was it jealousy she felt now? Again? On the very night before Dylan left?

"Stiff upper lip," she ordered herself.

Because part of her wanted to feel joy for Eden. Julio, too.

The rest of her wanted to bawl.

A remaining scrap or two wanted to slap herself.

"Selfish," she mumbled. She'd be losing a friend in some ways—but gaining a new...what? Stepgrandfather? At forty-something, small and dark, unlike her real grandfather who'd been big like Dylan, Julio didn't suit the role. He would come between her and Gran now, even if he didn't mean to. He already had.

With their rift over Julio and the apartment nearly healed, now this.

Darcie struggled with the champagne cork until Dylan covered her hand, and she gave him a blind smile of appeal. *Help me.*

"You just want an excuse for another kiss," she murmured.

"Good idea." Picking up his cue, he bent to her mouth then kissed each of Darcie's cheeks, blotting up twin tears that had escaped. The cork popped and bubbles flowed down the bottle's side.

She swallowed. "I propose a toast." Seeing nothing in

front of her, Darcie managed to pour the wine into four glasses. *Rise to the occasion.* "To Gran—Eden Marie Baxter—and Julio—" She didn't know his middle name and stumbled over the words.

He said, "Martin Perez."

"—and Julio Martin Perez...long life, and happiness."

"Thank you, dear." Eden raised her flute to her mauve-painted lips. She pressed her free hand to her throat and her cheeks went virginal white. "With your blessing, we're going to be married."

Then she slipped, unconscious, to the floor.

"Too much excitement," Darcie told Dylan. "That's all it was." They had just returned from the hospital where Gran was "resting comfortably," as the saying went.

"I'm sure her other tests tomorrow will be negative, too," Dylan agreed, "like her EKG was normal."

"She was just too excited over her engagement to Julio. And wasn't he wonderful with her in the E.R.? I do feel better," she said. "They're going to be happy together. I know he'll take care of her."

Dylan pulled her close as soon as she shut her apartment door. "Since you mention excitement..." In the darkened entryway he nuzzled her neck, then kissed her, his hands snaking up under her sweater to cup her breasts.

"You didn't have to delay your trip home," she said with a small moan. "You have the Stud to run, all those decisions..."

"My decision was to stay right here. Until Eden's home, you need someone to lean on." When she opened her mouth, he covered her lips with one finger. "No arguments, Matilda. There's no shame in needing someone..."

Darcie blinked. She'd done a lot of that during the evening. In the hospital waiting room she'd paced and worried and shed a few tears for her grandmother's well-being. She couldn't imagine Eden being seriously ill. She was one of the strongest women Darcie had ever known. It was Janet who took to her bed with the slightest cold. Eden bulldozed her way through without complaint, but if her heart no longer worked right...

"She's had angina for years. I don't know what I'd do without her," she murmured. "Without you."

"Fortunately, you won't need to face either one tomorrow."

He walked her into the bedroom, and Darcie didn't think of refusing him. She had promised Dylan a last night he wouldn't forget, promised herself the same. How could she renege on that promise, even if he wasn't leaving yet?

Exhausted from tension, still worried about Eden, she slipped off her shoes, then her skirt and sweater.

"You're a pretty good guy to have around. Thanks for tonight."

Dylan came up behind her. She felt his bare chest against her spine. Bending his head, he kissed first her left shoulder then the right.

"Don't thank me yet. I haven't started."

"I thought that's what foreplay is all about." She shivered when his lips grazed the nape of her neck, a sensitive spot Darcie hadn't noticed until she met Dylan.

"You call this foreplay?" His smile tickled her neck. "I feel like a man on death row who just got the governor's order of clemency. Two minutes before the warden threw the switch."

"You call that foreplay?" Darcie echoed. But she was smiling, too.

This, she thought, would be one of those playful times. Tonight, she didn't need to fight back tears after all, or store up memories. Until Gran came home, Dylan was staying. Staying in Darcie's bed.

She froze under his roaming hands.

Good grief. Was that what it took? Dylan, calling an ambulance, holding Gran's hand in the E.R., holding Darcie's at the same time, expediting paperwork at the admissions window, soothing Julio's worst fears, fetching everyone coffee? He was right. He made good decisions and he knew how to implement them. There were worse things than putting your trust in a man like that.

She turned in his arms. "I know this sounds terrible, but I almost hope Gran needs to stay in the hospital for a few more days. Just to make sure she's all right."

Dylan drew back to grin at her. "I haven't been in a hurry but I should get home. Why don't you just come with me, Matilda? Spend a couple of weeks at Rafferty Stud?"

"With *the* Rafferty Stud."

His voice went throaty, his eyes serious. "Never know where that might lead."

Catching her off balance in more ways than one, Dylan tumbled her onto the mattress. Darcie didn't fight him. Why should she? She'd seen the looks from everyone at Wunderthings when she showed up with Dylan yesterday. She was the envy of every woman in the office. Darcie wound her arms around his neck and hung on tight. At the moment she even envied herself.

She covered his mouth with hers, teased her way inside, dueled with his tongue until he groaned, and Darcie did, too.

He said hoarsely, "If you could have seen your face when Eden crumpled to the floor..."

"I was so afraid. I don't want to think about that now. Make love to me, Dylan."

They kissed awhile before he said, "You bet."

When he slid into her on a long, powerful stroke, his arms tight around her, his body filling hers by slow degrees, Darcie wondered how she would ever say goodbye.

As if he felt the same, he propped his elbows on the mattress, then framed her face in both hands. His dark eyes looked into hers and held. She saw a whole world in his gaze, a world she wanted fiercely on one hand, feared desperately on the other. He might be trainable—*might*—but their differences still existed.

She still didn't know how to bridge them. Distance. Lifestyles. Attitudes.

And yet, tonight, again...

Dylan's breathing sounded labored. "I can't wait, Matilda."

"Then don't."

Holding him close, she savored the rocking of his body into hers, faster, deeper, harder, then faster yet, until she realized he was way ahead of her, and Darcie stepped outside herself to relish his orgasm first. She felt his body pause, stiffen, begin to shudder...

Behind them, the fire escape vibrated with footsteps. Over Dylan's suddenly rigid shoulders, with widened eyes Darcie watched a dark figure appear at the glass. The window opened, and a man climbed through into the bedroom. Uh-oh, she thought, but it was too late.

With a groan, Dylan tensed. He rolled off Darcie. Before she could speak, Dylan launched himself at the intruder—and took him down onto the carpet. A shout rang out.

"Ouch! Christ. What the—"

It was an unwise move, Darcie told herself, still prone in bed, to interrupt an aroused male—specifically the Rafferty Stud—on the verge of a tumultuous climax.

Dylan's hands locked around a throat. His knee pressed into a polo-shirt clad chest. "*Got you*. Darcie, quick. Call 911!"

Chapter Nineteen

"Dylan, let him go. I *know* him."

Still apparently dazed, Dylan stared back at her. "But he—"

"This is my neighbor." She'd told him about Cutter but obviously Dylan had forgotten. He wasn't fully aware just now.

On the floor in his khakis and a navy V-neck sweater Cutter made a strangled sound. Dylan's hands were still at his throat and he straddled Cutter's prone body.

Dylan sent her a dubious look. "Let him up?"

"Absolutely."

Cutter slowly sat up and shook his head, as if he couldn't comprehend what he saw. Belatedly, Darcie realized she was naked. So was Dylan. No sense making silly excuses for his presence in her bed. She didn't owe Cutter an explanation.

As discreetly as possible, Darcie scooped up Dylan's shirt from a chair and slipped it on herself. She tossed him his jeans.

Cutter eyed Dylan with obvious suspicion. "Who the hell are you?" His fists loosely wadded at his sides and his spread-legged stance, though wobbly, indicated his readiness for further battle. "*I* ought to call 911 and have the cops arrest you for assault."

"Me?" Dylan zipped up his pants with apparent unconcern that he'd been caught with them down in the first place. Aussie culture, Darcie thought, like Lamington cake and beer and that heavy-duty damper. "You must be *bonza*—crazy—if you think I'm going to apologize. Throw a leg over the windowsill in a woman's apartment in the middle of the night and you have the balls to feel outraged?" He turned to glare at Darcie. "You *know* this bloke? And you *let* him enter your apartment like this?"

Darcie hastily introduced them before they killed each other.

"Remember what I said? Cutter sometimes forgets his key."

"Oh, yeah. Right," Dylan muttered.

"I live above Darcie," Cutter said with an edge to his tone. "It's a short flight from the ground up the fire escape."

"If you can open her window, why not do the same with your own?"

"Mine's locked. With a grate."

Dylan sent her another look of reproach. "Two women, living in New York. On the first floor, dammit, where anyone can walk in. If I had my way, Darcie would be in Cincinnati—or somewhere else safe." Another glance. "Since we haven't worked that out, if you ever even think again of using this bedroom window to settle your problem—"

"Who is this guy?" Cutter said again, obviously not meaning Dylan's name.

Dylan took a step forward, murder in his eyes, and Darcie laid a restraining hand on his arm. His muscles felt brick-hard. She could almost hear his teeth grinding.

"Let me take care of him," Dylan muttered.

"Will you two *stop?*"

The air seemed so thick with testosterone she could barely breathe. Eden might think that having two men

fight over you was a plus, but at 3:00 a.m. Darcie disagreed. If she didn't intervene, they would kill each other—
or try. After wrestling sheep and bales of hay in Australia,
Dylan's fitness was not in question, but she wasn't as sure
of Cutter. She didn't want to see them fight, especially
over her.

Cutter's equally hard gaze slashed down Dylan's frame
from his dark hair to his broad shoulders to his still-hard
groin.

"Sorry I intruded on your good time." He turned to
her before Dylan could answer. "Darcie, could I see you?
In private?"

Dylan tensed but Darcie released his arm.

"Wait here. I'll just be a moment."

"I'm leaving the door open," he called after her and
Cutter.

Leaving Dylan and his dark-as-the-pit-of-hell gaze behind, Darcie dragged Cutter into the living room by his
sleeve. She pointed at the sofa, then chose an armchair for
herself. This certainly wasn't the time to get cozy with
Cutter Longridge—not that she ever expected to now. Except for a few kisses, he hadn't tried to touch her. So why
this jealousy about Dylan?

Darcie folded her arms. "Now that the territorial displays are out of the way, do you mind telling me what
tonight's visit is all about?"

"The usual." But Cutter's gaze slid away. He laced his
hands together and stared at his intertwined fingers. A
thick strand of hair from his cowlick slipped down over
his forehead. *"Pahtly,"* he added. His Southern accent had
deepened.

"Spill it."

Cutter sighed. "Hell, I got fired yesterday. Remember
that 'make or break' project? Went out for a few drinks,
which became a lot of drinks, then ended up with a
woman I work—worked—with, someone I can't even
stand. I should have come here..." He trailed off. "No,
then I'd have had the dubious pleasure of meeting up
with—Jesus, that guy is like some cross between Keanu

Reeves and Crocodile Dundee. Only bigger, and younger. He's your Aussie?"

"Good bones, huh?"

He shook his head. "This city is all screwed up. It's screwed me up."

"It's not for everyone," Darcie agreed, feeling messed up herself—which she and Claire had already discussed.

Her pulse beat faster. Cutter had become a good friend, if an unusual companion, mostly late at night. He hadn't paid her a visit in some time, though; she hadn't even thought about him since Dylan arrived in New York.

"That was last night," she said. "What happened tonight?"

"How did you guess?"

Darcie smiled. "You don't look good, Cutter. Your hair's standing on end...your eyes are bleary."

"More drinking. Funny thing, when life is giving me the big shaft, alcohol becomes a moot point. Tonight I was with some other guys. We all drank too much. I'm the only one who made it home. The rest of 'em are bunked with the guy who lived closest to the last bar."

"You're really lucky Dylan didn't loosen your teeth. He's right. You have to stop using my window."

Cutter shrugged. "As if it would matter. The news gets worse."

Darcie held her breath.

"My father got wind of my unemployment. He's offered me a position in his bank. In Atlanta. It's an offer I can't refuse."

"The godfather, hmm?"

"Living under my mother's roof." He ran a hand through his hair. "Now I have to break my lease, pack my gear, and head south. Just when the weather's going to turn real hot and humid there. I hate summers in Atlanta."

"You could stay here, Cutter. I mean in New York, not with me."

"That's clear." He darted a glance toward her bedroom.

The door indeed stood open, and Darcie imagined Dylan just inside, monitoring her conversation with Cutter

Longridge. Which didn't endear Dylan to her at the moment. "This is my apartment," she said, as much to inform Dylan as to reassure herself. "Dylan Rafferty is my houseguest."

Cutter snorted. "Right, like I'm blind. Guess I can't blame the guy for coming at me like that." He rose to his feet, a little shaky but upright. "I better go. You still have the spare key I gave you?"

"I'll get it."

The key hung on a hook in her kitchen and Darcie retrieved it.

"When are you leaving New York, Cutter?"

"As soon as possible. Once the money stops coming in, I'm in trouble. I need that job on Peachtree Street. My mom's home cooking, too—for a while."

He didn't sound happy and neither was she. Darcie felt sad, as if she too had lost her job and was being forced to go back to Cincinnati.

"Don't make a mistake." She said, "You could look for a new job here. I'm sure you'd find something."

"Something," he said. "Know what? I'm no good at advertising, Darcie. If the industry was flying high, I'd still be no good. My portfolio looks like a schoolkid's in comparison to the other people in my office. Former office. No," he went on, "I might as well admit it. This isn't the career or the place for me."

"I'm sorry, Cutter."

In the entry hall, he hesitated. His gaze softened, and he brought both hands up to cup her face. "I'm sorry, too." He looked toward Dylan, now in her bedroom doorway, but Darcie refused to turn around. This was her life, her moment. Another first for her, she realized. "I thought you and I could...you know. Maybe have something."

"I thought so, too, at first. I think we make better friends than we would—"

He bent close to whisper against her mouth, "Lovers."

Then he kissed her. Gently, softly, tenderly.

And all Darcie felt was friendship.

Perhaps Dylan saw that, too, because he never moved from the bedroom doorway.

"Don't be a stranger." She hugged him tight. "Let me hear from you. Leave me your phone number in Atlanta and I'll call you. I promise."

"I hope you will. I'll see you again before I go."

He opened the apartment door and stepped out into the hall. Then he turned and smiled at her, his gaze blurry. Or was that Darcie's vision that wavered?

"Be happy," Cutter said.

"Whatever that means. You, too, Cutter Longridge."

Annie reached the top of the stairs just as Darcie went to shut the apartment door in her face. No surprise, after her flirtation with Dylan in the kitchen last week. Tired and a bit tipsy, she tried not to form any more rational thoughts about her decision as a result tonight. She reeled into Cutter on the landing.

"Oops."

"Steady, Miss Annie." He righted her, then kissed her on the cheek so quick Annie wondered if she'd imagined it. Why did she think it was a goodbye peck? Probably because her own mind was on the same page. He clattered up the steps to the floor above. His door slammed and Annie pushed into the apartment below.

"This place is like Newark, LaGuardia, JFK all rolled into one tonight," Darcie said.

Annie tossed her bag on the sofa, then herself. She stretched out her legs, which didn't quite seem to be attached to her body at the moment. "Landings, takeoffs, delays…" She looked around her. "Where's Dylan?"

Leaning against the bedroom door frame, he folded his arms over his chest. "You missed most of the action."

"What?" Annie said but she could feel tension all around. Thank heaven she'd had enough beer to blunt its effect. Annie hated tension. She had too much of her own to deal with.

Darcie frowned. "Cutter Longridge's defeat. You're very late tonight."

"Gee, Mom, the time just slipped away."

"Don't be cute. Janet may be on a plane to New York even as we speak."

"Oh, God. Why?"

Darcie filled her in on Eden's frightening "episode," ending with a statement that only increased Annie's discomfort. "Gran's probably fine but we won't know until tomorrow. Julio's with her now."

"All night?"

"In one of those hospital recliner chairs next to her bed."

Annie grinned, humor surfacing through the buzz of alcohol in her head.

"That's a hoot. I bet Julio's between the sheets with her right now. You know Gran. She'd rather go out having a good time than doing what the doctor says."

Darcie raised her eyebrows. She could hardly disagree.

"Where were you, Annie?"

"Here. There. Everywhere. We wound up in Chelsea…somewhere." She waved a hand in dismissal. It didn't matter.

By tomorrow, none of this would matter.

She had failed. And she knew it.

"Are you okay?" Darcie's expression gentled. She sat beside Annie on the sofa, and Dylan disappeared back into the bedroom, giving them privacy.

"After eight or ten beers and about a thousand pees in the crummy ladies' room of that lousy bar, after deciding that I am a total screwup and should admit it? I'm fine."

"Annie. You had too much beer. Go to bed."

"No, I am. Fine *and* a screwup. You know it, Darce. You've been telling me for weeks. 'Get a job, Annie.' Or 'get new friends, Annie.' Or 'don't pierce your belly button, Annie.' Well, I finally got the message."

"What happened tonight?" Darcie looked into her eyes and Annie held her gaze, unable to glance away. As sisters, they always guessed the truth before it was spoken.

"Some guys grabbed me in the rest room. The little hall that leads to the men's or women's, I mean."

"Did they hurt you?"

"No, but they got insistent. One of the guys I was with heard the commotion—heard me scream, I guess—and came running. Chairs flew. Bottles broke. Bodies crashed. The police showed up."

Darcie groaned. "Not again."

"It wasn't like our party. I had my clothes on. But a couple of people got arrested. We all have to pay damages. Mom's going to have another fit."

"Annie, this has to stop. You can't—"

"Yes. I know." She took a deep breath that didn't clear her head. Or ease her misery. "I thought if I could just *get* here—you know—everything would work. For once in my life *I'd* be the one who made it. Succeeded. But it's not going to happen. I even know why. I figured it out tonight after those jerks pushed me against the wall."

"I'm listening."

"I can't be you. I have to be me. Annie Baxter, mixed-up girl from Cincinnati." To her horror, her eyes filled. "I don't belong here, Darcie."

"First Cutter, now you. This seems to be the night for confessions."

"Know where I do belong?"

"I think I can guess."

"In Cincinnati—with Mom and Dad and the house where we grew up and the room I still love. That's why I've been homesick. I'm not ready to be on my own—not this much—and if I stay here, I'll get myself into serious trouble."

"That's possible," Darcie agreed.

"So you won't be mad if I leave?"

"I'll miss you," Darcie said, her voice thick so that Annie realized her sister didn't totally despise her. "Maybe you should get some sleep, and think about this in the morning."

"No, I'm sure," she said. "I miss Cliff, too. Every time he calls me, I cry afterward. Isn't that stupid? Last night I realized how silly it was to be here, missing Cliff while he's missing me in good old Porkopolis."

At the city's nickname, Darcie smiled. "You have a point."

"I've dated him, you know, since we were freshmen in high school. He just might be the love of my life—and what I thought was true, that finding him practically next door was just too neat and corny and convenient to be real love, is actually false. Maybe Cliff's the man for me exactly *because* he's from the same background I have. We like the same things. We have the same memories. Let's face it. What do I really have in common with Malcolm, or any other guy I met here?"

"Tattoos? You weren't skimming the cream, Annie."

"Maybe not. Or maybe I wasn't for a reason."

"What's that?"

"I didn't *want* to find the man of my dreams here. I wanted Cliff all along."

"Maybe you did." When Darcie held out her arms, Annie went into her embrace with a watery smile of her own. And a hiccup from too much yeast, hops and malt. "No more tattoos?" Darcie said, then touched Annie's brick-red hair. "No more garish color?"

"You won't have to feel responsible for me."

"Kid, I'll always be responsible for you. You're my baby sister."

With a grateful sigh, Annie settled deeper into Darcie's arms and held on until her misery faded and her beer settled and her decision to leave New York seemed absolutely right.

After Darcie had shepherded Annie to bed, she found her own room empty. Where was Dylan? Curious, she wandered back into the living room and discovered him in the entryway fiddling with the lock.

"You need a new dead bolt. A window grate, too," he said. "Since I'm staying another day or two, I can put them in tomorrow."

"Dylan, that's not necessary." She stood behind him, admiring the long line of his spine under his plain white T-shirt—a shirt they'd washed together only last night in the downstairs laundry. His briefs, her underpants and bras...that everyday intimate connection, that shared background they now had—leaving out geography, of course—would be broken soon, too. She tried not to feel depressed. "Annie's leaving," she said.

"Now? It's almost dawn. Doesn't she ever sleep?"

"No, I mean *leaving*. Like Cutter. He's going back to Atlanta so there's no reason for you to change my locks."

"He's not going today, is he?"

"No, but..."

"Then you need new locks. Because if I'm still here and that guy climbs through your bedroom window again, I'll be staying a lot longer. In—what's your big prison?"

"Sing-Sing."

Dylan straightened from his examination of her door. He turned around, slowly, his gaze intent and full of purpose. Darcie felt her heartbeat rise.

"You wouldn't want to visit me in jail. Would you?"

She remembered the erotic game they'd played about his sentence. "No. But why do violence? Cutter's harmless."

Dylan looked unconvinced. "Tell me Longridge doesn't mean anything to you."

"He's my friend."

"He didn't look like just a pal when his eyes ran down your body in the bedroom and he saw you were naked."

"Well, he is a functional male. Red-blooded, I assume." Not that she considered herself to be some femme fatale men couldn't resist...

"While I'm here," Dylan said, "I don't want him around."

Darcie planted both hands on her hips. "Are you being disgustingly macho? Or are you just tired and cranky?"

"I'm cranky and possessive." He smiled faintly. "I don't like to share."

"What about Deidre? If I have to share, so do you."

Dylan moved closer. He cocked his head to one side and studied her.

"Is that the green-eyed monster lurking again behind that this-is-just-for-kicks expression?"

"You're free to do as you please."

"So you say." Dylan's smile broadened. With satisfaction, Darcie thought.

"And that display in my bedroom was uncalled for. A complete overreaction."

"*I'm* jealous," he freely admitted. Then moved even closer. Darcie watched him, her gaze fixed on his darkening eyes. "And still hot. I have to hand it to Longridge. His timing couldn't have been more—no, *less*—perfect."

"Poor Dylan." Darcie wound her arms around his neck.

"You frustrated, too?"

"Desperate."

Dylan's head lowered and she felt the strong muscles in his shoulders flex. He wrapped her tight in his arms and touched his mouth to hers. With the first contact, Darcie felt her evening resolve itself. Gran would be all right. Cutter was leaving and so was Annie, but Darcie would find some way to pay the entire rent herself. When Dylan's tongue met hers, she felt sadness, anger, worry disappear. Dylan was still here. He still wanted her. They hadn't finished what they'd started.

"Let's go to bed," she whispered against his mouth.

"Let's stay right here."

He nudged her back against the wall in the dark entry hall, as far from Annie's room as they could get, but Darcie didn't resist. She realized why Dylan wanted to be here instead of in her soft, warm bed. It was here she'd said goodbye to Cutter, and in a continuing expression of male territorial rights, Dylan needed to take her in the same exact spot.

"You know this is juvenile, unworthy of the Rafferty Stud."

He trailed kisses along her throat, her collarbone, then the swell of her breasts—as much as they could swell when she wasn't wearing a bra.

"I don't care."

His hands swept up under her shirt (Dylan's shirt) and

found her nipples. He pushed the shirt higher until he could close his mouth over her breasts, first one, then the other in a ritual display of possession that thrilled rather than repulsed Darcie.

When Dylan dropped to his knees in front of her, when he kissed his way down her rib cage to her waist then her hips, when he nuzzled between her thighs, she nearly exploded.

"Not yet. Not yet," he said, doing such wicked, talented things to her body that she couldn't even speak, she could only gasp.

"Dylan…"

"This is *you*, Darcie." When he had her on the edge again, he took his mouth away.

Moaning, writhing under his hands, groping for his mouth to touch her elsewhere, to bring her up and up and up, she heard herself beg. "Please, Dylan."

"You," he said again and stood. She heard his zipper glide down, heard the rustle of denim when he pushed his jeans to the floor. Underneath them he was naked. He hadn't bothered with his briefs after Cutter climbed through the window. Like a jolt of Spanish fly increasing her desire, she felt him hard between her thighs, bare and smooth and silky-hot. "This is *me*."

Before she took another shaken breath, with her mouth swollen and tingling, her breasts aching and her thighs shaking, Dylan put both hands on her bottom and lifted her until she felt his erection at the juncture he sought. "Wrap your legs around me."

In the next instant he slid deep inside her, so deep Darcie knew he touched her womb. Then she knew nothing except the glide and pull, the push and tug of Dylan's body in hers, and out, and in again, their rhythm in perfect harmony, their mouths fastened tight together, her legs around him and his weight holding her to the wall, and all the sounds they made, soft but urgent, in the entry hall of her apartment.

When the climax hit, it hit them both. Hard. Long. Endless.

Finally, Dylan, still shuddering, dropped his head next to hers against the wall. "Oh, Matilda."

"That was...really good." Her heart thudded like a tire gone flat to the rim.

"Good?" He was silent for a while. Then he added, "Ass-kicking great."

Darcie kissed his damp temple. "And you're purged now?"

"Drained, all my strength gone like Samson with his hair shorn close as a sheep. I may not recover for months."

"I mean, of Cutter Longridge."

Dylan drew back. "You sure know how to break a mood. But since you have—" He broke off. "Or are you just trying to protect yourself here?"

Darcie untwined her arms from around his neck. She lowered her legs and slid to the floor, slowly down Dylan's body to show him she hadn't forgotten the mood.

"Protect myself?"

He put an arm around her neck and walked Darcie toward her bedroom. Yawning because, after all, it was nearly daylight and the sky was already pearly-gray, he said, "You do it all the time."

Her pulse leaped. Darcie didn't like the direction of this conversation. She'd had a hard enough night. Not just with Dylan.

"Can't this wait? Whatever axe you need to grind, let's do it later."

In her bedroom Dylan lifted her in his arms, then tucked her under the covers next to him. "Later will be Eden's tests, and your sister packing, and me putting in those new locks. Somehow we won't get around to it. I have things to say, and I need you to listen."

She wasn't ready. He could be stubborn—and persuasive. She needed to prepare. If that was self-protection, okay.

If he was about to dump her...after that awesome sex in the hall...

"I'm really tired, Dylan. I have to work this morning."

"So we'll go to bed early tomorrow night." He raised

an eyebrow at her. "We'll sleep, too," he added with a
half smile that died away in the next instant.

"I'm not going to like this." She lifted onto an elbow
and looked at him in the dim light. Gorgeous. Dark hair,
dark eyes, sun-browned skin. Lots of it. *What's to hate?*
Dread overwhelmed her.

Dylan drew a deep breath. "I run a lot of sheep on my
station," he admitted. "Every spring—my spring, your
fall—a bunch of lambs gets born. They frolick, gambol,
leap and play all that first season."

"Now you're getting poetic."

"Then they grow up," he went on, as if he hadn't heard
her. Dylan reached out to touch her cheek. "Those little
girl lambs are damn cute. Full of themselves. And pretty
soon, one day they're ready."

"Ready?"

"To breed. That's what it's all about, Darcie. Us, too."

She tried to rise. "You've been on the farm too long."

Dylan tugged her back down. "Maybe you should see
for yourself," he said.

"Are you asking me again to visit?"

"No. To stay."

Her pulse jumped. "You mean, live there? With your
mother in the house?"

"She'll love you."

"Me? A woman who picked you up in the Westin Sydney bar? Dylan, I don't belong in Australia." She felt sensitive to this subject, especially tonight after her talk with
Annie. "Like my sister 'forgetting' to get a job and going
back to Cincinnati, you belong at Rafferty Stud. You *are*
Rafferty Stud."

He groaned. "Not at the moment. I'm exhausted."

"I'm serious. I belong here," she said. "You should
marry Deidre."

His mouth tightened. "I don't want to marry Deidre."

But to Darcie, it made sense. "She lives next door. Like
Cliff for Annie. You could join your two stations into one
bigger operation. You understand each other, your way of
life is the same. You're compatible in bed...."

"I don't believe it. I'm with one woman who's trying to push me at another."

With every word she felt worse. But also right. "Deidre suits you. I don't."

"How do you know? You've never even seen her." Dylan's gaze held hers. "What do you think I was doing in the Westin bar that night myself?"

"Having a beer. Trolling for chicks."

"Wrong—except for the beer part. Know why I went in there? I'd had a rotten day. I was in the city on business, to buy prime livestock to expand my breeding operation, and it wasn't going well. I was tired, frustrated with the broker I use, disgusted. So I thought 'Why not? I'll have a few Foster's, fall into bed, try again in the morning. Once I get to town, which isn't often from the Outback, I stay until the business is done.'" He paused. "Then I looked across the room—and saw you."

His stare intensified. "I was glad I could stay with you those two weeks. I haven't been the same since."

She didn't know what to say. So she said nothing.

When he drew her into his arms, she didn't—couldn't—resist. So he wasn't dumping her. Wouldn't let her dump him, as if she could do that either. Her heart pounded furiously, whether in excitement or alarm, she couldn't distinguish.

"What I'm trying to tell you is, everything has its season, not to turn this into a sermon." He half smiled. "But it's true for people just like sheep. Why do you think nature gives a young woman glossy hair—" his tone rough, he ran gentle hands through Darcie's mane "—a ripe mouth—" he grazed her lips with a finger "—beautiful breasts, a slim waist, rounded hips..."

"Dylan." She would dissolve again if he didn't stop.

"Why do you think a man's shoulders get broad, his muscles hard, his beard coarse, his arms and thighs strong?"

Darcie was blushing.

"To attract a mate," he said.

"Did I ask for a biology lesson?" *This is you. This is me.*

"Listen. I'm thirty-four years old. I don't have time to

hang out in bars looking for women. I get to the city
twice, maybe three times a year. Hell, where I live a mail-
order bride's probably the best solution for a man.''

"Or Deidre."

He pulled back. "Don't throw her at me again."

"But can't you see *my* point? We've washed our underwear together, yes, but I *live* in Manhattan. I *love* Manhattan. It's not the wicked city to me, it's exciting, the
center of commerce and civilization. You live in the Outback, one of the most remote areas in the world. What
could be more different? What could make us more opposite?"

His jaw hardened. "Opposites attract. Like male and female."

"Yes, and I wouldn't change a minute of these past
weeks...or Sydney...but don't you see, Dylan? We're a
fantasy come true. I looked across the Westin bar and saw
this gorgeous guy wearing an Akubra—after Gran said
'bring one home for me, too—'"

"Great. Thanks."

"—and I did something I've never done before in my
life. I took a risk—and gave you a come-hither smile. And
you came."

"More than once," he said, but his weak smile twitched.
"I don't have time for courting games, Darcie. I want a
wife soon, some babies..."

She had to agree. "You need sons. To carry on the
Stud."

"I'm ready to settle down."

"I'm not."

"Why not?" he said.

Her heart drummed. In his roundabout way, was he
asking her to *marry* him? To live on a *farm?* His attitude,
like his earlier possessiveness, convinced her all over again
that he was, at heart, too much like her parents.

"I have the Wunderthings opening to think of...
Gran...the rest of my family here in the States, work..."

"Cutter Longridge," he said with a bitter edge. "Merrick Lowell. Do *they* make you happy?"

His touch rough yet tender, Dylan pulled her near and nuzzled her neck until she moaned. *He* made her happy. But he was all wrong for her, even if at times she wanted him to be The One. Hadn't he just proved that with his usual, traditional approach to a man with a woman?

"This is what it's all about, Matilda," he insisted. "Mating, procreation." When she didn't answer, he sighed but moved closer, behind her, his head next to hers on the same pillow. "Maybe I'm not saying this right," he murmured.

"Maybe you are." Which scared her.

Long after Dylan finally fell asleep, and his breathing sounded regular and deep in the quiet room, Darcie lay staring at her ceiling and her stars. Usually this worked. But when rosy dawn light bathed the walls, she still had no answers.

He hadn't said he loved her.

Oh, God, how could she lose him? How could she keep him?

"We'll work it out, Matilda" she remembered him saying. "We can."

Chapter Twenty

Her grandmother would survive, Eden assured Darcie the next afternoon. Dylan had gone to the cafeteria for coffee and doughnuts all around—violating Gran's new dietary restrictions, "but you only live once," she said—and the two women were alone. This was an opportunity not to be missed, and rare with Julio and Dylan always near. Darcie watched Gran check the doorway again to make sure it was empty. It didn't take her long to get to the point.

"You're *not* letting that man go," Eden persisted.

"Unless you can fake another heart attack before tomorrow, I am." Eden sent her a chiding look, and Darcie added, "What else can I do? I have a job here."

"Then why aren't you at Wunderthings now?"

Darcie smiled. It was only three o'clock. She'd left Walt fuming over a report at the same time he wished her well, and Greta most likely plotting against her, but this seemed more important. "Because my favorite grandmother is lying here in this icky hospital and I needed to make sure she was all right."

Eden picked up a hand mirror from her bed table and studied her face. "My tests were perfectly normal. My cholesterol's a bit high but the doctor has given me some wonderful new drug, without side effects, and in no time I'll be like a twenty-year-old virgin."

"That'll be the day." She grinned. "Not the twenty-something part."

Eden smiled slyly. Her auburn hair stood up in spikes, more mussed than Darcie had ever seen her. Not from illness, she suspected. Eden grappled it into place.

"I sent Julio home to feed Jane this morning—but we did have the most lovely interlude beforehand. Several, in fact," Eden said.

"Me, too." *The entryway, up against the wall, this morning, in bed, Dylan's hard weight along my back...*

"We are very lucky girls."

"Women," Darcie corrected her, as she always did Janet.

"At this age thinking of myself as a girl does wonders for my face." She smoothed lotion onto her skin, then used a dark pencil on her eyebrows.

"Whatever floats your boat, Gran."

"Full makeup. I was a ruin without it yesterday. What must those paramedics have thought when they lifted me onto the stretcher with those bulging muscles? Speaking of which..." Eden's smile disappeared. "I've met a number of your young men since you moved to New York—and Dylan is by far the best, despite Cutter Longridge. Dylan's honest, straightforward, sexy as a Chippendale dancer—"

"Better," Darcie could attest.

"—and he does something for that Akubra that could stop an old woman's heart. Not mine, of course." She applied powder-blue eyeshadow to her lids. "Dylan Rafferty cares deeply for you, dear. It's in his eyes, and the way he treats you."

"You seem to have done a thesis on the subject. Maybe he just likes doughnuts."

"No, he thinks of you before himself." She pursed her coral-painted lips. "Like Julio. Need I remind you of Merrick Lowell?"

Darcie leaned around the array of pots and jars and tubes

on Eden's table to hug her. "Merrick keeps calling but I won't talk. His choice seems clear enough. I won't play the fool a third time. I wish you the very best with Julio. I know I was less than enthusiastic at first, but I think he's just right for you after all."

"You don't mind our difference in age?"

Darcie beamed. "What do four decades matter when there's true love?"

"You adorable child." Gran held on tight. When she pulled away, her eyes were shining. "What will you do once Dylan's gone—Annie, too? I hate to see you live alone."

"You sound like Dylan."

"He's right. There's always room with me, you know. Julio likes you very much. He calls you my *niña linda*. My pretty little girl."

"I'm not a little girl, Gran."

Eden's expression softened even more. "So you keep reminding me—but you're wrong. A part of you will always be that little girl to me, and to Hank and Janet. One day you'll realize how lovely that is...to have memories with people who've known you all your life. As you really are."

Darcie blinked. "Are you trying to make me cry?"

"I'm trying to be sure you make the right choice."

"Dylan?" she said.

"If he makes you happy, yes. But don't think too much. Take happiness where you find it. Life is short, dear."

Feeling uncomfortable with Dylan's scrutiny last night, and Gran's today, Darcie drew back. When the time was right, she'd know about Dylan. About everything.

"Don't push," she said, then made a great show of smoothing Eden's blanket, rearranging her makeup bottles into neat rows as if to impose logic on her own life.

"No flat whites, sorry, ladies." *Lydies,* he said. Dylan came into the room carrying a tray full of hospital mugs and cream-filled doughnuts. His private smile for Darcie turned her knees weak.

"Flat whites?" Eden echoed.

"Ozspeak," Darcie said, "in other words, latte," fixing her grandmother's coffee the way she liked it, then handing her a paper plate with half a doughnut. "I don't think you should eat more than this, even with your new medication."

"I won't push. You won't fuss."

Dylan put an arm around Darcie's shoulders and stood beside Eden's bed, his coffee cup in his free hand. He seemed to have a need to touch Darcie all the time today. As if he knew he wouldn't be able to touch her tomorrow, or any day after that.

"Did I miss something?"

"Girl talk," Eden said.

"Womenspeak," Darcie corrected.

Dylan gave her a dark look, his smile fading. He obviously had more than touching in mind. "We'd better go. I need to pack."

Gran quickly agreed. "You two need to be alone. Julio and I spend as much time together as we can. Of course he lives right here in New York, in my own duplex—"

"Julio moved in with you?"

"Last week. Perhaps the thrill has been too much for me and explains my little 'episode' yesterday."

"I doubt it," Dylan said, grinning. "You could show us a thing or two."

"I'll be glad to. Anytime. Just call first—"

"Next time I'm in the States."

"Ah," Eden murmured, looking pleased. "And when will that be?"

"When Darcie invites me." So he was going to play hardball.

She marched to the door. "I'm leaving before this conspiracy gets worse. Gran, behave yourself. Give Julio my...love." She crooked a finger at Dylan, who had bent to kiss Eden goodbye. She said something to him that Darcie couldn't hear. Then he straightened and crossed the room to her. "I'll call tomorrow, Gran," she said. "Rest before you go home."

Dylan tipped his Akubra to her and they left.

"What was that all about?" he said in the hall.

"Guess."

"She thinks you should come to Australia, see how you like Rafferty Stud—"

"I like him very much."

"The station, Matilda." He stopped her to steal a kiss. "Eden thinks you should emigrate. See me every day. Think about babies..." He gave her another long, hot, melting kiss Darcie couldn't resist. "I agree with her," he whispered against her lips.

"Sandbagged," Darcie said to herself.

The next morning she watched Dylan toss underwear into his bag, lying open on her bed.

He wasn't as backward as she'd once imagined, but he still had a long way to go in his attitude toward men and women. Like Hank, with Janet. Darcie had to keep that in mind, or she'd be on her knees begging him to stay.

Dylan's gaze fixed on his suitcase. "I can still get you a ticket."

"This late? It would cost the earth. I couldn't even pay my rent." She couldn't pay it all anyway.

"*I'll* buy the ticket." His mouth hardened. "If you'd come with me, you wouldn't need to pay rent. I own the station free and clear."

"So your mother and I can stay as long as we want?"

Dylan closed the suitcase with a snap.

"As long as *you* want?" Darcie added.

"What's that supposed to mean?"

She could be stubborn, too. "It means I'm not ready to change my whole life. It means I'm not going to spend it in the Outback with a man who thinks I should walk three paces behind him."

He faced her, his eyes even darker. "I never said that."

"But Dylan, that's how it would be. I'd turn into my own mother—and I'm not even sure what you're offering."

"A free trip to Australia," he said, looking mulish. He

did it well, and Darcie knew she was up against a brick wall. "After that, we'll see."

"And if things didn't work out? I'd fly back to New York without a job waiting, or an apartment…" She hesitated. "I don't know if I'll ever want the traditional family you want, that my parents have had."

"That bad?"

"No, but it's not for me. Not now. I've made that clear from the start."

"And nothing has changed since we met in that bar?"

She recalled Dylan's words the other night. *We'll work it out.* And her own conjecture that maybe they could compromise. But this was all Dylan's show, his command request. Back to square one.

"I don't think so."

"Wrong. You're not that naive." Shaking his head, he avoided her gaze. "Well, since we're having a blue here— a fight—" Dylan hauled the bag off the bed and sent her a long look. "Know what I think?"

She was afraid to ask. Her throat wouldn't work. She was afraid for him to touch her. If he did, she'd give in.

"I think you're scared to death of life—and love. Do you care that much about defying your parents? Turning your back on your upbringing, your mother's way? Enough to risk your own happiness? With me," he said, "or anyone else?"

"Dylan…"

He started for the door. "I don't have a Buckley's chance here."

"What does *that* mean?" Even his slang pointed out their differences.

"No chance in hell, Matilda."

The nickname nearly undid her. What if she never heard it again? She reached out a hand to him but missed. He was already halfway down the hall to the front door. Halfway out of her life. Was that what she wanted?

But Darcie felt no closer to defining life on her own, even if she lost Dylan now. Could two people even find happiness, together? she wondered.

"You're not being fair," she said, following him when she knew she shouldn't. To her own ears, she sounded petulant. "Dylan, wait! You can't expect—"

He threw the words at her over his shoulder.

"If you want to talk, you know where to find me."

When she saw Darcie weaving her way through the lunchtime crowd at Phantasmagoria, Claire felt her mouth turn down. Uh-oh. This wasn't good. Here she'd been feeling so pleased and positive, not obsessing at all. Now, she didn't know what to say except the obvious. "You look destroyed."

"Me?" Darcie's expression perked up. "I'm fine. Never better." Her smile turned dangerously bright. "This is the first day of the rest of my life, etcetera." Claire fished in her bag for a tissue, just in case. "I think I'll have a T-shirt printed with that message."

"Dylan went home." Claire said it for her and Darcie sank onto a chair. Until that instant, Claire had thought she had life ironed out again. "You are in bad shape."

Darcie picked up her menu. "No, really. I'm okay." She studied the blank front page. "I mean, we had a great time. No denying that. But that's where it ends so he took a cab to JFK. Better for both of us."

"You told him that?"

"Many times."

"Darcie Baxter, you are an idiot. When does his flight leave?"

She didn't even have to check her watch. "Twenty minutes ago. He's probably right over our heads as we speak." She listened for a moment. "Nope. No 747s roaring above the clouds. Must be headed toward Cincinnati by now."

"Does he stop over there? You could get a Comair hop and meet him. Introduce him to your parents at the same time."

Darcie's gaze fell again. "They're coming here to take Annie home. This isn't some movie like *An Officer and a Gentleman* with one of those dopey endings."

"Richard Gere went after Debra Winger in that one."

"You've been renting movies."

"Every night. That is, when I'm not with Peter..."

Claire couldn't help it. The Cheshire grin broke across her face, in part as a diversion. Darcie shrieked, shattering the low conversations around them.

"You did it? *You did Peter?*"

The whole room turned to gape at them. Claire put her hand over Darcie's mouth. "Hush. You'll get us kicked out of here—and I'm starving. Let's order first. I'll give you the lurid details while your mouth's stuffed with shrimp salad and avocado."

"I can't believe you screwed Peter the Great."

"You should see *his* grin. Then you'd know."

Darcie clutched her hand across the table. "Claire, I'm so happy for you. I was afraid you and Peter wouldn't make it."

"Well. We did. Four times the first night."

Darcie snickered. At least her face had lost that forlorn look.

"Can you walk?"

"Yes, I can walk, thank you very much. Just a little limp now," she added. "Nothing serious. But permanent."

Darcie laughed and everyone turned toward them again.

"We talked," Claire said. Respecting Darcie's obvious heartbreak, she'd kept her news to herself as long as she could. "I'm going back to work."

"To Heritage? What about Samantha?"

"She and Peter are at the lake in Central Park right now, sailing a remote-control boat. Well, he's sailing, she's watching from her stroller. After we lunch, I'll do some shopping then meet them for dinner and the ferry home. It's Peter's day to parent. We've decided it's not fair for him to pursue his career while I abandon mine. I liked staying home, don't get me wrong." She hesitated. "And it's not fair to Samantha to be stuck in daycare. But there's more, Darcie. You were right. I *need* my job."

"What did Peter say?"

Claire leaned back in her chair, more satisfied than she'd

felt in months—since she'd delivered the baby—except, of course, for those hours with Peter the other night. "He said it was his turn. Until Sam starts nursery school, we'll juggle our hours. He said we could work it out."

Darcie winced. "That's what Dylan says—said."

"He did?" But Claire needed to finish her story first. "Peter agreed quickly after I finally laid my issues on the table—or, rather, our bed."

"What did you say?"

"That I have to be me, not just his wife or Sam's mom."

"Now you sound like Annie. She's given up playing second best to her big sister—that's me, good grief what a role model—and she's going home to find her true place. Being Annie."

"She's right. Doing what's best for me will help Sam grow into an independent, capable person, too. Peter will watch her when I work and vice versa. And I know I'll thrive with my new schedule. Three days each week at Heritage, my old title, same office. Which I'll be sharing from now on."

"With whom?"

"Another woman who just had a baby. Between us, we'll fill a full-time slot." Claire hailed their waitress to place two orders for the day's special. "And two glasses of your Chardonnay, please."

"The California—or the Australian?"

"Oh, God." Darcie's gaze dropped to the tablecloth and she blinked. Furiously. Claire could have kicked herself. The Look was back, dammit. "The Australian," Claire said for her. Hoping it was potent, like Dylan. Strong and full-bodied. Hoping it knocked Darcie to her knees, and to her senses. If that happened, she would be on the next plane, with Claire's help, to... "Where did you say he was flying?"

"To L.A. Then Sydney. I knew he was leaving," Darcie rushed on. "That was part of the deal from the start. I mean, he must be nuts to think I could walk away from everything here—"

Wait a minute. What am I not hearing? "Dylan proposed to you?"

"I don't know."

"Darcie, either he said 'marry me' or he didn't."

She gnawed her lip, waiting for the waitress to set down their entrees. As soon as she disappeared, Darcie grabbed her wine and chugged down half the glass. "He didn't. He said come visit the station. He said meet my namesake, the sheep. He said his mother would love me. He said, in effect, 'let's make babies.'"

Claire stared. "Well, it's an unusual proposal. But what else could it mean?"

"Dylan's not the most articulate guy," she admitted. "He has this laid-back, laconic style..."

"He's to die for. And you know it." Claire leaned closer. "I know I've been the last person in New York to give advice since Samantha was born. But I'm better now. Honest," she said when Darcie only shook her head. "So here's the thing. You're crazy about each other. Don't let thousands of miles or his views on being barefoot and pregnant or your climb up the ladder at Wunderthings destroy your possible happiness. It's time, Darcie."

"What if he's just been leading me on—like so many others? And I fly all the way to Australia, planning some *An Officer and a Gentleman* thing in reverse—sweep him off his feet right in the shearing shed—and Dylan says, 'Didn't you know I was using you?'"

"I think you've grown beyond Merrick Lowell. I think Dylan's good for you. When you do get married, can I be matron of honor?"

Darcie groaned and speared a shrimp. "He's good all right."

"He helped you with Eden. Didn't he? He stuck around and smoothed everything for you. He charmed her. She told me so. Julio likes him, too. I bet Hank and Janet would, and I know Annie thinks he could hang the moon—if you weren't involved with him instead."

"She's going back to Cliff. I'm no longer involved."

"Darcie Elizabeth Baxter, who are you trying to kid?"

Subsiding against her seat, Darcie rearranged her shrimp salad in its avocado shell. Finally, she threw down her fork with a sigh of defeat, and if it weren't for the lunch patrons all around them, Claire could have shouted "hurrah."

"You *can* have it all," Claire said, "just not the way you—we—expected it to be." With renewed satisfaction, she watched Darcie's lower lip tremble again just before her whole face crumpled.

"I am such a mess. I am a complete, utter, total, absolute wreck."

"So, now we're getting somewhere. What are you going to do about it?"

That evening, still thinking of Dylan, Darcie sat alone in the suite she'd shared with Merrick at the Grand Hyatt for more nights than she cared to admit. This time, it seemed appropriate. Even Gran couldn't object. The hotel had been Darcie's choice for this meeting, and channel surfing with the remote control, she waited for Merrick Lowell. On her terms now. She had to do this first.

When she heard his key card in the lock, she jumped anyway.

Dropping the remote, Darcie shot to her feet. She'd improved a lot in the last few months, become less naive and gullible and certainly less trusting, but she still dreaded confrontation.

"You got here first," he said. He walked across the room to kiss her cheek, his gaze disconnected, and Darcie took a long look at him. He seemed different tonight. His smooth blond hair, his blue eyes were the same. Even his suit didn't have a wrinkle. His mood, however, was another matter. She couldn't read it. Or could she?

"You can relax, Merrick. I didn't come here to screw."

Flushing, he finally lifted his gaze to hers. And smiled. Relieved, she could tell.

"I had a few bad moments with Geoff before I left the apartment."

"He's jealous?"

She retrieved the remote and clicked off the TV. She

sat back down. Life could become more bizarre than a sitcom.

"Not jealous, really. Insecure."

"Is this a problem for you? Being here?"

"Not any longer." His quiet tone held the rest of his smile.

That's what it was, Darcie realized. She hadn't seen him since the night she met Geoff, but oddly, he looked at peace with himself. Merrick's whole face had ironed out since his separation from Jacqueline. From the sofa Darcie watched him walk to the minibar where he pulled out a small bottle of scotch for himself, a white wine for her. That was amazing in itself, that he'd thought of her.

"Then why are we here?" he asked. "I thought you were still angry with me." Merrick clunked ice into his glass, splashed in some mineral water, poured in the scotch. Making his own drink first. Some things didn't change, which almost made Darcie smile. She wasn't ready to answer.

Merrick opened her wine and filled a stemmed glass. He carried both their drinks to the sitting area and handed hers to Darcie. Before he spoke again, he took a healthy swig of his scotch.

"I've been thinking. A lot, lately. Having flashbacks, too," he said, dropping down onto the sofa next to her.

Darcie inhaled his scent, a subtly spicy soap and the very expensive-smelling aftershave she'd never been able to identify. Blue Blood, she'd call it, add a little color to the mix. Darcie preferred clean skin and a sometime hint of male perspiration—like Dylan. She burrowed into the cushions and sipped her wine, hoping to anesthetize herself. She didn't want to talk about her problems yet. As if he'd listen.

"And what have your thoughts proved?"

"How wrong I was," he said after a moment. Merrick stretched out his legs, straightened the perfect creases in his cuffed pants. He ran a hand through his well-styled hair. "I spent most of my life trying to fit in…the right schools, the right clubs, the right job…even the 'right' wife. I've told you Jackie and I never had a passionate relationship." He flicked a glance at her, looking guilty. "Maybe that's why I turned to you. As if to prove the problem was with her. Jackie and I stayed together for the kids—a novel concept in the new millennium, I realize, but like our families we're both pretty conservative. God, I hated those stilted Sunday dinners in Greenwich with my in-laws."

Darcie swallowed more wine, trying not to choke. A mistress had fit right into his life, too. She'd come here to give herself closure, but of course Merrick was working things out for himself.

"I think I knew," he said, "a long time ago. Even when I was a kid in boarding school. I felt torn about me, who I really was, but couldn't recognize it then. So I kept on doing what my parents expected of me, and then Jackie. And I kept getting more confused." He looked at her again. "I need to tell you how sorry I am, Darce. I used you—"

"Well, I used you, too." Pragmatic sex.

"No, I mean emotionally. I thought if I could see you, here on Monday nights or whenever, I'd be okay. Okay according to the traditions of society...the class to which I'd been born." He shook his head, then finished the scotch. "It doesn't work that way."

"What doesn't?"

"Happiness."

Merrick stared into his empty glass. "Remember right after you came back from Sydney? When you were still pissed at me about Jackie, after that day in FAO? Didn't want to see me again?"

Darcie nodded. She'd been so hurt, which seemed long ago and less important now. "You were persistent."

"Because I saw you in the Wunderthings lobby—twice—then kissed you at Zoe's," he said, "and here was this beautiful woman who knew me. I hoped we'd...heal each other, build on what we already had and everything would fall into place. I was right, partly. At the time you were trying to forget the Australian guy—"

"Get back to my 'real life.'" Whatever that meant.

"Yes, but don't you see? We were just each other's comfort zones," he said.

"Guess that didn't work for long." Darcie straightened to study his expression. He looked…regretful, when she'd never seen him truly sorry before, but still okay with himself now. "That's why you didn't want to get 'close' again the night I moved. Well, neither did I, really, but you seemed…lost, Merrick."

"I was. Desperate."

"Then at my housewarming party, you left early and I thought I'd somehow hurt your feelings."

He half smiled. "I'd met Geoff the week before. I couldn't understand why he affected me the way he did, at first sight. When I saw you with your friend—"

"Cutter Longridge," Darcie remembered, then couldn't resist adding, "Why, he must have looked better to you than I did."

"No, only different." Merrick shifted on the sofa. "I left there feeling dazed but no longer mixed-up. I knew that the issue had been mine all along, not Jackie's or yours or even my family. I'm bisexual, Darce. I went home and called Geoff."

He sighed. "It…happened, and then there was no turning back. Do you know why?"

"No," she said. Since Dylan had left, she knew very little.

"Because I realized I'd been living my life by other people's rules. Geoff encouraged me to live for myself." Talk about change, Darcie thought. "He's right," Merrick added. He got up to fix himself another drink but turned toward her from the minibar with a smile. "I hope this doesn't hurt you, but I've never been happier."

Somehow, she returned his smile. He hadn't offered her a refill, but for once that oversight didn't faze Darcie. "I can see that."

Rejoining her on the sofa, Merrick put an arm around her shoulders. She didn't pull away. For years, they'd enjoyed each other's company—in some fashion—but in the past weeks, no, since her trip to Sydney, they had actually, gradually, become friends. An odd pairing, she supposed, like being roomies with Gran, or Gran with Julio…or Darcie with Dylan, but there it was.

Darcie said nothing. Her throat suddenly tight, she stared into her wine. *You're scared,* Dylan had said.

"All right. Let's hear it." Merrick's embrace tightened. "No, let me guess. From the downcast look on your face, the darker hazel of your eyes, I'd say the Aussie has gone home."

"You said it wouldn't work."

"Worse, he's dumped you."

"Even worse, I think he wants to marry me—eventually."

Merrick drew back to stare at her. "Serious?"

"I'm afraid so."

But when she finished telling Merrick about Dylan, he said, "I don't get the problem. It's not Wunderthings, is it? Because with the new Sydney store, you could transfer—run operations from there, expand all over the place into Asia. Make yourself a real star." He didn't mean like the ones on her bedroom ceiling.

"Do you think so?"

Merrick ruffled her hair. "Get out of the box, Darce. Living halfway around the world from this guy isn't an insurmountable issue—not in the jet age. You could even commute." He paused. "Your grandmother's not holding you back, is she? Or Annie?"

She waited a beat, listening to her own heart thud. "No, but Dylan's attitudes are another matter. He thinks women belong at home."

"What man doesn't, deep down? He wants you there just for him."

"He's…a throwback." She thought of his wrangle with Cutter. But then, he had come through for her with Gran, and Merrick surprised her by taking Dylan's side again.

"Or is it really your parents you're worried about? Your parents who expect—rigidly expect, like mine—things of you that you don't want to give? Shouldn't give. I've heard about Janet and Hank often enough to suspect I'm right."

"You heard what I said?"

"Often enough." That's all he would admit. Typical.

"Merrick, you really are a beast."

Which didn't bother him. It seemed, tonight, nothing did. She liked him this way.

He studied the amber liquor in his glass. "The real question is, are you going to keep caring what your family wants for you instead of what you need?"

She smiled. "But you're a nicer beast than I've thought you were lately."

He flushed. "I'm not saying you should marry this guy—" Setting his glass down, he held her face in his hands. "Darce, do you have the courage to make your own decisions? To go your own way?"

"I don't know."

But for reasons of her own, Darcie knew she'd better find out.

When Merrick drew her close, she leaned her head on his shoulder. He wasn't the man for her—never had been—but for a very different reason than she'd thought. He wasn't, after all, just like her parents. They sat together for a long time, sipping their drinks, and just *being*. It was the best night she'd ever spent with him. Then Darcie felt Merrick's lips on her hair.

"I hope you do," he said.

Chapter
Twenty-One

Merrick had more faith in her than Darcie did in herself. One of her usual problems. She watched Annie pile underwear into a soft bag, just as Dylan had done, but Darcie could see no organization to Annie's process. Still, she thought, Annie would go back to Cincinnati—and Cliff—with some new knowledge of herself. More important, her sister had made her decision and for two whole weeks had stuck to it.

At this point, with Janet and Hank in the kitchen sorting housewares back into boxes, Darcie had retreated to the bedroom with Annie. It seemed safer than having her mother and father deliver another lecture about her own future. The subject made Darcie weary.

Everything did these days.

"You're not yourself, Darce," Annie pointed out.

"It shows. I drag to work in the morning, crawl home at night," she said, lying across Annie's bed. "I'm no further in figuring out my life than I was before you came. No, when I started living with Gran four years ago."

"Before Merrick. Before Dylan."

"Long before Cutter, too."

She'd heard from none of them. When she'd called him in Atlanta, Cutter's mother had told her he was "focusing his energies," presumably meaning *don't call again, he's done with you*. That didn't bother Darcie, who had no romantic claim on him, but she did hate being stonewalled. Cutter listened to her. He might give her some advice she could use.

Not that she'd heeded the wisdom Gran, Claire, Merrick, even Dylan had offered.

Coward.

Maybe Dylan was right. She was afraid—more afraid of commitment in any form than Merrick had been before Geoff.

"Have you called him?"

"Merrick?"

"No," Annie muttered, "I meant Dylan. You can't kid me, Darce. It's him you're stewing about. I hear you every night tossing in bed, those loud sighs. And no wonder, he's *hot*. Beyond hot, he's really nice. You need to take the bull by the horns—or the ram, I suppose."

"I don't know how to deal with this."

"What?" Annie said. "The guy begs you to follow him home—"

"Like an orphaned puppy."

"No, like the woman he wants in his life."

"There's nothing like a born-again romantic."

"Just because I grew up practically next door to Cliff and we're like, soul mates—and you met Dylan on the other side of the world, doesn't mean that can't work for you, too."

"There's nothing like a born-again philosopher."

Annie frowned. "I've never seen you this miserable, and trust me, I've seen you miserable before."

Darcie straightened a clump of bras that Annie had thrown into her bag. "I'm sorry, I didn't intend to snap at you." She had a short temper lately, too. "I'm glad you and Cliff will be together again, and you've already lined up that job at Lazarus."

Once she decided to act, Darcie admitted, Annie didn't

waste time. The upscale department store might be the making of her.

"I think I'll be good at PR, don't you?"

"Definitely. You're a people person."

Annie grinned briefly. "I won't mention my tattoos. And did you notice? I've stopped wearing my rings."

Her nose ring. Her eyebrow ring. Three of the four earrings through her cartilage. Mired in her own misery, Darcie hadn't noticed—but today Annie, in jeans and a camp shirt, looked normal. Wholesome. Cincinnati-bound. It almost soothed Darcie.

"I can't wait to get home," Annie said. "I'm still worried about you, though."

Now this was an amazing development. Was Annie growing up at last? Thinking of someone beyond herself?

"I'm impressed. So many changes all at once…"

Darcie trailed off. She'd had a lot of changes, too, not for the better. Her heart thumped and she got off the bed just as Janet and Hank appeared in the doorway. Trapped, she thought.

Her mother wasn't a time-waster, either. She launched into her sole topic of conversation for the past twenty-four hours since she and Hank had driven in from Ohio.

"If you'd reconsider, Darcie…"

"I did. I'm staying here."

Janet smoothed her already well-combed hair. She was wearing her usual pumps (don't ask me why) and a dress. The perfect outfit for moving.

"Your father and I can have you packed in a couple of hours. You can sublease the apartment."

"I'll start on the living room—all those books yours, Darcie?" Her father stood there in his Dockers and boat shoes, neat as a pin except for the smear of kitchen grease across one cheek, which made Darcie almost grin.

My life can be reduced to a dozen cardboard boxes and a bunch of garbage bags. Janet had objected to those of course. Clothing belonged in wardrobes. Too bad they didn't have any. Darcie crossed her arms.

"Not that I'm seriously considering this, but what about my job?"

Janet answered. "Walter Corwin will find someone else. He can promote that terrible Greta Hinckley. Send her to Australia."

Greta? After all Darcie's hard work?

"It's filled with Leftists anyway," Hank murmured.

"I know we've had our differences," Janet reminded her. "But nothing would make us happier than to have our girls home with us again."

Hank put his arm around Darcie, awkward but firm. "We love you, baby."

Her throat closed. She leaned against him, needing something, feeling lonely. Even, yes, a little scared. They had their quirks, like everyone else, but they really weren't bad parents. In fact, very good ones.

What was it Gran had said? *Someday you'll realize how lovely it is to have memories with people who've known you all your life. Exactly as you are.*

For a moment she felt tempted to go with them, to stay with them forever. Yet she couldn't just leave.

"I love you, too." Knowing further discussion would be futile, Darcie backed toward the door to the hall. "But there's something I need to do."

She had made one decision. All she needed was Walt's cooperation.

The next morning Annie was on the road to Cincinnati with Janet and Hank, the apartment—and its full rent— belonged to Darcie again, but instead of preparing her pitch for Walt, she was leaving Greta a note at her desk.

Scrabbling for something to write with, she knocked over Greta's penholder. Pencils, erasers, a flash of silver tumbled onto the desktop. As she scribbled the message, instructing Greta to check on the Goolong designs—and *only* to verify production—Darcie became aware of Nancy Braddock passing by on her usual morning circuit of the department.

Nancy stopped cold. Her eyes snapped. She picked up the letter opener.

"Did this come from where I think it did?"

"Greta's mug of pencils."

"Wouldn't you just know."

At that moment Greta herself appeared, swinging down the aisle with a scowl and her usual bag of pastries. "You know, it's funny, Braddock—Baxter—but I thought this was my space. My desk."

Nancy waved the slim silver piece.

"What is this?" Darcie asked. It looked like a stiletto but distracted by her need to see Walt, she barely noticed.

"Walt bought his wife this letter opener in Taos. Their wedding anniversary trip—twenty years of marriage—just before she got sick. She loved the workmanship…"

Darcie examined the chased silver pattern more closely. "Did Walt give this to you, Greta?"

Nancy bristled. "He would *never* part with it. He certainly wouldn't let Greta have it—no matter what he's getting from *her*." She paused to take a breath while Darcie realized she had seen the opener before. *It belonged to my mother,* Greta had told her. "I can't believe Hinckley's still part of this organization," Nancy went on. "If I had a dollar for every time I've caught her stealing—"

Clearly, Nancy was in no shape to deal with the situation. Darcie gently took the opener from her shaking fingers, and said, "I was going in to see Walt anyway. I'll ask him about this, too."

"There's nothing to ask. Greta's a *thief!* You should know, Darcie. *Tell him.*"

Darcie disliked confrontation, especially about Greta and especially since she'd started seeing Walt. But it appeared that Nancy Braddock, too, had had enough.

"I'm not sure Walt will believe me," Darcie said.

Nancy glared at Greta, then looked at Darcie. "He'll believe you. And me."

Greta marched after them. "Walter will believe *me.*"

Darcie suspected this was true. Her mentor, she imagined, had other things on his mind these days—mainly

Greta. With Hinckley in her wake, she stalked into Walt's office without knocking. The silver letter opener stayed behind her back, clutched in one hand. She would ask about it later, once she'd posed her own question. Without having time to prepare, she came straight to the point. *Make yourself a star,* Merrick had said.

"Walt, I need to see you. Send *me* to Sydney."

He glanced up from his desk. His gaze went immediately to Greta, and she smiled. Although she felt sure Greta wanted to climb on his lap, she took a seat beside Darcie on one of the twin upholstered chairs in front of Walt's desk. Nancy hovered behind them.

Walt's eyes didn't look happy, Darcie noticed—one miserable person could spot another—and her senses went on alert. Had he heard the commotion in the hall? Was there trouble brewing between him and Greta?

Greta kept smiling but her eyes turned hard. "Take me with you, Walter."

Her tone sounded suggestive. He fidgeted with a stack of papers on his desk.

"I could help," Greta went on. "I know there've been problems with the store."

Some of which Greta had created, but Darcie didn't need to risk getting what she wanted by saying so. Or bring up the letter opener just yet.

"I'm familiar with those problems," she cut in. "I handled the display furniture crisis, the late order—" she looked at Greta "—and our labor troubles over the past two weeks. I'm sure Wunderthings would rather save money at this point than spend more."

Walt's mouth thinned. "Get to it, Baxter."

Hoping she didn't sound desperate, she said, "I can deal with the opening by myself. One plane ticket, one hotel room, one daily expense account. You could stay here to handle the department." And Greta, she thought.

Greta turned to her. "You've mismanaged the whole Sydney project. Why would he send you? If Walter had listened to me, we wouldn't have problems. If I hadn't tried to deal with Henry Goolong—"

302 *Leigh Riker*

With that, Darcie changed her mind. Too bad Greta wouldn't keep her mouth shut. Now, Darcie wouldn't stay quiet about their rivalry. Nancy was right. Darcie tightened her grip on the letter opener. "You overstepped your responsibilities, and if you hadn't stolen my other ideas—"

"You haven't had a good idea in your life. I'm surprised Walter hasn't fired you by now. You've ridden on *my* creative output long enough—"

"Greta." Walt looked increasingly unhappy.

Darcie studied Greta for a moment, taking in her new makeup and shinier hair, her simply cut but flattering dark suit. Even her shoes looked up-to-date with their chunky heels and sleek silhouette. She'd never be a beauty, but then neither was Walt. He'd definitely taken an interest in Greta. So what was wrong here? All Darcie knew was, she'd tried to help Greta, and her efforts had backfired. Now she had no choice but to confront her, to defend herself.

In the chair beside her, Greta eyed Darcie with alarm. Greta's palms turned sweaty. She gazed at Walter, willing him to glance her way, to see her love for him shining in her eyes.

"Walt, I know you have a personal relationship with Greta—" Darcie whipped a silver letter opener from behind her back "—and I'm sorry, but this was on—"

She hadn't even finished before Walter reached out to take it. "Greta's desk."

And her heartbeat surged with dismay. She'd forgotten all about the treasure she'd taken from this very office weeks ago, before Walter had even looked at her and really seen her at last. Greta tried to ignore the fact that his attention had been captured at Darcie's housewarming party. Now it fell on the prize found on her desk.

"Nancy was there," Darcie said. "She told me what it was. Did you give Greta—"

Shaking his head, Walter rotated the silver in his hands, spring sunlight flashing on its smooth surface. His mouth went grim. He avoided looking at Greta, who sat dying in her chair, and focused on Darcie instead. Greta felt her recent balloon of happiness deflate with his next words.

"You ready to leave for Sydney?" He wasn't talking to her.

Darcie said, "Well...yes. Sure. Any time."

"We'll both go," he said decisively, as if making up his mind on the spot.

"But Walter," Greta began. She jumped to her feet, her eyes burning.

"I apologize, Darcie. Nancy," he added with a nod at his assistant who was wringing her hands at the edge of Greta's peripheral vision. "It's taken me too long to recognize the truth here, even when it's been in front of me all this time." Still not looking at Greta, he restacked some papers in front of him, then laid the silver opener across them. The End, her pulse seemed to throb. What could she do?

"Walter—" she said more insistently.

"You've harassed Nancy for the last time. She threatened to quit yesterday and I can't lose her. I heard the shouting in the hall a few minutes ago. I've heard your harangues with her on the phone during the day, with Darcie, too, in her cubicle. I tried to overlook them because you and I..." He trailed off then finished, "But I've seen you going through my own papers, even my personal mail."

She put a hand to her heart. "Only to help you—"

"No," he said, "to gather useful information." He picked up the opener again as if he couldn't bear not to touch it another moment. "I won't give you the chance to sabotage me, too, sometime. Not after this." He held the silver in his hands, as if to let his memories warm him. "My wife's. Stolen. It's the last straw, Greta. You're done for the day. Go home. We'll talk tomorrow about your future with Wunderthings."

If she had one, Greta thought, fearing he could hear her thundering pulse.

"Don't do anything you'll regret, Walter. Remember

what we've meant to each other, the fresh *chance* we've discovered—'' Their few shared kisses, his touch…except that it had never gone far enough to suit Greta.

Now, she knew, it never would. She watched his finger poise over the intercom that could summon Security if need be, then spun around to Darcie, who looked stunned.

"This is your fault, Baxter!" Greta said. She whirled back to Walter. "And you…I gave you my love but you only used me!" With that small exaggeration, she considered a dozen threats but as he continued to gaze at her without emotion, she felt the energy to spew all her hurt and anger begin to drain from her until, seconds later, it was only a trickle of sorrow.

Walter didn't speak. In the long silence, neither did Darcie. Finally, Nancy turned and went out into the anteroom, leaving the door open.

"Make our reservations, please," he called after her. "Darcie and I leave as soon as possible. Thanks, Nancy." He didn't mean just her work for him, her value as his assistant. "You, too, Baxter."

Greta fixed a last, hard stare on Darcie.

"I'll just, uh…" Baxter had no need to say more. With a vague gesture, she drifted toward the exit, too.

Leaving Greta alone with Walter Corwin.

Walter smoothed a finger along the edge of the silver letter opener, along the memories he clearly preferred over Greta. For once in her life, given the opportunity, she had nothing to say, not even to save herself. The realization stole the rest of her spirit.

Without a word, she followed Darcie into the hall and slunk back to her own cubicle, taking her love, her obsession, with her, Greta's very posture a symbol of her utter defeat.

Three nights later, Darcie leaned back in her chair in the bar of the Westin Sydney—scene of her original crime, she thought—and while Walt downed his second Rob Roy, sipped her Perrier with lemon.

It didn't ease her stomach, which felt testy after the long

flight from New York to L.A. to Sydney. More jet lag. And it didn't soothe her guilt. Neither did the red licorice whip she gnawed on from the package on the table.

Greta lingered in her mind. So did this opportunity. Walt—and Wunderthings—must not be that strapped for cash, or didn't he trust her here to work on her own?

And that was just her professional life. If she'd never picked up Dylan...

But she had picked him up, singing "Waltzing Matilda," no less. She'd seen him right here, talking to this same bartender, with a beer in his hand, and she had willed him to her side.

Zing.

I've never been the same since, he'd said.

Well, neither had she. Thanks to Dylan, she never would be again.

Darcie straightened in her chair. For a moment, she entertained the wild notion of calling him tonight. She'd ask the waiter to bring her a phone—her cell didn't work this far from home—and lay the whole thing on Dylan's broad shoulders. *You creep, I fell for you and now...*

That wouldn't work. And right now she had the store to think of first.

Walt looked distinctly anxious, or depressed. Was he thinking about the Sydney opening, too? Or Greta?

Darcie reached out to cover his hand. "Are you okay?"

"Sure. Why not?" He drained the rest of his drink. Darcie chose another licorice.

"Well, I mean, I know you and Greta were..."

"It didn't work out. I gave her a new assignment. The Albany store's in trouble. Greta has good ideas—when she thinks of them herself. She'll relocate. Maybe the fresh start will help her."

"And Greta will work out her issues. I hope she will."

As if conceding that was possible, Walt lifted one shoulder. Darcie hadn't seen him signal the waiter, but when a fresh Rob Roy landed on the table in front of him, Walt took a long swallow. Darcie was still covering his other hand. She handed him a red licorice whip for comfort.

"I had really hoped," he said after a moment, "that we...but hell, I should have known. You told me about Greta. So did Nancy. I guess I had to learn for myself. I knew all along not to mix pleasure with business."

Darcie felt a twinge of fresh guilt. She followed Walt's gaze across the room, as if he were giving up a last chance to find happiness—or searching, too, as she was, for Dylan at the bar. Reminding her that she shouldn't make the same mistake. When his hand rotated to capture hers, Darcie's guilt turned to surprise then empathy, before Walt spoke again.

"Speaking of business and pleasure, what about your Aussie?"

Surprised again, she admitted, "I don't know what to do, Walt."

When he squeezed her hand, she blinked.

"But that's my problem," she assured him. "I'm here to work."

"So we are." He eased back with a last pat of her hand. "So we will, Baxter."

A few minutes later Walt went upstairs to bed. Darcie stayed, nursing her water and finishing her red licorice.

"I don't think I could sleep," she said to her glass. "I mean, I feel too sorry for Walt, who needs someone, sorry for myself if you want to know the truth." She pushed the glass aside. "What next, almost-thirty-year-old Darcie Elizabeth Baxter?"

When a man's laugh across the room reminded her of Dylan's, she glanced up, her heart suddenly pounding.

Even the thought of his name made her weak.

Or was the man laughing at her for talking to herself? Darcie didn't care.

"Hey, I'm here. Again." To work, she'd promised Walt. "But after that, *what?*" she wondered aloud. "I've already done misery. Annie sure noticed. So did Gran and Claire. And Merrick. Even Mom and Dad. When they left with Annie's cartons loaded in the van, they said, 'If you need us, Darcie...for anything...just call.'"

She cleared her throat, tried to clear her vision. Tried

not to see the curious glances from other people in the bar. Let them stare. Let them listen.

Muttering to herself might help. Laying an Australian ten-dollar bill on the table to pay for her water, Darcie eased her chair back. "Like Walt, I'll go up to bed—without Dylan this time—and figure out my best course overnight."

Without the beer he'd pushed on her before, without the sex, it should be simple. By morning, despite her fear, she would know what to do.

"For the first time in my life," she murmured, "everything will make sense."

She hoped.

"Please don't say that," Darcie told Rachel, her new manager, the day before the opening of Wunderthings Sydney. *"The rest of the salesclerks didn't show up?"*

"They're not coming in, Miss Baxter. Darcie."

"Then they're fired."

"They already quit. Not enough pay."

Walter—or could it be Greta?—strikes again. "Get me some new candidates."

Rachel's dark curls jiggled, like her perky little breasts. She glanced around, as if making sure Walt was busy elsewhere in the store.

"Beg pardon, but there are none. Mr. Corwin had us advertise in the newspaper when he was here last time. We put a sign outside the door, too, but…"

"Don't tell me." Grinding her molars, she realized she'd never been this nervous. "Set the sign out again and I'll call an employment service."

With a huffed-out breath, she went into the office at the rear of the store and shut the door. Darcie leaned against it and counted to fifty. Not enough. She was still counting when the desk phone jangled.

Who was she to criticize Walter? She still had no plan about Dylan.

"Darcie Baxter here." It was the building's management on the line and she groaned at the man's harsh tone of

voice, his biting words. "Of course we're planning to pay
our rent," she said and Darcie frowned. "I'll look into it
and get back to you immediately."

This had all the earmarks of Greta's fine hand. She dialed
again.

But on the phone a subdued Greta, wakened from sleep,
claimed no knowledge of the error. By midnight—all the
gods be praised—Nancy Braddock had arranged to wire
the funds, the QVB management was smiling again, and
Darcie was entertaining notions of actually having her job
when she got back to New York—providing the Sydney
opening went well, which remained to be seen.

For instance, the display windows.

Darcie marched outside to take a better look. But up
close and personal, the array of female mannequins in
Wunderthings bras and panties and filmy negligees—Walt's
idea—made Darcie groan.

"Bland, isn't it?" Rachel said beside her.

"Poor Walt must be pining for…well, never mind. We
need to get people into this store, not send them running
for the opposite end of the QVB. This is hopeless. Tear it
all down."

She stood, tapping one foot against the floor, thinking.
Praying, really. The fear of failure at this—the chance of a
lifetime to prove herself to Walt, but especially to the
Wunderthings board of directors—set her creative synapses
whirring like the innards of a mainframe computer. If only
Walt had sprung for a professional display person…

Then it hit her. They didn't need professional. They
needed…sex.

Darcie's first memory of Dylan Rafferty sped through
her mind. She'd had the fantasy even then. *Dylan, in a shop
window.*

"Find me some different models. Male mannequins."
Rachel's eyes lit up and knowing she was on the right path,
Darcie added, "Tall, dark, built, as gorgeous as you can
get. We need them here by 8:00 a.m. tomorrow."

"That's not much time."

"It's enough." She went back inside to search through

cartons of merchandise. "Where's the shipment of the new Aboriginal line?"

Rachel blinked. "I didn't know there was one."

Darcie's patience flew out the window onto King Street. She headed again for the phone. When the shipment finally showed up after a dozen calls, Darcie let out the pent-up breath she seemed to have been holding all day. But by the time this store opened, with a new contingent of salesclerks, including several males, she'd probably be hyperventilating. Still, while she and Rachel unpacked the prints fresh from the Canberra factory, it began to look as if everything could work out.

At least with Wunderthings Sydney. Her baby.

The designs from Henry Goolong and his son looked wonderful in silk and the microfiber version, too, with strong, dark colors and classic images. They felt soft and sensual. Darcie hoped they would be a hit. She needed one.

Inspired, she got her second wind and worked the rest of the evening with Rachel setting up displays of panties and bustiers, arranging shelves of nightshirts and gowns, organizing teddies and corsets and "minimizers" and Wunderthings' last season highlight, gel- and water-filled push-up brassieres.

Buying herself time.

After the opening, she thought. She would face Dylan then.

Darcie got up the next morning before her alarm rang or the backup call from the front desk at the Westin Sydney came through. Stumbling from bed, she hurried to take a shower.

She'd formed some beautiful memories here amid the green frosted glass and chrome. Not Room 3001's fault she had pursued the matter in New York—and wound up totally confused about her life.

When she came out, and put on her best power suit, her most expensive pumps, she felt better.

By the time she and Walt reached the QVB, she was at least ready for business.

Rachel had coffee waiting for them.

"Good news. The mannequins arrived. Five minutes to spare."

"Thank you, God. Get them out here. We open in an hour."

Snatching up some of the Aboriginal pieces, Darcie headed for the windows.

Even she couldn't believe the effect they produced.

"You were right," Walt said, nodding his approval, too.

The male models draped with transparent lingerie looked just about perfect. Darcie tried not to feel that something was missing. There was no time to ponder her personal life when her professional future was at stake right now. Still...

"Ack," she said, startling Rachel, who was adjusting a lacy bra to hang from one dark-haired mannequin's hand. "We need hats."

"Hats?"

"Akubras. There must be a store in this mall that sells hats."

"They won't open until ten."

"At the stroke of, you be there. Buy four of them. Different colors."

"To complement the Aboriginal lingerie."

Darcie said, "Brilliant woman."

Her heart beating fast with excitement—and terror—she helped Walt open the main doors to the store at precisely ten o'clock. With his help and Rachel's, she set the sandwich board signs on either side of the entry announcing the Opening Day Fair with its Two for One Sale on Select Items—not the new Aboriginal line—rechecked the snacks and drinks, the glass container of red licorice whips, then took a deep breath. And waited for business.

The day flew past.

The Akubra-ed mannequins, bare-chested and well-muscled, stopped traffic. The lingerie draped around their necks, over their shoulders, tucked into jeans waistbands and through belt loops brought smiles to the trendy shoppers' faces. The Aboriginal lingerie pulled them into the shop. Darcie's gleaming furniture even in pecan, Regency Stripe wallpaper, and Oriental rugs set the right tone.

By four o'clock Darcie was exhausted. Or, she would have been if she'd stopped long enough to let herself feel weary. She didn't have time. All day she had punched sales into the register, helped customers find their right sizes, restocked shelves.

"Wait until we total today's receipts," Rachel murmured, sweeping past her to show a middle-aged matron the latest in bustiers.

"I can't wait. I am beside myself with joy."

Rachel took a look at her—on the fly but long enough. She leaned to whisper in Darcie's ear. "Well, for someone who feels great, you look pasty. Take a break. The other girls, the guys and I can handle everything here. You deserve it. Go have a wine. If there are questions, Walt can answer."

Shaking with the release of tension, Darcie headed down the hall to the Italian restaurant at its end and chose a table in the ell outside the entrance from which she could watch passersby and everyone who went into Wunderthings.

Then a woman sat down with her to rave about the store, distracting her, and Darcie got swept up in congratulations—and satisfaction. It was going to work out.

Maybe not Dylan, but at least her career.

Would it be enough? She'd never wondered before.

After thanking the customer, Darcie walked back to the store, her heart heavy now, her mind on Dylan rather than the shop. Even success had lost its luster.

Gran was with Julio.

Claire was with Peter. And at work.

Merrick was at peace with Geoffrey.

Annie was home with Cliff by now.

Even Cutter was caught up with someone new, he'd reported in his one phone call to her.

As for herself...

Startled from her reverie, Darcie stopped dead in the hall. A crowd had gathered—an even bigger crowd than the one that had ebbed and flowed all day—in front of the display windows at Wunderthings. Her pulse jumped into her throat. What had gone wrong?

Expecting disaster, she pushed her way through the throng of shoppers murmuring among themselves. They weren't unhappy, she realized. Some laughed, a few giggled, and several fingers pointed at the glass.

Then Darcie saw why.

In the center of the display, surrounded by the mannequins that had been such a hit all afternoon, stood a real-live male in tight, worn blue jeans and a chambray shirt. A man with broad shoulders, dark eyes, and dark hair. He wore a gray-green Akubra on his head. Not one of those Rachel had bought.

Lacy lingerie dripped from his hands. Aboriginal design panties hung from both shoulders. And a matching bra was hooked over his index finger.

Dylan Rafferty.

He was grinning, talking, teasing the women through the window—beckoning them inside.

They flocked into the store. Walt and Rachel seemed as frantic as the salesclerks. Merchandise—what was left of it—winged off the shelves straight to the checkout line, which now snaked around the perimeter of the entire store. One woman tried to climb into the display window after Dylan but Darcie stepped in her path.

"Sorry, store property." *Mine.*

Where had that come from? Darcie had no idea. Her pulse racing, she hustled up into the display, moved aside a mannequin, and tapped Dylan on one shoulder. Before he even turned around, he was humming.

"Waltzing Matilda."

When he did turn and see her, the grin lit his dark eyes like black opals and morphed into a laugh. He held out both arms full of lingerie.

Darcie laughed, too. She laughed until the tears ran down her cheeks.

She laughed some more.

And then she knew. "I *know*."

Darcie flung her arms around his neck and scaled his long, lean frame as if he were the famed Ayers Rock, her personal sacred object. Up close, she stared into those black-opal eyes and Dylan stared into her hazel ones, just as silent as Darcie, oblivious of the crowd of envious women around them, oblivious of anything but each other.

Dylan was the first to recover.

"Hey, Matilda." He seemed to have trouble going on.

Darcie's eyes narrowed. "Did Walt Corwin call you?"

"No." Dylan cleared his throat. "I thought I could do it—not push you any further—but I got tired of waiting for you to come get me."

"You wasted the trip to Sydney. I was going to track you down tomorrow."

"What's wrong with today?"

"Not a thing. Now."

With a whoop that sent his Akubra flying, he swung her around and around, panties falling from his shoulders, a bra snagged on his belt, hanging over his fly. He kissed her, his mouth soft then hot, moving on hers, until she felt dizzy from his taste as much as from the motion.

"Down," she said.

"Or what? Chunder?"

"On the Paramatta."

After letting her slide down to solid ground, slide against his body the entire way, he folded his arms over his impressive chest and cocked his head. "I know you have to make decisions for yourself—"

"I just did."

Someone handed him the Akubra and he clamped it on his head. He kept staring while the crowd of shoppers milled and flowed around them and finally, with the jangle of the closing bell, drifted back into the hallway toward the mall exits.

Darcie didn't notice them. Or Walt and Rachel herding people out. She just stood there while the place emptied.

Go your own way, Darcie, Merrick had told her.

Claire had said, *You can have it all, just not like you—we—expected.*

Soul mates, Annie had said. *Next door or half the world away.*

And what had Gran advised? *Take happiness where you find it. Life is short.* She'd said something else, months ago, but Darcie couldn't recall what it was right now.

"Your store," Dylan said, looking around at the mostly bare shelves, the now empty checkout counter and the dry soda pitchers, the crumbs of cookies, the empty red licorice container. "It's great. Good on ya."

"Good for me?"

"Good for you," he agreed.

Darcie smiled. "I may never learn to speak your language."

"Oh, you speak my language just fine."

He had that dark look in his eyes and her pulse lurched. What was he saying? That he accepted her need to have this career, to be her own person? She swallowed, hard. She could tell him this, the words she'd denied him until now. One reason—a big reason—why she had flown back to Australia. To him.

"I love you, Dylan."

Startled, he stepped back, then came forward again. He put his arms around her and held her tight. "I love you, too. Matilda."

He kissed her again, took another step, then another, edging her backward across the floor, as if they were two-stepping in some Texas bar.

"Where are we going?"

"Somewhere private."

Darcie looked around. "This is a store."

"It's closed." Turning his head toward the register, he called out, "Thanks, Rachel. I appreciate your help. Any time you need a stand-in here, let me know."

She snickered, gave them both a wave, and went out the door, ready to lock it behind her. "My pleasure." She was dragging Walt with her, which made Darcie smile.

"Come on," Rachel told him, "I'll buy you a drink." She called back, "We're celebrating. The total our first day topped any store in Wunderthings' chain."

Darcie heard that—and part of her rejoiced—but the rest simply didn't care. Not now, anyway. The important thing was to be with Dylan. Wherever. It didn't make a lick of sense. It didn't have to.

In the nearest dressing room with Darcie, Dylan pressed her against the mirrored wall. "I have fond memories of this," he murmured, lowering his head to hers again. "Our first night at the Westin."

How could she forget? Maybe his traditional views not only weren't that much like her parents'; maybe they weren't a complete obstacle to change. Maybe she needn't fight against her upbringing so hard. Or her own until-now elusive happiness.

Love isn't logical. Life isn't rational. They're not meant to be.

And suddenly, Darcie remembered the rest. Gran was right. Any man who could make her laugh until she cried, until her ribs hurt, until her heart spun, had to be a keeper.

Darcie didn't know whether they could work things out, but she was no longer naive enough to think things could be fixed in stone. No longer as uncertain of her place as a woman. She would try—she suspected Dylan would, too. For now, Down Under and deep in Darcie's heart, he was the one. For her. But, "Dylan, we need to talk."

"First we make love," he said against her mouth, and Darcie subsided.

"Then we negotiate."

Engaging Men

by
Lynda Curnyn

When one ex-boyfriend gets married, a girl can laugh it off. With two, she begins to get nervous... But three? *Three?*

Angie DiFranco is starting to take it personally, and her nightmare of becoming that universally pitied cliché – The Unmarried Daughter – is looming scarily! What is it about her that fails to inspire men to lay down a month's wages for even a measly half-carat gesture of eternal love?

According to her one successfully married friend, men are like tight lids. The ex-girlfriend simply loosens him up, leaving him ready for the next woman to pop off the lid, no problem! Suddenly Angie looks at Kirk, her current boyfriend, with new eyes. Kirk, whose last girlfriend gave him The Ultimatum, and who suddenly seems primed to be popped right open... If the tight-lid theory is true, Angie could be married within a year – with a little effort. And some help from her friends!

RED DRESS INK

On sale 20th June 2003

Life's little curves.

0603/14(

RDI/WRITERS

RED DRESS INK

Life's little curves.

Did you enjoy this novel?

Think you can write one of your own . . . ?

At **Red Dress Ink™** we're looking for lively, talented writers. This exciting new imprint features many young, debut authors who had a story to tell, and weren't afraid to have a go!

We publish novels that reflect the lifestyles of today's urban, single women. Sassy, witty and irreverent, our authors show life as it is, with a strong touch of humour, hipness and energy.

✦ **You're climbing the corporate ladder in knee-high boots**
✦ **You have at least five first-date outfits**
✦ **Biological clock? You don't even own a watch!**

If you can relate to any of these statements,
Red Dress Ink™ is for you.

For more information, including authors' guidelines, write to:

The Senior Editor
Red Dress Ink
Eton House, 18-24 Paradise Road
Richmond, Surrey TW9 1SR